THE ROSARY GIRLS

RICHARD MONTANARI

DOUBLEDAY LARGE PRINT HOME LIBRARY EDITION

BALLANTINE BOOKS   NEW YORK

THE ROSARY GIRLS

A NOVEL

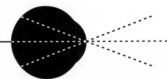

This Large Print Book carries the
Seal of Approval of N.A.V.H.

For DJC
Cuor forte rompe cattiva sorte.

THE ROSARY GIRLS

PALM SUNDAY, 11:55 PM

There is a wintry sadness about this one, a deep-rooted melancholy that belies her seventeen years, a laugh that never fully engages any sort of inner joy.

Perhaps there is none.

You see them all the time on the street; the one walking alone, books clutched tightly to her breast, eyes cast earthward, ever adrift in thought. She is the one strolling a few paces behind the other girls, content to accept the rare morsel of friendship tossed her way. The

*one who babysits her way through all the mile-
stones of adolescence. The one who refuses
her beauty, as if it were elective.*

Her name is Tessa Ann Wells.

She smells like fresh-cut flowers.

"I cannot hear you," I say.

*". . . lordaswiddee," comes the tiny voice
from the chapel. It sounds as if I have awakened her, which is entirely possible. I took her
early Friday morning, and it is now nearly midnight on Sunday. She has been praying in the
chapel, more or less nonstop.*

*It is not a formal chapel, of course, mere-
ly a converted closet, but it is outfitted
with everything one needs for reflection and
prayer.*

*"This will not do," I say. "You know that it is
paramount to derive meaning from each and
every word, don't you?"*

From the chapel: "Yes."

*"Consider how many people around the
world are praying at this very moment. Why
should God listen to those who are insincere?"*

"No reason."

*I lean closer to the door. "Would you want
the Lord to show you this sort of contempt on
the day of rapture?"*

"No."

"Good," I reply. "What decade?"

It takes a few moments for her to answer. In the darkness of the chapel, one must proceed by feel.

Finally, she says: "Third."

"Begin again."

I light the remainder of the votives. I finish my wine. Contrary to what many believe, the rites of the sacraments are not always solemn undertakings, but rather are, many times, cause for joy and celebration.

I am just about to remind Tessa when, with clarity and eloquence and import, she begins to pray once more:

"Hail Mary, full of grace, the Lord is with thee . . ."

Is there a sound more beautiful than a virgin at prayer?

"Blessed art thou amongst women . . ."

I glance at my watch. It is just after midnight.

"And blessed is the fruit of thy womb, Jesus . . ."

It is time.

"Holy Mary, mother of God . . ."

I take the hypodermic from its case. The needle gleams in the candlelight. The Holy Spirit is here.

"Pray for us sinners . . ."

The Passion has begun.
"Now and at the hour of our death . . ."
I open the door and step into the chapel.
Amen.

PART ONE

PART ONE

1

There is an hour known intimately to all who rouse to meet it, a time when darkness sheds fully the cloak of twilight and the streets fall still and silent, a time when shadows convene, become one, dissolve. A time when those who suffer disbelieve the dawn.

Every city has its quarter, its neon Golgotha.

In Philadelphia, it is known as South Street.

This night, while most of the City of Brotherly Love slept, while the rivers flowed mutely to the sea, the flesh peddler rushed down South Street like a dry, blistering wind. Between Third and Fourth Streets he pushed through a wrought-iron gate, walked down a narrow alleyway, and entered a private club called Paradise. The handful of patrons scattered about the room met his gaze, then immediately averted their eyes. In the peddler's stare they saw a portal to their own blackened souls, and knew that if they engaged him, even for a moment, the understanding would be far too much to bear.

To those who knew his trade, the peddler was an enigma, but not a puzzle anyone was eager to solve.

He was a big man, well over six feet tall, with a broad carriage and large, coarse hands that promised reckoning to those who crossed him. He had wheat-colored hair and cold green eyes, eyes that would spark to bright cobalt in candlelight, eyes that could take in the horizon with one glance, missing nothing. Above his right eye was a shiny keloid scar, a ridge of ropy tissue in the shape of an inverted *V*. He wore a long black leather coat that strained against the thick muscles in his back.

He had come to the club five nights in a row now, and this night he would meet his buyer. Appointments were not easily made at Paradise. Friendships were unknown.

The peddler sat at the back of the dank basement room at a table that, although not reserved for him, had become his by default. Even though Paradise was settled with players of every dark stripe and pedigree, it was clear that the peddler was of another breed.

The speakers behind the bar offered Mingus, Miles, Monk; the ceiling: soiled Chinese lanterns and rotary fans covered in wood-grain contact paper. Cones of blueberry incense burned, wedding the cigarette smoke, graying the air with a raw, fruity sweetness.

At three ten, two men entered the club. One was the buyer; the other, his guardian. They both met the eyes of the peddler. And knew.

The buyer, whose name was Gideon Pratt, was a squat, balding man in his late fifties, with flushed cheeks, restless gray eyes, and jowls that hung like melted wax.

He wore an ill-fitting three-piece suit and had fingers long-gnarled by arthritis. His breath was fetid. His teeth, ocher and spare.

Behind him walked a bigger man—bigger even than the peddler. He wore mirrored sunglasses and a denim duster. His face and neck were ornamented with an elaborate web of *ta moko,* the Maori tribal tattoos.

Without a word, the three men gathered, then walked down a short hallway to a supply room.

The back room at Paradise was cramped and hot, packed with boxes of off-brand liquor, a pair of scarred metal desks, and a mildewed, ragged sofa. An old jukebox flickered carbon-blue light.

Once in the room, door closed, the large man, who went by the street name of Diablo, roughly patted down the peddler for weapons and wires, attempting to establish a stratum of power. As he was doing this, the peddler noted the three-word tattoo at the base of Diablo's neck. It read: MONGREL FOR LIFE. He also noticed the butt of a chrome Smith & Wesson revolver in the large man's waistband.

Satisfied that the peddler was unarmed and wore no listening devices, Diablo stepped away, behind Pratt, crossed his arms, and observed.

"What do you have for me?" Pratt asked.

The peddler considered the man before answering him. They had reached the moment that occurs in every transaction, the instant when the purveyor must come clean and lay his wares upon the velvet. The peddler reached slowly into his leather coat—there would be no furtive moves here—and removed a pair of Polaroid pictures. He handed them to Gideon Pratt.

Both photographs were of fully clothed, suggestively posed teenaged black girls. The one called Tanya sat on the front stoop of her row house, blowing a kiss to the photographer. Alicia, her sister, vamped on the beach in Wildwood.

As Pratt scrutinized the photos, his cheeks flared crimson for a moment, his breath hitched in his chest. "Just . . . beautiful," he said.

Diablo glanced at the snapshots, registering no reaction. He turned his gaze back to the peddler.

"What is her name?" Pratt asked, holding up one of the photos.

"Tanya," the peddler replied.

"Tan-ya," Pratt repeated, separating the syllables, as if to sort the essence of the girl. He handed one of the pictures back, then glanced at the photograph in his hand. "She is adorable," he added. "A mischievous one. I can tell."

Pratt touched the photograph, running his finger gently over the glossy surface. He seemed to drift for a moment, lost in some reverie, then put the picture into his pocket. He snapped back to the moment, back to the business at hand. "When?"

"Now," the peddler replied.

Pratt reacted with surprise and delight. He had not expected this. "She is *here*?"

The peddler nodded.

"Where?" asked Pratt.

"Nearby."

Gideon Pratt straightened his tie, adjusted the vest over his bulging stomach, smoothed what little hair he had. He took a deep breath, finding his axis, then gestured to the door. "Shall we?"

The peddler nodded again, then looked to Diablo for permission. Diablo waited a moment, further cementing his status, then stepped to the side.

The three men exited the club, walked across South Street to Orianna Street. They continued down Orianna, emerging into a small parking lot between the buildings. In the lot were two vehicles: a rusted van with smoked-glass windows and a late-model Chrysler. Diablo put a hand up, strode forward, and looked into the windows of the Chrysler. He turned, nodded, and Pratt and the peddler stepped up to the van.

"You have the payment?" the peddler asked.

Gideon Pratt tapped his pocket.

The peddler looked briefly between the two men, then reached into the pocket of his coat and retrieved a set of keys. Before he could insert the key into the van's passenger door, he dropped them to the ground.

Both Pratt and Diablo instinctively looked down, momentarily distracted.

In the following, carefully considered instant, the peddler bent down to retrieve the keys. Instead of picking them up, he closed his hand around the crowbar he had placed behind the right front tire earlier in the evening. When he arose, he spun on his heels and slammed the steel bar into the center of Diablo's face, exploding the man's nose into a thick scarlet vapor of blood and ruined cartilage. It was a surgically delivered blow, perfectly leveraged, one designed to cripple and incapacitate but not kill. With his left hand the peddler removed the Smith & Wesson revolver from Diablo's waistband.

Dazed, momentarily bewildered, operating on animal instinct instead of reason, Diablo charged the peddler, his field of vision now clouded with blood and involuntary tears. His forward motion was met with the butt of the Smith & Wesson, swung with the full force of the peddler's considerable strength. The blow sent six of Diablo's teeth into the cool night air, then clacking to the ground like so many spilled pearls.

Diablo folded to the pitted asphalt, howling in agony.

A warrior, he rolled onto his knees, hesitated, then looked up, anticipating the deathblow.

"Run," the peddler said.

Diablo paused for a moment, his breath now coming in staggered, sodden gasps. He spit a mouthful of blood and mucus.

When the peddler cocked the hammer of the weapon and placed the tip of the barrel to his forehead, Diablo saw the wisdom of obeying the man's order.

With great effort, he arose, staggered down the road toward South Street, and disappeared, never once taking his eyes from the peddler.

The peddler then turned to Gideon Pratt.

Pratt tried to strike a pose of menace, but this was not his gift. He was facing a moment all murderers fear, a brutal computation of his crimes against man, against God.

"Wh-who are you?" Pratt asked.

The peddler opened the back door of the van. He calmly deposited the gun and the crowbar, and removed a thick, cowhide belt. He wrapped his knuckles in the hard leather.

"Do you dream?" the peddler asked.

"What?"

"Do . . . you . . . *dream*?"

Gideon Pratt fell speechless.

For Detective Kevin Francis Byrne of the Philadelphia Police Department's Homicide Unit, the answer was a moot point. He had tracked Gideon Pratt for a long time, and had lured him into this moment with precision and care, a scenario that had invaded *his* dreams.

Gideon Pratt had raped and murdered a fifteen-year-old girl named Deirdre Petti-grew in Fairmount Park, and the department had all but given up on solving the case. It was the first time Pratt had killed one of his victims, and Byrne had known that it would not be easy to draw him out. Byrne had in-vested a few hundred hours of his own time and many a night's sleep in anticipation of this very second.

And now, as dawn remained a dim rumor in the City of Brotherly Love, as Kevin Byrne stepped forward and landed the first blow, came his receipt.

Twenty minutes later they were in a cur-tained emergency room at Jefferson Hospi-tal. Gideon Pratt stood dead center, Byrne to one side, a staff intern named Avram Hirsch on the other.

Pratt had a knot on his forehead the size and shape of a rotted plum, a bloodied lip, a deep purple bruise on his right cheek, and what might have been a broken nose. His right eye was nearly swollen shut. The front of his formerly white shirt was a deep brown, caked with blood.

As Byrne looked at the man—humiliated, demeaned, disgraced, *caught*—he thought about his own partner in the Homicide Unit, a daunting piece of ironwork named Jimmy Purify. Jimmy would have loved this, Byrne thought. Jimmy loved the characters, of which Philly seemed to have an endless supply. The street professors, the junkie prophets, the hookers with hearts of marble.

But most of all, Detective Jimmy Purify loved catching the bad guys. The worse the man, the more Jimmy savored the hunt.

There was no one worse than Gideon Pratt.

They had tracked Pratt through an extensive labyrinth of informants, had followed him through the darkest veins of Philadelphia's netherworld of sex clubs and child pornography rings. They had pursued him with the same sense of purpose, the same focus and rabid intent with which they had stepped out of the academy so many years earlier.

Which was just the way Jimmy Purify liked it.

It made him feel like a kid again, he said.

In his day Jimmy had been shot twice, run over once, beaten far too many times to calculate, but it was a triple bypass that finally took him out. While Kevin Byrne was so pleasantly engaged with Gideon Pratt, James "Clutch" Purify was resting in a post-op room in Mercy Hospital, tubes and drip lines snaking out of his body like Medusa's snakes.

The good news was that Jimmy's prognosis looked good. The sad news was that Jimmy thought he was coming back to the job. He wasn't. No one ever did from a triple. Not at fifty. Not in Homicide. Not in Philly.

I miss you, Clutch, Byrne thought, knowing that he was going to meet his new partner later that day. *It just ain't the same without you, man.*

It never will be.

Byrne had been there when Jimmy went down, not ten, powerless feet away. They had been standing near the register at Malik's, a hole-in-the-bricks hoagie shop at Tenth and Washington. Byrne had been loading their coffees with sugar while Jimmy had been macking the waitress, Desiree, a young, cinnamon-skinned beauty at least three musical styles Jimmy's junior and five miles out of his league. Desiree was the only real reason they ever stopped at Malik's. It sure as hell wasn't the food.

One minute Jimmy had been leaning against the counter, his young-girl rap firing on all eight, his smile on high beam. The next minute he was on the floor, his face contorted in pain, his body rigid, the fingers of his huge hands curling into claws.

Byrne had frozen that instant in his mind, the way he had stilled few others in his life. Over his twenty years on the force, he had found it almost routine to accept the moments of blind heroism and reckless courage in the people he loved and admired. He had even come to accept the senseless, random acts of savagery delivered by and unto strangers. These things came with the job: the steep premium to justice sought. It was the moments of naked humanity and weakness of flesh, however, he could not elude, the images of body and spirit betrayed that burrowed beneath the surface of his heart.

When he saw the big man on the muddied tile of the diner, his body skirmishing with death, the silent scream slashed into his jaw, he knew that he would never look at Jimmy Purify the same way again. Oh, he would love him, as he had come to over the years, and he would listen to his preposterous stories, and he would, by the grace of God, once again marvel at Jimmy's lithe and fluid abilities behind a gas grill on those sweltering Philly summer Sundays, and he would, without a moment's thought or hesitation, take a bullet to the heart for the man, but he knew immediately that this thing they did—the unflinching descent into the maw of violence and insanity, night after night—was over.

As much as it brought Byrne shame and regret, that was the reality of that long, terrible night.

The reality of *this* night, however, found a dark balance in Byrne's mind, a delicate symmetry that he knew would bring Jimmy Purify peace. Deirdre Pettigrew was dead, and Gideon Pratt was going to take the full ride. Another family was shredded by grief, but this time the killer had left behind his DNA in the form of a gray pubic hair that would send him to the little tiled room at SCI Greene. There Gideon Pratt would meet the icy needle if Byrne had anything to say about it.

Of course, the justice system being what it was, there was a fifty–fifty chance that, if convicted, Pratt would get life without parole. If that turned out to be the case, Byrne knew enough people in prison to finish the job. He would call in a chit. Either way, the sand was running on Gideon Pratt. He was in the hat.

"The suspect fell down a flight of concrete steps while he attempted to evade arrest," Byrne offered to Dr. Hirsch.

Avram Hirsch wrote it down. He may have been young, but he was from Jefferson. He had already learned that, many times, sexual predators were also quite clumsy, and prone to tripping and falling. Sometimes they even had broken bones.

"Isn't that right, Mr. Pratt?" Byrne asked.

Gideon Pratt just stared straight ahead.

"Isn't that right, Mr. Pratt?" Byrne repeated.

"Yes," Pratt said.

"Say it."

"While I was running away from the police, I fell down a flight of steps and caused my injuries."

Hirsch wrote this down, too.

Kevin Byrne shrugged, asked: "Do you find that Mr. Pratt's injuries are consistent with a fall down a flight of concrete steps, Doctor?"

"Absolutely," Hirsch replied.

More writing.

On the way to the hospital, Byrne had had a discussion with Gideon Pratt, imparting the wisdom that what Pratt had experienced in that parking lot was merely a taste of what he could expect if he considered a charge of police brutality. He had also informed Pratt that, at that moment, Byrne had three people standing by who were willing to go on the record that they had witnessed the suspect tripping and falling down the stairs while being chased. Upstanding citizens, all.

In addition, Byrne disclosed that, while it was only a short ride from the hospital to the police administration building, it would be the longest few minutes of Pratt's life. To make his point, Byrne had referenced a few of the tools in the back of the van: the saber saw, the surgeon's rib-cracker, the electric shears.

Pratt *understood*.

And he was now on the record.

A few minutes later, when Hirsch pulled down Gideon Pratt's pants and stained underwear, what Byrne saw made him shake his head. Gideon Pratt had shaved off his pubic hair. Pratt looked down at his groin, back up at Byrne.

"It's a ritual," Pratt said. "A *religious* ritual."

Byrne exploded across the room. "So's *crucifixion,* shithead," he said. "What do you say we run down to Home Depot for some religious supplies?"

At that moment Byrne caught the intern's eyes. Dr. Hirsch nodded, meaning, they'd get their sample of pubic hair. Nobody could shave *that* close. Byrne picked up on the exchange, ran with it.

"If you thought your little ceremony was gonna stop us from getting a sample, you're officially an asshole," Byrne said. "As if that was in some doubt." He got within inches of Gideon Pratt's face. "Besides, all we had to do was hold you until it grew back."

Pratt looked at the ceiling and sighed.

Apparently that hadn't occurred to him.

Byrne sat in the parking lot of the police administration building, braking from the long day, sipping an Irish coffee. The coffee was cop-shop rough. The Jameson paved it.

The sky was clear and black and cloudless above a putty moon.

Spring murmured.

He'd steal a few hours sleep in the borrowed van he had used to lure Gideon Pratt, then return it to his friend Ernie Tedesco later in the day. Ernie owned a small meat packing business in Pennsport.

Byrne touched the wick of skin over his right eye. The scar felt warm and pliant beneath his fingers, and spoke of a pain that, for the moment, was not there, a phantom grief that had flared for the first time many years earlier. He rolled down the window, closed his eyes, felt the girders of memory give way.

In his mind, that dark recess where desire and revulsion meet, that place where the icy waters of the Delaware River raged so long ago, he saw the last moments of a young girl's life, saw the quiet horror unfold . . .

. . . *sees the sweet face of Deirdre Pettigrew. She is small for her age, naïve for her time. She has a kind and trusting heart, a sheltered soul. It is a sweltering day, and Deirdre has stopped for a drink of water at a fountain in Fairmount Park. A man is sitting on the bench next to the fountain. He tells her that he once had a granddaughter about her age. He tells her that he loved her very much and that his granddaughter got hit by a car and she died. That is so sad, says Deirdre. She tells him that a car had hit Ginger, her cat. She died, too. The man nods, a tear forming in his eye. He says that, every year, on his granddaughter's birthday, he comes to Fairmount Park, his granddaughter's favorite place in the whole world.*

The man begins to cry.

Deirdre drops the kickstand on her bike and walks to the bench.

Just behind the bench there are thick bushes.

Deirdre offers the man a tissue . . .

Byrne sipped his coffee, lit a cigarette. His head pounded, the images now fighting to get out. He had begun to pay a heavy price for them. Over the years he had medicated himself in many ways—legal and not, conventional and tribal. Nothing legal helped. He had seen a dozen doctors, heard all the diagnoses—to date, migraine with aura was the prevailing theory.

But there were no textbooks that described his auras. His auras were not bright, curved lines. He would have welcomed something like that.

His auras held monsters.

The first time he had seen the "vision" of Deirdre's murder, he had not been able to fill in Gideon Pratt's face. The killer's face had been a blur, a watery draft of evil.

By the time Pratt had walked into Paradise, Byrne knew.

He popped a CD in the player, a homemade mix of classic blues. It was Jimmy Purify who had gotten him into the blues. The real thing, too: Elmore James, Otis Rush, Lightnin' Hopkins, Bill Broonzy. You didn't want to get Jimmy started on the Kenny Wayne Shepherds of the world.

At first Byrne didn't know Son House from Maxwell House. But a lot of late nights at Warmdaddy's and trips to Bubba Mac's on the shore had taken care of that. Now, by the end of the second bar, third at the latest, he could tell the difference between Delta and Beale Street and Chicago and St. Louis and all the other shades of blue.

The first cut on the CD was Rosetta Crawford's "My Man Jumped Salty on Me."

If it was Jimmy who had given him the solace of the blues, it was Jimmy who had also brought him back into the light after the Morris Blanchard affair.

A year earlier, a wealthy young man named Morris Blanchard had murdered his parents in cold blood, blown them apart with a single shot each to the head from a Winchester 9410. Or so Byrne had believed, believed as deeply and completely as anything he had understood to be true in his two decades on the job.

He had interviewed the eighteen-year-old Morris five times, and each time the guilt had risen in the young man's eyes like a violent sunrise.

Byrne had directed the CSU team repeatedly to comb Morris's car, his dorm room, his clothing. They never found a single hair or fiber, nor a single drop of fluid that would place Morris in the room the moment his parents were torn apart by that shotgun.

Byrne knew that the only hope he'd had of getting a conviction was a confession. So he had pressed him. *Hard*. Every time Morris turned around, Byrne was there: concerts, coffee shops, studying in McCabe Library. Byrne had even sat through a noxious art house film called *Eating,* sitting two rows behind Morris and his date, just to keep the pressure on. The real police work that night had been staying awake during the movie.

One night Byrne parked outside Morris's dorm room, just beneath the window on the Swarthmore campus. Every twenty minutes, for eight straight hours, Morris had parted the curtains to see if Byrne was still there. Byrne had made sure the window of the Taurus was open, and the glow of his cigarettes provided a beacon in the darkness. Morris made sure that every time he peeked he would offer his middle finger through the slightly parted curtains.

The game continued until dawn. Then, at about seven thirty that morning, instead of attending class, instead of running down the stairs and throwing himself on Byrne's mercy, babbling a confession, Morris Blanchard decided to hang himself. He threw a length of towrope over a pipe in the basement of his dorm, stripped off all his clothes, then kicked out the sawhorse beneath him. One last *fuck you* to the system. Taped to his chest had been a note naming Kevin Byrne as his tormentor.

A week later the Blanchard's gardener was found in a motel in Atlantic City, Robert Blanchard's credit cards in his possession, bloody clothes stuffed into his duffel bag. He immediately confessed to the double homicide.

The door in Byrne's mind had been locked.

For the first time in fifteen years, he had been wrong.

The cop-haters came out in full force. Morris's sister Janice filed a wrongful death civil suit against Byrne, the department, the city. None of the litigation amounted to much, but the weight increased exponentially until it threatened to break him.

The newspapers had taken their shots at him, vilifying him for weeks with editorials and features. And while the *Inquirer* and *Daily News* and *CityPaper* had dragged him over the coals, they had eventually moved on. It was *The Report*—a yellow rag that fancied itself alternative press, but in reality was little more than a supermarket tabloid—and a particularly fragrant piece-of-shit columnist named Simon Close, who had made it personal beyond reason. For weeks after Morris Blanchard's suicide, Simon

Close wrote polemic after polemic about Byrne, the department, the police state in America, finally closing with a profile of the man Morris Blanchard would have become: a combination Albert Einstein, Robert Frost, and Jonas Salk, if one were to believe.

Before the Blanchard case, Byrne had given serious consideration to taking his twenty and heading to Myrtle Beach, maybe starting his own security firm like all the other burned-out cops whose will had been cracked by the savagery of inner-city life. He had done his time as interlocutor of the Bonehead Circus. But when he saw the pickets in front of the Roundhouse—including clever *bons mots* such as BURN BYRNE!—he knew he couldn't. He couldn't go out like that. He had given far too much to the city to be remembered that way.

So he stayed.

And he waited.

There would be another case to take him back to the top.

Byrne drained his Irish, got comfortable in his seat. There was no reason to head home. He had a full tour ahead of him, starting in just a few hours. Besides, he was all but a ghost in his own apartment these days, a dull spirit haunting two empty rooms. There was no one there to miss him.

He looked at the windows of the police administration building, the amber glow of the ever-burning light of justice.

Gideon Pratt was in that building.

Byrne smiled, closed his eyes. He had his man, the lab would confirm it, and another stain would be washed from the sidewalks of Philadelphia.

Kevin Francis Byrne wasn't a prince of the city.

He was *king*.

2

MONDAY, 5:15 AM

This is the other city, the one William Penn never envisioned when he surveyed his "green countrie town" between the Schuylkill and Delaware Rivers, dreaming of Greek columns and marble halls rising majestically from the pines. This is not the city of pride and history and vision, the place where the soul of a great nation was created, but rather a part of North Philadelphia where living ghosts hover in darkness, hollow-eyed and craven. This is a low place, a place of soot and feces and ashes and blood, a place where men hide from the eyes of their children, and remit their dignity for a life of relentless sorrow. A place where young animals become old.

If there are slums in hell, they will surely look like this.

But in this hideous place, something beautiful will grow. A Gethsemane amid the cracked concrete and rotted wood and ruined dreams.

I cut the engine. It is quiet.

She sits next to me, motionless, as if suspended in this, the penultimate moment of her youth. In profile, she looks like a child. Her eyes are open, but she does not stir.

There is a time in adolescence when the little girl who once skipped and sang with abandon finally dispatches these ways with a claim on womanhood, a time when secrets are born, a body of clandestine knowledge never to be revealed. It happens at different times with different girls—sometimes at a mere twelve or thirteen, sometimes not until sixteen or older—but happen it does, in every culture, to every race. It is a time not heralded by the coming of the blood, as many believe, but rather by the awareness that the rest of the world, especially the male of the species, suddenly sees them differently.

And, from that moment on, the balance of power shifts, and is never the same.

No, she is no longer a virgin, but she will be a virgin once again. At the pillar there will be a scourge and from this blight will come resurrection.

I exit the vehicle and look east and west. We are alone. The night air is chilled, even though the days have been unseasonably warm.

I open the passenger door and take her hand in mine. Not a woman, nor a child. Certainly not an angel. Angels do not have free will.

But a calm-shattering beauty nonetheless.

Her name is Tessa Ann Wells.

Her name is Magdalene.

She is the second.

She will not be the last.

3

Dark.

A breeze brought exhaust fumes and something else. A paint smell. Kerosene, maybe. Beneath it, garbage and human sweat. A cat shrieked, then—

Quiet.

He was carrying her down a deserted street.

She could not scream. She could not move. He had injected her with a drug that made her limbs feel leaden and frail; her mind, thick with a gauzy gray fog.

For Tessa Wells, the world passed by in a churning rush of muted colors and glimpsed geometric shapes.

Time stalled. Froze. She opened her eyes.

They were inside. Descending wooden steps. The smell of urine and rotting lunch meat. She hadn't eaten in a long time and the smell made her stomach lurch and a trickle of bile rise in her throat.

He placed her at the foot of a column, arranging her body and limbs as if she were some sort of doll.

He put something in her hands.

The rosary.

Time passed. Her mind swam away again. She opened her eyes once more as he touched her forehead. She could sense the cruciform shape he inscribed there.

My God, is he anointing me?

Suddenly, memories shimmered silver in her mind, a mercurial reflection of her childhood. She recalled—

—horseback riding in Chester County and the way the wind would sting my face

and Christmas morning and the way Mom's crystal captured the colored lights from the enormous tree Dad bought every year and Bing Crosby and that silly song about Hawaiian Christmas and its—

He stood in front of her, now, threading a huge needle. He spoke in a slow monotone—

Latin?

—as he tied a knot in the thick black thread and pulled it tight.

She knew she would not leave this place.

Who would take care of her father?

Holy Mary, mother of God . . .

He had made her pray in that small room for a long time. He had whispered the most horrible words in her ear. She had prayed for it to end.

Pray for us sinners . . .

He pushed her skirt up her thighs, then all the way to her waist. He dropped to his knees, spread her legs. The lower half of her body was completely paralyzed.

Please God, make it stop.

Now . . .

Make it stop.

And at the hour of our death . . .

Then, in this damp and decaying place, this earthly hell, she saw the steel drill bit glimmer, heard the whir of the motor, and knew her prayers were finally answered.

4

"Cocoa Puffs."

The man glared at her, his mouth set in a tight yellow rictus. He was standing a few feet away, but Jessica could feel the danger radiate from him, could suddenly smell the bitter tang of her own terror.

As he held her in his unwavering stare, Jessica sensed the edge of the roof approaching behind her. She reached for her shoulder holster but, of course, it was empty. She rummaged her pockets. Left side: something that felt like a barrette, along with a pair of quarters. Right side: air. Great. On her way down she would be fully equipped to put her hair up and make a long-distance call.

Jessica decided to employ the one bludgeon she had used her entire life, the one fearsome device that had managed to get her into, and out of, most of her troubles. Her words. But instead of anything remotely clever or threatening, all she could manage was a wobbly:

"What?"

Again, the thug said: "Cocoa Puffs."

The words seemed as incongruous as the setting: a dazzlingly bright day, a cloudless sky, white gulls forming a lazy ellipse overhead. It felt like it should be Sunday morning, but Jessica somehow knew it wasn't. No Sunday morning could shoulder this much peril, nor conjure this much fear. No Sunday morning would find her on top of the Criminal Justice Center in downtown Philadelphia, with this terrifying gangster moving toward her.

Before Jessica could speak, the gang member repeated himself one last time. "I made you Cocoa Puffs, Mommy."

Hello.

Mommy?

Jessica slowly opened her eyes. Morning sunlight burrowed in from everywhere, slim yellow daggers that poked at her brain. It wasn't a gangster at all. It was, instead, her three-year-old daughter Sophie, perched on her chest, her powder-blue nightie deepening the ruby glow of her cheeks, her face a soft pink eye in a hurricane of chestnut curls. Now, of course, it all made sense. Now Jessica understood the weight on her heart, and why the gruesome man in her nightmare had sounded a little bit like Elmo.

"Cocoa Puffs, honey?"

Sophie Balzano nodded.

"What about Cocoa Puffs?"

"I made you breakfess, Mommy."

"You did?"

"Uh-huh."

"All by yourself?"

"Uh-huh."

"Aren't *you* a big girl."

"I am."

Jessica offered her sternest expression. "What did Mommy say about climbing on the cabinets?"

Sophie's face went into a series of evasive maneuvers, attempting to conceive a story that might explain how she got the cereal out of the upper cabinets without climbing on the countertops. In the end, she just gave her mother a flash of the big browns and, as always, the discussion was over.

Jessica had to smile. She envisioned the Hiroshima that must be the kitchen. "Why did you make me breakfast?"

Sophie rolled her eyes. Wasn't it *obvious*? "You need breakfess on your first day of school!"

"That's true."

"It's the most 'portant meal of the day!"

Sophie was, of course, far too young to grasp the concept of work. Ever since her first foray into preschool—a pricey Center City facility called Educare—whenever her mother left the house for any extended period of time, for Sophie, it was *going to school.*

As morning toed the threshold of consciousness, the fear began to melt away. Jessica wasn't being held at bay by a criminal, a dream-scenario that had become all too familiar to her in the previous few months. She was in the arms of her beautiful baby. She was in her heavily mortgaged twin in Northeast Philadelphia; her heavily financed Jeep Cherokee was in the garage.

Safe.

Jessica reached over and clicked on the radio as Sophie gave her a big hug and a bigger kiss. "It's getting late!" Sophie said, then slid off the bed and rocketed across the bedroom. "C'*mon,* Mommy!"

As Jessica watched her daughter disappear around the corner, she thought that, in her twenty-nine years, she had never been quite so grateful to greet the day; never so glad to be over the nightmare she began having the day she heard she would be moving to the Homicide Unit.

Today was her first day as a murder cop.

She hoped it would be the last day she had the dream.

Somehow, she doubted it.

Detective.

Even though she had spent nearly three years in the Auto Unit, and had carried a badge the entire time, she knew that it was the more select units of the department— Robbery, Narcotics, and Homicide—that carried the true prestige of that title.

As of today, she was one of the elite. One of the chosen. Of all the gold-badge detectives on the Philadelphia police force, those men and women in the Homicide Unit were looked upon as gods. You could aspire to no more lofty a law enforcement calling. While it was true that dead bodies showed up in the course of every kind of investigation, from robberies and burglaries, to drug deals gone bad, to domestic arguments that got out of hand, whenever a pulse could not be found, the divisional detectives picked up the phone and called Homicide.

As of today, she would speak for those who could no longer speak for themselves.

Detective.

"You want some of Mommy's cereal?" Jessica asked. She was halfway through her huge bowl of Cocoa Puffs—Sophie had poured her nearly the entire box—which was rapidly turning into a sort of sugary, beige stucco.

"No sankoo," Sophie said through a mouthful of cookie.

Sophie was sitting across from her at the kitchen table, vigorously coloring what appeared to be an orange, six-legged version of Shrek, making roundabout work of a hazelnut biscotti, her favorite.

"You sure?" Jessica asked. "It's *really, really* good."

"No sankoo."

Damn, Jessica thought. The kid was as stubborn as she was. Whenever Sophie made up her mind about something, she was immovable. This, of course, was good news and bad news. Good news, because it meant that Jessica and Vincent Balzano's little girl didn't give up easily. Bad news, because Jessica could envision arguments with the teenaged Sophie Balzano that would make Desert Storm look like a sandbox fracas.

But now that she and Vincent were separated, Jessica wondered how it would affect Sophie in the long term. It was painfully clear that Sophie missed her daddy.

Jessica looked at the head of the table, where Sophie had set a place for Vincent. Granted, the silverware she selected was a small soup ladle and a fondue fork, but it was the effort that mattered. Over the past few months, whenever Sophie went about anything that involved a family setting—including her Saturday-afternoon tea parties in the backyard, soirees generally attended by her menagerie of stuffed bears, ducks, and giraffes—she had always set a place for her father. Sophie was old enough to know that the universe of her small family was upside down, but young enough to believe that little-girl magic just might make it better. It was one of the thousand reasons Jessica's heart ached every day.

Jessica was just starting to formulate a plan for distracting Sophie so she could get to the sink with her salad bowl full of Cocoa muck when the phone rang. It was Jessica's first cousin Angela. Angela Giovanni was a year younger, and was the closest thing to a sister Jessica had ever had.

"Hey, Homicide Detective Balzano," Angela said.

"Hey, Angie."

"Did you sleep?"

"Oh yeah. I got the full two hours."

"You ready for the big day?"

"Not really."

"Just wear your tailored armor, you'll be fine," Angela said.

"If you say so," Jessica said. "It's just that . . ."

"What?"

Jessica's dread was so unfocused, so general in nature, she had a hard time putting a name to it. It really *did* feel like her first day of school. Kindergarten. "It's just that this is the first thing in my life I've ever been afraid of."

"Hey!" Angela began, revving up her optimism. "Who made it through college in three years?"

It was an old routine for the two of them, but Jessica didn't mind. Not today. "Me."

"Who passed the promotion exam on her first try?"

"Me."

"And who kicked the living, screaming shit out of Ronnie Anselmo for copping a feel during *Beetlejuice*?"

"That would be me," Jessica said, even though she remembered not really minding all that much. Ronnie Anselmo was pretty cute. Still, there was a principle.

"Damn straight. Our own little Calista Braveheart," Angela said. "And remember what Grandma used to say: *Meglio un uovo oggi che una gallina domani*."

Jessica flashed on her childhood, on holidays at her grandmother's house on Christian Street in South Philly, on the aromas of garlic and basil and Asiago and roasting peppers. She recalled the way her grandmother would sit on her tiny front stoop in spring and summer, knitting needles in hand, the seemingly endless afghan spooling on the spotless cement, always green and white, the colors of the Philadelphia Eagles, spouting her witticisms to all who would listen. This one she used all the time. *Better an egg today than a chicken tomorrow*.

The conversation settled into a tennis match of family inquiries. Everyone was fine, more or less. Then, as expected, Angela said:

"You know, he's been asking about you."

Jessica knew exactly who Angela meant by *he*.

"Oh yeah?"

Patrick Farrell was an emergency room physician at St. Joseph's Hospital, where Angela worked as an RN. Patrick and Jessica had had a brief, if rather chaste affair before Jessica had gotten engaged to Vincent. She had met him one night when, as a uniformed cop, she brought a neighborhood boy into the ER, a kid who had blown off two fingers with an M-80. She and Patrick had casually dated for about a month.

Jessica was seeing Vincent at the time—himself a uniformed officer out of the Third District. When Vincent popped the question, and Patrick was faced with a commitment, Patrick had deferred. Now, with the separation, Jessica had asked herself somewhere in the neighborhood of a billion times if she had let the good one get away.

"He's pining, Jess," Angela said. Angela was the only person north of Mayberry who used words like *pining*. "Nothing more heartbreaking than a beautiful man in love."

She was certainly right about the *beautiful* part. Patrick was that rare black Irish breed—dark hair, dark blue eyes, broad shoulders, dimples. Nobody ever looked better in a white lab coat.

"I'm a married woman, Angie."

"Not that married."

"Just tell him I said . . . hello," Jessica said.

"Just hello?"

"Yeah. For now. The last thing I need in my life right now is a man."

"Probably the saddest words I've ever heard," Angela said.

Jessica laughed. "You're right. It does sound pretty pathetic."

"Everything all set for tonight?"

"*Oh* yeah," Jessica said.

"What's her name?"

"You ready?"

"Hit me."

"Sparkle Munoz."

"Wow," Angela said. "Sparkle?"

"Sparkle."

"What do you know about her?"

"I saw a tape of her last fight," Jessica said. "Powder puff."

Jessica was one of a small but growing coterie of Philly female boxers. What began as a lark at Police Athletic League gyms, while Jessica tried to lose the weight she had gained during her pregnancy, had grown into a serious pursuit. With a record of 3–0, all three wins by knockout, Jessica was already starting to get some good press. The fact that she wore dusty rose satin trunks with the words JESSIE BALLS stitched across the waistband didn't hurt her image, either.

"You're gonna be there, right?" Jessica asked.

"Absolutely."

"Thanks, cuz," Jessica said, glancing at the clock. "Listen, I gotta run."

"Me, too."

"Got one more question for you, Angie."

"Shoot."

"Why did I become a cop again?"

"That's easy," Angela said. "To molest and swerve."

"Eight o'clock."

"I'll be there."

"Love you."

"Love you back."

Jessica hung up the phone, looked at Sophie. Sophie had decided it was a good idea to connect the dots on her polka-dot dress with an orange Magic Marker.

How the *hell* was she going to get through this day?

With Sophie changed and deposited at Paula Farinacci's—the godsend babysitter who lived three doors down, and one of Jessica's best friends—Jessica walked back home, her maize-colored suit already starting to wrinkle. When she had been in Auto, she could opt for jeans and leather, T-shirts and sweatshirts, the occasional pantsuit. She liked the look of the Glock on the hip of her best faded Levi's. All cops did, if they were being honest. But now she had to look a little more professional.

Lexington Park was a stable section of Northeast Philadelphia that bordered Pennypack Park. It was also home to a lot of law enforcement types, and for that reason, there were not a lot of burglaries in Lexington Park these days. Second-story men seemed to have a pathological aversion to hollow points and slavering rottweilers.

Welcome to Cop Land.

Enter at your own risk.

Before Jessica reached her driveway, she heard the metallic growl and knew it was Vincent. Three years in Auto gave her a highly attuned logic when it came to engines, so when Vincent's throaty 1969 Shovelhead Harley rounded the corner and roared to a stop in the driveway, she knew her piston-sense was still fully functioning. Vincent also had an old Dodge van, but, like most bikers, the minute the thermometer topped forty degrees—and often before—he was on his Hog.

As a plainclothes narcotics detective, Vincent Balzano had an unfettered leeway when it came to his appearance. With his four-day beard, scuffed leather jacket, and Serengeti sunglasses, he looked a lot more like a perp than a cop. His dark brown hair was longer than she'd ever seen it. It was pulled back into a ponytail. The ever-present gold crucifix he wore on a gold chain around his neck winked in the morning sunlight.

Jessica was, and always had been, a sucker for the bad-boy, swarthy type.

She banished *that* thought and put on her game face.

"What do you want, Vincent?"

He took off his sunglasses and calmly asked: "What time did he leave?"

"I don't have time for this shit."

"It's a simple question, Jessie."

"It's also none of your business."

Jessica could see that this hurt but, at the moment, she didn't care.

"You are my *wife*," he began, as if giving her a primer on their life. "This is my house.

My daughter *sleeps* here. It *is* my fucking business."

Save me from the Italian-American male, Jessica thought. Was there a more possessive creature in all of nature? Italian-American men made silverback gorillas look reasonable. Italian-American cops were even worse. Like herself, Vincent was born and bred on the streets of South Philly.

"Oh, *now* it's your business? Was it your business when you were banging that *putana*? Huh? When you were banging that big-ass South Jersey frosted skank in my bed?"

Vincent rubbed his face. His eyes were red, his posture a little weary. It was clear he was coming off a long tour. Or maybe a long night doing something else. "How many times do I have to apologize, Jess?"

"A few million more, Vincent. Then we'll be too friggin' old to remember how you cheated on me."

Every unit has its badge bunnies, cop groupies who saw a uniform or a badge and suddenly had the uncontrollable urge to flop onto their backs and spread their legs. Narcotics and Vice had the most, for all the obvious reasons. But Michelle Brown was no badge bunny. Michelle Brown was an affair. Michelle Brown had fucked her husband in *her house*.

"Jessie."

"I need this shit today, right? I really need this."

Vincent's face softened, as if he'd just remembered what day this was. He opened his mouth to speak, but Jessica raised a hand, cutting him off.

"Don't," she said. "Not today."

"When?"

The truth was, she didn't know. Did she miss him? Desperately. Would she show it? Never in a million years.

"I don't know."

For all his faults—and they were legion—Vincent Balzano knew when to quit with his wife. "C'mon," he said. "Let me give you a ride, at least."

He knew she would refuse, opting out of the Phyllis Diller look a ride to the Round-house on a Harley would provide for her.

But he smiled that damn smile, the one that got her into bed in the first place, and she almost—almost—caved.

"I've got to go, Vincent," she said.

She walked around the bike and continued on toward the garage. As tempted as she was to turn around, she resisted. He had cheated on her and now she was the one who felt like shit.

What's wrong with this picture?

While she deliberately fumbled with the keys, drawing it out, she eventually heard the bike start, back up, roar defiantly, and disappear up the street.

When she started the Cherokee, she punched 1060 on the dial. KYW told her that I-95 was jammed. She glanced at the clock. She had time. She'd take Frankford Avenue into town.

As she pulled out of the drive, she saw an EMS van in front of the Arrabiata house across the street. Again. She made eye contact with Lily Arrabiata, and Lily waved. It seemed Carmine Arrabiata was having his weekly false-alarm heart attack, a regular event for as far back as Jessica could remember. It had gotten to the point that the city would no longer send an EMS rescue. The Arrabiatas had to call private ambulances. Lily's wave was twofold. One, to say good morning. The other to tell Jessica that

Carmine was fine. At least for the next week or so.

Heading toward Cottman Avenue, Jessica thought about the stupid fight she had just had with Vincent, and how a simple answer to his initial question would've ended the discussion immediately. The night before she had attended a Catholic Food Drive organizational meeting with an old friend of the family, little Davey Pizzino, all five foot one of him. It was a yearly occasion Jessica had attended since she was a teenager, and the farthest thing imaginable from a date, but Vincent didn't need to know that. Davey Pizzino blushed at Summer's Eve commercials. Davey Pizzino, at thirty-eight, was the oldest living virgin east of the Alleghenies. Davey Pizzino left at nine thirty.

But the fact that Vincent had probably spied on her pissed her off to no end.

Let him think what he wanted.

On the way into Center City, Jessica watched the neighborhoods change. No other city she could think of had a personality so split between blight and splendor. No other city clung to the past with more pride, nor demanded the future with more fervor.

She saw a pair of brave joggers working their way up Frankford, and the floodgates opened wide. A torrent of memories and emotions washed over her.

She had begun running with her brother when he was seventeen; she, just a gangly thirteen, loosely constructed of pointy elbows, sharp shoulder blades, and bony kneecaps. For the first year or so she hadn't a prayer of matching either his pace or his stride. Michael Giovanni stood just under six feet and weighed a trim and muscular 180.

In the summer heat, the spring rain, the winter snow they would jog through the streets of South Philly; Michael, always a few steps ahead; Jessica, always struggling to keep up, always in silent awe of his grace. She had beaten him to the steps of St. Paul's once, on her fourteenth birthday, a contest to which Michael had never wavered in his claim of defeat. She knew he had let her win.

Jessica and Michael had lost their mother to breast cancer when Jessica was only five, and from that day forward Michael had been there for every scraped knee, every young girl's heartbreak, every time she had been victimized by some neighborhood bully.

She had been fifteen when Michael had joined the Marine Corps, following in their father's footsteps. She recalled how proud they had all been when he came home in his dress uniform for the first time. Every one of Jessica's girlfriends had been desperately in love with Michael Giovanni, his caramel eyes and easy smile, the confident way he could put old people and children at ease. Everyone knew he would join the police force after his tour of duty, also following in their father's footsteps.

She had been fifteen when Michael, serving in the First Battalion, Eleventh Marines, was killed in Kuwait.

Her father, a thrice-decorated veteran of the police force, a man who still carried his late wife's internment card in his breast pocket, had closed his heart completely that day, a terrain he now tread only in the company of his granddaughter. Although small of stature, Peter Giovanni had stood ten feet tall in the company of his son.

Jessica had been headed to prelaw, then law school, but on the night they received word of Michael's death she knew that she would join the police force.

And now, as she began what was essentially an entirely new career in one of the most respected homicide units of any police department in the country, it looked like law school was a dream relegated to the realm of fantasy.

Maybe one day.

Maybe.

By the time Jessica pulled into the parking lot at the Roundhouse, she realized that she didn't recall any of it. Not a single thing. All the cramming in procedure, evidence, the years on the street, everything evacuated her brain.

Did the building get bigger? she wondered.

At the door she caught her reflection in the glass. She was wearing a fairly expensive skirt suit, her best sensible girl-cop shoes. A big difference from the torn jeans and sweatshirts she had favored as an undergrad at Temple, in those giddy years before Vincent, before Sophie, before the academy, before all . . . *this*. Not a care in the world, she thought. Now her world was built on worry, framed with concern, with a leaky roof shingled with trepidation.

Although she had entered this building many times, and although she could probably find her way to the bank of elevators blindfolded, it all seemed foreign to her, as if she were seeing it for the first time. The sights, the sounds, the smells all blended into the demented carnival that was this small corner of the Philadelphia justice system.

It was her brother Michael's beautiful face that Jessica saw as she grabbed the handle on the door, an image that would come back to her many times over the next few weeks as the things upon which she had based her whole life became redefined as madness.

Jessica opened the door, stepped inside, thinking:

Watch my back, big brother.
Watch my back.

5

The Homicide Unit of the Philadelphia Police Department was located on the first floor of the Roundhouse, the police administration building—or PAB, as it was often called—at Eighth and Race Streets, nicknamed for the round shape of its three-story structure. Even the elevators were round. Criminals were fond of pointing out that, from the air, the building looked like a pair of handcuffs. When a suspicious death occurred anywhere in Philadelphia County, the call came here.

Of the sixty-five detectives in the unit, only a handful were women, a stat the brass were desperate to change.

Everyone knew that, these days, in a department as politically sensitive as the PPD, it wasn't necessarily a person who was promoted, but quite often a statistic, a delegate of some demographic that made the cut.

Jessica knew this. But she also knew that her career on the street was exceptional, and that she had earned her slot on the Homicide Unit, even if she arrived there a few years ahead of the standard decade or so on the job. She had her degree in criminal justice; she had been a more-than-competent uniformed officer, garnering two commendations. If she had to knock a few old-school heads in the unit, so be it. She was ready. She had never backed down from a fight, and she wasn't going to begin now.

One of the three supervisors of the Homicide Unit was Sergeant Dwight Buchanan. If the homicide detectives spoke for the dead, it was Ike Buchanan who spoke for those who spoke for the dead.

When Jessica walked into the common room, Ike Buchanan noticed her and waved her over. The daywork shift began at eight, so at this hour the room was packed. Most of the last out shift was still on, which was not all that uncommon, making the already cramped half-circle space a snarl of bodies. Jessica nodded at the detectives sitting at desks, all men, all on the phone, all of whom returned her greeting with cool, perfunctory nods of their own.

She wasn't in the club *yet*.

"Come on in," Buchanan said, extending his hand.

Jessica shook his hand, then followed him, noticing his slight limp. Ike Buchanan had taken bullets in the Philly gang wars of the late 1970s and, according to legend, had endured half a dozen surgeries and a year of painful rehab to get back in blue. One of the last of the iron men. She had seen him with a cane a few times, but not today. Pride and grit, around this place, were more than luxuries. Sometimes they were the glue that held the chain of command together.

Now in his late fifties, Ike Buchanan was rail-thin, whipcord-strong, and sported a full head of cloud-white hair and bushy white eyebrows. His face was flushed and pocked by nearly six decades of Philly winters and, if the other legend was true, more than his share of Wild Turkey.

She entered the small office, sat down.

"Let's get the details out of the way." Buchanan closed the door halfway and walked behind his desk. Jessica could see him trying to cover the limp. He may have been a decorated cop, but he was still a man.

"Yes, sir."

"Your background?"

"Grew up in South Philly," Jessica said, knowing that Buchanan knew all this, knowing that this was a formality. "Sixth and Catharine."

"Schools?"

"I went to St. Paul's. Then N.A. Did my undergraduate work at Temple."

"You graduated Temple in three years?"

Three and a half, Jessica thought. *But who's counting?* "Yes, sir. Criminal justice."

"Impressive."

"Thank you, sir. It was a lot of—"

"You worked out of the Third?" he asked.

"Yes."

"How did you like working for Danny O'Brien?"

What was she supposed to say? That he was an overbearing, misogynistic, witless shithead? "Sergeant O'Brien is a good officer. I learned a lot from him."

"Danny O'Brien is a Neanderthal," Buchanan said.

"That's one school of thought, sir," Jessica said, trying her best to keep the smile inside.

"So tell me," Buchanan said. "Why are you *really* here?"

"I'm not sure what you mean," she said. Buying time.

"I've been a cop for thirty-seven years. Hard for me to believe, but true. Seen a lot of good people, a lot of bad people. On both sides of the law. There was a time when I was just like you. Ready to take on the world, punish the guilty, avenge the innocent." Buchanan turned around, faced her. "Why are you here?"

Be cool, Jess, she thought. *He's tossing you an egg.* "I'm here because . . . because I think I can make a difference."

Buchanan stared at her for a few moments. Impossible to read. "I thought the same thing when I was your age."

Jessica wasn't sure if she was being patronized or not. Up came the Italian in her. Up came the South Philly. "If you don't mind me asking, sir, *have* you made a difference?"

Buchanan smiled. This was good news for Jessica. "I haven't retired yet."

Good answer, Jessica thought.

"How is your father?" he asked, shifting gears on the fly. "Is he enjoying retirement?"

The truth was, he was climbing the walls. The last time she stopped by his house he was standing by the sliding glass door, looking out into his tiny backyard with a packet of Roma tomato seeds in his hand. "Very much, sir."

"He's a good man. He was a great cop."

"I'll tell him you said so. He'll be pleased."

"The fact that Peter Giovanni is your father won't help you or hurt you around here. If it ever gets in the way, you come see me."

Not in a million friggin' years. "I will. I appreciate it."

Buchanan stood up, leaned forward, pinned her with his intense gaze. "This job has broken a lot of hearts, Detective. I hope yours isn't one of them."

"Thank you, sir."

Buchanan looked over her shoulder, out into the common room. "Speaking of heart-breakers."

Jessica followed his gaze to the big man standing next to the assignment desk, reading a fax. They stood, exited Buchanan's office.

As they approached him, Jessica sized the man. He was in his early forties, about six three, maybe 240, solid. He had light brown hair, wintergreen eyes, huge hands, a thick, shiny scar over his right eye. Even if she hadn't known he was a homicide cop, she would have guessed. He met all the criteria: good suit, cheap tie, shoes that hadn't seen polish since they left the factory, along with the de rigueur trio of scents: tobacco, Certs, and the faint trace of Aramis.

"How's the baby?" Buchanan asked the man.

"Ten fingers, ten toes," the man said.

Jessica spoke the code. Buchanan was asking how a current case was going. The detective's response meant: *All is well.*

"Riff Raff," Buchanan said. "Meet your new partner."

"Jessica Balzano," Jessica said, extending her hand.

"Kevin Byrne," he replied. "Nice to meet you."

The name immediately dragged Jessica back a year or so. The Morris Blanchard affair. Every cop in Philly had followed the case. Byrne's image had been plastered all over the city, on every news show, newspaper, and local magazine. Jessica was surprised she hadn't recognized him. At first glance he seemed five years older than the man she remembered.

Buchanan's phone rang. He excused himself.

"Same here," she replied. Eyebrows up. "Riff Raff?"

"Long story. We'll get to it." They shook hands as the name registered with Byrne. "You're Vincent Balzano's wife?"

Jesus Christ, Jessica thought. Nearly seven thousand cops on the force and you could fit them all in a phone booth. She applied a few more foot-pounds—or, in this instance, hand-pounds—of pressure to her handshake. "In name only," she said.

Kevin Byrne got the message. He winced, smiled. "Gotcha."

Before letting go, Byrne held her gaze for a few seconds in the way that only veteran police officers can. Jessica knew all about it. She knew about the club, the territorial makeup of a unit, the way that cops bond and protect. When she was first assigned to Auto, she had to prove herself on a daily basis. After a year, though, she could roll with the best of them. After two years, she could pull a J-turn on two inches of solid ice, could tune up a Shelby GT in the dark, could read a VIN number through a smashed pack of Kools on the dashboard of a locked car.

When she caught Kevin Byrne's stare and threw it right back at him, something happened. She wasn't positive if it was a good thing, but it let him know that she was no probie, no boot, no damp-seated rookie who got here based on her plumbing.

They retrieved their hands as the phone rang at the assignment desk. Byrne answered, made a few notes.

"We're up on the wheel," Byrne said. The wheel was the duty roster of assignments for detectives on the Line Squad. Jessica's heart sank. How long had she been on the job, fourteen minutes? Wasn't there supposed to be a grace period? "Dead girl in crack town," he added.

Guess not.

Byrne fixed Jessica with a look afloat somewhere between a smile and a challenge. He said: "Welcome to Homicide."

"How do you know Vincent?" Jessica asked.

They had ridden in silence for a few blocks after pulling out of the lot. Byrne drove the standard-issue Ford Taurus. It was the same uneasy silence experienced on a blind date, which, in many ways, this was.

"A year ago we took down a dealer in Fishtown. We'd been looking at him for a long time. Liked him for the murder of one of our CIs. Real badass. Carried a hatchet on his belt."

"Charming."

"*Oh* yeah. Anyway, it was our case, but Narcotics set up a buy to draw the prick out. When it came time for entry, about five in the morning, there's six of us, four from

Homicide, two from Narcotics. We get out of the van, checking our Glocks, adjusting our vests, getting pumped for the door. You know the drill. All of a sudden, no Vincent. We look around, behind the van, under the van. Nothing. It's quiet as hell, then all of sudden we hear *'Get onna ground . . . get onna ground . . . hands behind yer back motherfucker!'* from *inside* the house. Turns out Vincent was off, through the door and up the guy's ass before any of us could move."

"Sounds like Vince," Jessica said.

"And how many times has he seen *Serpico*?" Byrne asked.

"Let's put it this way," Jessica said. "We've got it on DVD *and* VHS."

Byrne laughed. "He's a piece of work."

"He's a piece of something."

Over the next few minutes they went through their who-do-you-knows, where-did-you-go-to-schools, who-have-you-busted repartee. All of which brought them back to their families.

"So is it true that Vincent was in the seminary once?" Byrne asked.

"For about ten minutes," Jessica said. "You know how it is in this town. If you're male and Italian, you've got three choices. The seminary, the force, or cement contracting. He has three brothers, all in the building trades."

"If you're Irish, it's plumbing."

"There ya go," Jessica said. Although Vincent tried to posture himself as a swaggering South Philly homeboy, he had a BA from Temple with a minor in art history. On Vincent's bookshelves, next to the *PDR, Drugs in Society,* and *The Narc's Game,* sat a well-worn copy of H. W. Janson's *History of Art*. He wasn't all Ray Liotta and gold-plated *malocchio*.

"So what happened to Vince and the calling?"

"You've met him. Do you think he was built for a life of discipline and obedience?"

Byrne laughed. "Not to mention celibacy."

No friggin' comment, Jessica thought.

"So, you guys are divorced?" Byrne asked.

"Separated," Jessica said. "You?"

"Divorced."

It was a standard refrain for cops. If you weren't splitsville, you were en route. Jessica could count the happily married cops on one hand, with an empty ring finger left over.

"Wow," Byrne said.

"What?"

"I'm just thinking . . . two people on the job, under one roof. Damn."

"Tell me about it."

Jessica had known all about the challenges of a two-badge marriage from the start—the egos, the hours, the pressures, the danger—but love has a way of obscuring the truth you know, and molding a truth you seek.

"Did Buchanan give you his *why are you here* speech?" Byrne asked.

Jessica was relieved that it wasn't just her. "Yeah."

"And you told him you were here because you want to make a difference, right?"

Was he baiting her? Jessica wondered. Fuck *this*. She glanced over, ready to reveal a few talons. He was smiling. She let it slide. "What is that, the standard?"

"Well, it beats the truth."

"What's the truth?"

"The real reason we became cops."

"And what is *that*?"

"The big three," Byrne said. "Free meals, no speed limits, and the license to beat the shit out of bigmouthed assholes with impunity."

Jessica laughed. She had never heard it put quite so poetically. "Well, let's just say I didn't tell the truth, then."

"What did you say?"

"I asked him if he thought *he'd* made a difference."

"Oh, man," Byrne said. "Oh man, oh man, oh *man*."

"What?"

"You got in Ike's face the first *day*?"

Jessica thought about it. She imagined she did. "I guess so."

Byrne laughed, lit a cigarette. "We're gonna get along just fine."

The 1500 block of North Eighth Street, near Jefferson, was a blighted stretch of weed-blotted vacant lots and weather-blasted row houses—slanted porches, crumbling steps, sagging roofs. At the rooflines, the cornices wrote wavy contours of waterlogged white pine; the dentils were rotted to toothless scowls.

Two patrol cars flashed in front of the crime scene house, midblock. A pair of uniforms stood guard at the steps, both covertly cupping cigarettes in their hands, ready to flick and stomp the moment a superior officer arrived.

A light rain had begun to fall. The deep violet clouds to the west threatened storms.

Across the street from the house a trio of wide-eyed black kids hopped from one foot to the other, nervous, excited, as if they had to pee, their grandmothers hovering nearby, chatting and smoking, shaking their heads at this, yet another atrocity. To the kids, though, this was no tragedy. This was a live version of *COPS,* with a dose of *CSI* thrown in for dramatic value.

Behind them loitered a pair of Hispanic teenaged boys—matching hooded Rocawear sweatshirts, thin mustaches, spotless, unlaced Timberlands. They observed the unfolding scene with casual interest, fitting it into the stories they would pitch later that night. They stood close enough to the theatrics to observe, but far enough away to paint themselves into the backdrop of the urban canvas with a few quick strokes if it appeared they might be questioned.

Huh? What? No man, I was sleepin'.

Gunshots? No man, I had my 'phones on, wicked loud.

Like many of the houses on the street, the front of this row house had plywood nailed over the entrance and the windows, the city's attempt at closing the house to addicts and scavengers. Jessica took out her notebook, looked at her watch, noted their time of arrival. They exited the Taurus and approached one of the uniforms, badges out, just as Ike Buchanan rolled on the scene. Whenever there was a homicide and two supervisors were on shift, one went to the crime scene, one stayed at the Roundhouse to coordinate the investigation. Although Buchanan was the ranking officer, it was Kevin Byrne's show.

"What do we have this fine Philly morning?" Byrne asked with a pretty good Dublin brogue.

"Female juvenile DOA in the basement," said the officer, a stocky black woman in her late twenties. OFFICER J. DAVIS.

"Who found her?" Byrne asked.

"Mr. DeJohn Withers." She pointed to a disheveled, clearly homeless black man standing near the curb.

"When?"

"Sometime this morning. Mr. Withers is a bit unclear of the time frame."

"He didn't consult his Palm Pilot?"

Officer Davis just smiled.

"He touch anything?" Byrne asked.

"He says no," Davis said. "But he was down there scrapping for copper, so who knows?"

"He called it in?"

"No," Davis said. "He probably didn't have change." Another knowing smile. "He flagged us down, we called radio."

"Hang on to him."

Byrne glanced at the front door. It was sealed. "Which house is it?"

Officer Davis pointed to the row house on the right.

"And how do we get inside?"

Officer Davis pointed to the row house to the left. The front door was torn from its hinges. "You have to walk through."

Byrne and Jessica walked through the row house to the north of the crime scene, a long-since abandoned and stripped property. The walls were scarred with years of graffiti, pocked with dozens of fist-sized holes in the drywall. Jessica noticed that there wasn't a single item left that might be worth anything. Switch plates, outlet plates, outlets, fixtures, copper wire, even the baseboards were long gone.

"Serious feng shui problem here," Byrne said.

Jessica smiled, but a bit nervously. Her main concern at the moment was not falling through the rotted joists into the basement.

They emerged in the back and negotiated through the chain-link fence to the rear of the crime scene house. The tiny backyard, which abutted an alley that ran behind the block of houses, was besieged with derelict appliances and tires, all overgrown with a few seasons of weeds and scrub. A small doghouse at the rear of the fenced-in property stood guard over nothing, its chain rusted into the earth, its plastic dish filled to the brim with filthy rainwater.

A uniformed officer met them at the back door.

"You clear the house?" Byrne asked. *House* was a very loose term. At least a third of the rear wall of the structure was gone.

"Yes, sir," he said. His tag read R. VAN DYCK. He was in his early thirties, Viking blond, pumped, and heavily muscled. His arms strained the material of his coat.

They gave their information to this officer, who was taking the crime scene log. They entered through the back door and as they descended the narrow stairs to the basement, the stench greeted them first. Years of mildew and wood rot dallied beneath the smells of human by-products—urine, feces, sweat. Beneath that there was an ugliness suggesting an open grave.

The basement was long and narrow, mirroring the layout of the row house above, perhaps fifteen by twenty-four feet, with three support columns. As Jessica ran her Maglite over the space she saw it was littered with rotting drywall, spent condoms, crack bottles, a disintegrating mattress. A forensic nightmare. In the damp grime were probably a thousand smeary footprints if there were two; none, at first glance, pristine enough for a usable impression.

In the midst of this was a beautiful dead girl.

The young woman sat on the floor in the center of the room, her arms wrapped around one of the support pillars, her legs splayed on either side. It appeared that, at some point, a previous tenant had tried to make the supporting columns into Doric-style Roman columns with a material that might have been Styrofoam. Although the pillars had a cap and a base, the only entablature was a rusted I-beam above, the only frieze, a tableau of gang tags and obscenities spray-painted along the length. On one of the walls of the basement was a long-faded mural of what was probably supposed to be the Seven Hills of Rome.

The girl was white, young, perhaps sixteen or seventeen. She had flyaway strawberry-blond hair cut just above her shoulders. She wore a plaid skirt, maroon knee socks, and white blouse beneath a maroon V-neck with a school logo. In the center of her forehead was a cross made of a dark, chalky material.

At first glimpse Jessica could not see an immediate cause of death, no visible gunshot or stab wounds. Although the girl's head lolled to her right, Jessica could see most of the front of her neck, and it did not appear as if she had been strangled.

And then there were her hands.

From a few feet away, it appeared as if her hands were clasped in prayer, but there was a much darker reality. Jessica had to look twice just to be sure that her eyes were not playing tricks on her.

She glanced at Byrne. He had noticed the girl's hands at the same moment. Their eyes met and engaged a silent knowledge that this was no ordinary rage killing, no garden-variety crime of passion. They also silently communicated that they would not speculate for the time being. The horrible certainty of what was done to this young woman's hands could wait for the medical examiner.

The girl's presence, in the middle of this ugliness, was so out of place, jarring to the eye, Jessica thought; a delicate rose pushed through the musty concrete. The weak daylight that struggled through the small, hopper-style windows caught the highlights in her hair and bathed her in a dim sepulchral glow.

The one thing that was clear was that this girl had been posed, which was not a good sign. In 99 percent of homicides, the killer can't get away from the scene fast enough, which is usually good news for the investigators. The concept of blood simple—people getting stupid when they see blood, therefore leaving behind everything needed to convict them, scientifically speaking— was usually in effect. Anybody who stops to pose a dead body is making a statement, offering a silent, arrogant communication to the police who will investigate the crime.

A pair of officers from the Crime Scene Unit arrived, and Byrne greeted them at the base of the steps. A few moments later, Tom Weyrich, a longtime veteran from the medical examiner's office, arrived with his photographer in tow. Whenever a person died under violent or mysterious circumstances, or if it was determined that there might be a need for a pathologist to testify in a court of law at some later date, photos documenting the nature and extent of the external wounds or injuries were a routine part of the examination.

The medical examiner's office had its own staff photographer who took scene photos wherever indicated in homicides, suicides, fatal accidents. He was on call to travel anywhere in the city at any time of the day or night.

Dr. Thomas Weyrich was in his late forties, a meticulous man in all areas of his life, right down to the razor crease in his tan

Dockers and perfectly trimmed salt-and-pepper beard. He bagged his shoes, gloved his hands, and carefully stepped over to the young woman.

While Weyrich did his preliminary exam, Jessica hung close to the damp walls. She had always believed that simple observation of people who were good at their jobs was a lot more informative than any textbook. On the other hand, she hoped her behavior was not seen as reticence. Byrne took the opportunity to go back upstairs to consult with Buchanan and determine the path of entry for the victim and her killer or killers, as well as to direct the canvass.

Jessica assessed the scene, trying to plug in her training. Who was this girl? What happened to her? How did she get down here? Who did this? And, for what it was worth, why?

Fifteen minutes later, Weyrich cleared the body, meaning that the detectives could approach and begin their investigation.

Kevin Byrne returned. Jessica and Weyrich met him at the base of the steps.

Byrne asked: "You have an ETD?"

"No rigor yet. I'd say around four or five

this morning." Weyrich snapped off his rubber gloves.

Byrne glanced at his watch. Jessica made the note.

"What about a cause?" Byrne asked.

"Looks like a broken neck. I'm going to have to get her on the table to know for sure."

"Was she killed here?"

"Impossible to tell at this point. But my guess is she was."

"What about her hands?" Byrne asked.

Weyrich looked grim. He tapped his shirt pocket. Jessica could see the outline of a pack of Marlboros there. He would not, of course, smoke at a crime scene, even this crime scene, but the gesture told her that a cigarette was warranted. "Looks like a steel bolt and nut," he said.

"Was the bolt done postmortem?" Jessica asked, hoping the answer would be yes.

"I'd say it was," Weyrich said. "Very little blood. I'll get on it this afternoon. I'll know more then."

Weyrich looked at them, found no more immediate questions pending. Walking up the steps, his cigarette was out and lit by the time he reached the top tread.

Silence owned the room for a few moments. Many times, at a homicide scene, when the victim was a gang member shot by a rival warrior, or a tough guy laid out behind a bar by a fellow tough guy, the mood among the professionals delegated to probe, investigate, examine, and clean up after the carnage was one of brisk politeness, sometimes even lighthearted banter. The gallows humor, the off-color joke. Not this time. Everyone in this damp and hideous place went about his or her task with a grim determination, a common purpose that said: *This is wrong.*

Byrne broke the silence. He held out his hands, palms skyward. "Ready to check for ID, Detective Balzano?"

Jessica took a deep breath, centering herself. "Okay," she said, hoping she didn't sound as wobbly as she felt. She had anticipated this moment for months, but now that it was here, she found herself unprepared. Putting on a pair of latex gloves, she carefully approached the girl's body.

She had, of course, seen a number of corpses in her time on the street and in the

Auto Unit. One time she had babysat a dead body in the backseat of a stolen Lexus on a ninety-five-degree day on the Schuylkill Expressway, trying not to watch the body, which seemed to bloat by the minute in the stifling car.

In all those instances, she knew she was handing the investigation off.

Now it was her turn.

Someone was asking her for help.

In front of her was a dead young girl whose hands were bolted together in eternal prayer. Jessica knew that the victim's body, at this stage, had much to offer, by way of clues. She would never again be this close to the murderer: to his method, his pathology, his mind-set. Jessica opened her eyes wide, her senses on high alert.

In the girl's hands was a rosary. In Roman Catholicism, the rosary is a string of beads forming the shape of a circle, with a pendent crucifix, usually consisting of five sets of beads called decades, each composed of one large and ten smaller beads. On the large beads, the Lord's Prayer is said. On the smaller beads, the Hail Mary.

As Jessica approached, she saw that this rosary was made of black carved wood oval beads, with what appeared to be a Madonna of Lourdes center. The rosary was looped around the girl's knuckles. It appeared to be a standard, inexpensive rosary, but on closer inspection Jessica noted that two of the five decades were missing.

She gently examined the girl's hands. Her nails were short and clean, exhibiting no evidence of a struggle. No breakage, no blood. There appeared to be no material beneath her nails, although they would bag her hands anyway. The bolt that passed through her hands entered and exited at the center of the palms, and was made of galvanized steel. The bolt appeared to be new, and was about four inches in length.

Jessica looked closely at the mark on the girl's forehead. The smudge formed a blue cruciform, as the ashes did on Ash Wednesday. Although Jessica was far from devout, she still knew and observed the major Catholic holy days. It had been nearly six weeks since Ash Wednesday, but this mark was fresh. It seemed to be made of a chalky substance.

Lastly, Jessica looked at the label at the back of the girl's sweater. Sometimes dry cleaners left a tag with all or part of the patron's name. There was none.

She stood up a little shakily, but confident she had done a competent examination. At least for a preliminary look.

"Any ID?" Byrne stayed along the wall, his clever eyes scanning the scene, observing, absorbing.

"No," Jessica replied.

Byrne grimaced. Whenever a victim was not identified at the scene, it tacked hours, sometimes even days onto the investigation. Precious time that could never be recovered.

Jessica stepped away from the body as the CSU officers began their ceremony. They would slip on their Tyvek suits and make a grid of the space, taking detailed photographs of the scene, as well as a video. This place was a petri dish of subhumanity. There were probably prints of every derelict in North Philly here. The CSU team would be here all day. Probably well into the night.

Jessica headed up the steps, but Byrne stayed behind. She waited for him at the top of the stairs, partly because she wanted to see if there was anything else he wanted her to do, partly because she really didn't want to have to direct the investigation out front.

After a short while, she walked a few treads back down, peering into the basement. Kevin Byrne stood over the young girl's body, head down, eyes closed. He fingered the scar over his right eye, then dropped his hands to his waist, knit his fingers.

After a few moments, he opened his eyes, made the sign of the cross, and started toward the steps.

On the street more people had gathered, rubbernecking, drawn to the strobing police lights like moths to flame. Crime came often to this part of North Philly, but it never ceased to beguile and fascinate its residents.

Emerging from the crime scene house, Byrne and Jessica approached the witness who had found the body. Although the day was overcast, Jessica gulped the daylight like a starving woman, grateful to be out of that clammy tomb.

DeJohn Withers might have been forty or sixty; it was impossible to tell. He had no lower teeth, and only a few up top. He wore five or six flannel shirts and a pair of filthy cargo pants, each pocket bulging with some mysterious urban swag.

"How long I gotta stay here?" Withers asked.

"Got some pressing engagements, do you?" Byrne replied.

"I ain't gotta talk to you. I did the right thing by doing my civic duty and now I get treated like some criminal."

"Is this your house, sir?" Byrne asked, pointing to the crime scene house.

"No," Withers said. "It is *not*."

"Then you are guilty of breaking and entering."

"I didn't break nothin'."

"But you entered."

Withers tried to wrap his mind around the concept, as if breaking and entering, like country and western, were somehow inseparable. He remained silent.

"Now, I'm willing to overlook this serious crime if you answer a few questions for me," Byrne said.

Withers looked at his shoes, defeated. Jessica noted that he had a ripped black high-top on his left foot and an Air Nike on his right.

"When did you find her?" Byrne asked.

Withers screwed up his face. He pushed up the sleeves of his multitude of shirts, revealing thin, scabby arms. "It look like I got a watch?"

"Was it light out, or was it dark out?" Byrne asked.

"Light."

"Did you touch her?"

"What?" Withers barked with true outrage. "I ain't no goddamn pervert."

"Just answer the question, Mr. Withers."

Withers crossed his arms, waited a moment. "No. I didn't."

"Was anyone with you when you found her?"

"No."

"Did you see anyone else around here?"

Withers laughed, and Jessica caught a full blast of his breath. If you blended rotten mayonnaise and week-old egg salad, then tossed it with lighter fluid vinaigrette, it would have smelled a little bit better. "Who comes down *here*?"

It was a good question.

"Where do you live?" Byrne asked.

"I'm currently at The Four Seasons," Withers replied.

Byrne suppressed a smile. He kept his pen an inch over the pad.

"I stay at My Brother's House," Withers added. "When they got room."

"We may need to talk to you again."

"I know, I know. Don't leave town."

"We'd appreciate it."

"There a reward?"

"Only in heaven," Byrne said.

"I ain't *goin'* to heaven," Withers said.

"Look into a transfer when you get to Purgatory," Byrne said.

Withers scowled.

"When you bring him in to get his statement, I want him tossed and all of his things logged," Byrne said to Davis. Interviews and witness statements were taken at the Roundhouse. Interviews of homeless folks were generally brief, due to the lice factor and the shoe-box proportions of the interview rooms.

Accordingly, Officer J. Davis looked Withers up and down. The frown on her face fairly screamed: *I have to touch this bag of disease?*

"Get the shoes, too," Byrne added.

Withers was just about to object when Byrne raised a hand, stopping him. "We'll get you a new pair, Mr. Withers."

"They better be good ones," Withers said. "I do a lot of walkin'. I just got these broke in."

Byrne turned to Jessica. "We can extend the canvass, but I'd say there's a fairly good chance she didn't live in the neighborhood," he said, rhetorically. It was hard to believe anyone lived in these houses anymore, let alone a white family with a kid in a parochial school.

"She went to the Nazarene Academy," Jessica said.

"How do you know?"

"The uniform."

"What about it?"

"I still have mine in my closet," Jessica said. "Nazarene is my alma mater."

6

The Nazarene Academy was the largest Catholic girls school in Philadelphia, with more than a thousand students in grades nine through twelve. Situated on a thirty-acre campus in Northeast Philadelphia, it was opened in 1928 and, since that time, had graduated a number of city luminaries—among them industry leaders, politicians, doctors, lawyers, and artists. The administration offices for five other diocesan schools were located at Nazarene.

When Jessica had attended the school, it was number one in the city, academically speaking, winning every citywide scholastic challenge it entered: those locally televised knockoffs of College Bowl where a group of orthodontically challenged fifteen- and sixteen-year-olds sit at bunting-draped tables and rattle off the differences between Etruscan and Greek vases, or delineate the time line of the Crimean War.

On the other hand, Nazarene had also come in dead last in every citywide athletic challenge it ever entered. An unbroken record, and one not likely to ever be shattered. Thus they were known, among young Philadelphians, to this very day, as the Spazarenes.

As Byrne and Jessica entered the main doors, the dark-varnished walls and crown molding, combined with the sweet, doughy aroma of institutional food, dragged Jessica back to ninth grade. Although she had always been a good student, and had rarely been in trouble—despite her cousin Angela's many larcenous attempts—the rarefied air of the academic setting and the proximity to the principal's office still filled Jessica with a vague, formless dread. She had a nine-millimeter pistol on her hip, she was nearly thirty years old, and she was scared to death. She imagined she always would be when she entered this formidable building.

They walked through the halls toward the main office just as class broke, spilling hundreds of tartan-clad girls into the corridors. The noise was deafening. Jessica had already been five eight and had weighed 125 in ninth grade—a stat she mercifully maintained to this day, give or take 5 pounds, mostly give. Back then she had been taller than 90 percent of her classmates. Now it seemed that half the girls were her height or taller.

They followed a group of three girls down the corridor to the principal's office. As Jessica watched them, she sanded away the years. A dozen years earlier, the girl on the left, the one making a point a little too loudly, would have been Tina Mannarino. Tina was the first to get a French manicure, the first to sneak a pint of peach schnapps into a Christmas assembly. The stout one next to her, the one who rolled the top of her skirt to challenge the rule of hems being an inch from the floor when kneeling, would have been Judy Babcock. Last count, Judy, who was now Judy Pressman, had four daughters. So much for short skirts. Jessica would have been the girl on the right: a little too tall, too angular and thin, always listening, looking, observing, calculating, scared of everything, never showing it. Five parts attitude, one part steel.

The girls now carried MP3 players instead of Sony Walkmans. They listened to Christina Aguilera and 50 Cent instead of Bryan Adams and Boyz II Men. They mooned over Ashton Kutcher instead of Tom Cruise.

Okay, they probably *still* mooned over Tom Cruise.

Everything changes.

But nothing ever does.

In the principal's office Jessica noted that not much had changed, either. The walls were still a bland, eggshell enamel, the air was still fragrant with a mixture of lavender and lemon Pledge.

They met the principal, Sister Veronique, a bird-like woman in her sixties, with quick blue eyes and even quicker movements. When Jessica had attended the school, the principal had been Sister Isolde. Sister

Veronique might have been the older nun's twin—sturdy, pale, with a low center of gravity. She moved with the surety of purpose that can only come from years of chasing down and disciplining young girls.

They introduced themselves and took seats in front of her desk.

"How can I help you?" Sister Veronique asked.

"I'm afraid we may have some troubling news about one of your students," Byrne said.

Sister Veronique had grown up in the age of Vatican I. In those days the notion of trouble at a Catholic high school usually meant petty larceny, smoking, and drinking, maybe the occasional pregnancy. Now it was pointless to speculate.

Byrne handed her the Polaroid close-up of the girl's face.

Sister Veronique glanced at the picture, then quickly averted her eyes and crossed herself.

"Do you recognize her?" Byrne asked.

Sister Veronique forced herself to look again at the photograph. "No. I'm afraid I don't know her. But we have more than a thousand students. About three hundred are new this term."

She took a moment, then leaned over and pressed a button on the intercom on her desk. "Would you ask Dr. Parkhurst to step into my office?"

Sister Veronique was clearly shaken. Her voice trembled slightly. "Is she . . . ?"

"Yes," Byrne said. "She's dead."

Sister Veronique crossed herself again. "How did she . . . who would . . . why?" she managed.

"It's early in the investigation, Sister."

Jessica glanced around the office, which was pretty much as she remembered it. She felt the worn arms of the chair in which she sat, wondering how many girls had nervously perched in this chair over the past dozen years.

After a few moments, a man walked into the office.

"This is Dr. Brian Parkhurst," Sister Veronique said. "He is our head guidance counselor."

Brian Parkhurst was in his early thirties, a tall, slender man with fine features, close-cropped reddish gold hair, and the faint remnants of a faceful of childhood freckles.

Conservatively dressed in a deep gray tweed sport coat, button-down blue oxford shirt, and shiny kilty-and-tassel loafers, he wore no wedding ring.

"These people are with the police," Sister Veronique said.

"My name is Detective Byrne," Byrne said. "This is my partner, Detective Balzano."

Handshakes all around.

"How can I help you?" Parkhurst asked.

"You're the guidance counselor here?"

"Yes," Parkhurst said. "I'm also the school psychiatrist."

"You're an MD?"

"Yes."

Byrne showed him the Polaroid.

"My God," he said, the color draining from his face.

"Do you know her?" Byrne asked.

"Yes," Parkhurst said. "It's Tessa Wells."

"We're going to need to contact her family," Byrne said.

"Of course." Sister Veronique took another moment to compose herself, before turning to her computer and tapping a few keys. In a moment, Tessa Wells's school records appeared on the screen, along with her personal data. Sister Veronique regarded the screen as if it were an obituary, then hit a key and started the laser printer in the corner of the room.

"When was the last time you saw her?" Byrne asked Brian Parkhurst.

Parkhurst paused. "I believe it was Thursday."

"Thursday of last week?"

"Yes," Parkhurst said. "She stopped by the office to discuss college applications."

"What can you tell us about her, Dr. Parkhurst?"

Brian Parkhurst took a moment to organize his thoughts. "Well, she was very bright. A little on the quiet side."

"A good student?"

"Very," Parkhurst said. "Carried a 3.8 average if I'm not mistaken."

"Was she in school Friday?"

Sister Veronique tapped a few keys. "No."

"What time do classes start?"

"Seven fifty," Parkhurst said.

"And what time do you let out?"

"Generally around two forty-five," Sister Veronique said. "But intramural and extracurricular activities can sometimes keep students here until five and six o'clock."

"Was she a member of any clubs?"

Sister Veronique tapped a few more keys. "She's a member of the Baroque Ensemble. They're a small classical chamber group. But they only meet every two weeks. There were no rehearsals last week."

"Do they meet here on campus?"

"Yes," Sister Veronique said.

Byrne turned his attention back to Dr. Parkhurst. "Anything else you can tell us?"

"Well, her father is pretty sick," Parkhurst said. "Lung cancer, I believe."

"Is he living at home?"

"Yes, I believe so."

"And her mother?"

"She's deceased," Parkhurst said.

Sister Veronique handed Byrne the printout listing Tessa Wells's home address.

"Do you know who her friends were?" Byrne asked.

Brian Parkhurst again appeared to think carefully about this before answering. "Not . . . offhand," Parkhurst said. "Let me ask around."

The slight delay in Brian Parkhurst's reply was not lost on Jessica—and if he was as good as she knew he was, it was not lost on Kevin Byrne, either.

"We'll probably be back later today." Byrne handed Parkhurst a card. "But if you think of anything in the meantime, please give us a call."

"I sure will," Parkhurst said.

"Thanks for your time," Byrne said to both of them.

When they reached the parking lot, Jessica asked: "A little too much cologne for daytime, don't you think?" Brian Parkhurst had been wearing Polo Blue. A lot of it.

"Just a bit," Byrne replied. "Now why would a man over thirty need to smell that good around teenaged girls?"

"Good question," Jessica said.

The Wells house was a shabby trinity on Twentieth Street, near Parrish, a straight-through row house on the sort of typical North Philadelphia street where the working-class residents try to differentiate their homes from their neighbors' by the little details—the window boxes, the carved lintels, the decorative numbers, the pastel awnings. The Wells house had the look of a house maintained out of necessity, rather than any sense of vanity or pride of place.

Frank Wells was in his late fifties, a lumbering, raw-boned man with thinning gray hair that fell into his light blue eyes. He wore a patched flannel shirt and sun-faded khakis, along with a pair of hunter-green corduroy house slippers. His hands were dotted with liver spots, and he had the gaunt, spectral bearing of a man who had recently lost a lot of weight. His glasses had thick, black plastic frames, the type worn by math teachers in the 1960s. He also wore a nasal tube that led to a small oxygen tank on a stand next to his chair. Frank Wells, they would learn, had late-stage emphysema.

When Byrne had showed him the photo of his daughter, Wells had not reacted. Or rather, he had reacted by not visibly reacting. A crucial moment in all homicide investigations is when key players—spouses, friends, family, co-workers—are informed of the death. Reactions to the news are important. Few people are good enough actors to conceal their true feelings effectively upon receiving such tragic news.

Frank Wells took the news like a man who had survived a lifetime of tragedy with stony aplomb. He had not cried, or cursed, or railed against the horror of it all. He closed his eyes for a few moments, handed the photo back, and said: "Yes, that's my daughter."

They met in the small, tidy living room. A worn, oval braided rug sat in the center. Early American furniture lined the walls. An ancient color TV console hummed a fuzzy game show, volume low.

"When did you last see Tessa?" Byrne asked.

"Friday morning." Wells removed the oxygen tube from his nose and let the hose drape over the armrest of the recliner in which he sat.

"What time did she leave?"

"Just before seven."

"Did you speak to her at all during the day?"

"No."

"What time did she usually get home?"

"Three thirty or so," Wells said. "Sometimes later when she had band practice. She played the violin."

"And she did not come home or call?" Byrne asked.

"No."

"Did Tessa have any brothers or sisters?"

"Yes," Wells said. "One brother, Jason. He's much older. He lives in Waynesburg."

"Did you call any of Tessa's friends?" Byrne asked.

Wells took a slow, clearly painful breath. "No."

"Did you call the police?"

"Yes. I called the police around eleven on Friday night."

Jessica made a note to check on the missing-person report.

"How did Tessa get to school?" Byrne asked. "Did she take the bus?"

"Mostly," Wells said. "She had her own car. We got her the Ford Focus for her birthday. It helped with her errands. But she insisted on paying for her own gas, so she usually took the bus three or four days a week."

"Is it a diocese bus or did she take SEPTA?"

"A school bus."

"Where is the pickup?"

"Over on Nineteenth and Poplar. A few other girls take the bus from there, too."

"Do you know what time the bus passes there?"

"Five after seven," Wells said with a sad

smile. "I know that time well. It was a struggle every morning."

"Is Tessa's car here?" Byrne asked.

"Yes," Wells said. "It's out front."

Both Byrne and Jessica made notes.

"Did she own a rosary, sir?"

Wells thought for a few seconds. "Yes.
She got one from her aunt and uncle for her
first communion." Wells reached over, taking a small, framed photo from the end
table, handing it to Jessica. It was a picture
of the eight-year-old Tessa clasping a crystal bead rosary in her steepled hands. It was
not the rosary she held in death.

Jessica made a note of this as the game
show welcomed a new contestant.

"My wife, Annie, died six years ago,"
Wells said, out of the blue.

Silence.

"I'm sorry," Byrne said.

Jessica looked at Frank Wells. She saw
her own father in those years after her
mother had died, smaller in every way except his capacity for sorrow. She glanced at
the dining room and envisioned the word-
less dinners, heard the scrape of smooth-
edged silverware on chipped melamine.
Tessa had probably prepared the same

sorts of meals for her father that Jessica had: meat loaf with jar gravy, spaghetti on Friday, roast chicken on Sunday. Tessa had almost certainly done the ironing on Saturdays, growing taller each year, eventually standing on phone books instead of milk crates in order to reach the ironing board. Tessa, as had Jessica, had surely learned the wisdom of turning her father's work pants inside out to iron the pockets flat.

Now, suddenly, Frank Wells lived alone. Instead of home-cooked leftovers, the refrigerator would be colonized by the half can of soup, the half container of chow mein, the half-eaten deli sandwich. Now Frank Wells would buy the individual serving cans of vegetables. Milk by the pint.

Jessica took a deep breath and tried to concentrate. The air was cloying and close, nearly corporeal with solitude.

"It's like a clock." Wells seemed to hover a few inches over his La-Z-Boy, afloat on fresh grief, his fingers interlaced carefully on his lap. It was as if someone had positioned his hands for him, as if such a simple task were foreign to him in his bleak anguish. On the wall behind him was a skewed collage of photographs: family milestones of weddings, graduations, and birthdays. One showed Frank Wells in a fishing hat, his arm around a young man in a black windbreaker. The young man was clearly his son, Jason. The windbreaker bore an institutional crest Jessica could not immediately place. Another photograph showed a middle-aged Frank Wells in a blue hard hat in front of a coal-mine shaft.

Byrne asked: "I'm sorry? A clock?"

Wells stood, moving with an arthritic dignity from his chair to the window. He studied the street outside. "When you have a clock in the same place for years and years and years. You walk in that room and, if you want to know what time it is, you look at that space, because that's where the *clock* is. You look in that *particular space*." He fiddled with his shirt cuffs for the twentieth time. Checking the button, rechecking. "And then one day you rearrange the room. The clock is now in a *new* place, a *new* space in the world. And yet, for days, weeks, months—maybe even years—you look at the old place, expecting to find out the time. You know it's not there, but you look anyway."

Byrne let him talk. It was all part of the process.

"That's where I am now, Detectives. That's where I've been for six years. I look at that place where Annie was in my life, where she *always* was, and she isn't there. Somebody moved her. Somebody moved my Annie. Somebody rearranged. And now . . . and now Tessa." He turned to look at them. "Now the clock has stopped."

Having grown up in a cop family, having witnessed the nightly torment, Jessica was well aware that there were moments like these, times when someone had to question the closest relative of a murdered loved one, times when anger and rage became a twisting, savage thing within you. Jessica's father had once told her he sometimes envied doctors, for they were able to point to some incurable disease when they approached relatives in the hospital corridor, grim-faced and grimly cordial. All homicide cops ever had was a torn human body, and all they could ever point to were the same three things over and over and over again. *I'm sorry, ma'am, your son died of greed, your husband died of passion, your daughter died of revenge.*

Kevin Byrne edged ahead.

"Did Tessa have a best friend, sir? Someone she spent a lot of time with?"

"There was one girl who would come by the house now and then. Patrice was her name. Patrice Regan."

"Did Tessa have any boyfriends? Anyone she was seeing?"

"No. She was . . . she was a shy girl, you see," Wells said. "She did see this boy Sean for a while last year, but she stopped."

"Do you know why they stopped seeing each other?"

Wells blushed slightly, then regained his composure. "I think he wanted to . . . Well, you know how young boys are."

Byrne glanced at Jessica, signaling her to take the notes. People get self-conscious when police officers write down what they say, as they say it. While Jessica took notes, Kevin Byrne could maintain eye contact with Frank Wells. It was cop shorthand, and Jessica was pleased that she and Byrne, no more than a few hours into their partnership, were already speaking it.

"Do you know Sean's last name?" Byrne asked.

"Brennan."

Wells turned from the window, heading back to his chair. He then hesitated, steadying himself on the sill. Byrne shot to his feet, crossed the room in a few strides. Taking Frank Wells by the arm, Byrne helped him back to the overstuffed recliner. Wells sat down, positioning the oxygen tube into his nose. He picked up the Polaroid and glanced at it again. "She's not wearing her pendant."

"Sir?" Byrne asked.

"I gave her an angel pendant watch when she made her confirmation. She never took it off. Ever."

Jessica looked to the photo on the mantel, the Olan Mills–type shot of the fifteen-year-old high school student. Her eyes found the sterling pendant around the young woman's neck. Crazily, Jessica remembered when she was very young, in that strange and confusing summer when her mother became a skeleton, her mother had told her that she had a guardian angel who would look after her all her life, keeping her safe from harm. Jessica wanted to believe it was true for Tessa Wells, too. The crime scene photo made it very hard.

"Is there anything else you can think of that might help us?" Byrne asked.

Wells thought for a few moments, but it was clear he was no longer part of a dialogue, but rather adrift on his memories of his daughter, memories that had not yet turned into the specter of dreams. "You didn't know her, of course. You came to meet her in this terrible way."

"I know, sir," Byrne said. "I can't tell you how sorry we are."

"Did you know that, when she was really small, she would only eat her Alpha-Bits in alphabetical order?"

Jessica thought of how systematic her own daughter Sophie was about everything, the way she would line up her dolls by height when she played with them, the way she organized her clothes by color. Reds to the left, blues in the middle, greens on the right.

"And then she would skip when she was sad. Isn't that something? I asked her about it once when she was about eight or so. She said that she would skip until she was happy again. What sort of person skips when they are sad?"

The question hung in the air for a few moments. Byrne caught it, soft-pedaled it in.

"A special person, Mr. Wells," Byrne said. "A very special person."

Frank Wells stared blankly at Byrne for a few moments, as if he had forgotten the two police officers were there. Then he nodded.

"We are going to find whoever did this to Tessa," Byrne said. "You have my word on that."

Jessica wondered how many times Kevin Byrne had said something like that, and how many times he was able to make good. She wished she could be so confident.

Byrne, the veteran cop, moved on. Jessica was grateful. She didn't know how much longer she could sit in this room before the walls would begin to close in. "I have to ask you this question, Mr. Wells. I hope you understand."

Wells stared, his face an unvarnished canvas, primed with heartache.

"Can you think of anyone who would have wanted to do something like this to your daughter?" Byrne asked.

There was a proper moment of silence, the span of time needed for the appearance of deductive thought. The fact was, *no*body knew *any*one who could do what was done to Tessa Wells.

"No" was all Wells said.

A lot went with that *no,* of course; every side dish on the menu, as Jessica's late grandfather used to say. But for the moment, it went unsaid here. And as the spring day raged outside the windows of Frank Wells's tidy living room, as the body of Tessa Wells lay cooling in the medical examiner's office, already beginning to conceal its many mysteries, that was a good thing, Jessica thought.

A damn good thing.

They left Frank Wells standing in the doorway to his row house, his pain fresh and red and raw, a million exposed nerve endings waiting for the infection of silence. He would make a formal identification of the body later in the day. Jessica thought about the time Frank Wells had spent since his wife had died, the two thousand or so days that everyone else involved had gone about their lives, living and laughing and loving. She considered the fifty thousand or so hours of inextinguishable grief, each one populated by sixty horrible minutes, themselves counted off by sixty agonizing seconds apiece. Now the cycle of grief began again.

They had looked through some of the drawers and closets in Tessa's room, finding nothing of particular interest. A methodical young woman, organized and precise, even her junk drawer was orderly, separated into clear plastic boxes: matchbooks from weddings, ticket stubs from movies and concerts, a small collection of interesting buttons, a pair of plastic bracelets from hospital stays. Tessa favored satin sachets.

Her clothes were plain and of medium quality. On the walls had been a few posters, not of Eminem or Ja Rule or DMX or any of the current harvest of boy bands, but rather of maverick girl violinists Nadja Salerno-Sonnenberg and Vanessa-Mae. An inexpensive Skylark violin stood in a corner of her closet. They had searched her car and found nothing. They would examine the contents of her school locker later.

Tessa Wells was a working-class kid who took care of her sick father, got good grades, and probably had a scholarship to Penn State in her future. A girl who kept her clothes in dry-cleaning bags and her shoes in boxes.

And now she was dead.

Someone was walking the streets of Philadelphia, breathing the warm spring air, smelling the daffodils bursting through the soil, someone who had taken an innocent young girl to a filthy, decayed place and brutally ended her life.

In doing that monstrous thing, this someone had said:

There are one and a half million people in Philadelphia.

I am one of them.

Find me.

PART TWO

7

Simon Close, the star reporter for Philadelphia's leading weekly shock tabloid, *The Report,* had not set foot in a church in more than two decades and, although he didn't exactly expect the heavens to part and a bolt of righteous lightning to split the sky and rend him in half, leaving him a smoldering pile of fat and bone and gristle if he did so, there was enough residual Catholic guilt inside him to give him a moment's pause if he ever entered a church, dipped his finger in the holy water, and genuflected.

Born thirty-two years ago in Berwick-upon-Tweed in the Lake District, the rugged north of England that abuts the border of Scotland, a fell rat of the first order, Simon had never been one to put too much faith in anything, not the least of which was the church. The scion of an abusive father and a mother too drunk to notice or care, Simon had long ago learned to put whatever belief he had in himself.

He had lived in half a dozen Catholic group homes by the time he was seven—where he had learned many things, none of them reflecting the life of Christ—after which he was pawned off on the one and only relative willing to take him in, his spinster aunt Iris who lived in Shamokin, Pennsylvania, a small town about 130 miles northwest of Philadelphia.

Aunt Iris had taken Simon to Philadelphia many times when he was young. Simon recalled seeing the tall buildings, the vast bridges, smelling the city smells and hearing the bustle of urban life, and knew—knew as fully as the realization that he would, no matter what, hang on to his

Northumberland inflections at all costs—
that one day he would live there.

At sixteen, Simon interned as a copy dog
at the *News-Item,* the local Coal Township
daily paper, his eye, like everyone working
at any rag east of the Alleghenies, on the
city desk at *The Philadelphia Inquirer* or *The
Daily News*. But after two years of running
copy from the editorial office to the typeset-
ter in the basement, and writing the occasional listing and schedule for the Shamokin
Oktoberfest, he saw the light, a radiance
that had yet to dim.

On a storm-lashed New Year's Eve, at the
newspaper's offices on Main Street, Simon
was sweeping up when he saw a glow from
the newsroom. When he peeked in, he saw
two men. The paper's leading light, a man in
his fifties named Norman Watts, was poring
over the enormous Pennsylvania Code.

The man who covered arts and entertainment, Tristan Chaffee, was wearing a shiny
tux, his tie down, his feet up, a glass of
white Zinfandel in his hand. He was working
on a story about a local celebrity—an over-
rated singer of syrupy love songs, a low-
rent Bobby Vinton—who had apparently
been caught in a child porn sting.

Simon pushed his broom, covertly watching the two men work. The serious journalist pored over obscure details of land plots and abstracts and eminent domain rights, rubbing his eyes, butting out long-ashed cigarette after cigarette, forgetting to smoke them, making frequent trips to the loo to drain what must have been a pea-sized bladder.

And then there was the entertainment hack, sipping sweet wine, chatting on the phone with record producers, club owners, groupies.

The decision made itself.

Sod the hard news, Simon had thought.

Gimme the white Zin.

At eighteen, Simon enrolled at the Luzerne County Community College. A year after graduation, Aunt Iris passed silently in her sleep. Simon packed his few belongings and moved to Philly, at long last loping after his dream (that being, becoming the British Joe Queenan). For three years he lived on his small inheritance, trying to sell his free-lance articles to the major national glossies, with no luck.

Then, after three more years of writing freelance music and film reviews for the *In-*

quirer and *Daily News,* and eating his share of ramen noodles and hot ketchup soup, Simon landed a feature job at a new start-up tabloid called *The Report*. He worked his way up quickly, and for the past seven years Simon Close had written a weekly discourse of his own design called "Up Close!," a rather lurid crime beat column that covered the city of Philadelphia's more shocking crimes and, when he was so blessed, the transgressions of its more luminous citizens. In these areas Philadelphia rarely disappointed.

And while his venue at *The Report*—THE CONSCIENCE OF PHILADELPHIA read the tag— was not the *Inquirer* or *The Daily News* or even *CityPaper,* Simon had managed to file near the top of the news cycle on a number of big stories, much to the consternation of his far-better-paid colleagues in the so-called legitimate press.

So-called because, according to Simon Close, there *was* no such thing as the legitimate press. They were all knee deep in the cesspool, every hack with a spiral-bound notebook and acid reflux disease, and the ones who considered themselves solemn chroniclers of their times were seriously deluded. Connie Chung spending a week shadowing Tonya Harding and the "reporters" from *Entertainment Tonight* covering the JonBenet Ramsey and Laci Peterson cases were all the blur one needed.

Since when were dead little girls entertainment?

Since serious news was flushed down the toilet with an O. J. chaser, that's when.

Simon was proud of his work at *The Report*. He had good instincts and an almost photographic memory for quotes and details. He had been front and center on the story of the homeless man found in North Philly, his internal organs removed from his body, as well as the scene of the crime. On that one, Simon had bribed a night technician at the medical examiner's office with a joint of Thai stick for an autopsy photo, which, unfortunately, never saw the ink of print.

He had beaten the *Inquirer* to print on a scandal at the police department about a homicide detective who had hounded a man to suicide after the murder of the young man's parents, a crime of which the young man was innocent.

He'd even had a cover story on a recent adoption scam where a South Philly woman, owner of a shadow agency called Loving Hearts, was taking thousands of dollars for phantom children she never delivered. Although he would have preferred a higher body count in his stories, and grislier photos, he was nominated for an AAN award for "Phantom Hearts," as that adoption scam piece had been called.

Philadelphia Magazine had also run an exposé on the woman—a full month after Simon's piece in *The Report*.

When his stories broke after the paper's weekly deadline, Simon filed to the paper's website, which was currently logging nearly ten thousand hits per day.

And so it was when the phone rang around noon, rousing him from a rather vivid dream that included Cate Blanchett, a pair of Velcro handcuffs, and a riding crop, he was suffused with dread at the notion that he might once again have to revisit his Catholic roots.

"Yeah," Simon managed. His voice sounded like a mile of muddy culvert.

"Get the fuck out of bed."

There were at least a dozen people he knew who might greet him thusly. It wasn't even worth firing back. Not this early. He knew who it was: Andrew Chase, his old friend and co-conspirator in journalistic exposé. Although categorizing Andy Chase as a *friend* was a monumental stretch. The two men tolerated each other the way mold and bread might, a distasteful alliance that, for mutual profit, yielded the occasional benefit. Andy was a boor and a slob and an insufferable prig. And those were his selling points. "It's the middle of the night," Simon protested.

"In Bangladesh, maybe."

Simon wiped the crud from his eyes, yawned, stretched. Close enough to wakefulness. He glanced next to him. Empty. Again. "What's up?"

"A Catholic school girl was found dead."

The game, Simon thought.

Again.

On this side of the night, Simon Edward Close was a reporter, and thus the words were a spike of adrenaline in his chest. He was awake now. His heart began that rattle he knew and loved, the noise that meant: *story.* He rummaged the nightstand, found two empty packs of cigarettes, poked around the ashtray until he hooked a two-inch butt. He straightened it out, fired it, coughed. He reached over, hit RECORD on his trusted Panasonic recorder with its in-line microphone. He had long since abandoned the notion of trying to take coherent notes before his first *ristretto* of the day. "Talk to me."

"They found her on Eighth."

"Where on Eighth?"

"Fifteen hundreds."

Beirut, Simon thought. *This is good.* "Who found her?"

"Some wino."

"On the street?" Simon asked.

"In one of the row houses. In the basement."

"How old?"

"The house?"

"Jesus, Andy. It's too fucking early. Don't muck about. The girl. How old was the *girl*?"

"Teenager," Andy said. Andy Chase had been an EMS tech for the Glenwood Ambulance Group for eight years. Glenwood did a lot of the ambulance contract work for the city and, over the years Andy's tips had led Simon to a number of scoops, as well as to a great deal of inside dope on the cops. Andy never let him forget that fact. This one would cost Simon a lunch at The Plough & The Stars. If the story became a cover story, he owed Andy a hundred extra.

"Black? White? Brown?" Simon asked.

"White."

Not as good a story as a *little* white one, Simon thought. Dead little white girls were a guaranteed cover. But the Catholic school angle was great. A load of cheesy similes to cull from. "They take the body yet?"

"Yeah. They just moved it."

"What the hell was a white Catholic school girl doing on that part of Eighth?"

"Who am I, Oprah? How should I know?"

Simon computed the elements of the story. Drugs. And sex. Had to be. Bread and jam. "How did she die?"

"Not sure."

"Murder? Suicide? Overdose?"

"Well, the murder police were out there, so it wasn't an overdose."

"Was she shot? Stabbed?"

"I think she was mutilated."

Oh God, yes, Simon thought. "Who's the primary detective?"

"Kevin Byrne."

Simon's stomach flipped, did a brief pirouette, then settled. He had a history with Kevin Byrne. The notion that he might lock horns with him again both excited and scared the shit out of him. "Who's with him, that Purity?"

"Purify. No. Jimmy Purify is in the hospital," Andy said.

"Hospital? Gunshot?"

"Heart attack."

Fuck, Simon thought. No drama there. "He's working alone?"

"No. He's got a new partner. Jessica something."

"A woman?" Simon asked.

"No. A *guy* named Jessica. You sure you're a reporter?"

"What does she look like?"

"Actually, she's hot as hell."

Hot as hell, Simon thought, the excitement of the story heading south from his brain. No offense to female law enforcement officers, but some women on the force tended to look like Mickey Rourke in a pantsuit. "Blonde? Brunette?"

"Brunette. Athletic. Big brown eyes and great legs. Major babe."

This was shaping up. Two cops, beauty and the beast, dead white girls on crack alley. And he hadn't lifted cheek one out of bed yet.

"Give me an hour," Simon said. "Meet me at The Plough."

Simon hung up, threw his legs over the side of the bed.

He surveyed the landscape of his three-room apartment. What an eyesore, he thought. But, he mused further, it was—like Nick Carraway's West Egg rental—a *small* eyesore. One of these days he would hit. He was sure of it. One of these days he would wake up and not be able to see every room of his house from the bed. He would have a downstairs and a yard and a car that didn't sound like a Ginger Baker drum solo every time he turned it off.

Maybe this was the story that would do it.

Before he could stumble to the kitchen, he was greeted by his cat, a scrappy, one-eared cinnamon tabby named Enid.

"How's my girl?" Simon tickled her behind her one good ear. Enid curled twice, rolled over on his lap.

"Daddy's got a hot lead, dolly-doll. No time for loving this morning."

Enid purred her understanding, jumped to the floor and followed him to the kitchen.

The one spotless appliance in Simon's entire flat—besides his Apple PowerBook—was his prized Rancilio Silvia espresso machine. It was on a timer to turn on at 9:00 AM, even though its owner and chief operator never seemed to make it out of bed before noon. Still, as any coffee fanatic would aver, the key to a perfect espresso is a hot basket.

Simon filled the filter with freshly ground espresso roast, made his first *ristretto* of the day.

He glanced out his kitchen window into the square airshaft between the buildings. If he bent over, craned his neck to a forty-five-degree angle, pressed his face against the glass, he could see a sliver of sky.

Gray and overcast. Slight drizzle.

British sunshine.

He could just as well be back in the Lake District, he thought. But if he were back in Berwick, he wouldn't have this juicy story, now, would he?

The espresso machine hissed and rumbled, pouring a perfect shot into his heated demitasse cup, a precise seventeen-second pour, with luscious golden *crema*.

Simon pulled the cup, savoring the aroma, the start of a glorious new day.

Dead white girls, he mused, sipping the rich brown coffee.

Dead *Catholic* white girls.

In *crack* town.

Lovely.

8

They split up for lunch. Jessica returned to the Nazarene Academy in a department Taurus. The traffic was light on I-95, but the rain persisted.

At the school, she spoke briefly to Dottie Takacs, the school bus driver who picked up the girls in Tessa's neighborhood. The woman was still terribly upset by the news of Tessa's death, nearly inconsolable, but she managed to tell Jessica that Tessa was not at the bus stop on Friday morning, and that no, she didn't recall anyone strange who frequently hung around the bus stop or anywhere along the route. She added that it was her job to keep her eyes on the *road*.

Sister Veronique informed Jessica that Dr. Parkhurst had taken the afternoon off, but provided her with his home address and phone numbers. She also told her that Tessa's final class on Thursday had been French II. If Jessica recalled correctly, all Nazarene students were required to take two consecutive years of a foreign language to qualify for graduation. Jessica was not at all surprised that her old French teacher, Claire Stendhal, was still teaching.

She found her in the teachers' lounge.

"Tessa was a wonderful student," Claire said. "A dream. Excellent grammar, flawless syntax. Her assignments were always handed in on time."

Talking to *Madame* Stendhal hurtled Jessica back a dozen years, although she had never been inside the mysterious teachers' lounge before. Her concept of the room, like that of many of the other students, had been a combination nightclub, motel room, and fully stocked opium den. She was disappointed to discover that, all this time, it was merely a tired, ordinary room with a trio of tables surrounded by chipped cafeteria chairs, a small grouping of love seats, and a pair of dented coffee urns.

Claire Stendhal was another story. There was nothing tired or ordinary about her, never had been: tall and elegant, with to-die-for bone structure and smooth vellum skin. Jessica and her classmates had always been terribly envious of the woman's wardrobe: Pringle sweaters, Nipon suits, Ferragamo shoes, Burberry coats. Her hair was shocked with silver, a little shorter than she remembered, but Claire Stendhal, now in her midforties, was still a striking woman. Jessica wondered if *Madame* Stendhal remembered her.

"Did she seem troubled at all lately?" Jessica asked.

"Well, her father's illness was taking quite a toll on her, as you might expect. I understand she was responsible for taking care of the household. Last year she took nearly three weeks off to care for him. She never missed a single assignment."

"Do you remember when that was?"

Claire thought for a moment. "If I'm not mistaken, it was right around Thanksgiving."

"Did you notice any changes about her when she came back?"

Claire glanced out the window, at the rain falling on the commons. "Now that you mention it, I suppose she was a bit more introspective," she said. "Perhaps a little less willing to engage in group discussion."

"Did the quality of her work decline?"

"Not at all. If anything, she was even more conscientious."

"Was she close friends with anyone in her class?"

"Tessa was a polite and courteous young woman, but I don't think she had many close friends. I could ask around, if you like."

"I would appreciate it," Jessica said. She handed Claire a business card. Claire looked at it briefly, then slipped it into her purse, a slim Vuitton Honfleur clutch. *Naturellement*.

"She talked about going to France one day," Claire said.

Jessica remembered talking about the same thing. They all did. She didn't know a single girl in her class who had actually gone.

"But Tessa wasn't one of those who mooned about romantic walks along the Seine, or shopping on the Champs-Elysées," Claire continued. "She talked about working with underprivileged kids."

Jessica made a few notes about this, although she was not at all sure why. "Did she ever confide in you about her personal life? About someone who might have been bothering her?"

"No," Claire said. "But not all that much has changed since your high school days in that regard. Nor mine, for that matter. We are adults, and the students see us that way. They really are no more likely to confide in us than they are in their parents."

Jessica wanted to ask Claire about Brian Parkhurst, but it was only a hunch she had. She decided not to. "Can you think of anything else that might help?"

Claire gave it a few moments. "Nothing comes to mind," she said. "I'm sorry."

"That's quite all right," Jessica said. "You've been very helpful."

"It's just hard to believe that . . . that's she's gone," Claire said. "She was so young."

Jessica had been thinking the same thing all day. She had no response now. None that would comfort or suffice. She gathered her belongings, glanced at her watch. She had to get back to North Philly.

"Late for something?" Claire asked. Wry and dry. Jessica recalled the tone quite well.

Jessica smiled. Claire Stendhal *did* remember her. Young Jessica had always been tardy. "Looks like I'm going to miss lunch."

"Why not grab a sandwich in the cafeteria?"

Jessica thought about it. Perhaps it was a good idea. When she was in high school she was one of those weird kids who actually *liked* cafeteria food. She hiked her courage and asked: *"Qu' est-ce que vous . . . proposez?"*

If she wasn't mistaken—and she desperately hoped she wasn't—she had asked: *What do you suggest?*

The look on her former French teacher's face told her she got it right. Or close enough for high school French.

"Not bad, *Mademoiselle* Giovanni," Claire said with a generous smile.

"*Merci.*"

"*Avec plaisir,*" Claire replied. "And the sloppy joes are still pretty good."

Tessa's locker was only six units away from Jessica's old one. For a brief moment, Jessica was tempted to see if her old combination still worked.

When she had attended Nazarene, Tessa's locker belonged to Janet Stefani, the editor of the school's alternative newspaper and resident pothead. Jessica half expected to see a red plastic bong and a stash of Ho Hos when she opened the locker door. Instead she saw a reflection of Tessa Wells's last day of school, her life as she left it.

There was a Nazarene hooded sweatshirt on a hanger, along with what looked like a home-knit scarf. A plastic rain bonnet hung from the hook. On the top shelf, Tessa's gym clothes were clean and neatly folded. Beneath them was a short stack of sheet music. Inside the door, where most girls kept a collage of pictures, Tessa had a cat calendar. The previous months had been torn out. The days had been crossed off, right through the previous Thursday.

Jessica checked the books in the locker against Tessa's class list, which she had gotten from the front office. Two books were missing. Biology and algebra II.

Where were they? Jessica wondered.

Jessica riffled the pages of Tessa's remaining textbooks. Her communications media textbook offered a class syllabus on hot pink paper. Inside her theology text—*Understanding Catholic Christianity*—there was a pair of dry-cleaning coupons. The rest of the books were empty. No personal notes, no letters, no photographs.

At the bottom of the locker were a pair of calf-high rubber boots. Jessica was just about to close the locker when she decided to pick up the boots and turn them over. The left boot was empty. When she turned over the right boot, an item tumbled out and onto the highly polished hardwood floor.

A small, calfskin diary with gold leaf trim.

In the parking lot Jessica ate her sloppy joe and read from Tessa's diary.

The entries were sparse, with days between notations, sometimes weeks. Apparently, Tessa wasn't someone who felt compelled to commit every thought, every feeling, every emotion and interaction to her journal.

On the whole, she seemed a sad girl, seeing the poignant side of life as a rule. There were entries about a documentary she had seen on three young men whom, she believed, as did the filmmakers, were falsely convicted of murder in West Memphis, Tennessee. There was a long entry about the plight of hungry children in Appalachia. Tessa had donated twenty dollars to the Second Harvest program. There were a handful of entries about Sean Brennan.

What did I do wrong? Why won't you call?

There was one long, rather touching story about a homeless woman Tessa had met. A woman named Carla who lived in a car on Thirteenth Street. Tessa did not say how she'd met the woman, only how beautiful Carla was, how she might have been a model if life had not taken so many bad turns for her. The woman told Tessa that one of the worst parts of living out of a car was that there was no privacy, that she lived in constant fear that someone was watching her, someone intent on doing her harm. Over the following few weeks, Tessa thought long and hard about the problem, then realized there was something she could do to help.

Tessa paid a visit to her aunt Georgia. She borrowed her aunt's Singer sewing machine and, at her own expense, made curtains for the homeless woman, drapes that could be cleverly hooked into the fabric of the car's interior ceiling.

This was a special young lady, Jessica thought.

The last entry of note read:

Dad is very sick. He is getting worse, I think. He tries to be strong, but I know it is just an act for me. I look at his frail hands and I think about the times, when I was small, when he would push me on the swings. I felt as if my feet could touch the clouds! His hands are cut and scarred from all the sharp slate and coal. His fingernails are blunt from the iron chutes. He always said that he left his soul in Carbon County, but his heart is with me. And with Mom. I hear his terrible breathing every night. Even though I know how much it hurts, each breath comforts me, tells me he is still here. Still Dad.

Near the center of the diary, there were two pages torn out, then the very last entry, dated nearly five months earlier, read, simply:

I'm back. Just call me Sylvia.

Who is Sylvia? Jessica wondered.

Jessica went through her notes. Tessa's mother's name was Anne. She had no sisters. There was certainly no "Sister Sylvia" at Nazarene.

She flipped back through the diary. A few pages before the section that was removed was a quote from a poem that she didn't recognize.

Jessica turned once again to the final entry. It was dated right around Thanksgiving of the previous year.

I'm back. Just call me Sylvia.

Back from where, Tessa? And who is Sylvia?

9

Jimmy Purify had been nearly six feet tall in the seventh grade, and no one had ever called him skinny.

In his day, Jimmy Purify could walk into the toughest white bars in Gray's Ferry without uttering a word, and conversations would drop to a whisper; the hard cases would sit a little straighter.

Born and raised in West Philly, in the Black Bottom, Jimmy had endured travails from within as well as without, and he had handled it all with self-possession and a street dignity that would have broken a smaller man.

But now, as Kevin Byrne stood in the doorway of Jimmy's hospital room, the man in front of him looked like a sun-faded sketch of Jimmy Purify, a husk of the man he had once been. Jimmy had lost thirty or so pounds, his cheeks were sunken, his skin was ashen.

Byrne found that he had to clear his throat before speaking.

"Hey, Clutch."

Jimmy turned his head. He tried to frown, but the corners of his mouth turned up, betraying the game. "Jesus Christ. Doesn't this place have security?"

Byrne laughed, a little too loudly. "You look good."

"Fuck you," Jimmy said. "I look like Richard Pryor."

"Nah. Maybe Richard Roundtree," Byrne replied. "But all things considered—"

"All things considered, I should be in Wildwood with Halle Berry."

"You've got a better shot at *Marion* Barry."

"Fuck you again."

"However, Detective, you don't look as good as he does," Byrne said. He held up a Polaroid of the battered and bruised Gideon Pratt.

Jimmy smiled.

"Damn, these guys are clumsy," Jimmy said, bumping a weak fist with Byrne.

"It's genetic."

Byrne propped the photo against Jimmy's water pitcher. It was better than any get-well card. Jimmy and Byrne had been looking for Gideon Pratt for a long time.

"How's my angel?" Jimmy asked.

"Good," Byrne said. Jimmy Purify had three sons, all bruisers, all grown, and he lavished all his softness—what little there was of it—on Kevin Byrne's daughter, Colleen. Every year, on Colleen's birthday, some shamefully expensive, anonymous gift would show up via UPS. No one was fooled. "She's got a big Easter party coming up."

"At the deaf school?"

"Yeah."

"I've been practicing, you know," Jimmy said. "Getting pretty good."

Jimmy made a few feeble hand shapes.

"What was that supposed to be?" Byrne asked.

"It was *Happy Birthday*."

"Actually, it looked something like *Happy Sparkplug*."

"It did?"

"Yeah."

"Shit." Jimmy looked at his hands, as if it were their fault. He tried the hand shapes again, faring no better.

Byrne fluffed Jimmy's pillows, then sat down, arranging his weight on the chair. There followed a long comfortable silence only attainable between old friends.

Byrne left it to Jimmy to get down to business.

"So, I hear you got a virgin to sacrifice." Jimmy's voice was raspy and weak. This visit had already taken a lot out of him. The nurses at the cardiac desk had told Byrne he could stay five minutes, no longer.

"Yeah," Byrne replied. Jimmy was talking about Byrne's new partner being a first-day Homicide.

"How bad?"

"Actually, not bad at all," Byrne said. "She's got good instincts."

"She?"

Uh-oh, Byrne thought. Jimmy Purify was as old school as you could get. In fact, according to Jimmy, his first badge was in Roman numerals. If it were up to Jimmy Purify, the only women on the force would be meter maids. "Yeah."

"She a young-old detective?"

"I don't think so," Byrne replied. Jimmy was referring to the hotshot types who hit the unit running, dragging in suspects, bullying witnesses, trying to get on the clear sheet. Old detectives—like Byrne and Jimmy—pick their shots. There's a lot less untangling. It was something you either learned, or you didn't.

"She good-lookin'?"

Byrne didn't have to think about this one at all. "Yeah. She is."

"Bring her around sometime."

"Jesus. You get a dick transplant, too?"

Jimmy smiled. "Yeah. Big one, too. I figured, what the fuck. I'm here, might as well go for a whopper."

"Actually, she's Vincent Balzano's wife."

The name took a moment to register. "That fuckin' hothead from Central?"

"Yeah. The same."

"Forget I said anything."

Byrne saw a shadow near the door. A nurse poked her head in, smiled. *Time to go.* He stood, stretched, glanced at his watch. He had fifteen minutes until he had to meet Jessica in North Philly. "I've got to roll. We caught a case this morning."

Jimmy frowned, making Byrne feel like shit. He should've kept his mouth shut. Telling Jimmy Purify there was a new case on which he would not be working was like showing a retired thoroughbred a picture of Churchill Downs.

"Details, Riff."

Byrne wondered how much he should say. He decided to just spill. "Seventeen-year-old girl," he said. "Found in one of the abandoned row houses near Eighth and Jefferson."

The look on Jimmy's face needed no translation. Part of it said how he wished he were back in harness. The other part related how much he knew that these cases got to Kevin Byrne. If you killed a young girl on his watch, there was no rock big enough to hide under.

"Druggie?"

"I don't think so," Byrne said.

"She was dumped?"

Byrne nodded.

"What do we have?" Jimmy asked.

We, Byrne thought. This was hurting a lot more than he'd thought it was going to. "Not much."

"Keep me in the loop, eh?"

You got it, Clutch, Byrne thought. He grabbed Jimmy's hand, gave it a slight squeeze. "Need anything?"

"Slab of baby back ribs would be nice. Side of scrapple."

"And a Diet Sprite, right?"

Jimmy smiled, his lids drooping. He was tired. Byrne walked to the door, hoping he could reach the cool green sanctity of the hallway before he heard it, wishing that he was at Mercy to interview a witness, wishing that Jimmy was right behind him, smelling like Marlboros and Old Spice.

He didn't make it.

"I'm not coming back, am I?" Jimmy asked.

Byrne closed his eyes, then opened them, hoping his face was fashioned into something resembling faith. He turned. "Sure you are, Jimmy."

"For a cop, you're a terrible fuckin' liar,

you know that? I'm amazed we ever made case one."

"You just get strong. You'll be back on the street by Memorial Day. You'll see. We'll fill up Finnigan's and raise a glass to little Deirdre."

Jimmy waved a weak, dismissive hand, then turned his head to the window. Within seconds, he was asleep.

Byrne watched him for a full minute. There was more he wanted to say, a lot more, but he would have time.

Wouldn't he?

He would have time to tell Jimmy how much his friendship had meant over the years, and how he had learned what real police work was all about from him. He would have time to tell Jimmy that it just wasn't the same city without him.

Kevin Byrne lingered a few more moments, then turned, stepped into the hall, and headed to the elevators.

Byrne stood in front of the hospital, his hands shaking, his throat tight with emotion. It took him five turns of the wheel of his Zippo to light a cigarette.

He hadn't cried in many years, but the feeling in the pit of his stomach recalled a time in his life when he had seen his old man cry for the first time. His father had been as big as a house, a Two-Streeter, a Mummer of citywide repute, an original stick fighter who could carry four twelve-inch concrete blocks up a ladder without a hod. Seeing him cry made him small in the ten-year-old Kevin's eyes, made him into every other kid's father. Padraig Byrne had broken down behind their Reed Street row house on the day he learned his wife needed cancer surgery. Maggie O'Connell Byrne lived another twenty-five years, but no one had known that at the time. His old man had stood by his beloved peach tree and shook like a blade of grass in a storm that day, and Kevin had sat in his bedroom window on the second floor, watching him, crying along with him.

He never forgot that image, never would.

He had not cried since.

But he wanted to now.

Jimmy.

10

Girl talk.

Is there any more cryptic language to the male of the species? I think not. No man who had ever been privy to the conversations of young females, for any length of time, would fail to concede that there exists no task more challenging than trying to demystify a simple tête-à-tête among a handful of American teenaged girls. By comparison, the World War II Enigma code was a breeze.

I am sitting in a Starbucks on Sixteenth and Walnut, a cooling latte on the table in front of me. At the next table are three teenaged girls. Between bites of their biscotti and sips of their white chocolate mochas pours forth a stream of machine-gun gossip and innuendo and observation so serpentine, so unstructured, that it is all I can do to keep up.

Sex, music, school, movies, sex, cars, money, sex, clothes.

I am exhausted just listening.

When I was younger, there were four clearly defined "bases" as it related to sex. Now, it seems, if I hear correctly, there are pit stops in between. Between second and third, I gather, there is now "sloppy" second, which, if I am not mistaken, involves one's tongue on a girl's breast. Then there is "sloppy" third, which means oral sex. None of the above, thanks to the 1990s, is considered sex at all, but rather "hooking up."

Fascinating.

The girl sitting closest to me is a redhead, perhaps fifteen or so. Her clean, shiny hair is pulled back into a ponytail and secured with a black velvet band. She wears a tight pink T-shirt and beige hip-hugger jeans. She is sitting with her back to me and I can see that her jeans are cut low and, in the posture she is in—leaning forward to make a point to her two friends—reveal an area of downy white skin beneath the top of her black leather belt and the bottom of her shirt. She is so close to me—inches away, really—that I can see the small dimples of gooseflesh caused by the draft of the air-conditioning, the ridges of the base of her spine.

Close enough, in fact, for me to touch.

She prattles on about something to do with her job, about someone named Corinne always being late and leaving the cleaning up to her, about how the boss is such a jerk and has really bad breath and, like, thinks he's really hot but in reality looks like that fat guy on The Sopranos *who takes care of Tony's uncle, or father, or whoever he is.*

I do so love this age. No detail is so small or insignificant that it will escape their scrutiny. They know enough to use their sexuality to get what they want, but have no idea that what they wield is so powerful, so devastatingly halting to the male psyche that, if they only knew what to ask for, it would be theirs on a platter. The irony is that, for most of them, when that under-

standing dawns, they will no longer possess the looks to achieve their goals.

As if scripted, they all manage to look at their watches at the same time. They gather their trash and make their way to the door.

I will not follow.

Not these girls. Not today.

Today belongs to Bethany.

The crown sits in the bag at my feet, and although I am not a fan of irony—irony is a dog that bays at the moon while pissing on graves, according to Karl Kraus—it is no small mockery that the bag is from Bailey Banks & Biddle.

Cassiodorus believed the crown of thorns was placed upon Jesus's head in order that all the thorns of the world might be gathered together and broken, but I don't believe that to be true. The crown for Bethany is anything but broken.

Bethany Price gets out of school at two twenty. Some days she stops at a Dunkin' Donuts for a hot chocolate and a cruller, sitting in a booth, reading a book by Pat Ballard or Lynne Murray, novelists who specialize in romances featuring larger women.

Bethany is heavier than the other girls, you see, and terribly self-conscious about it.

She buys her Zaftique and Junonia brand items on the Internet, still uncomfortable shopping in the plus-size departments at Macy's and Nordstrom, lest she be seen by her classmates. Unlike some of her thinner friends, she does not try to shorten the hem of her school uniform skirt.

It has been said that vanity blossoms but bears no fruit. Perhaps, but my girls sit at the school of Mary and therefore, despite their sins, will receive abundant grace.

Bethany does not know it, but she is perfect just the way she is.

Perfect.

Except for one thing.

And I will correct that.

1 1

They spent the afternoon recanvassing the route that Tessa Wells had walked to get to her bus stop in the morning. While a few of the houses yielded no response to their knocks, they spoke to a dozen people who were familiar with the Catholic schoolgirls who caught the bus on the corner. None recalled anything out of the ordinary on Friday, or any other day for that matter.

Then they caught a small break. As it often does, it came at the last stop. This time, at a ramshackle row house with olive-green awnings and a grimy brass door knocker in the shape of a moose head. The house was less than half a block from where Tessa Wells caught her school bus.

Byrne approached the door. Jessica hung back. After half a dozen knocks, they were about to move on when the door cracked an inch.

"Ain't buying nothin'," a man's thin voice offered.

"Ain't selling." Byrne showed the man his badge.

"Whatcha want?"

"For starters, I want you to open the door more than an inch," Byrne replied, as diplomatically as possible when one is on one's fiftieth interview of the day.

The man closed the door, unhooked the chain, then opened it wide. He was in his seventies, dressed in plaid pajama bottoms and a garish mauve smoking jacket that may have been fashionable sometime during the Eisenhower administration. He wore unlaced broughams on his feet, no socks. His name was Charles Noone.

"We're talking to everyone in the neighborhood, sir. Did you happen to see this girl on Friday?"

Byrne proffered a photograph of Tessa Wells, a copy of her high school portrait. The man fished a pair of off-the-rack bifocals out of his jacket pocket, then studied the photo for a few moments, adjusting his glasses up and down, back and forth. Jessica could see the price sticker still on the lower part of the right lens.

"Yeah. I seen her," Noone said.

"Where?"

"She walked to the corner like every other day."

"Where did you see her?"

The man pointed to the sidewalk, then swept a bony forefinger left to right. "She come up the street like always. I remember her because she always looks like she's off somewheres."

"Off?"

"Yeah. You know. Like off somewheres on her own planet. Eyes down, thinkin' about stuff."

"What else do you remember?" Byrne asked.

"Well, she stopped for a little while right

in front of the window. Right about where that young lady is standing."

Noone pointed to where Jessica stood.

"How long was she there?"

"Didn't time her."

Byrne took a deep breath, exhaled, his patience walking a tightrope, no net. "Approximately."

"Dunno," Noone said. He looked at the ceiling, eyes closed. Jessica noted that his fingers twitched. It appeared that Charles Noone was counting. If the number was more than ten, she wondered if he would be taking off his shoes. He looked back at Byrne. "Twenty seconds, maybe."

"What did she do?"

"Do?"

"While she was in front of your house. What did she do?"

"She didn't *do* nothin'."

"She just stood there?"

"Well, she was lookin' up the street at something. No, not exactly up the *street*. More like at the driveway next to the house." Charles Noone pointed to his right, at the driveway that separated his house from the tavern on the corner.

"Just looking?"

"Yeah. Like she seen something interesting. Like she seen somebody she knows. She blushed, like. You know how young girls are."

"Not really," Byrne said. "Why don't you tell me?"

At this, all body language changed, affected those little shifts that tell the parties involved they have entered a new phase of the conversation. Noone stepped back half an inch and tied the sash on his smoking jacket a little tighter, his shoulders stiffening slightly. Byrne shifted his weight onto his right foot, peered past the man into the gloom of his living room.

"I'm just saying," Noone said. "She just kinda went red for a second is all."

Byrne held the man's gaze until the man had to look away. Jessica had only known Kevin Byrne for a few hours, but already she had seen the cold green fire of those eyes. Byrne moved on. Charles Noone wasn't their man. "Did she say anything?"

"I don't think so," Noone replied, a new measure of respect in his voice.

"Did you see anybody in that driveway?"

"No, sir," the man said. "I don't have no

window over there. Besides, it's none of my business."

Yeah, right, Jessica thought. *Want to come down to the Roundhouse and explain why you watch young girls walk to school every day?*

Byrne gave the man a card. Charles Noone promised to call if he remembered anything.

The building next to Noone's house was an abandoned tavern called the Five Aces, a square, one-story brick-and-mortar blot on the cityscape that offered a drive-way to both Nineteenth Street and Poplar Avenue.

They knocked on the door to the Five Aces, but there was no response. The build-ing was boarded and tagged five senti-ments deep in graffiti. They checked the doors and windows, all of which were well nailed and bolted from the outside. What-ever happened to Tessa had not happened in this building.

They stood in the driveway and looked up and down the street, as well as across the street. There were two row houses with a clear view of the driveway. They canvassed both. Neither tenant recalled seeing Tessa Wells.

On the way back to the Roundhouse, Jessica assembled the puzzle of Tessa Wells's last morning.

At approximately six fifty on Friday morning, Tessa Wells left her house, walking to the bus stop. The route she took was the one she took always—down Twentieth to Poplar, over a block, then crossing to the other side of the street. At about 7:00 AM she was seen in front of a row house at Nineteenth and Poplar, where she hesitated for a short while, perhaps seeing someone she knew in the driveway to a long-shuttered tavern.

On most mornings she met her friends from Nazarene. At about five minutes after seven, the bus would pick them up and take them to school.

But Friday morning, Tessa Wells did not meet with her friends. Friday morning, Tessa simply vanished.

Approximately seventy-two hours later her body was found in an abandoned row house in one of the worst neighborhoods in Philadelphia, her neck broken, her hands mutilated, her body embracing a mockery of a Roman column.

Who had been in that driveway?

Back at the Roundhouse, Byrne ran an NCIC and PCIC check on everyone they had encountered. Everyone of interest, that is. Frank Wells, DeJohn Withers, Brian Parkhurst, Charles Noone, Sean Brennan. The National Crime Information Center is a computerized index of criminal justice information available to federal, state, and local law enforcement and other criminal justice agencies. The Philadelphia Crime Information Center was the local version.

Only Dr. Brian Parkhurst yielded results.

At the end of their tour they met with Ike Buchanan to give him a status report.

"Guess who has a sheet?" Byrne asked.

For some reason, Jessica didn't have to give it too much thought. "Dr. Cologne?" she replied.

"You got it," Byrne said. "Brian Allan Parkhurst," he began, reading from the computer printout. "Thirty-five years old, single, currently residing on Larchwood Street in the Garden Court area. Got his BS at John Carroll University in Ohio, his MD at Penn."

"What are the priors?" Buchanan asked. "Jaywalking?"

"You ready for this? Eight years ago he was charged with kidnapping. But it was no-billed."

"Kidnapping?" Buchanan asked, a little incredulous.

"He was a counselor at a high school and it turns out he was having an affair with one of the seniors. They went away for a weekend without telling the girl's parents, the parents called the police, and Dr. Parkhurst was picked up."

"Why was it no-billed?"

"Lucky for the good doctor, the girl turned eighteen the day before they left, and claimed that she went along willingly. The DA had to drop all charges."

"And where did this happen?" Buchanan asked.

"In Ohio. The Beaumont School."

"What is the Beaumont School?"

"A Catholic girls school."

Buchanan looked at Jessica, then at Byrne. He knew what they both were thinking.

"Let's tread lightly on this," Buchanan said. "Dating young girls is a long way from what was done to Tessa Wells. This is going to be a high-profile case, and I don't want Monsignor Brass Balls up my ass for harassment."

Buchanan was referring to Monsignor Terry Pacek, the very vocal, very telegenic, some would say militant spokesman for the Archdiocese of Philadelphia. Pacek oversaw all media relations concerning Philadelphia's Catholic churches and schools. He had butted heads with the department many times during the Catholic priest sex scandal in 2002, usually coming out on top in the public relations battles. You didn't want to go to war with Terry Pacek unless you had a full quiver.

Before Byrne could press the issue of shadowing Brian Parkhurst, his phone rang. It was Tom Weyrich.

"What's up?" Byrne asked.

Weyrich said: "There's something you better see."

The medical examiner's office was a gray monolith on University Avenue. Of the six thousand or so cases of death that were reported in Philadelphia every year, nearly half required a postmortem, and all were performed in this building.

Byrne and Jessica entered the main autopsy theater at just after six o'clock. Tom Weyrich wore his apron and a look of deep concern. Tessa Wells was laid out on one of the stainless steel tables, her skin a pallid gray, the powder blue sheet pulled up to her shoulders.

"I'm ruling this a homicide," Weyrich said, stating the obvious. "Spinal shock due to a transected cord." Weyrich slipped an X-ray into a light board. "The transection occurred between C5 and C6."

His initial assessment had been correct. Tessa Wells had died from a broken neck.

"At the scene?" Byrne asked.

"At the scene," Weyrich said.

"Any bruising?" Byrne asked.

Weyrich returned to the body and indicated the two small contusions on Tessa Wells's neck.

"This is where he grabbed her, then snapped her head to the right."

"Anything usable?"

Weyrich shook his head. "The doer wore latex gloves."

"What about the cross on her forehead?" The blue, chalky material on Tessa's forehead was faint, but still visible.

"I've swabbed it," Weyrich said. "It's at the lab."

"Any signs of a struggle? Defensive wounds?"

"None," Weyrich said.

Byrne considered this. "If she was alive when she was brought into that basement, why was there no sign of a fight?" he asked. "Why weren't her legs and thighs covered with cuts?"

"We found a small quantity of midazolam in her system."

"What is that?" Byrne asked.

"Midazolam is similar to Rohypnol. We're starting to see it show up on the streets more and more these days because it's still colorless and odorless."

Jessica knew, through Vincent, that the use of Rohypnol as a date rape drug was beginning to slack off due to the fact that it was now being formulated to turn blue when dropped into liquids, thereby tipping off the unsuspecting prey. But leave it to science to replace one horror with another.

"So you're saying our doer slipped this midazolam into a drink?"

Weyrich shook his head. He lifted the hair on the right side of Tessa Wells's neck. There was a small puncture wound. "She was injected with it. Small-bore needle."

Jessica and Byrne found each other's eyes. This changed things. Putting a drug in a drink was one thing. A lunatic roaming the streets with a hypodermic needle was quite another. He wasn't concerned with finessing his victims into his web.

"Is it particularly difficult to administer properly?" Byrne asked.

"It would take some knowledge not to hit muscle," Weyrich said. "But it's nothing that couldn't be learned with a little practice. An LPN could do it without too much of a problem. On the other hand, you can make a nuclear weapon with what you can find on the Internet these days."

"What about the drug itself?" Jessica asked.

"Ditto the Internet," Weyrich said. "I get Canadian spam for OxyContin every ten minutes. But the presence of midazolam doesn't explain the lack of defensive wounds. Even sedated, the natural instinct is to fight back. There wasn't enough of the drug in her system to totally incapacitate her."

"So what are you saying?" Jessica asked.

"I'm saying that there's something else. I'm going to have to run more tests."

Jessica noticed a small evidence bag on the table. "What is this?"

Weyrich held up the envelope. It contained a small picture, a reproduction of an old painting. "This was between her hands."

He extracted the picture with rubber-tipped forceps.

"It was rolled up between her palms," he continued. "It's been dusted for prints. There were none."

Jessica looked closely at the reproduction, which was about the size of a bridge playing card. "Do you know what it is?"

"CSU took a digital photograph of it and sent it to the head librarian at the fine arts department of the Free Library," Weyrich said. "She recognized it right away. It is called *Dante and Virgil at the Gates of Hell* by William Blake."

"Any idea what it means?" Byrne asked.

"Sorry. No idea at all."

Byrne stared at the picture for a few moments, then put it back into the evidence bag. He turned back to Tessa Wells. "Was she sexually assaulted?"

"Yes and no," Weyrich said.

Byrne and Jessica exchanged a glance. Tom Weyrich was not given to theatrics, so there must be a good reason he was putting off what he had to tell them.

"What do you mean?" Byrne asked.

"My preliminary findings are that she wasn't raped and, as far as I can tell, she didn't have intercourse in the past few days," Weyrich said.

"Okay. That's the *no* part," Byrne said. "What's the *yes*?"

Weyrich hesitated a second, then pulled the sheet down to Tessa's thighs. The young woman's legs were slightly spread. What Jessica saw took her breath away. "My God," she said, before she could stop herself.

The room fell silent, its living occupants adrift on their own thoughts.

"When was this done?" Byrne finally asked.

Weyrich cleared his throat. He'd been at this a while and it appeared that, even for him, this was a new one. "At some point in the past twelve hours."

"Premortem?"

"Premortem," Weyrich replied.

Jessica looked back at the body, the image of this young girl's final indignity finding, and settling, in a place in her mind where she knew it would live for a very long time.

Not only was Tessa Wells kidnapped from the street on her way to school. Not only was she drugged and taken to a place where someone broke her neck. Not only were her hands mutilated by a steel bolt, sealing them in prayer. Whoever had done these had finished the job with a final disgrace that turned Jessica's stomach.

Tessa Wells's vagina was sewn shut.

And the crude stitching, which was done with a thick black thread, was in the sign of the cross.

1 2

If J. Alfred Prufrock measured his life in coffee spoons, Simon Edward Close measured his in deadlines. He had less than five hours to make the deadline for the next day's print edition of *The Report*. And as of the opening credits of the evening local news, he had nothing to report.

When he moved among the reporters from the so-called legitimate press he was an exile. They regarded him the way you might a Mongoloid child, with looks of spurious compassion and ersatz sympathy, but also with an expression that said: *We can't kick you out of the party, but please don't touch the Hummels.*

The half a dozen reporters lingering near the cordoned-off crime scene on Eighth Street barely gave him a glance as he arrived in his ten-year-old Honda Accord. Simon would have liked to be a little more discreet in his arrivals, but his muffler—which was attached to the manifold pipe by a recently performed Pepsi-canectomy—insisted on announcing him first. He could almost hear the smirks from half a block away.

The block was cordoned off with yellow crime scene tape. Simon turned the car around, drove down to Jefferson, left to Ninth. Ghost town.

Simon got out, checked the batteries in his recorder. He smoothed his tie, the creases in his trousers. He had often thought that, if he didn't spend all his money on clothes, he might be able to upgrade his car or his flat. But he always rationalized that he spent most of his time on the street so, if no one saw his car or apartment, they would think him in the chips.

After all, in this business of show, image was everything, yes?

He found the access path he needed, cut through. When he saw the uniformed officer standing, behind the crime scene house—but not a solitary reporter, not yet, anyway—he made his way back to his car, and tried a trick he had learned from a wizened old paparazzo he knew from years ago.

Ten minutes later, he approached the officer behind the house. The officer, a huge black linebacker with enormous hands, held up one of those hands stopping him.

"How ya doing?" Simon asked.

"This is a crime scene, sir."

Simon nodded. He held up his press ID. "Simon Close with *The Report*."

No reaction. He could have just as well said, *Captain Nemo with the* Nautilus.

"You'll have to speak to the detective in charge of the case," the cop said.

"Of course," Simon said. "Who would that be?"

"That would be Detective Byrne."

Simon made a note, as if this information was new to him. "What is her first name?"

The uniform screwed up his face. "Who?"

"Detective Byrne."

"*Her* first name is Kevin."

Simon tried to look appropriately confused. Two years of high school drama, including the part of Algernon in *The Importance of Being Earnest,* helped somewhat. "Oh, I'm sorry," he said. "I heard a female detective was working on this case."

"That would be Detective Jessica Balzano," the officer said, with punctuation and a narrowing of brow that told Simon that this conversation was over.

"Thanks so much," Simon said, heading back down the alley. He turned, snapped a quick photograph of the cop. The cop got immediately on his radio, which meant that within a minute or two the area behind the row houses would be officially sealed.

By the time Simon got back to Ninth Street, there were already two reporters lingering behind the yellow tape across the access passageway—yellow tape Simon himself put there a few minutes earlier.

When he came strolling out, he could see the look on their faces. Simon ducked under the tape, tore it from the wall, handed it to Benny Lozado, a staffer from the *Inquirer.*

The yellow tape read: DEL-CO ASPHALT.

"Fuck you, Close," Lozado said.

"Dinner first, love."

Back in his car, Simon rummaged his memory.

Jessica Balzano.

Where did he know that name from?

He picked up a copy of last week's *Report,* thumbed through it. When he got to the meager sports page, he saw it. A small quarter-column ad for prizefights at the Blue Horizon. An all-female fight card.

At the bottom:

Jessica Balzano v. Mariella Munoz.

1 3

He found himself on the waterfront before his mind had the opportunity or the inclination to say no. How long had it been since he had been here?

Eight months, one week, two days.

The day Deirdre Pettigrew's body was found.

He knew the answer just as clearly as he knew the reason he had come back. He was here to recharge, to once again tap into the vein of madness that pulsed just beneath the asphalt of his city.

Deuces was a protected drug house that occupied an old waterfront building beneath the Walt Whitman Bridge, near Packer Avenue, just a few feet from the banks of the Delaware River. The steel front door was covered by gang graffiti and manned by a mountainous thug named Serious. Nobody accidentally wandered into Deuces. In fact, it had been more than a decade since the public had called it Deuces. Deuces was the name of the long-shuttered bar in which a very bad man named Luther White had been sitting and drinking the night Kevin Byrne and Jimmy Purify had entered, fifteen years earlier; the night that left two of them dead.

It was on this spot that Kevin Byrne's dark time began.

It was on this spot he began to see.

Now it was a crack house.

But Kevin Byrne wasn't here for the drugs. While it was true that he had flirted with every substance known to mankind over the years in order to stop the visions rumbling in his head, none had ever taken control. It had been years since he had dallied with anything other than Vicodin or bourbon.

He was here to reclaim the mind-set.

He broke the seal on a bottle of Old Forester, considered his day.

On the day his divorce had become final, nearly a year earlier, he and Donna had vowed that they would have dinner, as a family, one night every week. Despite the many obstacles both their jobs tossed in the way, they had not missed a week in a year.

This night they had muddled and mumbled their way through another dinner, his wife an uncluttered horizon, the dining room chatter a parallel monologue of perfunctory questions and stock answers.

For the past five years Donna Sullivan Byrne had been the white-hot agent for one of the largest and most prestigious Realtors in Philadelphia, and the money had rolled in. They weren't living in a row house in Fitler Square because Kevin Byrne was such a great cop. On his pay grade, they would have lived in Fishtown.

Back in the day, in the summer of their marriage, they would meet for lunch in Center City two or three times a week, and

Donna would tell him of her triumphs, her infrequent failures, her clever maneuvering through the jungles of escrow, closing costs, amortization, arrears, and appurtenances. Byrne had always glazed over at the terms—he couldn't tell a basis point from a balloon payment—just as he had always marveled at her energy, her zeal. She had come to her career well into her thirties, and she was happy.

But just about eighteen months earlier, Donna had simply shut down communication channels with her husband. The money still came in, and Donna was still an incredible mother to Colleen, still active in the community, but when it came to talking to him, sharing anything resembling a feeling, a thought, an opinion, she was gone. Walls up, turrets armed.

No note. No explanation. No rationale.

But Byrne knew why. When they had gotten married, he had promised her that he had ambitions within the department, that he was on a steady track to lieutenant, perhaps captain. Beyond that, politics? He had ruled it out within, but never without. Donna had always been skeptical. She knew enough cops to know that homicide detectives were lifers, and that you rode the unit right until the end.

And then Morris Blanchard was found swinging from the end of a towrope. Donna looked at Byrne that night and, without asking a single question, knew that he would never give up the chase to get back on top. He was Homicide, and that's all he would ever be.

A few days later, she filed.

After a long, tearful talk with Colleen, Byrne decided not to fight it. They had been watering a dead plant for a long time anyway. As long as Donna didn't poison his daughter against him, and as long as he got to see her when he wanted, it was okay.

This night, while her parents postured, Colleen had dutifully sat with them at their pantomimed dinner, lost in a book by Nora Roberts. Sometimes Byrne envied Colleen her inner silence, her cottony refuge from her childhood, such as it was.

Donna had been two months' pregnant with Colleen when she and Byrne had gotten married in a civil ceremony. When Donna had given birth, a few days after Christmas that year, and Byrne had seen Colleen for the first time, so pink and shriveled and helpless, he suddenly could not recall a single second of his life before that moment. In that instant, everything else was prelude, a blurry overture to the duty he felt at that moment, and he knew—knew as if it had been branded onto his heart—that no one would ever come between himself and that little girl. Not his wife, not his fellow officers, and God help the first-droopy-pantsed, sideways-hat-wearing, disrespectful little shit that came by for her first date.

He also recalled the day they found out Colleen was deaf. It was on Colleen's first Fourth of July. They had been living in a cramped three-room apartment at the time. The eleven o'clock news had just come on and there had been a small explosion, seemingly just outside the tiny bedroom where Colleen slept. Instinctively, Byrne had drawn his service weapon and made his way down the hall and into Colleen's room in a three giant steps, his heart slamming in his chest. When he pushed open her door, relief came in the form of a pair of kids on the fire escape, tossing firecrackers. He would deal with them later.

The horror, though, came in the form of stillness.

As the firecrackers continued to explode, not five feet from where his six-month-old daughter slept, she didn't react. She didn't wake up. When Donna arrived in the doorway, and took in the situation, she began to cry. Byrne held her, feeling at that moment that the road in front of them had just been repaved with trial, and that the fear he faced on the streets every day was nothing by comparison.

But now, Byrne often coveted his daughter's world of inner calm. She would never know the silver hush of her parents' marriage, ever oblivious to Kevin and Donna Byrne—once so passionate that they could not keep their hands off each other—saying "excuse me" as they passed in the narrow hallway of the home, like strangers on a bus.

He thought about his pretty, distant exwife, his Celtic rose. Donna, with her mysterious ability to clog a lie in his throat with just a glance, her perfect social pitch. She knew how to reap wisdom from disaster. She had taught him the grace of humility.

Deuces was quiet at this hour. Byrne sat

in an empty room on the second floor. Most drug houses were filthy places, littered with empty crack bottles, fast-food trash, thousands of spent kitchen matches, quite often vomit, sometimes excrement. Pipeheads didn't subscribe to *Architectural Digest* as a rule. The customers who frequented Deuces—a shadowy consortium of cops, civil servants, city officials who couldn't be seen cruising the corners—paid a little extra for the ambience.

He positioned himself cross-legged on the floor near the window, his back to the river. He sipped the bourbon. The sensation wrapped him in a warm amber embrace, easing the impending migraine.

Tessa Wells.

She had left her house Friday morning, a contract with the world in hand, a promise that she would be safe, that she would go to school, hang out with her friends, laugh at some silly jokes, cry at some silly love song. The world had broken that treaty. She was just a teenager, and she had already lived out her life.

Colleen had just become a teenager. Byrne knew that, psychologically speaking, he was probably way behind the curve, that the "teenaged years" began somewhere around eleven these days. He was also fully aware that he had long ago decided to resist that particular piece of Madison Avenue sexual propaganda.

He looked around the room.

Why was he here?

Again, the *question*.

Twenty years on the streets of one of the most violent cities in the world put him on the block. He didn't know a single detective who didn't drink, hadn't rehabbed, didn't gamble, didn't frequent the whores, didn't raise a hand to his children, his wife. With this job came excess, and if you didn't balance the excess of horror with an excess of passion for something—even domestic violence—the valves creaked and moaned until you imploded one day and put the barrel against your palate.

In his time as a homicide detective he had stood in dozens of parlors, hundreds of driveways, a thousand vacant lots, the voiceless dead waiting for him like a gouache of rainy watercolor in the near distance. Such bleak beauty. He could sleep with distance. It was detail that sullied his dreams.

He recalled every detail of that sweltering August morning he had been called to Fairmount Park: the thick buzz of flies overhead, the way Deirdre Pettigrew's skinny legs emerged from the bushes, her bloodied white panties bunched around one ankle, the bandage on her right knee.

He knew then, as he had known every single time he had seen a murdered child, that he had to step up, regardless how eroded his soul, how diminished his instincts. He had to brave the morning, no matter what demons tracked him through the night.

In the first half of his career it had been about the power, the inertia of justice, the rush of the capture. It was about *him*. But somewhere along the way, it became bigger. It became about all the dead girls.

And now, Tessa Wells.

He closed his eyes, again felt the frigid waters of the Delaware River eddy around him, the breath being wrenched from his chest.

Below him, the gang gunships cruised. The sound of the hip-hop bass chords shook the floor, the windows, the walls, rising from the city streets like steel steam.

The deviant's hour was coming. Soon he would walk among them.

The monsters were sliding out of their lairs.

And as he sat in a place where men traded their self-respect for a few moments of numbed silence, a place where animals walk erect, Kevin Francis Byrne knew that a new monster had stirred in Philadelphia, a dark seraph of death that would lead him to an uncharted dominion, summoning him to a depth to which men like Gideon Pratt only aspired.

1 4

It is night in Philadelphia.

I am standing on North Broad Street, looking toward Center City and the commanding figure of William Penn, craftily lighted atop city hall, feeling the warmth of the spring day fading into the sizzle of red neon and long, de Chirico shadows, marveling once more at the two faces of the city.

This is not the egg tempera of daytime Philly, the bright colors of Robert Indiana's

Love or the Mural Arts Program. This is Philly at night, a city rendered in thick, violent brushstrokes, an impasto of sedimentary pigments.

The old building on North Broad has witnessed many nights, its cast pilasters standing silent guard for almost a century. In many ways, it is the stoic face of the city: the old wooden seats, the coffered ceiling, the carved medallions, the worn canvas where a thousand men have spat and bled and fallen.

We file in. We smile at each other, raise eyebrows, clap shoulders.

I can smell the copper of their blood.

These men might know my deeds, but they do not know my face. They think I am a madman, that I pounce from the darkness like some horror movie villain. They will read about the things I have done, at their breakfast tables, on SEPTA, in the food courts, and they will shake their heads and ask why.

Could it be they know why?

If one were to peel back the phyllo layers of wickedness and pain and cruelty, could it be that these men might do the same if they had the chance? Might they lure each other's daughters to the dark street corner, the empty building, the deep-shadowed heart of the park? Might they wield their knives and pistols and bludgeons and finally utter their rage? Might they spend the currency of their wrath and then scurry off to Upper Darby and New Hope and Upper Merion and the safety of their lies?

There is always a morbid contest in the soul, a struggle between the loathing and the need, between the darkness and the light.

The bell rings. We rise from our stools. We meet in the center.

Philadelphia, your daughters are not safe.

You are here because you know that. You are here because you do not have the courage to be me. You are here because you are afraid of becoming *me.*

I know why I am here.

Jessica.

15

Forget Caesar's Palace. Forget Madison Square Garden. Forget the MGM Grand. The best place in America—some would argue, the world—to watch a prizefight, was The Legendary Blue Horizon on North Broad Street. In a town that had spawned the likes of Jack O'Brien, Joe Frazier, James Shuler, Tim Witherspoon, Bernard Hopkins—not to mention Rocky Balboa—The Legendary Blue Horizon was a treasure, and, as goes the Blue, so goes Philly fisticuffs.

Jessica and her opponent—Mariella "Sparkle" Munoz—dressed and warmed up in the same room. As Jessica waited for her great-uncle Vittorio, a former heavyweight himself, to tape her hands, she glanced over at her opponent. Sparkle was in her late twenties, with big arms and what looked like a seventeen-inch neck. A real shock absorber. She had a flat nose, scar tissue over both eyes, and what seemed to be a perpetual game face: a permanent grimace that was supposed to intimidate her opponents.

I'm shakin' over here, Jessica thought.

When she wanted to, Jessica could affect the posture and demeanor of a shrinking violet, a helpless woman who might have trouble opening a carton of orange juice without a big strong man to come to her rescue. This, Jessica hoped, was just honey for the grizzlies.

What it really meant was:

Bring it on, baby.

The first round began with what's known in boxing parlance as the "feeling out" process. Both women jabbing lightly, stalking each other. A clinch or two. A little bit of mugging and intimidation. Jessica was a few inches taller than Sparkle, but Sparkle made up for it in girth. She looked like a Maytag in knee socks.

About midround the action started to pick up, with the crowd starting to get into it. Every time Jessica landed even a jab, the crowd, led by a contingent of cops from Jessica's old district, went appropriately nuts.

When the bell rang at the end of the first round, Jessica stepped away clean and Sparkle threw a body shot, clearly, and deliberately, late. Jessica pushed her and the ref had to get between them. The ref for this fight was a short black guy in his late fifties. Jessica guessed that the Pennsylvania Athletic Commission thought they didn't need a big guy for the bout because it was just a lightweight bout, and female lightweights at that.

Wrong.

Sparkle threw a shot over the ref's head, glancing off Jessica's shoulder; Jessica retaliated with a hard jab that caught Sparkle on the side of the jaw. Sparkle's corner rushed in, along with Uncle Vittorio and although the crowd was cheering them on—some of the best fights in Blue Horizon history took place between rounds—they managed to separate the women.

Jessica plopped down on the stool as Uncle Vittorio stepped in front of her.

"Muckin bidge," Jessica muttered through the mouthpiece.

"Just relax," Vittorio said. He pulled the mouthpiece out, wiped her face. Angela grabbed one of the water bottles in the ice bucket, popped the plastic top, and held it near Jessica's mouth.

"Yer droppin' yer right hand every time you throw a hook," Vittorio said. "How many times we go over this? Keep yer right hand *up*." Vittorio slapped Jessica's right glove.

Jessica nodded, rinsed her mouth, spat in the bucket.

"Seconds out," yelled the referee from center ring.

Fastest damn sixty seconds ever, Jessica thought.

Jessica stood as Uncle Vittorio eased out of the ring—when you're seventy-nine, you ease out of everything—and grabbed the stool out of the corner. The bell rang, and the two fighters approached each other.

For the first minute of round two, it was much the same as it was in the first round. At the midway point, however, everything changed. Sparkle worked Jessica against the ropes. Jessica took the opportunity to launch a hook and, sure enough, she dropped her right hand. Sparkle countered with a left hook of her own, one that started somewhere in the Bronx, made its way down Broadway, across the bridge, and onto I-95.

The shot caught Jessica flush on the chin, stunning her, driving her deep into the ropes. The crowd fell silent. Jessica always knew that someday she might meet her match, but, before Sparkle Munoz moved in for the kill, Jessica saw the unthinkable.

Sparkle Munoz grabbed her crotch and yelled:

"Who's godda balls now?"

As Sparkle stepped in, preparing to throw what Jessica was certain would be the knockout blow, a montage of blurry images unspooled in her mind.

Like the time, on a drunk and disorderly call on Fitzwater Street, on her second week on the job, the wino puked into her holster.

Or the time Lisa Cefferati called her "Giovanni Big Fanny" on the playground of St. Paul's.

Or the day she came home early and saw Michelle Brown's dog-piss-yellow, cheap-ass, size ten Payless-looking shoes at the foot of the stairs, right next to her husband's boots.

At this moment the rage came from another place, a place where a young girl named Tessa Wells lived and laughed and loved. A place now silenced by the dark waters of a father's grief. *That* was the picture she needed.

Jessica cranked up every one of her 130 pounds, rolled her toes into the canvas, and unleashed a right cross that caught Sparkle on the tip of her chin, turning her head for a second like a well-oiled doorknob. The sound was massive, echoing throughout the Blue Horizon, mingling with the sounds of all the other great shots ever thrown in the building. Jessica saw Sparkle's eyes flash *Tilt!* and roll back into her head for a second before she collapsed to the canvas.

"Geddup!" Jessica shouted. *"Geddafuggup!"*

The referee ordered Jessica to a neutral corner before returning to the supine form of Sparkle Munoz and resuming his count. But the count was moot. Sparkle rolled onto her side like a beached manatee. This fight was *over*.

The crowd at the Blue Horizon shot to its collective feet with a roar that shook the rafters.

Jessica raised both hands in the air and did her victory dance as Angela ran into the ring and threw her arms around her.

Jessica looked around the room. She spotted Vincent in the front row of the balcony. He had attended every one of her fights when they were together, but Jessica hadn't been sure if he'd be at this one.

A few seconds later Jessica's father stepped into the ring, Sophie in his arms. Sophie never watched Jessica fight in the ring, of course, but she seemed to like the spotlight after a victory every bit as much as her mother. This night, Sophie wore her matching raspberry fleece separates and little Nike sweatband, looking like a toddler-weight contender herself. Jessica smiled, gave her father and daughter a wink. She was okay. Better than okay. The adrenaline hit her in a rush and she felt as if she could take on the world.

She held her cousin tighter as the crowd continued to bellow, chanting, *"Balls, Balls, Balls, Balls . . ."*

Over the roar, Jessica shouted into Angela's ear. "Angie?"

"Yeah?"

"Do me a favor."

"What?"

"Don't ever let me fight this fuckin' gorilla again."

Forty minutes later, on the sidewalk in front of the Blue, Jessica signed a few autographs for a pair of twelve-year-old girls who looked at her with a mixture of admiration and idol worship. She gave them the standard *stay-in-school, stay off drugs* sermons and they promised they would.

Jessica was just about to head to her car when she sensed a presence nearby.

"Remind me never to get you mad at me." The deep voice came from behind her.

Jessica's hair was wet with sweat and heading in six directions. She smelled like Seabiscuit after a mile-and-a-quarter run and she could feel the right side of her face swelling to the approximate size, shape, and color of a ripe eggplant.

She turned around to see one of the most beautiful men she had ever known.

It was Patrick Farrell.

And he was holding a rose.

While Peter took Sophie to his house, Jessica and Patrick sat in a dark corner of the Quiet Man Pub on the lower floor of Finnigan's Wake, a popular Irish pub and cop hangout on Third and Spring Garden Streets, their backs to the Strawbridge's wall.

It was not, however, dark enough for Jessica, even though she had done a quick remodeling of her face and hair in the ladies' room.

She nursed a double scotch.

"That was one of the most amazing things I've ever seen in my life," Patrick said.

He wore a charcoal cashmere turtleneck and black pleated slacks. He smelled great, which was one of the many things that time-tunneled her back to the days when they had been an item. Patrick Farrell always smelled great. And those *eyes*. Jessica wondered how many women over the years had tumbled headfirst into those deep blue eyes.

"Thanks," she said, instead of something remotely witty or minutely intelligent. She held her drink glass against her face. The swelling was down. Thank God. She didn't relish looking like the Elephant Woman in front of Patrick Farrell.

"I don't know how you do it."

Jessica shrugged her best *aw shucks*. "Well, the hard part is learning how to take a shot with your eyes open."

"Doesn't it hurt?"

"Of course it hurts," she said. "You know what it feels like?"

"What?"

"It feels like getting punched in the face."

Patrick laughed. "Touché."

"On the other hand, there's no feeling I can think of like the one you get from decking your opponent. God help me, I love that part."

"So, do you know it when you land it?"

"The knockout punch?"

"Yes."

"*Oh* yeah," Jessica said. "It's just like when you catch a baseball on the fat part of the bat. Remember that? No vibration, no effort. Just . . . contact."

Patrick smiled, shaking his head as if to concede that she was a hundred times braver than he. But Jessica knew this wasn't true. Patrick was an ER physician, and she couldn't think of any job tougher than that.

What took even more courage, Jessica thought, was that Patrick long ago stood up to his father, one of the most renowned heart surgeons in Philadelphia. Martin Farrell had expected Patrick to pursue a career as a cardiac surgeon. Patrick grew up in Bryn Mawr, attended Harvard Medical School, did his residency at Johns Hopkins, the path to stardom all but furrowed in front of him.

But when his kid sister Dana was killed in a Center City drive-by shooting, an innocent bystander in the wrong place at the wrong time, Patrick decided to devote his life to working as a trauma physician at an inner-city hospital. Martin Farrell all but disowned his son.

It was something Jessica and Patrick

shared—a career selecting them, as a result of a tragedy, instead of the other way around. Jessica wanted to ask how Patrick was getting along with his father now that so much time had passed, but she didn't want to open any old wounds.

They fell silent, listening to the music, catching each other's eyes, mooning like a pair of teenagers. A few cops from the Third District stopped by with congratulations for Jessica, drunkenly shadowboxing their way to the table.

Eventually, Patrick brought the conversation around to work. Safe territory for a married woman and an old flame.

"How is it working in the big leagues?"

Big leagues, Jessica thought. *The big leagues have a way of making you seem small.* "It's still early days, but it's a long way from my days in a sector car," she said.

"So, what, you don't miss chasing down purse snatchers, breaking up bar fights, and shuttling pregnant women to the hospital?"

Jessica smiled a little wistfully. "Purse snatchers and bar fights? No love lost there. As far as pregnant women go, I guess I retired with a record of one and one in that department."

"What do you mean?"

"When I was in a sector car," Jessica said, "I had one baby born in the backseat. Lost one."

Patrick sat a little straighter. Interested, now. This was *his* world. "What do you mean? How did you lose one?"

This was not Jessica's favorite story. She was already sorry she brought it up. It looked like she had to tell it. "It was Christmas Eve, three years ago. Remember that storm?"

It had been one of the worst blizzards in a decade. Ten inches of fresh snow, howling winds, temperatures around zero. The city all but shut down.

"Oh, yeah," Patrick said.

"Anyway, I was on last-out. It's just after midnight and I'm in a Dunkin' Donuts, getting coffee for me and my partner."

Patrick raised an eyebrow, meaning: *Dunkin' Donuts?*

"Don't even say it," Jessica said, smiling.

Patrick zipped his lips.

"I was just about to leave, when I hear this moaning. Turns out there was a pregnant woman in one of the booths. She was seven or eight months pregnant, and something was definitely wrong. I called for a rescue but all the EMS units were on runs, skidded out, frozen fuel lines. A nightmare. We were just a few blocks from Jefferson so I got her in the squad car and we took off. We get to around Third and Walnut and we hit this patch of ice, skidded into a line of parked cars. We got stuck."

Jessica sipped her drink. If telling the story made her feel bad, wrapping it up made her feel worse. "I called for assistance but by the time they got there, it was too late. The baby was stillborn."

The look in Patrick's eyes said he understood. It is never easy to lose one, no matter what the circumstances. "Sorry to hear it."

"Yeah, well, I made up for it a few weeks later," Jessica said. "My partner and I delivered a big baby boy down on South. And I mean *big*. Nine pounds and change. Like delivering a calf. I still get a Christmas card every year from the parents. After that, I applied for the Auto Unit. I had my fill of ob-gyn work."

Patrick smiled. "God has a way of evening the score, doesn't he?"

"He does," Jessica said.

"If I remember correctly, there was a lot of craziness that Christmas Eve, wasn't there?"

It was true. Generally, when a blizzard hits, it keeps the nut jobs indoors. But for some reason, the stars lined up that night and they were all out. Shootings, arson, muggings, vandalism.

"Yeah. We were running all night," Jessica said.

"Didn't somebody throw blood on the door of some church, or something like that?"

Jessica nodded. "St. Katherine's. Up in Torresdale."

Patrick shook his head. "So much for peace on earth, huh?"

Jessica had to agree. Although if there suddenly *was* peace on earth, she'd be out of a job.

Patrick sipped his drink. "Speaking of insanity, I hear you caught that homicide on Eighth Street."

"Where did you hear that?

With a wink: "I have my sources."

"Yeah," Jessica said. "My first case. Thank you, Lord."

"Bad as I heard?"

"Worse."

Jessica gave him a brief rundown of the scene.

"My God," Patrick said, reacting to the litany of horrors that befell Tessa Wells. "Every day I think I've heard it all. Every day I hear something new."

"I really feel for her father," Jessica said. "He's pretty sick. He lost his wife a few years ago. Tessa was his only daughter."

"I can't imagine what he's going through. Losing a child."

Jessica couldn't either. If she ever lost Sophie, her life would be over.

"Pretty tough assignment right out of the box," Patrick said.

"Tell me about it."

"Are you okay?"

Jessica thought about it before answering. Patrick had a way of asking questions like that. You got the feeling he really cared. "Yeah. I'm okay."

"How's your new partner?"

This one was easy. "Good. *Really* good."

"How so?"

"Well, he's got this way of handling people," Jessica said. "This way of getting people to talk to him. I don't know if it's fear or respect, but it works. And I've asked around about his solve rate. It's off the charts."

Patrick looked around the room, back at Jessica. He formed a half-smile, the one that had always made her stomach go a bit spongy.

"What?" she asked.

"Mirabile visu," Patrick said.

"That's what I always say," Jessica said.

Patrick laughed. "It's Latin."

"Latin for what? *Who beat the crap out of you*?"

"Latin for *You are wonderful to behold.*"

Doctors, Jessica thought. Smooth talk in Latin.

"Well . . . *sono sposato,*" Jessica replied. "That's Italian for *My husband would shoot us both in the friggin' forehead if he walked in here right now.*"

Patrick put both hands up in surrender.

"Enough about me," Jessica said, silently berating herself for even bringing up Vincent. He wasn't invited to this party. "Tell me what's up with you these days."

"Well, it's always busy at St. Joseph's. Never a dull moment," Patrick said. "Also, I might have a showing lined up at the Boyce Gallery."

Besides being a hell of a doctor, Patrick played the cello and was a talented painter. He had done a pastel sketch of Jessica one night when they were dating. Needless to say, Jessica had it well buried in the garage.

Jessica nursed her drink while Patrick had another. They caught up fully, effortlessly flirting just like the old days. The hand touching, the electric brush of feet under the table. Patrick also told her that he was donating his time to a new free clinic opening on Poplar. Jessica told him that she was thinking about painting the living room. Whenever she was around Patrick Farrell, she felt like she was a drain on society.

At around eleven Patrick walked her to her car, which was parked on Third Street. Then came the moment, as she knew it would. The scotch helped smooth it over.

"So . . . dinner next week, maybe?" Patrick asked.

"Well, I . . . you know . . ." Jessica hemmed and hawed.

"Just friends," Patrick added. "Nothing untoward."

"Well, then, forget it," Jessica said. "If we can't be toward, what's the point?"

Patrick laughed again. Jessica had forgotten how magical that sound could be. It had been a long time since she and Vincent had found anything to laugh about.

"Okay. Sure," Jessica said, trying, and failing, to find a single reason not to go to dinner with an old friend. "Why not?"

"Great," Patrick said. He leaned over and gently kissed the bruise on her right cheek. "Irish preop," he added. "It'll be better in the morning. Wait and see."

"Thanks, Doc."

"I'll call you."

"Okay."

Patrick winked, setting loose a few hundred sparrows in Jessica's chest. He put up his hands, in a defensive boxing posture, then reached out, smoothed her hair. He turned and walked to his car.

Jessica watched him drive away.

She touched her cheek, felt the lingering warmth of his lips. And was not at all surprised to discover that her face was starting to feel better already.

1 6

Simon Close was in love.

Jessica Balzano was absolutely incredible. Tall and slender and sexy as hell. The way she dispatched her opponent in the ring gave him, perhaps, the single most feral charge he had ever felt just looking at a woman. He felt like a schoolboy watching her.

She was going to make great copy.

She was going to make even better artwork.

He had flashed his smile and press ID at the Blue Horizon and gotten in with relative ease. Granted, it wasn't like getting into the Linc for an Eagles game, or the Wachovia Center to see the Sixers, but still, it gave him a sense of pride and purpose whenever he was treated like part of the mainstream press. Tabloid writers rarely got free tickets, never went on the press junkets, had to beg for press kits. He had misspelled many names in his career, due to the fact that he never got a decent press kit.

After Jessica's fight, Simon parked half a block from the crime scene tape on North Eighth Street. The only other vehicles were a Ford Taurus, parked inside the perimeter, along with a Crime Scene Unit van.

He watched the eleven o'clock news on his Watchman. The lead story was the murdered young girl. The victim's name was Tessa Ann Wells, seventeen, of North Philly. Immediately, Simon had his Philadelphia white pages open on his lap, his Maglite in his teeth. There were a total of twelve possibilities in North Philly: eight spelled *Welles,* four spelled *Wells*.

He pulled out his cell phone, dialed the first number.

"Mr. Welles?"

"Yes?"

"Sir, my name is Simon Close. I'm a writer with *The Report*."

Silence.

Then: "Yes?"

"First off, I just want to say how sorry I was to hear about your daughter."

A sharp intake of air. "My daughter? Something has happened to Hannah?"

Oops.

"I'm sorry, I must have the wrong number."

He clicked off, dialed the next number.

Busy.

Next. A woman this time.

"Mrs. Welles?"

"Who is this?"

"Madam, my name is Simon Close. I'm a writer with *The Report*."

Click.

Bitch.

Next.

Busy.

Jesus, he thought. Doesn't anyone in Philly sleep anymore?

Then Channel 6 did a recap. They called

the victim "Tessa Ann Wells of Twentieth Street in North Philly."

Thank you, Action News, Simon thought.

Check this *action.*

He looked up the number. Frank Wells on Twentieth Street. He dialed, but the line was busy. Again. Busy. Again. Same result. Redial. Redial.

Damn.

He thought about driving over there, but what happened next, like a crack of righteous thunder, changed everything.

1 7

Death had come here unbidden, and, for its penance, the block mourned in silence. The rain had diminished to a thin mist, whispering off the rivers, slicking the pavement. Night had buried its day in a glassine shroud.

Byrne sat in his car across the street from the Tessa Wells crime scene, his exhaustion now a living thing within. Through the fog he could see a faint orange glow coming from the basement window of the row house.

The CSU team would be there all night, and probably most of the next day.

He slipped a blues CD into the player. Soon, Robert Johnson scratched and crackled from the speakers, talking about that hellhound on his trail.

I hear you, Byrne thought.

He considered the short block of dilapidated row houses. The once graceful façades swooned beneath the yoke of weather and time and neglect. For all the drama that had unfolded behind these walls over the years, both petty and grand, it was the perfume of death that would remain. Long after the footers were plowed back into the earth, madness would dwell here.

Byrne saw movement in the field to the right of the crime scene. A slum dog regarded him from the cover of a small pile of discarded tires, his only worry his next bite of spoiled meat, his next tongueful of rainwater.

Lucky dog.

Byrne shut off the CD, closed his eyes, absorbed the silence.

There had been no fresh footprints through the weed-thick field behind the death house, no recently snapped branches on the low scrub. Whoever killed Tessa Wells had probably not parked on Ninth Street.

He felt the breath catch in his chest, the way it had the night he had plunged into the icy river, locked in death's caress with Luther White—

The images slammed into the back of his skull—brutal and vile and base.

He saw Tessa's final moments.

The approach comes from the front . . .

The killer turns off his headlights, decelerates, rolls slowly, cautiously, to a stop. Cuts the engine. He exits the vehicle, sniffs the air. He finds this place ripe for his insanity. A bird of prey is most vulnerable when it eats, mantling its catch, exposed to attack from above. He knows he is about to put himself at momentary risk. He has chosen his quarry with care. Tessa Wells is that thing that is missing within him; the very idea of beauty that he must destroy.

He carries her across the street, into the empty row house on the left. Nothing with a soul stirs here. It is dark inside, borrowing no moonlight. The rotted floor is a danger, but he does not risk a flashlight. Not yet.

She is light in his arms. He is full of a terrible power.

He exits the rear of the house.

(But why? Why not dump her in the first house?)

He is sexually aroused, but he does not act on it.

(Again, why?)

He enters the death house. He takes Tessa Wells down the stairs into the dank and putrid cellar.

(Has he been here before?)

Rats scurry, frightened off their meager carrion. He is in no hurry. Time does not come here anymore.

He is in complete control at this moment.

He is . . .

He is—

Byrne tried, but he could not see the killer's face.

Not yet.

The pain flashed with a bright, savage intensity.

It was getting worse.

Byrne lit a cigarette, smoked it down to the filter without the curse of a single thought, or the blessing of a single idea. The rain began again in earnest.

Why Tessa Wells? he wondered, turning her photograph over and over in his hands.

Why not the next shy young girl? What did Tessa do to deserve this? Did she refuse the advances of some teenaged Lothario? No. As crazy as every new crop of young men seemed to be, tagging each successive generation with some hyperbolic level of larceny and violence, this was far beyond the pale of some jilted teenager.

Was she chosen at random?

If that was the case, Byrne knew it was unlikely that this was going to stop.

What was so special about this place?

What was he failing to see?

Byrne felt the rage build. The pain tangoed at his temples. He split a Vicodin, swallowed it dry.

He hadn't slept more than three or four hours in the past forty-eight, but who needed sleep? There was work to be done.

The wind kicked up, fluttering the bright yellow crime scene tape—grand-opening pennants at Death Mart.

He looked into the rearview mirror; saw the scar over his right eye and the way it glistened in the moonlight. He ran his finger over it. He thought about Luther White and the way his .22 had glimmered in the moonlight on the night they both died, the way the barrel exploded and painted the world red, then white, then black; the full palette of lunacy, the way the river had embraced them both.

Where are you, Luther?
I could do with a little help.

He got out of the car, locked it. He knew he should go home, but somehow, this place filled him with the sense of purpose he needed at the moment, the peace he used to feel when he was sitting in the living room on some crisp fall day, watching an Eagles game, Donna on the couch next to him, reading a book, Colleen in her room, studying.

Maybe he should go home.

But go home to what? His empty two-room apartment?

He would drink another pint of bourbon, watch the talk shows, probably a movie. At three o'clock he would slip into bed, waiting for a sleep that would not come. At six he would concede to the pre-alarm dawn, and get up.

He glanced at the glow of light from the basement window, saw the shadows moving purposefully about, felt the pull.

These were his brothers, his sisters, his family.

He crossed the street to the death house. *This* was his home.

1 8

MONDAY, 11:08 PM

Simon had been aware of the two vehicles. The blue-and-white Crime Scene Unit van nestled against the side of the row house, and the Taurus parked down the street, the Taurus containing his nemesis, as it were: Detective Kevin Francis Byrne.

When Simon had broken the story on Morris Blanchard's suicide, Kevin Byrne had waited for him one night outside Downey's, a raucous Irish pub on Front and South Streets. Byrne had cornered him and had thrown him around like a rag doll, finally picking him up by the collar of his jacket and slamming him up against a wall. Simon was no bruiser, but he did go six feet tall, eleven stone, and Byrne had lifted him clean off the ground with a single hand. Byrne had smelled like a distillery after a flood, and Simon had prepared himself for a serious donnybrook. Okay, a serious beating. Who was he kidding?

But luckily, instead of punching him flat—which, Simon had to admit, he might have had coming—Byrne just stopped, looked at the sky, and dropped him like a spent tissue, letting him off with sore ribs, a banged up shoulder, and a knit shirt stretched beyond all attempts at resizing.

For his penance Byrne had gotten another half a dozen scathing articles out of Simon. For a year Simon had traveled with a Louisville Slugger in his car and an eye over his shoulder. Still did.

But all of that was ancient history.

There was a new wrinkle.

Simon had a pair of stringers he used from time to time, Temple University students who had the same notions about journalism that Simon had once held. They did research and the occasional stakeout, all for a pittance, usually just enough to keep them in iTunes downloads and X.

The one who had some potential, the one who could actually write, was Benedict Tsu. He called at ten after eleven.

"Simon Close."

"It is Tsu."

Simon wasn't sure if it was an Asian thing or a college thing, but Benedict always called himself by his last name. "What's up?"

"That place you asked about, the place on the waterfront?"

Tsu was talking about the dilapidated building under the Walt Whitman Bridge into which Kevin Byrne had mysteriously disappeared for a few hours earlier in the night. Simon had followed Byrne, but had to keep a discreet distance. When Simon had to leave to get to the Blue Horizon, he called Tsu and asked him to look into it. "What about it?"

"It's called Deuces."

"What's Deuces?"

"It's a crack house."

Simon's world began to spin. "A *crack house*?"

"Yes, sir."

"Are you sure?"

"Absolutely."

Simon let the possibilities wash over him. The excitement was overwhelming.

"Thanks, Ben," Simon said. "I'll be in touch."

"Bukeqi."

Simon clicked off, considered his good fortune.

Kevin Byrne was on the *pipe*.

Which meant that what had become a casual endeavor—following Byrne to get a story—would now become a grand obsession. Because, from time to time, Kevin Byrne had to score his drugs. Which meant that Kevin Byrne had a brand-new partner. Not a tall, sexy goddess with smoldering dark eyes and a freight-train right cross, but rather a skinny white boy from Northumberland.

A skinny white boy with a Nikon D100 camera and a Sigma 55-200mm DC zoom lens.

19

Jessica huddled in the corner of a dank cellar, watching a young woman kneeling in prayer. The girl was about seventeen, blond, freckled, blue-eyed, and innocent.

The moonlight streaming through the small window cast brusque shadows across the rubble in the cellar, creating buttes and chasms amid the gloom.

When the girl was done praying, she sat down on the damp floor and produced a hypodermic needle and, without ceremony or preparation, stuck the needle in her arm.

"Wait!" Jessica screamed. She made her way quickly across the debris-strewn basement with relative ease, considering the shadow and the clutter. No barked shins, no stubbed toes. It was as if she floated. But by the time she reached the young woman, the young woman was already depressing the plunger.

You don't have to do that, Jessica said.

Yes I do, the girl dream-replied. *You don't understand.*

I do understand. You don't need it.

But I do. There is a monster after me.

Jessica stood a few feet away from the girl. She saw that the girl was barefoot; her feet were red and raw and blistered. When Jessica looked back up—

The girl was Sophie. Or, more accurately, the young woman Sophie would become. Gone were her daughter's roly-poly little body and chubby cheeks, replaced instead by a young woman's curves: long legs, slender waist, a discernible bust beneath the ragged V-neck sweater with the Nazarene crest.

But it was the girl's face that horrified

Jessica. Sophie's face was drawn and haggard, with dark violet smudges beneath her eyes.

Don't, sweetie, Jessica implored. *God, no.*

She looked again and saw that the girl's hands were now bolted together and bleeding. Jessica tried to take a step forward but her feet seemed frozen to the ground, her legs leaden. She felt something at her breastbone. She looked down to see an angel pendant hanging around her neck.

Then, suddenly, a bell sounded. Loud and intrusive and insistent. It seemed to come from above. Jessica looked at the Sophie-girl. The drug was just taking hold of the girl's nervous system, and as her eyes rolled back, her head tilted upward. Suddenly, there was no ceiling above them, no roof. Just the black sky. Jessica followed her gaze as the bell pounded through the firmament again. A sword of golden sunlight split the night clouds, catching the sterling silver of the pendant, blinding Jessica for a moment, until—

Jessica opened her eyes and sat upright, her heart rattling around in her chest. She looked at the window. Pitch black. It was the middle of the night and the phone was ringing. Only bad news made the trip at this hour.

Vincent?

Dad?

The phone rang a third time, offering no details, no comfort. She reached for it, disoriented, frightened, her hands shaking, her head still throbbing. She lifted the receiver.

"H-hello?"

"It's Kevin."

Kevin? Jessica thought. Who the hell is Kevin? The only Kevin she knew was Kevin Bancroft, the weird kid who lived on Christian Street when she was growing up. Then it hit her.

Kevin.

The job.

"Yeah. Right. Okay. What's up?"

"I think we should catch the girls at the bus stop."

Greek. Maybe Turkish. Definitely some foreign language. She had no idea what these words meant.

"Can you hang on a sec?" she asked.

"Sure."

Jessica sprinted to the bathroom, splashed cold water on her face. The right side was still slightly swollen, but much less painful than it was last night, due to an hour of ice packs when she'd gotten home. Along with Patrick's kiss, of course. The thought made her smile, the smile made her face hurt. It was a good hurt. She ran back to the phone, but before she could say anything, Byrne added:

"I think we'll get more out of them there than we will at the school."

"Sure," Jessica replied, and she suddenly realized that he was talking about Tessa Wells's friends.

"I'll pick you up in twenty," he said.

For a minute, she thought he meant twenty minutes. She glanced at the clock. Five forty. He *did* mean twenty minutes. Luckily, Paula Farinacci's husband left for work in Camden by six, so she was up. Jessica could drop Sophie off at Paula's and have just enough time for a shower. "Right," Jessica said. "Okay. Great. No problem. See you then."

She hung up, threw her legs over the side of the bed, ready for a nice, brisk nap.

Welcome to Homicide.

20

Byrne had been waiting for her with a large coffee and a sesame seed bagel. The coffee was strong and hot, the bagel fresh.

Bless him.

Jessica hurried through the rain and slipped into the car, nodded a token greeting. To put it mildly, she was not a morning person, especially a six-o'clock-in-the-morning person. Her fondest hope was that she was wearing matching shoes.

They rode into the city in silence, Kevin

Byrne respecting her space and waking ritual, realizing he had forced the shock of the new day upon her unceremoniously. He, on the other hand, looked wide-awake. A little ragged, but wide-eyed and alert.

Men had it *so* easy, Jessica thought. Clean shirt, shave in the car, a spritz of Binaca, a drop of Visine, ready for the day.

They made the ride to North Philly in short order. They parked near the corner of Nineteenth and Poplar. Byrne put on the radio at the half hour. The Tessa Wells story was mentioned.

With half an hour to wait, they hunkered down. Occasionally, Byrne flipped the ignition to start the wipers, the defrosters.

They tried to talk about the news, the weather, the job. The subtext kept bulling forward.

Daughters.

Tessa Wells was someone's daughter.

This realization hardwired them both into the brutal soul of this crime. It might have been *their* child.

"She'll be three next month," Jessica said.

Jessica showed Byrne a picture of Sophie. He smiled. She *knew* he had a marsh-mallow center. "She looks like a handful."

"Two hands," Jessica said. "You know how it is when they're that age. They look to you for everything."

"Yeah."

"You miss those days?"

"I *missed* those days," Byrne said. "I was working double tours in those days."

"How old is your daughter now?"

"She's thirteen," Byrne said.

"Uh-oh," Jessica said.

"Uh-oh is an understatement."

"So . . . she have a house full of Britney CDs?"

Byrne smiled again, thinly this time. "No."

"*Oh* boy. Don't tell me she's into rap."

Byrne spun his coffee a few times. "My daughter is deaf."

"Oh my," Jessica said, suddenly morti-fied. "I'm . . . I'm sorry."

"That's okay. Don't be."

"I mean . . . I just didn't—"

"It's okay. Really. She hates sympathy. And she's a lot tougher than you and me combined."

"What I meant was—"

"I know what you meant. My wife and I

went through *years* of sorry. It's a natural reaction," Byrne said. "But to be quite honest, I've yet to meet a deaf person who thinks of herself as handicapped. Especially Colleen."

Seeing as she had opened this line of questioning, Jessica figured she might as well continue. She did, gently. "Was she born deaf?"

Byrne nodded. "Yeah. It was something called Mondini dysplasia. Genetic disorder."

Jessica's mind turned to Sophie, dancing around the living room to some song on *Sesame Street*. Or the way Sophie would sing at the top of her lungs amid the bubbles in the tub. Like her mother, Sophie couldn't tow a tune with a tractor, but she was earnest in the attempt. Jessica thought about her bright, healthy, beautiful little girl and considered how lucky she was.

They both fell silent. Byrne ran the wipers, the defroster. The windshield began to clear. The girls had yet not arrived at the corner. Traffic on Poplar was beginning to thicken.

"I watched her once," Byrne said, sounding a little melancholy, as if he had not spoken of his daughter to anyone in a while.

The longing was obvious. "I was supposed to pick her up at her deaf school, and I was a little early. So I pulled over to the side of the street to grab a smoke, read the paper.

"Anyway, I see this group of kids on the corner, maybe seven or eight of them. They're twelve, thirteen years old. I'm not really paying them any mind. They're all dressed like homeless people, right? Baggy pants, big shirts hanging out, untied sneakers. Suddenly I see Colleen standing there, leaning against the building, and it's like I don't know her. Like she's some kid who kind of *resembles* Colleen.

"All of a sudden, I'm *really* interested in all the other kids. Who's doing what, who's holding what, who's wearing, what, what their hands are doing, what's in their pockets. It's like I'm patting them all down from across the street."

Byrne sipped his coffee, threw a glance at the corner. Still empty.

"So she's holding her own with these older boys, smiling, yakking away in sign language, flipping her hair," he continued. "And I'm thinking: *Jesus Christ. She's flirting.* My little girl is flirting with these *boys*. My little girl who, just a few weeks ago, climbed into her Big Wheel and went pedaling down the street wearing her little yellow I HAD A WILD TIME IN WILDWOOD T-shirt is flirting with *boys*. I wanted to cap the horny little pricks right there.

"And then I watched one of them light a joint, and my fucking heart stops. I actually heard it wind down in my chest like a cheap watch. I'm ready to get out of the car with my cuffs in my hand when I realized what it would to do to Colleen, so I just watch.

"They pass it around, casual, right on the corner, like it's legal, right? I'm waiting, watching. Then one of the kids offers the joint to Colleen and I knew, I *knew* she was going to take it and smoke it. I knew she would grab it and take a long, slow hit off this blunt, and I suddenly saw the next five years of her life. Pot and booze and coke and rehab and Sylvan to get her grades back up and more drugs and the pill and then . . . then the most incredible thing happened."

Jessica realized she was staring at Byrne, rapt, waiting for him to finish. She snapped out of it, prodded. "Okay. What happened?"

"She just . . . shook her head," Byrne

said. "Just like that. *No thanks*. I doubted her at that moment, I completely broke faith with my little girl, and I wanted to tear my eyes out of my head. I was given the opportunity to trust her, completely unobserved, and I failed. *I* failed. Not her."

Jessica nodded, trying not to think about the fact that she was going to have to deal with a moment like that with Sophie in about ten years, not looking forward to it at all.

"And it suddenly occurred to me," Byrne said, "after all these years of worry, all these years of treating her as if she were fragile, all these years of walking on the street side of the sidewalk, all these years of staring down the idiots watching her sign in public and thinking she was a freak, all of it was unnecessary. She's ten times tougher than I am. She could kick my ass."

"Kids will surprise you." Jessica realized how inadequate it sounded when she said it, how completely uninformed she was on this subject.

"I mean, of all the things you fear for your kid: diabetes, leukemia, rheumatoid arthritis, cancer—my little girl was deaf. That's it. Other than that, she's perfect in every way.

Heart, lungs, eyes, limbs, mind. Perfect. She can run like the wind, jump high. And she has this smile . . . this smile that could melt the glaciers. All this time I thought she was handicapped because she couldn't hear. It was me. I'm the one who needs a freakin' telethon. I didn't realize how lucky we are."

Jessica didn't know what to say. She had mistakenly summed up Kevin Byrne as a streetwise guy who muscled his way through his life and his job, a guy who ran on instinct instead of intellect. There was quite a bit more at work here than she realized. She suddenly felt like she had won the lottery in being partnered with him.

Before Jessica could respond, two teenaged girls approached the corner, umbrellas up and open against the drizzle.

"There they are," Byrne said.

Jessica capped her coffee, buttoned her raincoat.

"This is more your turf." Byrne nodded toward the girls, lighting a cigarette, hunkering down in the comfortable—read: dry—seat. "You should handle the questions."

Right, Jessica thought. *I suppose it has nothing to do with standing in the rain at seven o'clock in the morning.* She waited for a break in the traffic, got out of the car, crossed the street.

On the corner were two girls in Nazarene school uniforms. One was a tall, dark-skinned black girl with the most elaborate network of corn-rowed hair Jessica had ever seen. She was at least six feet tall and stunningly beautiful. The other girl was white, petite, and small-boned. They both carried umbrellas in one hand, wadded-up tissues in the other. Both had red, puffy eyes. Obviously, they had already heard about Tessa.

Jessica approached, showed them her badge, told them she was investigating Tessa's death. They agreed to talk to her. Their names were Patrice Regan and Ashia Whitman. Ashia was Somali.

"Did you see Tessa at all on Friday?" Jessica asked.

They shook their heads in unison.

"She didn't come to the bus stop?"

"No," Patrice said.

"Did she miss a lot of days?"

"Not a lot," Ashia said between sniffles. "Once in a while."

"Was she the type to bag school?" Jessica asked.

"Tessa?" Patrice asked, incredulous. "No way. Like, *never.*"

"What did you think when she didn't show?"

"We just figured she wasn't feeling good or something," Patrice said. "Or it had something to do with her dad. Her dad's pretty sick, you know. Sometimes she has to take him to the hospital."

"Did you call her or talk to her during the day?" Jessica asked.

"No."

"Do you know anybody who might have talked to her?"

"No," Patrice said. "Not that I know of."

"What about drugs? Was she into the drug scene?"

"*God,* no," Patrice said. "She was like Sister Mary Narc."

"Last year, when she took off three weeks, did you talk to her much?"

Patrice glanced at Ashia. There were secrets entombed in that look. "Not really."

Jessica decided not to push. She consulted her notes. "Do you guys know a boy named Sean Brennan?"

"Yeah," Patrice said. "I do. I don't think Ashia ever met him."

Jessica looked at Ashia. She shrugged.

"How long were they seeing each other?" Jessica asked.

"Not sure," Patrice said. "Maybe a couple of months or so."

"Was Tessa still seeing him?"

"No," Patrice said. "His family moved away."

"Where to?"

"Denver, I think."

"When?"

"I'm not sure. About a month ago, I think."

"Do you know where Sean went to school?"

"Neumann," Patrice said.

Jessica made notes. Her pad was getting wet. She put it in her pocket. "Did they break up?"

"Yeah," Patrice said. "Tessa was pretty upset."

"What about Sean? Did he have a temper?"

Patrice just shrugged. In other words, yes, but she didn't want to get anybody in trouble.

"Did you ever see him hurt Tessa?"

"No," Patrice said. "Nothing like that. He was just . . . just a guy. You know."

Jessica waited for more. More was not forthcoming. She moved on. "Can you think of anyone Tessa didn't get along with? Anyone who might have wanted to do her harm?"

This question started the waterworks again. Both girls began to cry, wiping at their eyes. They shook their heads.

"Was she seeing anyone else after Sean? Anyone who might have been bothering her?"

The girls thought for a few seconds, and again shook their heads in unison.

"Did Tessa ever see Dr. Parkhurst at school?"

"Sure," Patrice said.

"Did she like him?"

"I guess."

"Did Dr. Parkhurst ever see her outside of school?" Jessica asked.

"Outside?"

"As in socially."

"What, like a date or something?" Patrice asked. She screwed up her face at the idea of Tessa dating a man as ancient as thirty or so. As *if.* "Uh, *no.*"

"Do you guys ever go to him for guidance counseling?" Jessica asked.

"Sure," Patrice said. "Everybody does."

"What sorts of things do you talk about?"

Patrice thought about it for a few seconds. Jessica could see that the girl was concealing something. "School, mostly. College apps, SATs, stuff like that."

"Ever talk about anything personal?"

Eyes earthward. Again.

Bingo, Jessica thought.

"Sometimes," Patrice said.

"What sort of personal things?" Jessica asked, recalling Sister Mercedes, the guidance counselor at Nazarene when she attended. Sister Mercedes was built like John Goodman and had a perpetual scowl. The only personal thing you talked about with Sister Mercedes was your promise not to have sex until you were forty.

"I don't know," Patrice said, getting interested in her shoes again. "Stuff."

"Did you talk about the boys you were seeing? Things like that?"

"Sometimes," Ashia answered.

"Did he ever ask you to talk about things that you found embarrassing? Or maybe a little bit too personal?"

"I don't think so," Patrice said. "Not that I can, you know, remember."

Jessica could see that she was losing her. She pulled out a pair of business cards and handed one each to the two girls. "Look," she began. "I know this is tough. If you think of anything that can help us find the guy who did this, give us a call. Or if you just want to talk. Whatever. Okay? Day or night."

Ashia took the card, remained silent, the tears building again. Patrice took the card, nodded. In unison, like synchronized mourners, the two girls lifted the balled tissues in their hands and dabbed at their eyes.

"I went to Nazarene," Jessica added.

The two girls looked at each other, as if she had just told them she had once attended the Hogwart School.

"Seriously?" Ashia asked.

"Sure," Jessica said. "Do you guys still carve stuff under the stage in the old auditorium?"

"*Oh* yeah," Patrice said.

"Well, if you look right under the newel post on the stairs leading under the stage, on the right-hand side, there is a carving that reads JG AND BB 4EVER."

"That was you?" Patrice looked quizzically at the business card.

"I was Jessica Giovanni then. I carved that in tenth grade."

"Who was BB?" Patrice asked.

"Bobby Bonfante. He went to Father Judge."

The girls nodded. Father Judge boys were, for the most part, pretty irresistible.

Jessica added: "He looked like Al Pacino."

The two girls glanced at each other, as if to say: *Al Pacino? Isn't he, like, grandpa old?* "Is that the old guy who was in *The Recruit* with Colin Farrell?" Patrice asked.

"A young Al Pacino," Jessica added.

The girls smiled. Sadly, but they smiled.

"So did it last forever with Bobby?" Ashia asked.

Jessica wanted to tell these young girls that it never does. "No," she said. "Bobby lives in Newark now. Five kids."

The girls nodded again in deep understanding of love and loss. Jessica had them back. Time to cut it off. She'd take another run at them later.

"By the way, when do you guys get off for Easter break?" Jessica asked.

"Tomorrow," Ashia said, her sobs all but dried.

Jessica flipped up her hood. The rain had already ruined whatever style her hair had held, but now it was starting to come down hard.

"Can I ask you something?" Patrice asked.

"Sure."

"Why . . . why did you become a cop?"

Even before Patrice's question, Jessica had a feeling that the girl was going to ask her that. It still didn't make the answer any easier. She wasn't entirely sure herself. There was legacy; there was Michael's death. There were reasons even *she* didn't know yet. In the end she said, modestly: "I like to help people."

Patrice dabbed her eyes again. "Does it ever, you know, creep you out?" she asked. "You know, to be around . . ."

Dead people, Jessica finished, in her mind. "Yeah," she said. "Sometimes."

Patrice nodded, finding common ground

with Jessica. She pointed at Kevin Byrne, sitting in the Taurus across the street. "Is he your boss?"

Jessica looked over, looked back, smiled. "No," she said. "He's my partner."

Patrice absorbed this. She smiled through her tears, perhaps in the understanding that Jessica was her own woman, and said, simply: "Cool."

Jessica shook off as much rain as she could, then slipped into the car.

"Anything?" Byrne asked.

"Not really," Jessica said, consulting her notepad. It was soaked. She tossed it into the backseat. "Sean Brennan's family moved to Denver about a month ago. They said Tessa wasn't seeing anyone else. Patrice said he was kind of a hothead."

"Worth looking at?"

"I don't think so. I'll put in a call to the Denver Board of Ed. See if young Mr. Brennan has missed any days recently."

"What about Dr. Parkhurst?"

"There's something there. I can feel it."

"What's your gut?"

"I think they talk about personal things with him. I think *they* think he's a little *too* personal."

"Do you think Tessa was seeing him?"

"If she was, she didn't confide in her friends," Jessica said. "I asked them about Tessa's three-week sabbatical from school last year. They got hinky. Something happened to Tessa around Thanksgiving last year."

For a few moments, the investigation halted, their separate thoughts met only by the staccato rhythms of the rain on the roof of the car.

Byrne's phone chirped as he started the Taurus. He flipped the cell open.

"Byrne . . . yeah . . . yeah . . . out*standing*," he said. "Thanks." He flipped the phone closed.

Jessica looked at Byrne, waiting. When it became clear that he was not about to share, she asked. If reticence was his nature, nosiness was hers. If this relationship was going to work, they would have to find a way to jigsaw the two.

"Good news?"

Byrne glanced over at her, as if he had forgotten she was in the car. "Yeah. The lab just made a case for me. They matched a hair with evidence found on a vic," he said. "This fucker is *mine*."

Byrne gave her a recap of the Gideon Pratt case. Jessica heard the passion in his voice, the deep sense of subdued rage as he talked about the brutal, senseless death of Deirdre Pettigrew.

"Gotta make a quick stop," he said.

A few minutes later they came to a rolling rest in front of a proud but struggling row house on Ingersoll Street. The rain was coming down in broad, cold sheets. As they exited the car and drew near the house, Jessica saw a frail, light-skinned black woman in her forties standing in the doorway. She wore a quilted magenta housecoat and tinted, oversized glasses. Her hair was in a multicolored African wrap; her feet were clad in white plastic sandals at least two sizes too large.

The woman put her hand to her breastbone when she saw Byrne, as if the sight of him stole her ability to breathe. A lifetime of bad news had walked up these steps, it seemed, and it probably all came from the lips of people who looked like Kevin Byrne.

Big white men who were cops, tax assessors, welfare agents, landlords.

As they climbed the crumbling steps, Jessica noticed a sun-faded eight-by-ten photo in the living room window, a leached print made on a color copier. The photo was an enlargement of a school snapshot of a smiling black girl of about fifteen. There was a loop of fat pink yarn in her hair, beads in her braids. She wore a retainer and seemed to be smiling despite the serious hardware in her mouth.

The woman did not invite them in, but mercifully there was a small awning over her front stoop, shielding them from the downpour.

"Mrs. Pettigrew, this is my partner, Detective Balzano."

The woman nodded at Jessica, but continued to bunch her housecoat to her throat.

"Have you . . . ," she began, trailing off.

"Yes," Byrne said. "We caught him, ma'am. He's in custody."

Althea Pettigrew's hand covered her mouth. Tears welled in her eyes. Jessica could see that the woman wore a wedding ring, but the stone was gone.

"What . . . what happens now?" she

asked, her body vibrating with anticipation. It was clear that she had prayed for and dreaded this day for a long time.

"That's up to the DA's office and the man's attorney," Byrne replied. "He'll be arraigned, and then there will be a preliminary hearing."

"Do you think he might . . .?"

Byrne took her hand in his, shaking his head. "He's not getting out. I'm going to do everything I can to make sure he never walks free again."

Jessica knew how many things could go wrong, especially in a capital murder case. She appreciated Byrne's optimism and at this moment it was the right sentiment to convey. When she was in Auto, she'd had a hard time telling people she was sure they were going to get their *cars* back.

"Bless you, sir," the woman said, then all but threw herself into Byrne's arms, her whimpers morphing into full-grown sobs. Byrne held her gingerly, as if she were made of porcelain. His eyes met Jessica's, saying: *This is why.* Jessica glanced over at the picture of Deirdre Pettigrew in the window. She wondered if the photo would come down today.

Althea composed herself somewhat, then said: "Wait right here, would you?"

"Sure," Byrne said.

Althea Pettigrew disappeared inside for a few moments, reappeared, then placed something into Kevin Byrne's hand. She wrapped her hand around his, closing it. When Byrne opened his hand, Jessica could see what the woman had handed him.

It was a well-worn twenty-dollar bill.

Byrne stared at it for a few moments, a bit bewildered, as if he had never seen American currency before. "Mrs. Pettigrew, I . . . I can't take this."

"I know it isn't much," she said, "but it would mean so much to me."

Byrne straightened out the bill as he appeared to organize his thoughts. He waited a few moments, then handed the twenty back. "I can't," he said. "Knowing that the man who did that terrible thing to Deirdre is in custody is enough payment for me, believe me."

Althea Pettigrew scrutinized the big police officer in front of her with a look of disappointment and respect on her face. Slowly, reluctantly, she took the money back. She put it into the pocket of her housecoat.

"Then you will have this," she said. She reached behind her neck and took off the delicate silver chain. The chain held a small silver crucifix.

When Byrne tried to decline this, the look in Althea Pettigrew's eyes told him she would not be refused. Not this time. She held it out until Byrne took it.

"I, uh . . . thank you, ma'am," was all that Byrne could manage.

Jessica thought: Frank Wells yesterday, Althea Pettigrew today. Two parents separated by worlds and just a few blocks, joined in unimaginable grief and sorrow. She hoped they would have the same results for Frank Wells.

Although he was probably doing his best to mask it, as they walked back to the car Jessica noticed a slight spring in Byrne's step, despite the downpour, despite the grimness of their current case. She understood it. All cops did. Kevin Byrne was riding a wave, a small ripple of satisfaction known to law enforcement professionals when, after a lot of hard work, the dominoes fall and they spell out a beautiful pattern, a clean, borderless image called justice.

Then there was the other side of the business.

Before they could get in the Taurus, Byrne's phone rang again. He answered, listened for a few seconds, his face void of expression. "Give us fifteen minutes," he said.

He snapped the phone shut.

"What is it?" Jessica asked.

Byrne made a fist, poised to smash it into the windshield, stopped himself. Barely. Everything he had just felt was gone in an instant.

"What?" Jessica repeated.

Byrne took a deep breath, exhaled slowly, said: "They found another girl."

TUESDAY, 8:25 AM

Bartram Gardens was the oldest botanical garden in the United States, having been frequented by Benjamin Franklin, after whom John Bartram, the garden's founder, had named a genus of plant. Located at Fifty-fourth Street and Lindbergh, the forty-five-acre site boasted a landscape of wildflower meadows, river trails, wetlands, stone houses, and farm buildings. Today it hosted death.

A police cruiser and an unmarked were

parked near the River Trail when Byrne and Jessica arrived. A perimeter had already been established around what appeared to be half an acre of daffodils. As Byrne and Jessica approached the scene, it was easy to see how the body could have been over-looked.

The young woman lay on her back amid the bright flowers, her hands clasped in prayer at her waist, holding a black rosary. Jessica could see immediately that one of the decades of beads was missing.

Jessica looked around. The body was placed about fifteen feet into the field and, except for a narrow path of tramped flow-ers, probably caused by the medical exam-iner, there was no obvious ingress into the field. The rain had certainly washed away any footprints. If there was an abundance of forensic possibilities in the row house on Eighth, out here, after hours of torrential rain, there would be none.

Two detectives stood at the edge of the immediate crime scene: a slender Hispanic man in an expensive-looking Italian suit and a shorter, powerfully built man whom Jes-sica recognized. The cop in the Italian suit seemed equally concerned with the rain ruining his Valentino as with the investigation. At least at the moment.

Jessica and Byrne approached, considered the victim.

The girl wore a navy blue and green plaid skirt, blue knee socks, penny loafers. Jessica recognized it as the uniform belonging to Regina High School, a Catholic girls school on Broad Street in North Philly. She had raven-black hair cut into a pageboy style and, from what Jessica could see, had about a half dozen piercings in her ears and one in her nose, piercings that bore no jewelry. It was clear that this girl played the Goth role on weekends, but, due to the strict dress code at her school, wore none of her hardware in class.

Jessica looked at the young woman's hands and although she didn't want to accept the truth, there it was. The hands were bolted together in prayer.

Out of earshot of the others, Jessica turned to Byrne and asked, softly: "Have you ever had a case like this before?"

Byrne didn't have to think long about it. "No."

The two other detectives approached,

thankfully bringing their big golf umbrellas with them.

"Jessica, this is Eric Chavez, Nick Palladino."

Both men nodded. Jessica returned the greeting. Chavez was the Latin pretty boy, long lashes, smooth skin, midthirties. She had seen him at the Roundhouse the day before. It was clear that he was the unit's fashion plate. Every squad had one: the type of cop who, on a stakeout, would bring along a fat wooden hanger on which to hang his suit coat in the backseat, along with a beach towel he would tuck into his shirt collar when he ate the crap food you were forced to eat on a stakeout.

Nick Palladino was well dressed, too, but in a South Philly style—leather coat, tailored slacks, polished loafers, gold ID bracelet. He was about forty, with deep-set dark chocolate eyes, stone-set features; his black hair was combed straight back. Jessica had met Nick Palladino a few times before; he had partnered with her husband in Narcotics before moving over to Homicide.

Jessica shook hands with both men. "Nice to meet you," she said to Chavez.

"Likewise," he responded.

"Nice to see you again, Nick."

Palladino smiled. There was much danger in that smile. "How are you, Jess?"

"I'm good."

"The family?"

"All good."

"Welcome to the Show," he added. Nick Palladino had been with the squad less than a year himself, but he was solid blue. He had probably heard about her and Vincent separating, but he was a gentleman. Now was neither the time nor place.

"Eric and Nick work out of the Fugitive Squad," Byrne added.

The Fugitive Squad was one-third of the Homicide Unit. Special Investigations and the Line Squad—that section that handled the new cases—were the other two. When a big case came along, or whenever the wheel began to spin out of control, every homicide cop caught.

"Any ID?" Byrne asked.

"Nothing yet," Palladino said. "Nothing in her pockets. No purse or wallet."

"She went to Regina," Jessica said.

Palladino wrote it down. "That's the school on Broad?"

"Yeah. Broad and CB Moore."

"This the same MO as your case?" Chavez asked.

Kevin Byrne just nodded.

The idea, the very notion, that they might be up against a serial killer set all their jaws tight, throwing an even heavier pall over the day.

It had been less than twenty-four hours since this scene had played out in a dank and putrid basement of a row house on Eighth Street, and here they were again in a lush garden of cheerful flowers.

Two girls.

Two *dead* girls.

All four detectives watched as Tom Weyrich knelt next to the body. He pushed up the girl's skirt, examined her.

When he stood and turned to look at them, his face was grim. Jessica knew what it meant. This girl had suffered the same indignity in death as had Tessa Wells.

Jessica looked at Byrne. There was a deep anger rising within him, something primal and unrepentant, something that reached far beyond the job, his sense of duty.

A few moments later Weyrich joined them.

"How long has she been here?" Byrne asked.

"At least four days," Weyrich said.

Jessica did the math and a cold frost crept over her heart. This girl was dumped here right around the time Tessa Wells was kidnapped. This girl was killed first.

One decade of beads was missing from this girl's rosary. Two were missing from Tessa's.

Which meant that, of the hundreds of questions that floated above them, like the dense gray clouds, there was one truth here, one reality, one horrific fact apparent in this morass of uncertainties.

Someone was killing the Catholic school-girls of Philadelphia.

From all appearances, the rampage had just begun.

PART THREE

22

The Rosary Killer task force was assembled by noon.

As a rule, task forces were organized and authorized by the big bosses in the department, and always after an assessment of the political impact of the victims. Despite all the rhetoric regarding how all homicides are equal, manpower and resources are always made more readily available when the victims are important. If someone is knocking off drug dealers or gangbangers or streetwalkers, it's one thing. If someone is killing Catholic schoolgirls, it's quite another. Catholics vote.

By noon a good deal of the initial legwork and preliminary lab work had been rushed through the channels. The rosaries both girls held in death were identical, available at a dozen religious article retail stores in Philadelphia. Investigators were currently compiling a customer list. The missing beads were not found at either scene.

The preliminary report from the medical examiner's office concluded that the killer had used a carbon bit drill to bore the hole in the hands of the victims, and that the bolt used to secure their hands together was also a common item, a four-inch galvanized carriage bolt available at any Home Depot, Lowe's, or corner hardware store.

No fingerprints were found on either victim.

The cross on Tessa Wells's forehead was of blue chalk. The lab had not yet concluded a type. There was trace evidence of the same material on the second victim's forehead. In addition to the small William Blake print found on Tessa Wells, there was also an object found clasped between the hands of the other victim. It was a small segment of bone, approximately three inches in length. It appeared to be very sharp, and had not yet been identified by type or species. These two facts were not given to the media.

Neither was the fact that both victims were drugged. But now there was new evidence. In addition to the midazolam, the lab had confirmed the presence of an even more insidious drug. Both victims had a drug called Pavulon in their systems, a powerful paralytic that induced paralysis in the victim but did nothing for pain.

Reporters from the *Inquirer* and *The Daily News,* as well as the local television and radio stations, had so far been cautious about calling the murders the work of a serial killer, but there was no such restraint with *The Report,* the birdcage liner published out of two cramped rooms on Sansom Street.

WHO IS KILLING THE ROSARY GIRLS? screamed the headline on their website.

The task force met in the common room on the first floor of the Roundhouse.

There were six detectives in all. In addition to Jessica and Byrne, there was Eric Chavez, Nick Palladino, Tony Park, and

John Shepherd, the latter two detectives from the Special Investigations Unit.

Tony Park was Korean American, a long-time veteran of the Major Case Squad. The Auto Unit was part of Major Case, and Jessica had worked with Tony before. He was in his midforties, quick and intuitive, a family man. She had always known he would make his way to Homicide.

John Shepherd was an all-star point guard for Villanova in the early 1980s. Denzel-handsome and just graying around the temples, at an intimidating six eight he had his conservative suits custom tailored at Boyds on Chestnut Street. Jessica had never seen him without a tie.

Whenever a task force was assembled, the effort was made to staff it with detectives who brought a unique ability to the table. John Shepherd was good "in the room," a seasoned and skilled interrogator. Tony Park was a wizard with databases— NCIC, AFIS, ACCURINT, PCBA. Nick Palladino and Eric Chavez were good on the street. Jessica wondered what she brought to the table, hoping it was something other than her gender. She knew she was a born organizer, good with coordinating, arranging, scheduling. She hoped this would be the opportunity to prove it.

Kevin Byrne headed the task force. Even though he was clearly the right person for the job, Byrne had told Jessica that it had taken every bit of his persuasive powers to get Ike Buchanan to give it to him. Byrne knew that it wasn't any lack of confidence in his abilities, but rather that Ike Buchanan had to think about the bigger picture, that being the possibility of another firestorm of negative press if things, God forbid, went wrong the way they had in the Morris Blanchard case.

Ike Buchanan, as supervisor, would act as liaison to the big bosses, but Byrne would run the briefings and submit the status reports.

Byrne stood at the assignment desk as the team assembled, taking any available seat in the cramped space. Jessica thought Byrne looked a little shaky, a little burned around the cuffs. She had only known him a short while, but he hadn't struck her as the kind of cop to get rattled in a situation like this. It had to be something else. He looked like a haunted man.

"We have more than thirty sets of partial prints from the Tessa Wells crime scene, none from the Bartram site," Byrne began. "No hits yet. Neither victim has yielded any DNA in the form of semen or blood or saliva."

As he spoke, he placed pictures on the white board behind him. "The underlying signature here is a Catholic schoolgirl being taken right off the street. The killer puts a galvanized-steel bolt and nut through a drilled hole in the center of their hands. He is using a thick nylon thread—probably the sort used in sail making—and is sewing shut their vaginas. He is leaving a mark, in the shape of a cross, on their foreheads, made of a blue chalk. Both victims died of a broken neck.

"The first victim found was Tessa Wells. Her body was discovered in the basement of an abandoned house on Eighth and Jefferson. The second victim found, in a field at Bartram Gardens, had been dead for at least four days. In both instances, the doer wore nonporous gloves.

"Both victims were drugged with a short-acting benzodiazepine called midazolam, which is similar in effect to Rohypnol. In addition, there was a good amount of a drug called Pavulon. We have someone looking into the street availability of Pavulon now."

"What does this Pavulon do?" Park asked.

Byrne scanned the ME's report. "Pavulon is a paralytic. It produces skeletal muscle paralysis. Unfortunately, according to the report, for the victim, it has no effect at all on pain threshold."

"So our boy stabbed and plunged with this midazolam, then injected the Pavulon after the victims were sedated," John Shepherd said.

"That's probably how it happened."

"How available are these drugs?" Jessica asked.

"It seems that this Pavulon's been around for a while," Byrne said. "The background report says that it was used in a whole series of animal experiments. In the experiments, researchers thought that because the animal couldn't move, it wasn't in pain. They didn't give them any analgesic or hypnotic. Turns out the animals were in agony. It seems the role of drugs like Pavulon in torture are well known by the NSA/CIA. The amount of psychic horror you could introduce is about as extreme as it gets."

The implications of what Byrne was saying began to sink in, and it was chilling. Tessa Wells felt everything her killer was doing to her, but could not move.

"There is some street availability of Pavulon, but I think we need to look inside the medical community for a connection," Byrne said. "Hospital workers, doctors, nurses, pharmacists."

Byrne taped a pair of photos on the board.

"Our doer is also leaving an object on each victim," he continued. "In the case of the first victim we found a small piece of bone. In the case of Tessa Wells, a small reproduction of a painting by William Blake."

Byrne pointed to the two photos on the board, the images of the rosaries.

"The rosary found on the first victim had one set of ten beads—called a decade—missing. The typical rosary has five decades. Tessa Wells's rosary had two decades missing. As much as we don't want to do the math here, I think it's obvious what's happening. We have to shut this bad actor down, people."

Byrne leaned against the wall, turned to Eric Chavez. Chavez was the primary on the Bartram Gardens homicide.

Chavez stood, flipped open his notebook, began. "The Bartram victim's name was Nicole Taylor, seventeen, late of Callowhill Street in the Fairmount section. She was a student at Regina High School on Broad and CB Moore Avenue.

"The preliminary report from the ME's office is that the cause of death was identical to Tessa Wells, that being a broken neck. As to the other signatures, which were identical as well, we're running them through VICAP now. We'll know about the blue chalky material on Tessa Wells's forehead today. There were only trace amounts on Nicole's forehead, due to exposure.

"The only recent bruising to the body was on Nicole's left palm." Chavez pointed to a photo taped to the white board, a close-up of Nicole's left hand. "These cuts were made by pressure from her fingernails. Traces of her nail polish were found in the grooves." Jessica looked at the photo, subconsciously digging her short fingernails into the fleshy part of her hand. There appeared to be half a dozen crescent-shaped indentations on Nicole's palm, in no discernible pattern.

Jessica imagined the girl clenching her fist in fear. She banished the image. It was not the time for rage.

Eric Chavez proceeded to rebuild Nicole Taylor's last day.

Nicole left her apartment building on Callowhill at approximately seven twenty on Thursday morning. She walked alone down Broad Street to Regina High School. She attended all her classes, then had lunch with her friend, Domini Dawson, in the cafeteria. At two twenty she left the school, walking south on Broad. She stopped in at the Hole World body-piercing salon. There, she looked at some jewelry. According to the owner, Irina Kaminsky, Nicole seemed happy, even chattier than usual. Ms. Kaminsky had done all of Nicole's piercings and said that Nicole had her eye on a ruby nose stud, and was saving for it.

From the salon, Nicole continued up Broad Street to Girard Avenue, then over to Eighteenth Street, entering St. Joseph's Hospital, where her mother worked as a housekeeping supervisor. Sharon Taylor told the detectives that her daughter was in particularly good spirits because one of her favorite musical groups, Sisters of Mercy, was playing the Trocadero Theatre on Friday night, and she had tickets to see them.

Mother and daughter shared a fruit cup in the cafeteria. They talked about the wedding of one of Nicole's cousins, which was coming up in June, and the necessity of Nicole to "look like a lady." It was an ongoing battle between the two, due to Nicole's penchant for a Goth appearance.

Nicole kissed her mother, then left the hospital at approximately four o'clock, via the Girard Avenue exit.

At that point, Nicole Theresa Taylor simply vanished.

The next time anyone saw her, as far as the investigation could determine, was when the security guard at Bartram Gardens found her in the field of daffodils nearly four days later. Canvassing the area near the hospital was ongoing.

"Did her mother report her missing?" Jessica asked.

Chavez flipped through his notes. "The call came in at one twenty on Friday morning."

"No one saw her after she walked out of the hospital?"

"No one," Chavez said. "But there are surveillance cameras on the entrances and parking lot. The tapes are on the way here."

"Boyfriends?" Shepherd asked.

"According to Sharon Taylor, her daughter had no current boyfriend," Chavez said.

"What about her father?"

"Mr. Donald P. Taylor is a long-haul trucker, currently somewhere between Taos and Santa Fe.

"As soon as we're done here, we're going to visit the school and see if we can get a list of her circle of friends," Chavez added.

There were no more immediate questions. Byrne walked forward.

"Most of you know Charlotte Summers," Byrne said. "To those of you who don't, Dr. Summers is a professor of criminal psychology at the University of Pennsylvania. From time to time she consults with the department in the area of profiling."

Jessica knew Charlotte Summers by reputation only. Her most celebrated case had been the dead-on profiling of Floyd Lee Castle, a psychopath who had preyed upon prostitutes in and around Camden during the summer of 2001.

The fact that Charlotte Summers was already front and center told Jessica that this investigation had greatly broadened in the past few hours, and it might only be a matter of time until the FBI was called in to either assist with manpower or provide assistance in the forensic investigation. Everyone in the room wanted to get a solid lead before the suits showed up and took credit for everything.

Charlotte Summers stood and walked to the white board. In her late forties, she was elfin and slender, with pale blue eyes, a bobbed haircut. She wore a tasteful chalk-stripe suit, lavender silk blouse. "I know the temptation here is to assume that whoever we are looking for is a religious zealot of some sort," Summers said. "There is no reason to think he isn't. With one caveat. The inclination to think of zealots as impulsive or reckless is incorrect. This is a highly organized killer.

"Here's what we know: He is taking his victims right off the street, holding them for a while, then taking them to a place where he kills them. These are high-risk abductions. Broad daylight, public places. There is no evidence of ligature bruising on their wrists or ankles.

"Wherever he takes them initially, he is not restraining or shackling them. Both victims were given a dose of midazolam, as well as the paralytic that facilitated the vaginal sewing. The sewing is being done premortem, so it's clear that he wants them to be aware of what is happening to them. And to feel it."

"What's the significance of the hands?" Nick Palladino asked.

"Perhaps he is posing them to match some religious iconography. Some painting or sculpture on which he is fixated. The bolt might indicate an obsession with the stigmata, or the crucifixion itself. Whatever the significance, these specific acts have meaning. Usually, if you want someone dead, you walk up to them and strangle them or shoot them. The fact that our subject takes the time to do these things is, in and of itself, noteworthy."

Byrne threw a glance at Jessica, which she read loud and clear. He wanted her to look into the religious symbol angle. She made a note.

"If he isn't sexually assaulting the victims, what's his point?" Chavez asked. "I mean, with all this rage, why no rape? Is this about revenge?"

"We could be looking at some manifestation of grief or loss," Summers said. "But this is clearly about control. He wants to control them physically, sexually, emotionally, three areas where girls of this age are most confused. Perhaps he lost a girlfriend to a sex crime at this age. Perhaps a daughter or sister. The fact that he is sewing their vaginas might mean he believes he is returning these young women to some twisted sort of virginal state, a state of innocence."

"What would make him stop?" Tony Park asked. "There are a lot of Catholic girls in this town."

"I don't see any escalation of violence," Summers said. "In fact, his method of murder is fairly humane, all things considered. They are not lingering in death. He is not trying to take away femininity from these girls. Just the opposite. He is trying to secure it, preserve it for eternity, if you will.

"His hunting ground seems to be this part of North Philly," she said, indicating a highlighted twenty-block area. "Our unknown subject is probably white, between twenty and forty, physically strong, but probably not fanatical about it. Not a bodybuilder type. He was most likely raised a Catholic, of above-average intelligence, mostly likely with an undergraduate degree at the very least, probably more. He drives a van or a station wagon, perhaps an SUV of some sort. This would make it easier to get the girls in and out of his vehicle."

"What do we get from the location of the crime scenes?" Jessica asked.

"At this point, I have no idea, I'm afraid," Summers said. "The Eighth Street house and Bartram Gardens are about as disparate a pair of sites as one could imagine."

"Then you believe they are random?" Jessica asked.

"I don't believe they are. In both instances, it appears the victim is carefully posed. I don't believe our unknown subject does anything in a haphazard manner. Tessa Wells was chained to that column for a reason. Nicole Taylor was not randomly dumped in that field. These locations are definitely significant.

"At first there may have been the temptation to think that Tessa Wells was put in that row house on Eighth Street to hide her body, but I don't believe this to be the case. Nicole Taylor was carefully placed in the open a few days earlier. There was no attempt to hide the body. This guy is operating in daylight. He wants us to find his victims. He is arrogant and he wants us to think he's smarter than we are. The fact that he placed objects between their hands furthers this theory. He is clearly challenging us to understand what he's doing.

"As far as we can tell at this time, these girls did not know each other. They moved in different social circles. Tessa Wells liked classical music; Nicole Taylor was into the Goth rock scene. They attended different schools, had different interests."

Jessica looked at the photos of the two girls, side by side, on the board. She recalled how cliquish things were when she went to Nazarene. The cheerleader types would have nothing to do with the rock and rollers, and vice versa. There were the nerds who spent their free time hovering over the few computers in the library, the fashion queens who were always buried in the current issue of *Vogue* or *Marie Clare* or *Elle*.

Then there was her crowd, the South Philly contingent.

On the surface, what connected Tessa Wells and Nicole Taylor was that they were Catholic and they went to Catholic schools.

"I want every corner of these girls' lives turned inside out," Byrne said. "Who they hung around with, where they went on weekends, their boyfriends, relatives, acquaintances, what clubs they belonged to, what movies they've gone to, what churches they belong to. Somebody knows something. Somebody saw something."

"Can we keep the mutilation and the found items from the press?" Tony Park asked.

"Maybe for twenty-four hours," Byrne said. "After that, I doubt it."

Chavez spoke up. "I spoke to the school psychiatrist who handles the counseling at Regina. He works out of the offices at the Nazarene Academy in the Northeast. Nazarene is the administrative office for five diocesan schools, including Regina. The diocese employs one psychiatrist for all five schools, who rotates on a weekly basis. He might be able to help."

At this, Jessica felt her stomach fall.

There *was* a connection between Regina and Nazarene, and she now knew what that connection was.

"They only have one psychiatrist for that many kids?" Tony Park asked.

"They have half a dozen counselors," Chavez said. "But only one psychiatrist for the five schools."

"Who is that?"

While Eric Chavez looked through his notes, Byrne found Jessica's eyes. By the time Chavez located the name, Byrne was already out of the room and on the phone.

TUESDAY, 2:00 PM

"I really appreciate you coming in," Byrne said to Brian Parkhurst. They were standing in the middle of the wide, semicircular room that housed the Homicide Unit.

"Anything I can do to help." Parkhurst was dressed in a black-and-gray nylon jogging outfit and what looked like brand-new Reeboks. If he was at all nervous about being called in to talk to the police on this matter, it didn't show. Then again, Jessica thought, he was a psychiatrist. If he could read anxiety, he could write composure. "Needless to say, we're all devastated at Nazarene."

"Are the students taking it hard?"

"I'm afraid so."

The human traffic picked up around the two men. It was an old trick—make the witness look for somewhere to sit down. The door to Interview Room A was wide open; all chairs in the common room were occupied. On purpose.

"Oh, I'm sorry." Byrne's voice was dripping with concern and sincerity. He was good, too. "Why don't we sit in here?"

Brian Parkhurst sat in the upholstered chair across from Byrne in Interview Room A, the small, scruffy room where suspects and witnesses were questioned, made statements, provided information. Jessica observed through the two-way mirror. The door to the interview room remained open.

"Once again," Byrne began, "we appreciate you taking the time."

There were two chairs in the room. One was an upholstered desk chair; the other was a battered metal folding chair. Suspects never got the good chair. Witnesses did. Until they *became* suspects, that is.

"Not a problem," Parkhurst said.

The murder of Nicole Taylor had led the noon news, with live break-ins on all the local TV stations. Camera crews were at Bartram Gardens. Kevin Byrne had not asked Dr. Parkhurst if he had heard the news.

"Are you any closer to finding the person who killed Tessa?" Parkhurst asked in a practiced, conversational manner. It was the sort of tone he might use to start a therapy session with a new patient.

"We have a few leads," Byrne said. "It's still early in the investigation."

"Great," Parkhurst said. The word sounded cold and somewhat strident, given the nature of the crime.

Byrne let the word circle the room a few times, then float to the floor. He sat down opposite Parkhurst, dropped a file folder on the battered metal table. "I promise not to keep you too long," he said.

"I have all the time you need."

Byrne picked up the folder, crossed his legs. He opened the folder, carefully shielding the contents from Parkhurst. Jessica could see it was a 229, a basic biographical report. Nothing threatening to Brian Parkhurst, but he didn't have to know that. "Tell me a little more about your work at Nazarene."

"Well, it's mostly consultation in the areas of learning and behavior," Parkhurst said.

"You counsel students on their behavior?"

"Yes."

"How so?"

"All children and adolescents face problems from time to time, Detective. They have fears about starting at a new school, they feel depressed, they quite often lack self-discipline or self-esteem, they lack social skills. As a result, they often experiment with drugs or alcohol, or think about suicide. I let my girls know that my door is always open to them."

My girls, Jessica thought.

"Do the students you counsel find it easy to open up to you?"

"I like to think so," Parkhurst said.

Byrne nodded. "What else can you tell me?"

Parkhurst continued. "Part of what we do is attempt to isolate potential learning difficulties in students, as well as design programs for those who may be at risk of failure. Things like that."

"Are there a lot of students who fall into that category at Nazarene?" Byrne asked.

"Which category?"

"Students who are at a risk for failure."

"No more than any other parochial high school, I would imagine," Parkhurst said. "Probably fewer."

"Why is that?"

"There is a legacy of high academic achievement at Nazarene," he said.

Byrne scribbled a few notes. Jessica saw Parkhurst's eyes roam the notepad.

Parkhurst added: "We also try to provide parents and teachers with the skills to cope with disruptive behavior, encourage tolerance, understanding, appreciation of diversity."

This was strictly brochure copy, Jessica thought. Byrne knew it. Parkhurst knew it. Byrne shifted gears, making no attempt to mask it. "Are you a Catholic, Dr. Parkhurst?"

"Of course."

"If you don't mind me asking, why do you work for the archdiocese?"

"Excuse me?"

"I would imagine you could make a lot more money in private practice."

Jessica knew that to be true. She had made a call to an old schoolmate who worked in personnel at the archdiocese. She knew exactly what Brian Parkhurst made. He earned $71,400 per year.

"The church is a very important part of my life, Detective. I owe it a great deal."

"By the way, what's your favorite William Blake painting?"

Parkhurst leaned back, as if trying to focus on Byrne more clearly. "My favorite William Blake painting?"

"Yeah," Byrne said. "Me, I like *Dante and Virgil at the Gates of Hell.*"

"I, well, I can't say I know very much about Blake."

"Tell me about Tessa Wells."

It was a gut shot. Jessica watched Parkhurst closely. He was smooth. Not a tic.

"What would you like to know?"

"Did she ever mention someone who might have been bothering her? Someone she might have been afraid of?"

Parkhurst seemed to think about this for a moment. Jessica wasn't buying. Neither was Byrne.

"Not that I can recall," Parkhurst said.

"Did she seem particularly troubled of late?"

"No," Parkhurst said. "There was a period last year when I saw her a little more often than some of the other students."

"Did you ever see her outside of school?"

Like right around Thanksgiving? Jessica wondered.

"No."

"Were you a little closer to Tessa than some of the other students?" Byrne asked.

"Not really."

"But there was some sort of bond."

"Yes."

"Is that how it all started with Karen Hillkirk?"

Parkhurst's face reddened, then cooled instantly. He was clearly expecting this. Karen Hillkirk was the student with whom Parkhurst had had the affair in Ohio.

"It wasn't what you think, Detective."

"Enlighten us," Byrne said.

On the word *us,* Parkhurst threw a glance at the mirror. Jessica thought she saw the slightest smile. She wanted to slap it off his face.

Parkhurst then lowered his head for a

moment, penitent now, as if this was a story he had told many times, if only to himself.

"It was a mistake," he began. "I . . . I was young myself. Karen was mature for her age. It just . . . happened."

"Were you her counselor?"

"Yes," Parkhurst said.

"So then you can see how there are those who would say that you abused a position of power, can't you?"

"Of course," Parkhurst said. "I understand that."

"Did you have the same sort of relationship with Tessa Wells?"

"Absolutely not," Parkhurst said.

"Are you acquainted with a Regina student named Nicole Taylor?"

Parkhurst hesitated for a second. The rhythm of the interview was starting to pick up in tempo. It appeared that Parkhurst was trying to slow it down. "Yes, I know Nicole."

Know, Jessica thought. Present tense.

"You've counseled her?" Byrne asked.

"Yes," Parkhurst said. "I work with the students at five diocesan schools."

"How well do you know Nicole?" Byrne asked.

"I've seen her a few times."

"What can you tell me about her?"

"Nicole has some self-image issues. Some . . . troubles at home," Parkhurst said.

"What sort of self-image issues?"

"Nicole is a loner. She's really into the whole Goth scene and that has somewhat isolated her at Regina."

"Goth?"

"The Goth scene is loosely made up of kids who, for one reason or another, are spurned by the 'normal' kids. They tend to dress differently, listen to their own kinds of music."

"Dress differently how?"

"Well, there are all kinds of Goth styles. The typical, or stereotypical Goth dresses in all black. Black fingernails, black lipstick, numerous piercings. But some kids dress in a Victorian manner, or an industrial style, if you will. They listen to everyone from Bauhaus to the old-school bands like the Cure and Siouxsie and the Banshees."

Byrne just stared at Parkhurst for a few moments, fixing him in his chair. Parkhurst responded by rearranging his weight on the seat, straightening his clothes. He waited Byrne out. "You seem to know a lot about these things," Byrne finally said.

"It's my job, Detective," Parkhurst said. "I

can't help my girls if I don't know where they're coming from."

My girls again, Jessica noted.

"In fact," Parkhurst continued, "I confess to owning a few Cure CDs myself."

I'll bet you do, Jessica mused.

"You mentioned Nicole had some troubles at home," Byrne said. "What kind of troubles?"

"Well, for one, there is a history of alcohol abuse in her household," Parkhurst said.

"Any violence?" Byrne asked.

Parkhurst paused. "Not that I recall. But even if I did, we're getting into confidential matters here."

"Is that the sort of thing students would necessarily share with you?"

"Yes," Parkhurst said. "Those who are predisposed to do so."

"Are many of the girls *predisposed* to discussing intimate details of their home lives with you?"

Byrne put a false emphasis on the word. Parkhurst caught it. "Yes. I like to think that I am good at putting young people at ease."

Defensive now, Jessica thought.

"I don't understand all these questions

about Nicole. Has something happened to her?"

"She was found murdered this morning," Byrne said.

"Oh my God." Parkhurst's face drained of color. "I saw the news . . . I had no . . ."

The news had not released the name of the victim.

"When was the last time you saw Nicole?"

Parkhurst thought for a few crucial moments. "It's been a few weeks."

"Where were you on Thursday and Friday mornings, Dr. Parkhurst?"

Jessica was certain that Parkhurst knew that the questioning had just crossed a barrier, the one that separated witness from suspect. He remained silent.

"It's simply a routine question," Byrne said. "We have to cover all bases."

Before Parkhurst could answer, there was a soft rap on the open door.

It was Ike Buchanan.

"Detective?"

As they approached Buchanan's office, Jessica could see a man standing with his back to the door. He was about five eleven, wearing a black overcoat, a dark fedora in his right hand. He was athletically built, wide-shouldered. His shaved head glistened beneath the fluorescents. They stepped into the office.

"Jessica, this is Monsignor Terry Pacek," Buchanan said.

Terry Pacek, by reputation, was a fierce defender of the Archdiocese of Philadelphia, a self-made man from the hardscrabble hills of Lackawanna County. Coal country. In an archdiocese where there were nearly one and a half million Catholics and close to three hundred parishes, no one was a more vocal or staunch advocate than Terry Pacek.

He had come into his own in 2002 during a brief sex scandal where six Philadelphia priests were dismissed, along with a few from Allentown. Granted, the scandal paled in comparison to what had taken place in Boston, but still, with its large Catholic population, Philadelphia reeled.

Terry Pacek had been front and center in the media during those few months, visiting every local talk show, every radio station, and showing up in every newspaper account. Jessica's image of him, at the time, had been that of a well-spoken, well-educated pit bull. What she was not prepared for, now that she had met him in person, was the smile. At one moment, he looked like a compact version of a WWF wrestler ready to pounce. The next moment, his entire face changed, lighting up the room. She could see how he had charmed not only the media, but also the vicariate. She had the feeling that Terry Pacek could write his own future in the ranks of the church's political hierarchy.

"Monsignor Pacek." Jessica extended her hand.

"How is the investigation going?"

The question was directed at Jessica, but Byrne stepped forward. "It's still early," Byrne said.

"I understand that there has been a task force formed?"

Byrne knew that Pacek already knew the answer to this question. The look on Byrne's face told Jessica—and, perhaps, Pacek himself—that he didn't appreciate it.

"Yes," Byrne said. Flat, succinct, tepid.

"Sergeant Buchanan tells me that you have brought in Dr. Brian Parkhurst?"

Here we go, Jessica thought.

"Dr. Parkhurst volunteered to help us with the investigation. It turns out that he was acquainted with both victims."

Terry Pacek nodded. "So Dr. Parkhurst is not a suspect?"

"Absolutely not," Byrne said. "He is here merely as a material witness."

For now, Jessica thought.

Jessica knew that Terry Pacek was walking a tightrope. On one hand, if someone was killing the Catholic schoolgirls of Philadelphia, he had an obligation to stay on top of the situation, making sure that the investigation was given a high priority.

On the other hand, he could not stand idly by and have archdiocese personnel brought in for questioning without counsel, or at least a show of support from the church.

"As spokesperson for the archdiocese, you can certainly understand my concern over these tragic events," Pacek said. "The archbishop himself has communicated with me directly and authorized me to put all of the diocese's resources at your disposal."

"That's very generous," Byrne said.

Pacek handed Byrne a card. "If there is anything my office can do, please don't hesitate to call us."

"I sure will," Byrne said. "Just out of curiosity, Monsignor, how did you know Dr. Parkhurst had come in?"

"He called my office after you called him."

Byrne nodded. If Parkhurst gave the archdiocese a heads-up about a witness interview, it was pretty clear that he knew the conversation might turn into an interrogation.

Jessica glanced at Ike Buchanan. She saw him look over her shoulder and make a subtle move with his head, the sort of gesture you would make to tell someone that whatever they were looking for was in the room on the right.

Jessica followed Buchanan's gaze into the common room, just outside Ike's door, and found Nick Palladino and Eric Chavez there. They headed to Interview Room A, and Jessica knew what the nod meant.

Cut Brian Parkhurst loose.

24

The main branch of the Free Library was the largest library in the city, located on Vine Street and the Benjamin Franklin Parkway.

Jessica sat in the fine arts section, poring over a huge collection of Christian art tomes, looking for something, anything, that resembled the tableaux they had uncovered at the two crime scenes, scenes to which they had no witnesses, no fingerprints, as well as two victims who, as far as they knew, were unrelated: Tessa Wells, sitting at the column in that filthy basement on North Eighth Street; Nicole Taylor reposing in the field of spring flowers.

With the assistance of one of the librarians, Jessica did a catalog search using various keywords. The results were overwhelming.

There were books on the iconography of the Virgin Mary, books on mysticism and the Catholic Church, books on relics, the Shroud of Turin, the *Oxford Companion to Christian Art*. There were countless guides to the Louvre, to the Uffizi, to the Tate. She skimmed books on the stigmata, on Roman history as it applied to crucifixion. There were pictorial Bibles, books on Franciscan, Jesuit, and Cistercian art, sacred heraldry, Byzantine icons. There were color plates of oil paintings, watercolors, acrylics, woodcuts, pen-and-ink drawings, murals, frescoes, sculptures in bronze, marble, wood, stone.

Where to begin?

When she found herself thumbing through a coffee table book on ecclesiastical embroidery, she knew she was getting a little off course. She tried keywords like *prayer* and *rosary,* and got hundreds of hits.

She learned some basics, including that the rosary is Marian in nature, centered on the Virgin Mary, and is meant to be said while contemplating the face of Christ. She took as many notes as she could.

She checked out a few of the circulating books—many she had looked at were reference—and headed back to the Roundhouse, her mind reeling with religious imagery. Something in these books pointed to the inspiration for the madness of these crimes. She just had no idea how to ferret it out.

For the first time in her life she wished she had paid more attention in religion class.

2 5

The blackness was complete, seamless, a perpetual night that ignored time. Beneath the darkness, very faint, was the sound of the world.

For Bethany Price, the veil of consciousness came and went like waves on the beach.

Cape May, she thought through the deep haze in her mind, the images fighting up from the depths of her memory. She hadn't thought of Cape May in years. When she was small, her parents would take the family to Cape May, a few miles south of Atlantic City on the Jersey shore. She used to sit on the beach, her feet buried in the wet sand. Dad in his crazy Hawaiian trunks, Mom in her modest one-piece.

She remembered changing in the beach cabana, even then terribly self-conscious about her body, her weight. The thought made her touch herself. She was still fully clothed.

She knew she had ridden in a car for about fifteen minutes. It might have been longer. He had stuck her with a needle that had taken her to the grasp of sleep, but not quite into its arms. She had heard city sounds all around her. Buses, car horns, people walking and talking. She wanted to cry out to them, but she couldn't.

It was quiet.

She was afraid.

The room was small, maybe five feet by three feet. Not a room at all, really. More like a closet. On the wall opposite the door she had felt a large crucifix. On the floor was a padded confessional kneeler. The carpeting on the floor was new; she smelled the petroleum scent of the new fiber. Beneath the door she could see a meager bar of yellow light. She was hungry and thirsty, but she dared not ask.

He wanted her to pray. He had stepped into the darkness and given her a rosary, and told her to begin with the Apostle's Creed. He hadn't touched her in a sexual way. Not that she knew of, anyway.

He had left for a while, but was now back. He was pacing outside the closet, upset about something it seemed.

"I can't hear you," he said from the other side of the door. "What did Pope Pius the Sixth say about this?"

"I . . . I don't know," Bethany said.

"He said that, without contemplation, the rosary is a body without a soul, and its recitation runs the risk of becoming a mechanical repetition of formulas, in violation of the admonition of Christ."

"I'm sorry."

Why was he doing this? He had been nice to her before. She had gotten into trouble and he had treated her with respect.

The sound of the machine grew louder.

It sounded like a drill.

"Now!" boomed the voice.

"Hail Mary full of grace, the Lord is with

thee," she began for what was probably the hundredth time.

The Lord is with thee, she thought, her mind beginning to fog again.

Is the Lord with me?

2 6

The black-and-white videotape was grainy, but clear enough to see the comings and goings through the parking lot at St. Joseph's Hospital. The traffic—both automotive and pedestrian—was what one would expect: ambulances, police cars, delivery vans from medical and maintenance supply houses. A majority of the personnel were hospital employees: doctors, nurses, orderlies, housekeeping. Through this entrance came a few visitors, a handful of police officers.

Jessica, Byrne, Tony Park, and Nick Pal-ladino were jammed into the small room that doubled as a snack room and video room. At the 4:06:03 point of the tape, they saw Nicole Taylor.

Nicole walks out of the door marked SPE-CIAL HOSPITAL SERVICES, hesitates for a few moments, then ambles slowly toward the street. She has a small purse on a strap over her right shoulder and what looks like a bot-tle of juice or perhaps a Snapple in her left hand. There was no purse or bottle found at the crime scene in Bartram Gardens.

At the street, Nicole seems to notice something at the top of the frame. She cov-ers her mouth, perhaps in surprise, then walks over to a car parked at the very left edge of the screen. It appears to be a Ford Windstar. No occupant of the car is visible.

Just as Nicole reaches the passenger side of the car, a delivery truck from Allied Medical pulls between the camera and the minivan.

"Shit," Byrne said. Come on, come on . . ."

The time on the tape is 4:06:55.

The driver of the Allied Medical truck gets out of the driver's side and heads into the hospital. A few minutes later he returns, enters the cab.

When the truck pulls away, the Windstar and Nicole are gone.

They let the tape run for five more minutes, then fast-forwarded. Neither Nicole nor the Windstar returned.

"Can you rewind it to the point where she walks up to the van?" Jessica asked.

"No problem," Tony Park said.

They watched the tape over and over again. Nicole leaving the building, walking beneath the canopy, approaching the Windstar, each time freezing it at the moment the truck pulls up and obscures them.

"Can you get us in closer?" Jessica asked.

"Not on this machine," Park replied. "The lab can do all kinds of tricks, though."

The AV Unit, located in the basement of the Roundhouse, was capable of all kinds of video enhancement. The tape they were watching had been dubbed from the original, due to the fact that surveillance tape is recorded at a very slow speed, rendering it impossible to play on a normal VCR.

Jessica leaned close to the small black-and-white monitor. It appeared that the Windstar's license plate was Pennsylvania issue, ending in 6. It was impossible to tell what numbers, letters, or combinations thereof preceded this. If they had the beginning numbers on the plate, it would make it a lot easier to match the plate with the make and model of the car.

"Why don't we try to cross-reference Windstars with that number?" Byrne asked. Tony Park turned to walk from the room. Byrne stopped him, wrote something on his pad, tore it off, and handed it to Park. With that, Park was out the door.

The remaining detectives continued to watch the tape as traffic came and went; as personnel walked lazily toward their jobs or spryly away. Jessica found it excruciating to know that, behind the truck obscuring her view of the Windstar, Nicole Taylor was quite likely talking to someone who would soon end her life.

They watched the tape another six times, failing to glean any new information.

Tony Park returned with a thick stack of computer printouts in hand. Ike Buchanan followed.

"There are twenty-five hundred Windstars registered in Pennsylvania," Park said. "Two hundred or so end in the number six."

"Shit," Jessica said.

He then held up the printout, beaming. One of the lines was highlighted in bright yellow. "One of them is registered to Dr. Brian Allan Parkhurst of Larchwood Street."

Byrne was on his feet in an instant. He glanced at Jessica. He ran a finger over the scar on his forehead.

"It's not enough," Buchanan said.

"Why *not*?" Byrne asked.

"Where do you want me to start?"

"He knew both victims, and we can put him at the scene where Nicole Taylor was last seen—"

"We don't know that it was him. We don't know that she even got *in* that car."

"He had opportunity," Byrne plowed ahead. "Maybe even motive."

"Motive?" Buchanan asked.

"Karen Hillkirk," Byrne said.

"He didn't *kill* Karen Hillkirk."

"He didn't have to. Tessa Wells was underage. Maybe she was going to go public with their affair."

"What affair?"

Buchanan was, of course, right.

"Look, he's an MD," Byrne said, selling hard. Jessica got the sense that even Byrne was not convinced that Parkhurst was their doer. But Parkhurst knew *something*. "The ME's report said both girls were subdued with midazolam and then given a paralytic drug by injection. He drives a minivan, which is also right on. He fits the profile. Let me put him back in the chair. Twenty minutes. If he doesn't tip, we cut him loose."

Ike Buchanan briefly considered the idea. "If Brian Parkhurst sets foot in this building again, he's coming in with a lawyer from the archdiocese. You know it, and I know it," Buchanan said. "Let's do a little more legwork before we connect these dots. Let's find out if that Windstar belongs to an employee of the hospital before we start hauling people in. Let's see if we can account for every minute of Parkhurst's day."

Most police work is mind- and ass-numbingly dull. Much of the time is spent at a wobbly gray desk with sticky drawers full of paper, a phone in one hand, cold coffee in the other. Calling people. Calling people back. Waiting for people to call *you* back. Hitting dead ends, roaring up blind alleys, walking dejectedly out. People interviewed saw no evil, heard no evil, spoke no evil— only to discover that they remember a key fact two weeks later. Detectives talk to funeral parlors to see if they had a procession on the street that day. They talk to newspaper deliverymen, school crossing guards, landscapers, painters, city workers, street cleaners. They talk to junkies, hookers, alkies, dealers, panhandlers, vendors, anyone who makes a habit or vocation of simply hanging around the corner in which they are interested.

And then, after all the phone calls prove worthless, the detectives get to drive around the city, asking the same questions to the same people in person.

By midafternoon, the investigation had settled into a lethargic drone, like the seventh-inning dugout of a team down 5–0. Pencils tapped, phones stood mute, eye contact was avoided. The task force, with the help of a handful of uniformed officers, had managed to contact all but a handful of the Windstar owners. Two of them worked at St. Joseph's, one of them in housekeeping.

At five o'clock they held a press conference behind the Roundhouse. The police commissioner and the district attorney were front and center. All the expected questions were asked. All the expected answers were given. Kevin Byrne and Jessica Balzano were on camera and identified to the media as leading the task force. Jessica was hoping she wouldn't have to speak on camera. She didn't.

By five twenty they were back at their desks. They flipped through the local channels until they found a replay of the press conference. Brief applause, hoots, and hollers greeted the close-up of Kevin Byrne. A local anchor's voiceover accompanied the footage of Brian Parkhurst's exit from the Roundhouse earlier in the day. Parkhurst's name was plastered on the screen beneath the slow-motion image of him getting into his car.

Nazarene Academy had called back with the information that Brian Parkhurst had left early the previous Thursday and Friday, and that he had arrived at the school no earlier than 8:15 AM on Monday. He would have had ample time to abduct both girls, dump both bodies, and still maintain his schedule.

At five thirty, just after Jessica received a call back from the Denver Board of Education, effectively eliminating Tessa's old boyfriend Sean Brennan from the suspect pool, she and John Shepherd drove down to the forensic lab, the new state-of-the-art facility just a few blocks from the Roundhouse at Eighth and Poplar. There was new information. The bone found in Nicole Taylor's hands was a section cut from a leg of lamb. It appeared to have been cut with a serrated blade and sharpened on an oilstone.

So far their victims had been found holding a sheep bone and a reproduction of a William Blake painting. The information, although helpful, shed no light into any corner of the investigation.

"We've also got matching carpet fibers from both victims," Tracy McGovern said. Tracy was the deputy director of the lab.

All across the room, fists clenched, pumping the air. They had evidence. Synthetic fibers could be traced.

"Both girls had the same nylon fibers along the hem of their skirts," Tracy said.

"Tessa Wells had more than a dozen. Nicole Taylor's skirt yielded only a few, due to the fact that she had been out in the rain, but they were there."

"Is it residential? Commercial? Automotive?" Jessica asked.

"Probably not automotive. I'd say mid-range residential carpeting. Dark blue. But the pattern of the fibers was spread out along the very bottom of the hem. It wasn't anywhere else on their clothing."

"So they weren't lying down on the carpet?" Byrne asked. "Or sitting on it?"

"No," Tracy said. "For this kind of pattern, I'd say they were—"

"Kneeling," Jessica said.

"Kneeling," Tracy echoed.

At six o'clock Jessica sat at a desk, spinning a cup of cold coffee, thumbing through her books on Christian art. There were some promising leads, but nothing that duplicated the postures of the victims at the crime scenes.

Eric Chavez had a dinner date. He stood in front of the small two-way mirror in Interview Room A, tying and retying his tie, searching for the perfect double Windsor.

Nick Palladino was finishing up the calls to the remaining few Windstar owners.

Kevin Byrne stared at the wall of photographs like Easter Island statuary. He seemed rapt, consumed by the minutiae, replaying the time line over and over in his mind. Images of Tessa Wells, images of Nicole Taylor, snapshots of the death house on Eighth Street, pictures of the daffodil garden at Bartram. Hands, feet, eyes, arms, legs. Pictures with rulers to provide scale. Pictures with grids to provide context.

The answers to all Byrne's questions were directly in front of him, and to Jessica he looked like a man in a catatonic state. She would have given a month's salary to be privy to Kevin Byrne's private thoughts at that moment.

Late afternoon slogged toward evening. And yet Kevin Byrne stood motionless, scanning the board, left to right, top to bottom.

Suddenly he removed a close-up photograph of Nicole Taylor's left palm. He took it over to the window and held it up to the graying light. He looked at Jessica, but it appeared he was looking right through her. She was just an object in the path of his thousand-yard stare. He removed a magnifying glass from a desk and turned back to the photo.

"Christ," he finally said, drawing the attention of the handful of detectives in the room. "I can't believe we didn't see it."

"See what?" Jessica asked. She was glad Byrne was finally talking. She had been beginning to worry about him.

Byrne pointed to the indentations in the fleshy part of the palm, the marks that Tom Weyrich said were caused by pressure from Nicole's fingernails.

"These marks." He picked up the ME's report on Nicole Taylor. "Look," he continued. "There was trace evidence of burgundy fingernail polish in the grooves on her left hand."

"What about it?" Buchanan asked.

"The polish was *green* on her left hand," Byrne said.

Byrne pointed to the close-up of the fingernails on Nicole Taylor's left hand. The color was a forest green. He held up a photograph of her right hand.

"The polish on her *right* hand was burgundy."

The remaining three detectives looked at each other, shrugged.

"Don't you see it? She didn't make those grooves by clenching her left fist. She made them with her *opposite hand*."

Jessica tried to see something in the photograph, as if examining the positive and negative elements in an M. C. Escher print. She saw nothing. "I don't understand," she said.

Byrne grabbed his coat and headed for the door. "You will."

Byrne and Jessica stood in the small digital imaging room in the crime lab.

The imaging specialist was working on enhancing the photographs of Nicole Taylor's left hand. Most crime scene photographs were still taken on thirty-five-millimeter film and then transferred to digital format, after which they could then be enhanced, enlarged, and, if needed, prepared for trial. The area of interest in this photograph was the small, crescent-shaped indentations in the lower left portion of Nicole's palm. The technician enlarged and clarified the area, and when the image became clear, there was a collective gasp in the small room.

Nicole Taylor had sent them a message.

The slight cuts were not random at all.

"Oh my God," Jessica said, her first adrenaline rush as a homicide detective beginning to hum in her ears.

Before she died, Nicole Taylor had used the fingernails on her right hand to begin spelling a word on her left palm, a dying girl's plea in the final, desperate moments of her life. There could be no debate. The cuts spelled P A R.

Byrne flipped open his cell phone, called Ike Buchanan. Within twenty minutes, an affidavit of probable cause would be typed and submitted to the chief of the Homicide Unit at the district attorney's office. Within an hour, with any luck, they'd have a search warrant for the premises of Brian Allan Parkhurst.

2 7

Simon Close stared at the front page of *The Report,* sitting proudly on the screen of his Apple PowerBook.

WHO IS KILLING THE ROSARY GIRLS?

Is there anything better than seeing your byline beneath a screamingly provocative headline?

Maybe one or two things, tops, Simon thought. And both of those things cost him money, rather than lining his pocket with it.

The Rosary Girls.

His idea.

He had kicked around a few others. This one kicked back.

Simon loved this part of the night. The preen before the prowl. Although he dressed well for work—always in a shirt and tie, usually a blazer and slacks—it was at night that his tastes ran to the European cut, the Italian craftsmanship, the exquisite cloths. If it was Chaps during the day, it was Ralph Lauren proper at night.

He tried on Dolce & Gabbana and Prada, but he bought Armani and Pal Zileri. Thank God for that semiannual sale at Boyds.

He caught a glimpse of himself in the mirror. What woman could resist? While there were a lot of well-dressed men in Philadelphia, few really carried off the European style with any panache.

And then there were the women.

When Simon had struck out on his own, after Aunt Iris's death, he had spent some time in Los Angeles, Miami, Chicago, and New York City. He had even considered living in New York—albeit fleetingly—but within a few months he was back in Philadelphia. New York was too fast, too crazy. And while he believed that Philly girls were every bit as sexy as Manhattan girls, Philly girls had something going for them that New York girls never would.

You had a *shot* at Philly girls.

He had just gotten the perfect dimple in his tie when there was a knock at the door. He crossed the small flat, opened the door.

It was Andy Chase. Perfectly happy, terribly disheveled Andy.

Andy wore a backward, soiled Phillies cap and a royal blue Members Only jacket—*do they still make Members Only?* Simon mused—complete with epaulets and zippered pockets.

Simon gestured to his burgundy jacquard tie. "Does this make me look too gay?" he asked.

"No." Andy flopped onto the couch, hoisting a copy of *Macworld* magazine, chomping a Fuji apple. "Just gay enough."

"Piss off."

Andy shrugged. "I don't know how you can spend so much money on clothes. I mean, you can only wear one suit at a time. What's the point?"

Simon spun and walked across the living room, runway style. He pivoted, posed, vogued. "You can look upon me and still ask that question? Style is its own reward, *mon frère.*"

Andy affected a huge, mock yawn, then took another gnaw of his apple.

Simon poured himself a few ounces of Courvoisier. He opened a can of Miller Lite for Andy. "Sorry. No Beer Nuts."

Andy shook his head. "Mock me all you want. Beer Nuts are a lot better than that *fwa gra* shit you eat."

Simon made a grand gesture of covering his ears. Andy Chase offended at the cellular level.

They caught up on the day's events. For Simon, these chats were part of the overhead of doing business with Andy. Penance given and said, it was time to go.

"So how is Kitty?" Simon asked, perfunctorily, with as much enthusiasm as he could fake. *The wee cow,* he thought. Kitty Bramlett had been a petite, nearly pretty cashier at Wal-Mart when Andy fell for her. That was seventy pounds and three chins ago. Kitty and Andy had settled into that childless, early-middle-age nightmare of marriage built on habit. Microwave dinners, birthdays at the Olive Garden, and rutting twice a month in front of Jay Leno.

Kill me first, Lord, Simon thought.

"She is exactly the same." Andy tossed the magazine and stretched. Simon caught a glimpse of the top of Andy's trousers. They were safety-pinned together. "For some reason she still thinks you should try to get together with her sister. As if she would have anything to do with you."

Kitty's sister Rhonda looked like a distaff vision of Willard Scott, but not nearly as feminine.

"I'll be sure to give her a call soon," Simon replied.

"Whatever."

It was still raining. Simon would have to ruin the entire look with his tasteful, yet drearily functional London Fog raincoat. It was the one piece that sorely needed updating. Still, it was better than rain spotting the Zileri.

"No mood for your shite," Simon said, making exit gestures. Andy got the hint, stood up, headed toward the door. He had left his apple core on the couch.

"You can't harsh my vibe tonight," Simon added. "I look good, I smell great, I have a cover story in the oven, and life is *dolce.*"

Andy pulled a face: *Dolce?*

"Good lord," Simon said. He reached into

his pocket, removed the hundred-dollar bill, and handed it to Andy. "Thanks for the tip," he said. "Keep them coming."

"Anytime, bro," Andy said. He pocketed the bill, walked out the door, and headed down the stairs.

Bro, Simon thought. *If this is Purgatory, I truly fear Hell.*

He gave himself one last look in the full-length mirror inside the coat closet.

Perfect.

The city was his.

2 8

Brian Parkhurst wasn't home. Nor was his Ford Windstar.

The six detectives fanned out in the three-story Garden Court row house. The first floor held a small living room and dining room, kitchen at the back. Between the dining room and the kitchen, a steep set of stairs led to the second floor, which had a bathroom and a bedroom converted to office space. The third floor, which had once been two small bedrooms, had been renovated into a master suite. None of the rooms had dark blue nylon carpeting.

The furnishings were modern for the most part: leather sofa and chair, teak hutch and dining table. The office desk was older, probably pickled oak. His bookshelves spoke of an eclectic taste. Philip Roth, Jackie Collins, Dave Barry, Dan Simmons. The detectives noted the presence of *William Blake: The Complete Illuminated Books.*

I can't say I know very much about Blake, Parkhurst had said during his interview.

A quick riffling through the Blake book showed that nothing had been cut out of it.

A scan of the refrigerator, freezer, and kitchen garbage produced no evidence of leg of lamb. The *Joy of Cooking* in the kitchen was bookmarked on caramel flan.

There was nothing unusual in his closets. Three suits, a pair of tweed blazers, half a dozen pairs of dress shoes, a dozen dress shirts. All conservative and of good quality.

The walls of his office boasted his three certificates of higher education: one from John Carroll University and two from the University of Pennsylvania. There was also a well-framed poster for the Broadway production of *The Crucible*.

Jessica took the second floor. She went through the closet in the office, which seemed to be dedicated to Parkhurst's sporting endeavors. It appeared that he played tennis and racquetball, as well as engaging in a little sailboarding. There was also an expensive wet suit.

She went through his desk drawers, finding all the expected supplies. Rubber bands, pens, paper clips, Tic Tacs. Another drawer held LaserJet toner cartridges and a spare keyboard. All the drawers opened with no problem, except for the file drawer.

The file drawer was locked.

Odd, for a man who lived alone, Jessica thought.

A quick but thorough scan of the top drawer yielded no key.

Jessica looked out of the office door, listened to the chatter. All the other detectives were busy. She returned to the desk, quickly took out her pick set. You don't work in the Auto Unit for three years without picking up *some* locksmithing skills. Within seconds, she was in.

Most of the files were for household and

personal business. Tax records, business receipts, personal receipts, insurance policies. There was also a stack of paid Visa bills. Jessica wrote down the card number. A quick perusal of purchases yielded nothing suspicious. There was no charge to a religious supply house.

She was just about to close and lock the drawer when she saw the tip of a small manila envelope peeking out from behind the drawer. She reached back as far as she could and pulled the envelope out. It had been taped out of sight, but never properly sealed.

Inside the envelope were five photographs. They had been taken in Fairmount Park during the fall. Three of the pictures were of a fully clothed young woman, shyly posing in a faux-glamour pose. Two of them were the same young woman posing with a smiling Brian Parkhurst. The young woman sat on his lap. The pictures were dated October of the previous year.

The young woman was Tessa Wells.

"Kevin!" Jessica yelled down the stairs.

Byrne was up in a flash, taking four steps at a time. Jessica showed him the photographs.

"Son of a *bitch,*" Byrne said. "We had him and we let him go."

"Don't worry. We'll get him again." They had found a complete set of luggage beneath the stairs. He wasn't on a trip.

Jessica summed up the evidence. Parkhurst was a doctor. He knew both victims. He claimed to have known Tessa Wells in a professional sense, only as her counselor, and yet he had personal photographs of her. He had a history of sexual involvement with students. One of the victims had begun to spell his last name on her palm, just before her death.

Byrne got on Parkhurst's desk phone and called Ike Buchanan. He put the phone on speakerphone and briefed Buchanan on what they had found.

Buchanan listened, then uttered the three words for which Byrne and Jessica were hoping and waiting: "Pick him up."

2 9

If Sophie Balzano was the most beautiful little girl in the world when she was wide awake, she was positively angelic in that moment when day became night, in that sweet twilight of half sleep.

Jessica had volunteered to take the first watch on Brian Parkhurst's home in Garden Court. She was told to go home, get some rest. As was Kevin Byrne. There were two detectives on the house.

Jessica sat on the edge of Sophie's bed, watching her.

They had taken a bubble bath together. Sophie had washed and conditioned her own hair. No help needed, *thank you very much*. They had dried off, shared a pizza in the living room. It was breaking a rule—they were supposed to eat at the table—but now that Vincent wasn't around, a lot of rules seemed to be slipping by the wayside.

No more of that, Jessica thought.

As she got Sophie ready for bed, Jessica found herself hugging her daughter a little more closely, a little more often. Even Sophie had given her the fish eye, as if to say: *What's up, Mom?* But Jessica knew what was up. The way Sophie felt at these times was her salvation.

And now that Sophie was tucked in, Jessica allowed herself to relax, to start to unwind from the horrors of the day.

A little.

"Story?" Sophie asked, her tiny voice riding on the wings of a big yawn.

"You want me to read a story?"

Sophie nodded.

"Okay," Jessica said.

"Not the Hoke," Sophie said.

Jessica had to laugh. The Hoke was Sophie's bogeyman *du jour*. It all began with a trip to the King of Prussia mall, about a year earlier, and the presence of the fifteen-foot-tall inflatable green Hulk they had erected to promote the release of the DVD. One look at the giant figure and Sophie had immediately taken trembling refuge behind Jessica's legs.

"What's *that*?" Sophie had asked, lips aquiver, fingers clutching Jessica's skirt.

"It's only the Hulk," Jessica had said. "It's not real."

"I don't like the Hoke."

It had gotten to the point where anything green and more than four feet tall inspired panic these days.

"We don't have any Hoke stories, honey," Jessica said. She'd figured that Sophie had forgotten about the Hoke. Some monsters died hard, it seemed.

Sophie smiled and scrunched down under the covers, ready for a Hoke-free dream.

Jessica went to the closet, got out the book box. She perused the current slate of toddler lit. *The Runaway Bunny; You're the Boss, Baby Duck!; Curious George.*

Jessica sat down on the bed, looked at the spines of the books. They were all for children two and under. Sophie was nearly three. She was actually too mature for *The Runaway Bunny*. Dear God, Jessica thought, she's growing up way too fast.

The book on the bottom was *How Do I Put It On?,* a primer on getting dressed. Sophie could easily dress herself, and had been able to do so for months. It had been a long time since she had put her shoes on the wrong feet, or slipped her OshKosh overalls on backward.

Jessica decided on *Yertle the Turtle,* the Dr. Seuss story. It was one of Sophie's favorites. Jessica's, too.

Jessica began to read, chronicling the adventures and life lessons of Yertle and the gang on the island of Sala-ma-Sond. After a few pages she looked over at Sophie, expecting to see a big smile. Yertle was a laugh riot, usually. Especially the part where he becomes King of the Mud.

But Sophie was already fast asleep.

Lightweight, Jessica thought with a smile.

She flipped the three-way bulb onto the

lowest setting, bunched the covers around Sophie. She put the book back in the box.

She thought about Tessa Wells and Nicole Taylor. How could she not? She had the feeling that these girls would not be far from her conscious thoughts for a long time.

Had their mothers sat on the edges of their beds like this, marveling at the perfection of their daughters? Had they watched them sleep, thanking God for every breath in, and every breath out?

Of course they had.

Jessica looked at the photo frame on Sophie's nightstand, the Precious Moments frame covered in hearts and bows. There were six photos displayed. Vincent and Sophie at the shore when Sophie was just over a year old. Sophie wore a floppy orange bonnet and sunglasses. Her chubby little legs were caked with wet sand. There was a picture of Jessica and Sophie in the backyard. Sophie was holding the one and only radish they got out of the container garden that year. Sophie had planted the seed, watered the plant, harvested her crop. She had insisted on eating the radish, even though Vincent had warned her she wouldn't like it. Being a trouper, and stubborn as a little mule, Sophie had tasted the radish, trying not to make a face. Eventually her face went cabbage-patch with the bitterness, and she spit it into a paper towel. That marked the end of her agricultural curiosity.

The picture in the lower right-hand corner was of Jessica's mother, taken when Jessica had been a toddler herself. Maria Giovanni looking spectacular in a yellow sundress, her tiny daughter on her knee. Her mother looked so much like Sophie. Jessica wanted Sophie to know her grandmother, although Maria was barely a lucid memory to Jessica these days, more like an image glimpsed through a glass block.

She flipped off Sophie's light, sat in the dark.

Jessica had been on the job two full days, and it already seemed like months. The entire time she had been on the force, she had looked at homicide detectives the way many cops did: They only had one job to do. Divisional detectives handled a much broader range of crimes. As the saying goes, a homicide is just an aggravated assault gone wrong.

Boy, was she mistaken.

If this was only one job to do, it was enough.

Jessica wondered, as she had every day for the past three years, if it was fair to Sophie that she was a cop, that she put her life on the line every day when she left the house. She had no answer.

Jessica went downstairs, checked the front and the back door to the house for the third time. Or was it the fourth?

She was off on Wednesday, but she hadn't the slightest idea what to do with herself. How was she supposed to relax? How was she supposed to go about her life when two young girls had been brutally murdered? Right now she didn't care about the wheel, the duty roster. She didn't know a cop who would. At this point, half the force would donate their overtime to take this son of a bitch down.

Her father always had his yearly Easter get-together on Wednesday of Easter Week. Maybe that would get her mind off things. She would go and try to forget about the job. Her father always had a way of putting things in perspective for her.

Jessica sat on the couch, ran through the cable channels five or six times. She turned the set off. She was just about to climb into bed with a book when the phone rang. She really hoped it wasn't Vincent. Or maybe hoped it was.

It wasn't.

"Is this Detective Balzano?"

It was a man's voice. Loud music in the background. Disco beat.

"Who is calling?" Jessica asked.

The man didn't answer. Laughter and ice cubes in glasses. He was in a bar.

"Last chance," Jessica said.

"It's Brian Parkhurst."

Jessica glanced at the clock, noted the time on a notepad she kept near the phone. She looked at the screen on her caller ID. Private number.

"Where are you?" Her voice sounded high and nervous. Reedy.

Calm, Jess.

"Not important," Parkhurst said.

"It kinda is," Jessica said. Better. Conversational.

"I'm doing the talking."

"That's good, Dr. Parkhurst. Really. Because we'd really like to talk to you."

"I know."

"Why don't you come to the Round-house? I'll meet you there. We can talk."

"I'd rather not."

"Why?"

"I'm not a stupid man, Detective. I know you were at my house."

He was slurring his words.

"Where are you?" Jessica asked a second time.

No answer. Jessica heard the music morph into a Latin disco beat. She made another note. *Salsa club.*

"Meet me," Parkhurst said. "There are things you need to know about these girls."

"Where and when?"

"Meet me at *The Clothespin*. Fifteen minutes."

Next to *salsa club* she wrote: *within 15 min. of city hall.*

The Clothespin was the huge, Claes Oldenburg sculpture at the Center Square Plaza, right next to city hall. In the old days, people in Philly would say *Meet me at the eagle at Wanamaker,* the late, great department store with the mosaic of the eagle in the floor. Everyone knew the eagle at Wanamaker's. Now, it was *The Clothespin.*

Parkhurst added: "And come alone."

"Not gonna happen, Dr. Parkhurst."

"If I see anyone else there, I'm leaving," he said. "I'm not talking to your partner."

Jessica didn't blame Parkhurst for not wanting to be in the same room as Kevin Byrne at this point. "Give me twenty minutes," she said.

The line went dead.

Jessica called Paula Farinacci who, once again came through for her. There was certainly a special place in Babysitter Heaven for Paula. Jessica bundled a drowsy Sophie into her favorite blanket and shuttled her three doors down. When she got back home, she called Kevin Byrne on his cell phone, got his voice mail. She called him at home. Ditto.

Come on, partner, she thought.

I need you.

She put on jeans and running shoes, her rain slicker. She grabbed her cell phone, popped a fresh mag into her Glock, snapped on her holster, and headed into Center City.

Jessica waited near the corner of Fifteenth and Market Streets in the pouring rain. She decided not to stand directly beneath *The Clothespin* sculpture for all the obvious reasons. She didn't need to be a sitting target.

She glanced around the square. Few pedestrians were out, due to the storm. The lights on Market Street formed a shimmering red-and-yellow watercolor on the pavement.

When she was small, her father used to take her and Michael to Center City and the Reading Terminal Market for cannoli from Termini's. Granted, the original Termini's in South Philly was only a few blocks from their house, but there was something about riding SEPTA downtown and walking to the market that made the cannoli taste better. It still did.

In those days they used to saunter up Walnut Street after Thanksgiving, window-shopping at all the exclusive shops. They could never afford anything they saw in the windows, but the beautiful displays had sent her little-girl fantasies adrift.

So long ago, Jessica thought.

The rain was relentless.

A man approached the sculpture, snapping Jessica out of her reverie. He wore a green rain slicker, hood up, hands in pocket. He seemed to linger near the foot of the giant art piece, scanning the area. From where Jessica stood, he looked to be Brian Parkhurst's height. As to weight and hair color, it was impossible to tell.

Jessica drew her weapon, kept it behind her back. She was just about to head over when the man suddenly walked down into the subway stop.

Jessica drew a deep breath, holstered her weapon.

She watched the cars circle the square, headlights cutting the rain like cat's eyes.

She called Brian Parkhurst's cell phone number.

Voice mail.

She tried Kevin Byrne's cell phone.

Ditto.

She pulled the hood of her rain slicker tighter.

And waited.

3 0

He is drunk.

That will make my job easier. Slower reflexes, diminished capacity, poor depth perception. I could wait for him outside the bar, walk up to him, announce my intentions, then cut him in half.

He wouldn't know what hit him.

But where's the fun in that?

Where is the lesson?

No, I think it is best for people to know. I realize that there is a good chance I will be stopped before I can complete this passion play. And if I am, one day, walked down that long corridor, and into an antiseptic room, and strapped to a gurney, I will accept my fate.

I know that I will be judged by a much greater power than the commonwealth of Pennsylvania when my time comes.

Until then, I will be the one sitting next to you in church, the one who offers you a seat on the bus, the one who holds the door for you on a windy day, the one who bandages your daughter's scraped knee.

That is the grace of living in God's long shadow.

Sometime the shadow turns out to be nothing more than a coat tree.

Sometimes the shadow is everything you fear.

TUESDAY, 9:00 PM

Byrne sat at the bar, oblivious to the music, the din of the pool table. All he heard, for the moment, was the roar in his head.

He was at a run-down corner tavern in Gray's Ferry called Shotz, the farthest thing from a cop bar he could imagine. He could've hit the hotel bars downtown, but he didn't like paying ten dollars a drink.

What he *really* wanted was a few more minutes with Brian Parkhurst. If only he could take another run at him, he would know for sure. He downed his bourbon, ordered one more.

Byrne had turned off his cell phone earlier, but he had left his pager on. He checked it, seeing the number of Mercy Hospital. Jimmy had called for the second time that day. Byrne checked his watch. He'd stop by Mercy and charm the cardiac nurses into a brief visit. There are never any visiting hours when a cop is in the hospital.

The other calls were from Jessica. He'd call her in a little while. He just needed a few minutes to himself.

For now, he just wanted the peace of the noisiest bar in Gray's Ferry.

Tessa Wells.

Nicole Taylor.

The public thinks that when a person is murdered, cops show up at the scene, make a few notes, then go home to their lives. Nothing could be further from the truth. Because the unavenged dead never stay dead. The unavenged dead *watch* you. They watch you when you go to the movies or have dinner with your family, or lift a few pints with the boys at the corner tavern. They watch you when you make love. They watch and they wait and they question.

What are you doing for me? they whisper in your ear, softly, as your life unfolds, as your kids grow and prosper, as you laugh and cry and feel and believe. Why are you out having a good time? they ask. Why are you living it up while I'm laying here on the cold marble?

What are you doing for me?

Byrne's solve rate was one of the highest in the unit, partially, he knew, because of the synergy he'd had with Jimmy Purify, partially due to the waking dreams he'd begun having, courtesy of four slugs from Luther White's pistol and a trip beneath the surface of the Delaware.

The organized killer, by nature, believed himself superior to most people, but especially superior to the people tasked with finding him. It was this egotism that drove Kevin Byrne, and in this case, the Rosary Girl case, it was becoming an obsession. He knew that. He had probably known that the moment he had walked down those rotted steps on North Eighth Street and seen the brutal humiliation that had befallen Tessa Wells.

But he knew it was as much a sense of duty as it was the horror of Morris Blanchard. He had been wrong many times earlier in his career, but it had never led to the death of an innocent. Byrne wasn't sure if the arrest and conviction of the Rosary Girl killer would expiate the guilt, or if it would square him once again with the city of Philadelphia, but he hoped it would fill an emptiness inside.

And then he could retire with his head held high.

Some detectives follow the money. Some follow the science. Some follow the motive. Kevin Byrne trusted the door at the end of his mind. No, he couldn't predict the future, nor divine the identity of a killer just by laying hands. But sometimes it *felt* like he could, and maybe that was what made the difference. The nuance detected, the intention discovered, the path chosen, the thread followed. In the past fifteen years, ever since he had drowned, he had only been wrong once.

He needed sleep. He paid his tab, said goodbye to a few of the regulars, stepped out into the endless rain. Gray's Ferry smelled clean.

Byrne buttoned his raincoat, assessed his driving ability, considering the five bourbons. He pronounced himself fit. More or less. When he approached his car, he knew that something didn't look right, but the image didn't register immediately.

Then it did.

The driver's window was smashed in, broken glass shimmering on the front seat. He looked inside. His CD player and CD wallet were gone.

"Mother*fucker*," he said. "This fucking *city*."

He walked around the car a few times, a rabid dog chasing his tail in the rain. He sat down on the hood, actually considering the folly of calling this in. He knew better. You'd have as much chance of recovering a stolen radio in Gray's Ferry as Michael Jackson had of getting a job at a day care center.

The stolen CD player didn't bother him as much as the stolen CDs. He had a choice collection of classic blues in there. Three years in the making.

He was just about to leave when he noticed someone watching him from the vacant lot across the street. Byrne couldn't see who it was, but there was something about the posture that told him all he needed to know.

"Hey!" Byrne yelled.

The man took off, rabbiting behind the buildings on the other side of the street.

Byrne took off after him.

The Glock felt heavy in his hand, like a deadweight.

By the time Byrne got across the street, the man was lost in the miasma of pouring rain. Byrne still-hunted through the debris-strewn lot, then up to the alley that ran behind the row houses that spanned the length of the block.

He did not see the thief.

Where the hell did he go?

Byrne holstered his Glock, sidled up to the alleyway, peered to the left.

Dead end. A Dumpster, a pile of garbage bags, broken wooden crates. He eased into the alley. Was someone standing behind the Dumpster? A crack of thunder made Byrne spin, his heart trip-hammering in his chest.

Alone.

He continued, minding every night-shadow. The machine gun of raindrops on the plastic garbage bags obscured every other sound for a moment.

Then, beneath the rain, he heard a whimper, a rustling of plastic.

Byrne looked behind the Dumpster. It was a black kid, maybe eighteen or so. In the moonlight Byrne could see the nylon cap, Flyers jersey, a gang tat on his right arm that identified him as a member of JBM: Junior Black Mafia. He had tats of prison sparrows on his left arm. He was kneeling, bound, and gagged. There were bruises on his face from a recent beating. His eyes were ablaze with fear.

What the hell is going on here?

Byrne sensed movement to his left. Before he could turn, a huge arm reached around him from behind. Byrne felt the ice of a razor-sharp knife blade at his throat.

Then, in his ear: "Don't fuckin' move."

3 2

Jessica waited. People came and went, hurrying through the rain, hailing cabs, running to the subway stop.

None of them was Brian Parkhurst.

Jessica reached under her rain slicker, keyed her rover twice.

At the entrance to Center Square Plaza, less than fifty feet away, a disheveled man came out of the shadows.

Jessica looked at him, hands out, palms up.

Nick Palladino shrugged back. Before leaving the Northeast, Jessica had tried Byrne twice more, then called Nick on her way into the city; Nick had instantly agreed to back her play. Nick's vast experience working undercover in Narcotics made him a natural for covert surveillance. He wore a ratty hooded sweatshirt and stained chinos. For Nick Palladino, this was the true sacrifice to the job.

John Shepherd was under the scaffolding on the side of city hall, directly across the street, binoculars in hand. A pair of uniformed officers were stationed at the Market Street subway stop, both carrying the yearbook faculty photo of Brian Parkhurst, in case he showed up via that route.

He had not showed. And it looked as if he wasn't going to.

Jessica called the station house. The team sitting on Parkhurst's house reported no activity.

Jessica ambled over to where Palladino stood.

"Still can't reach Kevin?" he asked.

"No," Jessica said.

"He's probably crashed. He could use the rest."

Jessica hesitated, not knowing how to ask. She was new to this club and didn't want to step on any toes. "He seem okay to you?"

"Kevin's tough to read, Jess."

"He seems completely exhausted."

Palladino nodded, lit a cigarette. They were *all* tired. "He tell you about his . . . experience?"

"You mean about Luther White?"

From what Jessica could glean, Kevin Byrne had been involved in an arrest gone bad fifteen years earlier, a bloody confrontation with a rape suspect named Luther White. White had been killed; Byrne had nearly died himself.

It was the *nearly* part that confused Jessica.

"Yeah," Palladino said.

"No, he hasn't," Jessica said. "I haven't had the guts to ask him about it."

"It was a close call for him," Palladino said. "About as close as you can get. The way I understand it, he was, well, *dead* for a little while."

"Then I did hear it right," Jessica said, incredulous. "So, what, he's like psychic or something?"

"Oh, *God* no." Palladino smiled, shook his head. "Nothing like that. Don't ever even utter that *word* around him. In fact, it would be better if you never even brought it up."

"Why is that?"

"Let me put it this way. There's a big-mouthed detective over at Central who gave him some shit about it one night at Finnigan's Wake. I think the guy is still eating his dinner through a straw."

"Gotcha," Jessica said.

"It's just that Kevin's got a . . . sense about the really bad ones. Or he used to, anyway. The whole Morris Blanchard thing was pretty bad for him. He was wrong about Blanchard, and it almost destroyed him. I know he wants out, Jess. He's got his twenty in. He just can't find the door."

The two detectives looked out over the rain-swept plaza.

"Look," Palladino began, "this is probably not my place to say this, but Ike Buchanan went out on a limb with you. You know that, right?"

"What do you mean?" Jessica asked, although she had a fairly good idea.

"When he formed this task force, and gave it to Kevin, he could have moved you to the back of the pack. Hell, maybe he should have. No offense."

"None taken."

"Ike's a stand-up guy. You might think he's letting you stay at the front of the pack for political reasons—I don't think it will come as a shock to you that there's a few assholes in the department who think so— but he believes in you. You wouldn't be here if he didn't."

Wow, Jessica thought. *Where the hell did all this come from?*

"Well, I hope I can justify that faith," she said.

"You'll do fine."

"Thanks, Nick. That means a lot." She meant it, too.

"Yeah, well, I don't even know why I told you."

For some unknown reason, Jessica hugged him. After a few seconds they broke, smoothed their hair, coughed into their fists, got over the show of emotion.

"So," Jessica said, a little awkwardly, "what do we do right now?"

Nick Palladino scoured the block—city hall, over to South Broad, over to Center Square Plaza, down Market. He found John

Shepherd under the canopy to the entrance to the subway. John caught his eye. The two men shrugged. The rain poured.

"Fuck it," he said. "Let's shut it down."

3 3

Byrne didn't have to turn around to know who it was. The wet sounds coming from the man's mouth—the missing sibilance, the destroyed plosive, along with the deep nasal quality of the voice—said that it was someone who had recently had a number of upper teeth removed and his nose recently demolished.

It was Diablo. Gideon Pratt's bodyguard.

"Be cool," Byrne said.

"Oh, I'm cool, cowboy," Diablo said. "I'm dry fuckin' ice."

Then Byrne felt something much worse than the cold blade at his throat. He felt Diablo pat him down and take away his service Glock: the worst nightmare in the litany of bad dreams for a police officer.

Diablo put the barrel of the Glock to the back of Byrne's head.

"I'm a cop," Byrne said.

"No shit," Diablo said. "Next time you commit aggravated assault, you should stay off TV."

The press conference, Byrne thought. Diablo had seen the press conference, and then he had staked the Roundhouse and followed him.

"You don't want to do this," Byrne said.

"Shut the fuck up."

The tied-up kid looked between them, back and forth, his eyes shifting, looking for a way out. The tattoo on Diablo's forearm told Byrne he belonged to the P-Town Posse, an odd conglomerate of Vietnamese, Indonesians, and disaffected thugs who, for one reason or another, didn't fit elsewhere.

The P-Town Posse and the JBM were natural enemies, a hatred that ran ten years deep. Byrne now knew what was happening here.

Diablo was setting him up.

"Let him go," Byrne said. "We'll settle this between ourselves."

"This won't be settled for a long time, motherfucker."

Byrne knew he had to make a move. He swallowed hard, tasted the Vicodin at the back of his throat, felt the spark in his fingers.

Diablo made the move for him.

Without warning, without a modicum of conscience, Diablo stepped around him, leveled Byrne's Glock, and shot the kid point blank. One to the heart. Instantly, a spray of blood and tissue and flecks of bone hit the dirty brick wall, foaming deep scarlet, then washing to the ground in the heavy rain. The kid slumped.

Byrne closed his eyes. In his mind, he saw Luther White pointing the pistol at him so many years ago. He felt icy water swirl around him, sinking deeper, deeper.

Thunder clapped, lightning flashed.

Time crawled.

Stopped.

When the pain did not come, Byrne opened his eyes and saw Diablo turn the corner, then disappear. Byrne knew what

came next. Diablo would dump the weapon
nearby—Dumpster, garbage can, drainpipe.
Cops would find it. They always did. And
Kevin Francis Byrne's life would be over.

Who would come for him, he wondered?

Johnny Shepherd?

Would Ike volunteer to bring him in?

Byrne watched the rain hitting the dead
kid's body, washing his blood into the rutted
concrete, unable to move.

His thoughts scaled a tangled deadfall.
He knew that, if he called this in, if he put
this on the record, then all of this was just
beginning. The Q&A, the forensic team, the
detectives, the ADAs, the preliminary hearing, the press, the accusations, the Internal
Affairs witch hunt, the administrative leave.

Fear ripped through him—shiny and
metallic. The smiling, mocking face of Morris Blanchard danced behind his eyes.

The city would never forgive him for this.

The city would never forget.

He was standing over a dead black kid,
no witnesses and no partner. He was drunk.
A dead black gangbanger, killed execution
style with a slug from his service Glock, a
weapon that, at the moment, he could not

account for. For a white cop in Philly, the nightmare couldn't get much deeper.

There was no time to think about it.

He squatted down, looked for a pulse. There was none. He got out his Maglite, cupping it in his hand to keep the light as hidden as possible. He looked closely at the body. From the angle, and the appearance of the entry wound, it looked like a through and through. He found the shell casing in short order, pocketed it. He searched the ground between the kid and the wall for the slug. Fast-food trash, sodden cigarette ends, a pair of pastel condoms. No bullet.

Above his head, in one of the rooms overlooking the alley, a light flipped on. Soon there would be a siren.

Byrne picked up the pace of his search. He tossed garbage bags, the foul stench of rotted food nearly making him gag. Sodden newspapers, wet magazines, orange peels, coffee filters, eggshells.

Then the angels smiled on him.

Next to the broken shards of a smashed beer bottle, was the slug. He picked it up, put it in his pocket. It was still warm. He then took out a plastic evidence bag. He always had a few in his coat. He turned it inside out and laid the bag over the entrance wound on the kid's chest, making sure that he got a thick smear of blood. He stepped away from the body and turned the Baggie right-side out, sealing it.

He heard the siren.

By the time he turned to run, something other than rational thought had taken over Kevin Byrne's mind, something much darker, something that had nothing to do with the academy, the manual, the job.

Something called survival.

He started down the alley, absolutely certain he had overlooked something. He was sure of it.

At the mouth of the alley, he glanced both ways. Deserted. He sprinted across the vacant lot, slipped into his car, reached into his pocket, and turned on his cell phone. It rang immediately. The sound nearly made him jump. He answered.

"Byrne."

It was Eric Chavez.

"Where are you?" Chavez asked.

He wasn't here. *Couldn't* be here. He wondered about cell phone tracking. If it came to it, could they track where he was when he received this call? The siren grew closer. Could Chavez hear it?

"Old City," Byrne said. "What's up?"

"Call just came in. Nine-one-one. Some-one saw a guy carrying a body up to the Rodin Museum."

Jesus.

He had to go. Now. No time to think. This was how and why people got caught. But he had no choice.

"I'm on my way."

Before he left, he glanced down the alley, at the dark vista on display there. In the center was a dead kid dropped into the middle of Kevin Byrne's nightmare, a kid whose own nightmare had just breached the dawn.

3 4

He had fallen asleep. Ever since he had been a child in the Lake District, where the sound of rain on the roof was a lullaby, Simon had been soothed by the clatter of a storm. It was the car backfiring that awakened him.

Or maybe it was a shot.

This *was* Gray's Ferry, after all.

He looked at his watch. An hour. He had been asleep an *hour*. Some surveillance expert. More like Inspector Clouseau.

The last thing he remembered, before being startled awake, was Kevin Byrne disappearing into a rough Gray's Ferry bar called Shotz, the kind of place where, when you walk in, you go down two steps. Physically and socially. A ramshackle Irish bar full of House of Pain types.

Simon had parked on a side street, partly to keep out of Byrne's line of sight, partly because there wasn't a space in front of the bar. His intention was to wait for Byrne to emerge from the bar, follow him, see if he pulled over on some dark street and lit up a crack pipe. If all went well, Simon would have snuck up on the car and snapped a picture of the legendary detective Kevin Francis Byrne with a five-inch glass shooter between his lips.

Then he would own him.

Simon had gotten out his small, collapsible umbrella, opened the car door, spread the umbrella, and sidled up to the corner of the building. He peered around. Byrne's car was still parked there. It looked as if someone had broken the driver's window in. *Oh Lord,* Simon thought. *I pity the fool who picked the wrong car on the wrong night.*

The bar was still packed. He could hear

the dulcet strains of an old Thin Lizzy tune rattling the windows.

He was just about to head back to his car when a shadow caught his attention, a shadow darting across the vacant lot directly across from Shotz. Even in the dim light thrown by the bar's neon, Simon could recognize Byrne's huge silhouette.

What the hell was he doing over there?

Simon raised the camera, focused, snapped a few pictures. He wasn't sure why, but when you shadowed someone with a camera and tried to assemble the collage of images the next day, every image helped in establishing a time line.

Besides, digital images were erasable. It wasn't like the old days when every snap of a thirty-five millimeter camera cost money.

Back in the car, he had checked the images on the camera's small LCD screen. Not bad. A little dark, of course, but it was clearly Kevin Byrne coming out of that alley and across the lot. Two of the photographs had been against the side of a light-colored van, and there was no mistaking the man's hulking profile. Simon made sure that the image was imprinted with date and time.

Done.

Then his police band scanner—a Uniden BC250D, a handheld model that had more than once gotten him to a crime scene ahead of the detectives—crackled to life. He couldn't make out the details, but a few seconds later, when Kevin Byrne took off, Simon knew that whatever it was he belonged on the scene.

Simon turned the ignition key, hoping that the job he had done securing his muffler would hold. It did. He wouldn't be sounding like a Cessna aircraft while trying to shadow one of the city's savviest detectives.

Life was good.

He put the car in gear. And followed.

3 5

Jessica sat in her driveway, exhaustion beginning to take its toll. Rain hammered the roof of the Cherokee. She thought about what Nick had said. It had crossed her mind that she not had gotten The Talk after the task force was formed, the sit-down that would've started: *Look, Jessica, this has nothing to do with your abilities as a detective . . .*

That talk never happened.

She turned off the engine.

What had Brian Parkhurst wanted to tell her? He hadn't said that he wanted to tell her what he'd *done,* but rather that there were things about *these girls* that she needed to *know.*

Like what?

And where was he?

If I see anyone else there, I'm leaving.

Had Parkhurst made Nick Palladino and John Shepherd as cops?

Not likely.

Jessica got out, locked the Jeep, and ran to the back door, splashing in puddles along the way. She was soaked. It seemed as if she had been soaked forever. The light over the back porch had burned out a few weeks earlier, and as she fumbled for her house key she chided herself for the hundredth time for not replacing the bulb. Above her, the branches of the dying maple creaked. It really needed to get trimmed before those branches smashed into the house. These things had generally been Vincent's job, but Vincent wasn't around, was he?

Get it together, Jess. You are mom and *dad for the time being, as well as cook, re-pairman, landscaper, chauffeur, and tutor.*

She got her house key in hand and was

just about to open the back door when she heard a noise above her, the scrape of aluminum twisting, shearing, moaning under an enormous weight. She also heard leather-soled shoes scrape across the floor, saw a hand reach for her.

Draw your weapon Jess—

The Glock was in her purse. *Rule number one never keep your weapon in your purse—*

The shadow formed a body. A man's body.

A priest.

He closed his hand around her arm.

And pulled her into the darkness.

3 6

The scene around the Rodin Museum was a madhouse. Simon hung at the back of the gathering crowd, rubbernecking with the unwashed. What was it that drew ordinary citizens to scenes of misery and chaos like flies to a pile of dung, he wondered.

I should talk, he thought with a smile.

Still, in his own defense, he felt that, in spite of his penchant for the dreadful and predilection for the morbid, he still hung on to a scrap of dignity, still guarded closely that morsel of grandeur regarding the work he did, and the public's right to know. Like it or not, he was a journalist.

He worked his way toward the front of the crowd. He pulled his collar up, slipped on his tortoiseshell glasses, brushed his hair over his forehead.

Death was here.

So was Simon Close.

Bread and jam.

TUESDAY, 9:50 PM

It was Father Corrio.

Father Mark Corrio was the pastor of St. Paul's when Jessica was growing up. He was newly installed as pastor when Jessica was around nine, and she remembered how all the women swooned over his dark good looks at the time, how they all commented on what a waste it was that he had entered the priesthood. The dark hair had gone ice gray, but he was still a good-looking man.

On her porch, in the dark, in the rain, however, he was Freddie Krueger.

What happened was, one of the gutters over the porch was perched precariously overhead, about to break off under the weight of a waterlogged branch that had fallen from a nearby tree. Father Corrio had grabbed Jessica to get her out of harm's way. A few seconds later, the gutter had ripped free of the gutter board and crashed to the ground.

Divine intervention? Perhaps. But that didn't prevent Jessica from being scared shitless for a few seconds.

"I'm sorry if I frightened you," he said.

Jessica almost said, *I'm sorry I almost punched your freakin' lights out, Padre.*

"Come on inside," she offered instead.

Dried off, coffee made, they sat in the living room and got the pleasantries out of the way. Jessica called Paula and told her she'd be there shortly.

"How is your father?" the priest asked.

"He's great, thanks."

"I haven't seen him at St. Paul's lately."

"He's kind of short," Jessica said. "He might be in the back."

Father Corrio smiled. "How do you like living in the Northeast?"

When Father Corrio said it, it sounded like this part of Philadelphia was a foreign country. On the other hand, Jessica thought, to the cloistered world of South Philly, it probably was. "Can't get any good bread," she said.

Father Corrio laughed. "I wish I had known. I would have stopped at Sarcone's."

Jessica remembered eating warm Sarcone's bread as a little girl. Cheese from DiBruno's, pastries from Isgro's. These thoughts, along with the proximity of Father Corrio, filled her with a deep sadness.

What the hell *was* she doing in the 'burbs?

More important, what was her old parish priest doing up here?

"I saw you on television yesterday," he said.

For a moment, Jessica almost told him that he must be mistaken. She was a police officer. Then, of course, she remembered. The press conference.

Jessica wasn't sure what to say. Somehow she knew Father Corrio had stopped by because of the murders. She just wasn't sure if she was ready for a homily.

"Is that young man a suspect?" he asked.

He was referring to the circus surrounding Brian Parkhurst's departure from the Roundhouse. He had walked out with Monsignor Pacek, and—perhaps as an opening salvo in the PR wars to come—Pacek had deliberately and dramatically declined comment. Jessica had seen the constant replay of the scene at Eighth and Race. The media managed to get Parkhurst's name and plaster it all over the screen.

"Not exactly," Jessica lied. To her *priest,* yet. "We'd sure like to talk to him again, though."

"I understand he works for the archdiocese?"

It was a question and a statement. The sort of thing priests and shrinks were really good at.

"Yes," Jessica said. "He counsels students from Nazarene, Regina, and a few others."

"Do you think he is responsible for these . . .?"

Father Corrio trailed off. He clearly had trouble saying the words.

"I really don't know for sure," Jessica said.

Father Corrio absorbed this. "This is such a terrible thing."

Jessica just nodded.

"When I hear of crimes such as these," Father Corrio continued, "I have to wonder just how civilized a place we live in. We like to think that we have become enlightened through the centuries. But this? It's barbaric."

"I try not to think of it that way," Jessica said. "If I think about the horrors of it all, there's no way I can do my job." It sounded easy when she said it. It wasn't.

"Have you ever heard of the *Rosarium Virginis Mariae*?"

"I think so," Jessica said. It sounded like something she had run across in her research at the library, but like most of the information it was lost in a bottomless chasm of data. "What about it?"

Father Corrio smiled. "Don't worry. There won't be a pop quiz." He reached into his briefcase and produced an envelope. "I think you should read this." He handed her the envelope.

"What is this?"

"The *Rosarium Virginis Mariae* is an apostolic letter regarding the rosary of the Virgin Mary."

"Does it have something to do with these murders?"

"I don't know," he said.

Jessica glanced at the folded papers inside. "Thanks," she said. "I'll read it tonight."

Father Corrio drained his cup, looked at his watch.

"Would you like some more coffee?" Jessica asked.

"No thanks," Father Corrio said. "I really should get back."

Before he could rise, the phone rang. "Excuse me," she said.

Jessica answered. It was Eric Chavez.

As she listened, she looked at her reflection in the night-black window. The night threatened to open up and swallow her whole.

They had found another girl.

38

The Rodin Museum was a small museum dedicated to the French sculptor at Twenty-second Street and the Benjamin Franklin Parkway.

When Jessica arrived, there were already a number of patrol cars on the scene. Two lanes of the parkway were blocked. A crowd was gathering.

Kevin Byrne huddled with John Shepherd.

The girl sat on the ground, her back against the bronze gates leading into the museum courtyard. She looked about sixteen. Her hands were bolted together, just like the others. She was heavyset, red-haired, pretty. She wore a Regina uniform.

In her hands was a black rosary, with three decades of beads missing.

On her head was a crown of thorns, fashioned out of concertina wire.

Blood trickled down her face in a delicate crimson web.

"God*damn* it," Byrne yelled, slamming his fist into the hood of the car.

"I put out an all-points on Parkhurst," Buchanan said. "There's a BOLO on the van."

Jessica had heard it go out on her way into the city, her third trip of the day.

"A crown?" Byrne asked. "A fucking *crown*?"

"Gets better," John Shepherd said.

"What do you mean?"

"You see the gates?" Shepherd pointed his flashlight toward the inner gates, the gates leading to the museum itself.

"What about them?" Byrne asked.

"Those gates are called *The Gates of*

Hell," he said. "This fucker is a real piece of work."

"The picture," Byrne said. "The Blake painting."

"Yeah."

"He's telling us where the next victim is going to be found."

For a homicide detective, the only thing worse than having no leads was being played with. The collective rage at this crime scene was palpable.

"The girl's name is Bethany Price," Tony Park said, consulting his notes. "Her mother reported her missing this afternoon. She was at the Sixth District station when the call came in. That's her over there."

He pointed to a woman in her late thirties, dressed in a tan raincoat. She reminded Jessica of those shell-shocked people you see on foreign news footage, just after a car bomb has gone off. Lost, numb, hollowed out.

"How long had she been missing?" Jessica asked.

"She didn't make it home from school today. Everybody with a daughter in high school and junior high is pretty jumpy."

"Thanks to the media," Shepherd said.

Byrne began to pace.

"What about the guy who called in the nine-one-one?" Shepherd asked.

Park pointed to a man standing behind one of the patrol cars. He was about forty, well dressed in a three-button navy suit, club tie.

"His name is Jeremy Darnton," Park said. "He said he was driving about forty miles an hour when he went by. All he saw was the victim being carried on a man's shoulder. By the time he could pull over and double back, the man was gone."

"No description of the man?" Jessica asked.

Park shook his head. "White shirt or jacket. Dark pants."

"That's it?"

"That's it."

"That's every waiter in Philly," Byrne said. He went back to his pacing. "I want this guy. I want to put this fucker down."

"We all do, Kevin," Shepherd said. "We'll get him."

"Parkhurst played me." Jessica said. "He knew I wouldn't come alone. He knew I'd bring the cavalry. He tried to draw us off."

"And he did," Shepherd said.

A few minutes later, they all approached the victim as Tom Weyrich stepped in to do his preliminary exam.

Weyrich searched for a pulse, pronounced her dead. He then looked at her wrists. On each wrist was a long-healed scar, a snaky gray ridge, crudely cut, laterally, about an inch below the heel of her palm.

At some point in the last few years, Bethany Price had attempted suicide.

As the lights from the half dozen patrol cars strobed against the statue of *The Thinker,* as the crowd continued to gather, as the rain picked up in intensity, washing away precious knowledge, one man in the crowd looked on, a man who carried a deep and secret knowledge of the horrors that were befalling the daughters of Philadelphia.

39

The lights on the face of the statue are beautiful.

But not as beautiful as Bethany. Her delicate white features give her the appearance of a sad angel, as radiant as the winter moon.

Why don't they cover her?

Of course, if they only realized how tormented a soul Bethany was, they wouldn't be quite so upset.

I have to admit that I get a deep chill of

excitement standing among the good citizens of my city, watching it all.

I've never seen so many police cars in my life. The flashing racks illuminate the parkway like a carnival midway. It is almost a festive atmosphere. There are about sixty or so people gathered. Death is always an attraction. Like a roller-coaster. Let's get close, but not too close.

Unfortunately, we all get closer one day, whether we like it or not.

What would they think if I opened my coat and showed them what I am carrying? I look to my right. There is a married couple standing next to me. They appear to be in their midforties, white, affluent, well dressed.

"Do you have any idea what happened here?" I ask the husband.

He looks at me, a quick up and down. I do not offend. I do not threaten. "I'm not sure," he says. "But I think they found another girl."

"Another girl?"

"Another victim of that . . . rosary psycho."

I cover my mouth in horror. "Seriously? Right here?"

They nod solemnly, mostly out of a smug sense of pride in being the ones to tell me *the news. They are the sort people who watch* Entertainment Tonight *and immediately race to the phone to be the first to tell their friends about the celebrity death* du jour.

"I do hope they catch him soon," I say.

"They won't," the wife says. She is wearing an expensive white wool cardigan. She carries an expensive umbrella. She has the tiniest teeth I've ever seen.

"Why do you say that?" I ask.

"Between you and me," she says, "the police are not always the sharpest knives in the drawer."

I look at her jawline, the slightly sagging skin on her neck. Does she know that I could reach out, right now, take her face in my hands and snap her spinal cord in one second?

I feel like it. I really do.

Arrogant, self-righteous bitch.

I should. But I won't.

I have work to do.

Perhaps I'll follow them home, and pay her a visit when this is all over.

40

The crime scene stretched fifty yards in all directions. The traffic on the parkway was now bottlenecked to a single lane. Two uniformed officers directed the flow.

Byrne and Jessica watched Tony Park and John Shepherd instruct the Crime Scene Unit. They were the primary detectives on this case, although it was clear that the case would soon fall under the purview of the task force. Jessica leaned against one of the patrol cars, trying to sort out this nightmare. She glanced at Byrne. He was zoned, off on one of his mind jaunts.

Just then a man stepped forward from the crowd. Jessica saw him approaching out of the corner of her eye. Before she could react, he was upon her. She turned, defensive.

It was Patrick Farrell.

"Hey there," Patrick said.

At first his presence at the scene was so out of place that Jessica thought it was a man who *looked* like Patrick. It was one of those moments when someone who represents one part of your life steps into the other part of your life, and suddenly everything is a little off, a little skewed toward the unreal.

"Hi," Jessica said, surprised at the sound of her voice. "What are you doing here?"

Standing just a few feet away, Byrne gave Jessica a look of concern, as if to ask: *Everything okay?* At moments like this, considering what they were there for, everyone was a little on edge, a little less trustful of the strange face.

"Patrick Farrell, my partner, Kevin Byrne," Jessica said a little stiffly.

The two men shook hands. For an

odd instant, Jessica was apprehensive about their meeting, although she had no idea why. This was compounded by a momentary flicker in Kevin Byrne's eyes as the two men shook hands, a fleeting misgiving that dissolved as quickly as it had appeared.

"I was on my way to my sister's house in Manayunk. I saw flashing lights, I stopped," Patrick said. "It's Pavlovian, I'm afraid."

"Patrick is an ER physician at St. Joseph's," Jessica said to Byrne.

Byrne nodded, perhaps acknowledging the difficulties of a trauma room doctor, perhaps conceding their common ground as two men who patched the bloodied wounds of the city on a daily basis.

"A few years ago I saw an EMS rescue on the Schuylkill Expressway. I stopped and did an emergency trach. Ever since, I've never been able to pass a strobing rack."

Byrne stepped closer, lowered his voice. "When we catch this guy, and if he just happens to get seriously injured in the process, and he just happens to get sent to your ER, take your time fixing him up, okay?"

Patrick smiled. "No problem."

Buchanan approached. He looked like a man with the weight of a ten-ton mayor on his back. "Go home. Both of you," he said to Jessica and Byrne. "I don't want to see either of you until Thursday."

He got no arguments from either detective.

Byrne held up his cell phone, said to Jessica: "Sorry about this. I turned it off. It won't happen again."

"Don't worry about it," Jessica said.

"You want to talk, day or night, you call."

"Thanks."

Byrne turned to Patrick. "Nice to meet you, Doctor."

"Pleasure," Patrick said.

Byrne turned on his heels, ducked under the yellow tape, and walked to his car.

"Look," Jessica said to Patrick. "I'm going to stick around here for a little while, in case they need a warm body to canvass."

Patrick glanced at his watch. "That's cool. I'm off to my sister's house anyway."

Jessica touched his arm. "Why don't you call me later? I shouldn't be too long."

"You sure?"

Absolutely not, Jessica thought.

"Absolutely."

.   .   .

Patrick had a bottle of Merlot in one hand, a box of Godiva chocolate truffles in the other.

"No flowers?" Jessica asked with a wink. She opened her front door, let Patrick in.

Patrick smiled. "I couldn't get over the fence at Morris Arboretum," he said. "But not for lack of effort."

Jessica helped him take his dripping raincoat off. His black hair was mussed from the wind, glistening with droplets of rain. Even windblown and wet, Patrick was dangerously sexy. Jessica tried to derail the thought, although she had no idea why.

"How's your sister?" she asked.

Claudia Farrell Spencer was the cardiac surgeon Patrick was supposed to become, a force of nature that had fulfilled every one of Martin Farrell's ambitions. Except the part about being a boy.

"Pregnant and bitchy as a pink poodle," Patrick said.

"How far along is she?"

"According to her, about three years,"

Patrick said. "In reality, eight months. She's about the size of a Humvee."

"Gee, I hope you told her that. Pregnant women simply adore being told they're huge."

Patrick laughed. Jessica took the wine and the chocolates and put them on the foyer table. "I'll get some glasses."

As she turned to go, Patrick grabbed her hand. Jessica turned back, facing him. They found themselves face to face in the small foyer, a past between them, a present hanging in the balance, a moment drawing out in front of them.

"Better watch it, Doc," Jessica said. "I'm packin' heat."

Patrick smiled.

Somebody better do something, Jessica thought.

Patrick did.

He slipped his hands around Jessica's waist and pulled her closer. The gesture was firm, but not forceful.

The kiss was deep, slow, perfect. At first, Jessica found it hard to believe that she was kissing someone in her house other than her husband. But then she reconciled that Vincent hadn't had too much trouble getting over that hurdle with Michelle Brown.

There was no point to wondering about the right or wrong of it.

It felt right.

When Patrick led her over to the couch in the living room, it felt even better.

41

Ocho Rios, a small reggae spot in Northern Liberties, was winding down. The DJ was spinning music more as background at the moment. There were only a few couples on the dance floor.

Byrne crossed the room and talked to one of the bartenders, who disappeared through a door behind the bar. After a short while, a man emerged from behind the plastic beads. When the man saw Byrne, his face lit up.

Gauntlett Merriman was in his early forties. He had flown high with the Champagne Posse in the eighties, at one time owning a row house in Society Hill and a beach house on the Jersey shore. His long dreadlocks, streaked with white, even in his twenties, had been a staple on the club scene, as well as at the Roundhouse.

Byrne recalled that Gauntlett had once owned a peach Jaguar XJS, a peach Mercedes 380 SE, and a peach BMW 635 CSi, all at the same time. He would park them all in front of his place on Delancey, resplendent in their gaudy chrome wheel covers and custom gold hood ornaments in the shape of a marijuana leaf, just to drive the white people crazy. It appeared he had not lost the taste for the color. This night he wore a peach linen suit and peach leather sandals.

Byrne had heard the news, but he was not prepared for the specter that was Gauntlett Merriman.

Gauntlett Merriman was a ghost.

He had bought the whole package, it seemed. His face and hands were dotted with Kaposi's, his wrists emerged like knotted twigs from the sleeves of his coat. His flashy Patek Phillipe watch looked as if it might fall off at any second.

But, despite it all, he was still Gauntlett. Macho, stoic, *rude bwoi* Gauntlett. Even at this late date, he wanted the world to know he had ridden the needle to the virus. The second thing Byrne noticed, after the skeletal visage of the man crossing the room toward him, arms outstretched, was that Gauntlett Merriman wore a black T-shirt with big white letters proclaiming:

I'M NOT FUCKING GAY!

The two men embraced. Gauntlett felt brittle beneath Byrne's grasp. Like dry kindling, about to snap with the slightest pressure. They sat at a corner table. Gauntlett called over a waiter, who brought Byrne a bourbon and Gauntlett a Pellegrino.

"You quit drinking?" Byrne asked.

"Two years," Gauntlett said. "The meds, mon."

Byrne smiled. He knew Gauntlett well enough. "Man," he said. "I remember when you could snort the fifty-yard line at the Vet."

"Back in the day, I could fuck all night, too."

"No, you couldn't."

Gauntlett smiled. "Maybe an hour."

The two men adjusted their clothing, felt out each other's company. It had been a while. The DJ spun into a song by Ghetto Priest.

"How about all dis, eh?" Gauntlett asked, wanding his spindly hand in front of his face and sunken chest. "Some fuckery, dis."

Byrne was at a loss for words. "I'm sorry."

Gauntlett shook his head. "I had my time," he said. "No regrets."

They sipped their drinks. Gauntlett fell silent. He knew the drill. Cops were always cops. Robbers were always robbers. "So, to what do I owe the pleasure of your visit, Detective?"

"I'm looking for someone."

Gauntlett nodded again. This much he had figured.

"Punk named Diablo," Byrne said. "Big fucker, tats all over his face," Byrne said. "You know him?"

"I do."

"Any idea where I can locate him?"

Gauntlett Merriman knew enough not to ask why.

"Is this in the light or the shadow?" Gauntlett asked.

"Shadow."

Gauntlett looked out over the dance floor, a long, slow scan that endowed his favor with the weight it deserved. "I believe I can help you in this matter."

"I just need to talk to him."

Gauntlett held up a bone-thin hand. *"Ston a riva battan nuh know sun hat,"* he said, slipping deep into his Jamaican patois.

Byrne knew this one. *A stone at the bottom of the river doesn't know the sun is hot.*

"I appreciate this," Byrne added. He didn't bother to add that Gauntlett should keep all this to himself. He wrote his cell phone number on the back of a business card.

"Not at all." He sipped his water. "Ever' ting cook and curry."

Gauntlett rose from the table, a little unsteadily. Byrne wanted to help him, but he knew that Gauntlett was a proud man. Gauntlett found his balance. "I will call you."

The two men embraced again.

When he got to the door, Byrne turned, found Gauntlett in the crowd, thinking: *A dying man knows his future.*

Kevin Byrne envied him.

4 2

"Is this Mr. Amis?" the sweet voice on the phone inquired.

"Hello, love," Simon said, pouring on the North London. "How are you?"

"Fine, thanks," she said. "What can I do for you tonight?"

Simon used three different outcall services. For this one, StarGals, he was Kingsley Amis. "I'm frightfully lonely."

"That's why we're here, Mr. Amis," she said. "Have you been a naughty boy?"

"Terribly naughty," Simon said. "And I deserve to be punished."

While he waited for the girl to arrive, Simon looked at a tearsheet of the front page of the next day's *Report*. He had the cover, as he would have until the Rosary Killer was caught.

A few minutes later, as he sipped his Stoli, he imported the photos from his camera into his laptop. God, he loved this part, when all of his equipment was synched up and working.

His heart beat a little faster as the individual photos popped up on the screen.

He had never used the motor drive function on his digital camera before, the feature that allowed him to take a rapid series of photographs without resetting. It worked perfectly.

In all, he had six photographs of Kevin Byrne coming out of that vacant lot in Gray's Ferry, along with a handful of telephoto shots at the Rodin Museum.

No back alley meetings with crack dealers.

Not yet.

Simon closed his laptop, took a quick

shower, poured himself a few more inches of Stoli.

Twenty minutes later, as he prepared to open the door, he thought about who would be on the other side. As always, she would be blond and leggy and slender. She would be wearing a plaid skirt, navy blazer, white blouse, knee socks, and penny loafers. She would even carry a book bag.

He was a very naughty boy, indeed.

WEDNESDAY, 9:00 AM

"Whatever you need," Ernie Tedesco said.

Ernie Tedesco owned Tedesco and Sons Quality Meats, a small meatpacking company in Pennsport. He and Byrne had formed a friendship years earlier when Byrne had solved a series of truck hijackings for him.

Byrne had gone home with the intention of showering, grabbing something to eat, and rousting Ernie out of bed. Instead, he showered, sat on the edge of the bed, and the next thing he knew it was six o'clock in the morning.

Sometimes the body says no.

The two men gave each other the macho version of a hug—clasp hands, step forward, strong pat on the back. Ernie's plant was closed for renovations. When he left, Byrne would be alone there.

"Thanks, man," Byrne said.

"Anything, anytime, anywhere," Ernie replied. He stepped through the huge steel door and was gone.

Byrne had monitored the police band all morning. The call had not gone out about a body found in an alley in Gray's Ferry. Not yet. The siren he had heard the night before was another call.

Byrne entered one of the huge meat storage lockers, the frigid room where sides of beef were hung from hooks, and attached to ceiling tracks.

He put on gloves and moved a beef carcass a few feet from the wall.

A few minutes later, he propped open the outside door, went to his car. He had stopped at a demolition site on Delaware, where he had taken a dozen or so bricks.

Back inside the processing room, he

carefully stacked the bricks on an aluminum cart, and positioned the cart behind the hanging carcass. He stepped back, studied the trajectory. All wrong. He rearranged the bricks again, and yet again, until he had it right.

He took off the wool gloves and put on a pair of latex. He took the weapon out of his coat pocket, the silver Smith & Wesson he had taken off Diablo the night he brought in Gideon Pratt. He gave another quick glance around the processing room.

He took a deep breath, stepped back a few feet, and assumed a shooting stance, his body bladed to the target. He cocked the weapon, then squeezed a shot. The blast was loud, ringing off the stainless steel fixtures, caroming off the ceramic tile walls.

Byrne approached the swinging carcass, examined it. The entry hole was small, barely noticeable. The exit wound was impossible to find in the folds of fat.

As planned, the slug had hit the stacked bricks. Byrne found it on the floor, right near a drain.

It was then that his handheld radio crackled to life. Byrne turned it up. It was the radio call he had been expecting. The radio call he had been dreading.

The report of a body found in Gray's Ferry.

Byrne rolled the beef carcass back to where he had found it. He washed off the slug first in bleach, then in the hottest water his hands could stand, then dried it. He had been careful to load the Smith and Wesson pistol with a full-metal-jacketed slug. A hollow point would have brought fiber with it as it passed through the victim's clothing, and there was no way Byrne could have duplicated that. He wasn't sure how much effort the CSU team was going to put into the murder of another gangbanger, but he had to be careful nonetheless.

He took out the plastic bag, the bag in which he had collected the blood the night before. He tossed the clean slug inside, sealed the bag, collected the bricks, scanned the room one more time, then left.

He had an appointment in Gray's Ferry.

4 4

The trees bordering the bridle trail that snaked its way through Pennypack Park were straining at their buds. It was a popular jogging path, and this brisk spring morning had brought runners out in droves.

While Jessica jogged, the events of the previous night ran through her mind. Patrick had left a little after three. They had taken their encounter about as far as two consenting adults could without making love, a step for which they both wordlessly agreed they were not ready.

Next time, Jessica thought, she might not be so adult about the whole thing.

She could still smell him on her body. She could still feel him on her fingertips, her lips. But these sensations were overruled by the horrors of the job.

She picked up her pace.

She knew that most serial murderers had a pattern, a cooling down period between killings. Whoever was doing this was on a rampage, the final leg of a spree, a binge that, in all likelihood, would end in his own death.

The victims couldn't have been more different physically. Tessa was thin and blond. Nicole had been a Goth girl in her jet-black hair and piercings. Bethany had been heavy.

He *had* to know them.

Add to that the pictures of Tessa Wells found in his apartment, and it made Brian Parkhurst a prime suspect. Had he been seeing all three girls?

Even if he was, the biggest question remained. Why was he doing it? Had these girls rebuffed his advances? Threatened to go public? No, Jessica thought. There would have been a pattern of violence somewhere in his past.

On the other hand, if she could understand a monster's mind-set, she would *know* why.

Still, anyone whose pathology of religious insanity ran this deep must have acted on it before. And yet none of the crime databases had yielded even a remotely similar MO in the Philadelphia area, or anywhere nearby for that matter.

Yesterday Jessica had driven up Frankford Avenue in the Northeast, near Primrose Road, and had passed St. Katherine of Siena. St. Katherine was the church that had been defaced with blood three years earlier. She made a note to look into the incident. She knew she was grasping at straws, but straws were all they had at the moment. Many a case had been made on such a tenuous connection.

If anything, their doer had uncanny luck. He had picked three girls off the streets in Philly without anyone noticing.

Okay, Jessica thought. *Start at the beginning.* His first victim was Nicole Taylor. If it was Brian Parkhurst, they knew where he met Nicole. At school. If it was someone else, then he must have met Nicole elsewhere. But where? And why was she targeted? They had interviewed the two people at St. Joseph's who owned a Ford Windstar. Both were women; one in her late sixties, the other a single mother of three. Neither exactly fit the profile.

Was it someone along the route Nicole took to school? The route had been thoroughly canvassed. No one had seen anyone hanging around Nicole.

Was it a friend of the family?

And if it was, how did the doer know the other two girls?

All three girls had different doctors, different dentists. None of them played sports, so coaches and physical trainers were out. They had different tastes in clothes, in music, in just about everything.

Every question brought the answer closer to one name: Brian Parkhurst.

When had Parkhurst lived in Ohio? She made a mental note to check with Ohio law enforcement to see if there were any unsolved homicides with a similar MO in that time period. Because if there were—

Jessica never finished the thought because, as she rounded a bend in the bridle trail, she tripped over a branch that had fallen from one of the trees during the previous night's storm.

She tried, but she couldn't regain her balance. She fell, face-first, and rolled onto the wet grass, onto her back.

She heard people approaching.

Welcome to Humiliation Village.

It had been a while since she had taken a spill. She found that her appreciation for being on the wet ground, in public, had not grown in the intervening years. She moved slowly, carefully, trying to determine if anything was broken or, at the very least, strained.

"Are you okay?"

Jessica looked up from her earthbound vantage. The man doing the asking approached with a pair of middle-aged women, both sporting iPods on their waist packs. They were all dressed in quality jogging clothes, the kind of matching outfits with reflective stripes and zippered closures at the hem of the pants. Jessica, in her fuzzy, pilled sweats and well-worn Pumas, felt like a slob.

"I'm fine, thanks," Jessica said. She was.

Certainly nothing was broken. The soft grass had cushioned her fall. Except for a few grass stains and a contused ego, she was unharmed. "I'm the city acorn inspector. Just doing my job."

The man smiled, stepped forward, offered a hand. He was in his early thirties, blond and fair, nice looking in a collegiate way. She accepted the offer, rose to her feet, brushed herself off. The two women smiled in understanding. They had been jogging in place the whole time. When Jessica shrugged a *we've all taken a header, haven't we?* response, they continued on down the path.

"I just took a nasty fall myself the other day," the man said. "Down by the band shell. Tripped over a child's little plastic pail. Thought I'd fractured my right arm for sure."

"Embarrassing, isn't it?"

"Not at all," he said. "It gave me a chance to be one with nature."

Jessica smiled.

"I got a smile!" the man said. "I'm usually far more inept with pretty women. Usually takes months to get a smile."

Now, there's *a line,* Jessica thought. Still, he looked harmless.

"Mind if I jog along with you?" he asked.

"I'm just about done," Jessica said, although this wasn't true. She had the feeling that this guy was the chatty type and, in addition to the fact that she didn't like to talk while she ran, she had enough on her mind to think about.

"No problem," the man said. His face said otherwise. It looked as if she had slapped him.

Now she felt bad. He had stopped to lend a hand, and she shut him down rather unceremoniously. "I've got about a mile left in me," she said. "What kind of pace do you keep?"

"I like to keep the meter just under myocardial infarction."

Jessica smiled again. "I don't know CPR," she said. "If you grab your chest, I'm afraid you'll be on your own."

"Not to worry. I've got Blue Cross," he said.

And with that, they took off down the path at a leisurely pace, artfully dodging road apples, the warm, dappled sunlight blinking through the trees. The rain had stopped for a while, and the sunshine dried the earth.

"Do you celebrate Easter?" the man asked.

If he could see her kitchen, with its half a dozen egg-coloring kits, its bags of Easter grass, the jelly beans, cream eggs, chocolate bunnies, and little yellow Marshmallow Peeps, he would never ask that question. "I sure do."

"Personally, it's my favorite holiday of the year."

"Why is that?"

"Don't get me wrong. I like Christmastime. It's just that Easter is a time of . . . rebirth, I suppose. Of growth."

"That's a nice way of looking at it," Jessica said.

"Ah, who am I kidding?" he said. "I'm just addicted to Cadbury chocolate eggs."

Jessica laughed. "Join the club."

They jogged in silence for about a quarter mile, then rounded a soft curve, and headed into a long straightaway.

"Can I ask you a question?" he asked.

"Sure."

"Why do you think he's picking Catholic girls?"

The words were a sledgehammer to Jessica's chest.

In one fluid move she had her Glock out of her holster. She pivoted, lashed out with her right foot, and swept the man's legs out from under him. In a split second she had him on his face, in the dirt, the weapon to the back of his head.

"Don't fucking move."

"I just—"

"Shut up."

A few other joggers caught up to them. The expressions on their faces wrote the whole story.

"I'm a police officer," Jessica said. "Back up, please."

Joggers became sprinters. They all looked at Jessica's gun and took off as fast as they could down the path.

"If you just let me—"

"Did I stutter? I told you to shut up."

Jessica tried to catch her breath. When she did, she asked: "Who are you?"

There was no reason to wait for an answer. Besides, the fact that her knee was on the back of his head and his face was smashed into the turf probably precluded a response.

Jessica unzipped the back pocket of the man's jogging pants, pulled out a nylon wallet. She flipped it open. She saw the press card and wanted to pull the trigger even more.

Simon Edward Close. *The Report.*

She kneeled on the back of his head a little longer, a little harder. It was at times like these that she wished she weighed in at about 210.

"You know where the Roundhouse is?" she asked.

"Yes, of course. I—"

"Good," Jessica said. "Here's the deal. If you want to talk to me, you go through the press office there. If that's too much trouble, then stay the *fuck* out of my face."

Jessica eased the pressure on his head by a few ounces.

"Now, I'm going to get up and go to my car. Then I'm going to leave the park. You are going to remain in this position until I am gone. Do you understand me?"

"Yes," Simon replied.

She put all her weight on his head. "I mean it. If you move, if you even lift your head, I'm going to take you in for questioning on the Rosary Killings. I can lock you up for seventy-two hours without having to explain myself to anyone. Capeesh?"

"Ga-beetch," Simon said, the fact that he had a pound of wet sod in his mouth inhibiting his attempt at speaking Italian.

A little while later, when Jessica started her car and headed for the park exit, she glanced back at the trail. Simon was still there, facedown.

God, what an asshole.

45

Crime scenes always looked different in daylight. The alley looked benign and peaceful. A pair of uniforms stood at its entrance.

Byrne badged the officers, slipped under the tape. When the two detectives saw him, they each gave the homicide wave—palm down, a slight dip to the ground, then straight out. *Everything's cool.*

Xavier Washington and Reggie Payne had been partnered so long, Byrne thought, they were beginning to dress alike and finish each other's sentences, like an old married couple.

"We can all go home," Payne said with a smile.

"What do you have?" Byrne asked.

"Just a little thinning of the gene pool." Payne pulled back the plastic sheet. "This is the late Marius Green."

The body was in the precise position it had been in when Byrne left it the previous night.

"It's a through and through." Payne pointed to Marius's chest.

"Thirty-eight?" Byrne asked.

"Could be. Looks more like a nine, though. Haven't found the brass or the slug yet."

"He's JBM?" Byrne asked.

"Oh yeah," Payne replied. "Marius was a very bad actor."

Byrne glanced at the uniformed officers looking for the slug. He looked at his watch. "I have a few minutes."

"Oh, now we can really go home," Payne said. "The face is on the case."

Byrne walked a few feet toward the Dumpster. The mound of plastic trash bags obscured him from view. He picked up a short piece of lumber, began poking around. When he was sure he was unobserved, he took the baggie from his pocket, opened it, turned it upside down, and dropped the bloodied slug to the ground. He continued to nose around, but not too carefully.

After a minute or so, he returned to where Payne and Washington stood.

"I've got my own psycho to catch," Byrne said.

"Catch *you* at the house," Payne replied.

"*Got* it," one of the uniforms standing by the Dumpster bellowed.

Payne and Washington looked at each other, high-fived, walked over to where the uniform stood. They had found the slug.

Facts: Marius Green's blood was on the slug. It had caromed off brick. End of story.

There would be no reason to look farther or dig deeper. The slug would now be bagged and tagged, taken down to ballistics, where a property receipt would be issued. Then it would be compared to other bullets recovered from crime scenes. Byrne had the distinct feeling that the Smith &

Wesson he had taken off Diablo was used in other unsavory undertakings in the past.

Byrne exhaled, looked heavenward, slipped into his car. Only one more detail to address. Finding Diablo and imparting to him the wisdom of leaving Philadelphia forever.

His pager went off.

The call was from Monsignor Terry Pacek.

The hits just keep on coming.

The Sporting Club was Center City's biggest fitness club, located on the eighth floor at the historic Bellevue, the beautifully ornate building at Broad and Walnut Streets.

Byrne found Terry Pacek on one of the LifeCycles. The dozen or so stationary bikes were arranged in a square, facing each other. Most were occupied. Behind Byrne and Pacek, the slap and shriek of Nikes on the basketball court below offset the whir of the treadmills and hiss of the cycles, as well as the grunts and groans and grumbles of the fit, near fit, and ain't never gonna *be* fit.

"Monsignor," Byrne said in greeting.

Pacek didn't break rhythm, nor seem to acknowledge Byrne in any way. He was perspiring, but he wasn't breathing hard. A quick glance at the readout on the cycle showed that he had already put in forty minutes, and was still maintaining a ninety-rpm pace. Incredible. Byrne knew Pacek to be in his midforties, but he was in great shape, even for a man ten years younger. In here, out of his cassock and collar, dressed in stylish, Perry Ellis jogging pants and sleeveless T-shirt, he looked more like a slowly aging tight end than a priest. Actually, a slowly aging tight end is precisely what Pacek was. As Byrne understood it, Terry Pacek still held the Boston College record for receptions in a single season. They didn't call him the Jesuit John Mackey for nothing.

Looking around the club, Byrne saw a well-known news anchor puffing away on a StairMaster, a pair of city councilmen plotting on parallel treadmills. He found himself self-consciously sucking in his stomach. He would start a cardio regimen tomorrow. Definitely tomorrow. Or maybe the day after.

He had to find Diablo first.

"Thanks for meeting with me," Pacek said.

"Not a problem," Byrne said.

"I know you're a busy man," Pacek added. "I won't keep you too long."

Byrne knew that *I won't keep you long* was code for *Get comfortable, you're gonna be here a while*. He just nodded, waited for a moment. The moment played out empty. Then: "What can I do for you?"

The question was as rhetorical as it was rote. Pacek hit the COOL DOWN button on the cycle, rode it out. He slipped off the seat, threw a towel around his neck. And although Terry Pacek was far more toned than Byrne, he was at least four inches shorter. Byrne found cheap solace in this.

"I'm a man who likes to cut through the layers of bureaucracy when possible," Pacek said.

"What makes you think it's possible in this instance?" Byrne asked.

Pacek stared at Byrne for a few, uncomfortable seconds too long. Then he smiled. "Walk with me."

Pacek led the way to the elevator, which they took to the third floor mezzanine and its jogging track. Byrne found himself hoping that *Walk with me* meant precisely that.

Walking. They got out on the carpeted track, which ringed the fitness room below.

"How is the investigation going?" Pacek asked as they began their way around at a reasonable pace.

"You didn't call me here for a status report."

"You're right," Pacek replied. "I understand that there was another girl found last night."

This was no secret, Byrne thought. It was even on CNN, which meant that no doubt people in Borneo knew. Great publicity for Philly's tourism board. "Yes," Byrne said.

"And I understand that your interest in Brian Parkhurst remains high."

An understatement. "We'd like to talk to him, yes."

"It is in everyone's interest—especially the heartbroken families of these young girls—that this madman be caught. And that justice is done. I know Dr. Parkhurst, Detective. I find it hard to believe that he has had anything to do with these crimes, but that is not for me to decide."

"Why am I here, Monsignor?" Byrne was in no mood for palace politics.

After two full circuits of the jogging track, they were back at the door. Pacek wiped the sweat from his head, and said: "Meet me downstairs in twenty minutes."

Zanzibar Blue was a chic jazz club and restaurant in the basement of the Bellevue, just beneath the lobby of the Park Hyatt, nine floors beneath the Sporting Club. Byrne ordered a coffee at the bar.

Pacek entered, bright-eyed, flushed with his workout.

"Vodka rocks," he said to the bartender.

He leaned against the bar next to Byrne. Without a word, he reached into his pocket. He handed Byrne a slip of paper. On it was an address in West Philly.

"Brian Parkhurst owns a building on Sixty-first Street, near Market. He's renovating it," Pacek said. "He's there now."

Byrne knew that nothing was free in this life. He pondered Pacek's angle. "Why are you telling me this?"

"It's the right thing to do, Detective."

"But your bureaucracy is no different from mine."

"I have done judgment and justice: leave

me not to mine oppressors," Pacek said with a wink. "Psalms, One Hundred and Ten."

Byrne took the piece of paper. "I appreciate this."

Pacek sipped his vodka. "I wasn't here."

"I understand."

"How are you going to explain obtaining this information?"

"Leave it to me," Byrne said. He would have one of his CIs make a call to the Roundhouse, logging it in about twenty minutes.

I seen him . . . that guy youse are lookin' for . . . I seen him up around Cobbs Creek.

"We all fight the good fight," Pacek said. "We choose our weapons early in life. You chose a gun and a badge. I chose the cross."

Byrne knew this wasn't easy for Pacek. If Parkhurst turned out to be their doer, Pacek would be the one to take the flak for the Archdiocese having hired him in the first place—a man who'd had an affair with a teenaged girl being put in proximity to, perhaps, a few thousand more.

On the other hand, the sooner the Rosary Killer was caught—not only for the sake of the Catholic girls in Philadelphia, but also for the church itself—the better.

Byrne slid off the stool, towering over the priest. He dropped a ten on the bar.

"Go with God," Pacek said.

"Thanks."

Pacek nodded.

"And, Monsignor?" Byrne added, slipping on his coat.

"Yes?"

"It's Psalms One Nineteen."

46

Jessica was in her father's kitchen, washing dishes, when the "talk" came. Like all Italian American families, anything of any importance was discussed, dissected, resected, and solved in only one room of the house. The kitchen.

This day would be no different.

Instinctively, Peter picked up a dish towel and stationed himself next to his daughter. "You having a good time?" he asked, the real conversation he wanted to have hiding just beneath his policeman's tongue.

"Always," Jessica said. "Aunt Carmella's cacciatore brings me back." She said this, lost, for the moment, in a pastel nostalgia of her childhood in this house, in memories of those carefree years at family functions with her brother; of Christmas shopping at the May Company, of Eagles games at a frigid Veterans Stadium, of seeing Michael in his uniform for the first time: so proud, so fearful.

God, she missed him.

". . . the *sopressata*?"

Her father's question yanked her back to the present. "I'm sorry. What did you say, Dad?"

"Did you try the *sopressata*?"

"No."

"Out of this world. From Chickie's. I'll make you a plate."

Jessica had never once left a party at her father's house without a plate. Nor had anyone else for that matter.

"You want to tell me what's wrong, Jess?"

"Nothing."

The word fluttered around the room for a while, then took a nosedive, as it always did when she tried it with her father. He always knew.

"Right, sweetie," Peter said. "Tell me."

"It's nothing," Jessica said. "Just, you know, the usual. Work."

Peter took a plate, dried it. "You nervous about the case?"

"Nah."

"Good."

"*Way* beyond nervous," Jessica said, handing her father another dinner plate. "Scared to death is more like it."

Peter laughed. "You'll catch him."

"You seem to be overlooking the fact that I've never worked a homicide in my life."

"You'll do fine."

Jessica didn't believe it, but, somehow, when her father said it, it sounded like the truth. "I know." Jessica hesitated, then asked, "Can I ask you something?"

"Sure."

"And I want you to be completely honest with me."

"Of course, honey. I'm a policeman. I always tell the truth."

Jessica glared at him over the top of her glasses.

"Okay. Point taken," Peter said. "What's up?"

"Did you have anything to do with me getting into Homicide?"

"Not a thing, Jess."

"Because, if you did . . ."

"What?"

"Well, you might think you're helping me, but you're not. There's a very good chance I'm gonna fall flat on my face here."

Peter smiled, reached over with a squeaky-clean hand, and grabbed Jessica's cheek, the way he had since she was a baby. "Not this face," he said. "This is an angel's face."

Jessica blushed and smiled. "Pa. Yo. I'm pushing thirty here. A little too old for the *visa bella* routine."

"Never," Peter said.

They fell silent for a little while. Then, as dreaded, Peter asked: "You getting everything you need from the labs?"

"Well, so far, I guess," Jessica said.

"Want me to make a call?"

"No!" Jessica replied, a little more force-

fully than she wanted. "I mean, not yet. I mean, I'd like to, you know . . ."

"You'd like to do it on your own."

"Yeah."

"What, we just met over here?"

Jessica blushed again. She could never fool her father. "I'll be okay."

"You sure?"

"Yeah."

"I'll leave it up to you then. Somebody drags their feet, you call me."

"I will."

Peter smiled, gave Jessica a sloppy kiss on the top of her head, just as Sophie came tearing into the room with her second cousin Nanette, both little girls wild-eyed with all the sugar. Peter beamed. "All my girls under one roof," he said. "Who's got it better than me?"

WEDNESDAY, 11:25 AM

The little girl giggles as she chases the puppy around and around the small, crowded park on Catharine Street, weaving through the forest of legs. We adults watch her, hovering nearby, ever vigilant. We are shields against the evils of the world. If you think about all the tragedy that could befall such a little one, the mind staggers.

She stops for a moment, reaches to the ground, retrieving some little-girl treasure. She examines it closely. Her interest is pure and untainted by greed or possession or self-indulgence.

What did Laura Elizabeth Richards say about purity?

"The lovely light of holy innocence shines like a halo 'round her bended head."

The clouds threaten rain but, for the moment, a blanket of golden sunlight covers South Philadelphia.

The puppy runs past the little girl, turns, nips at her heels, perhaps wondering why the game had stopped. The little girl doesn't run or cry. She has her mother's toughness. And yet there is something inside of her that is vulnerable and sweet, something that speaks of Mary.

She sits on a bench, primly arranges the hem of her dress, pats her knees.

The puppy leaps onto her lap, licks her face.

Sophie laughs. It is a marvelous sound.

But what if one day soon her little voice was silenced?

Surely all the animals in her stuffed menagerie would weep.

4 8

WEDNESDAY, 11:45 AM

Before she left her father's house, Jessica had slipped into his small office in the basement, sat down at his computer, accessed the Internet, and navigated to Google. She found what she was looking for in short order, then printed it out.

While her father and aunts watched Sophie at the small park next to the Fleisher Art Memorial, Jessica walked down the street to a cozy café on Sixth Street called Dessert. It was much quieter than a park full of sugar-amped toddlers and Chianti-primed adults. Besides, Vincent had shown up and she really didn't need the fresh hell.

Over a Sacher torte and coffee she perused her findings.

Her first Google search had been the lines from the poem she found in Tessa's diary.

Jessica had her answer instantly.

Sylvia Plath. The poem was called "Elm."

Of course, Jessica thought. Sylvia Plath was the patron saint of all melancholy teenaged girls, the poet who committed suicide in 1963 at the age of thirty.

I'm back. Just call me Sylvia.

What had Tessa meant by that?

The second search she performed was about the incident regarding the blood that had been thrown on the door of St. Katherine on that crazy Christmas Eve three years earlier. There wasn't much about it in the archives of either the *Inquirer* or *The Daily News*. Not surprisingly, *The Report* had done the longest piece on it. Written by none other than her favorite muckraker, Simon Close.

It turned out that the blood had not been thrown on the door at all, but rather painted on with a brush. And it had been done while the congregation had been inside celebrating midnight mass.

The picture that accompanied the article was of the double doors leading into the church, but it was not clear. It was impossible to tell if the blood on the doors represented anything or nothing. The article didn't say.

According to the item, police investigated the incident, but when Jessica searched further, she found no follow-up.

She made a call and found out that the detective who looked into the incident was a man named Eddie Kasalonis.

4 9

Except for the pain in his right shoulder and the grass stains on his new jogging suit, it had been a very productive morning.

Simon Close sat on his couch, contemplating his next move.

Although he hadn't expected the warmest greeting when he had revealed himself as a reporter to Jessica Balzano, he had to admit he was a little surprised by her violent reaction.

Surprised and, he also had to admit, extremely aroused. He had done his best Eastern Pennsylvania accent and she hadn't suspected a thing. Until he hit her with the bombshell question.

He fished the tiny digital voice recorder out of his pocket.

"Good . . . if you want to talk to me, you go through the press office there. If that's too much trouble, then stay the fuck out of my face."

He opened his laptop, checked his e-mail—more spam for Vicodin, penis enlargement, great mortgage rates, and hair restoration, along with the usual fan mail from readers ("rot in hell you fukin hack").

A lot of writers resist technology. Simon knew quite a few who still wrote on yellow legal pads with a ballpoint pen. A few others who worked on ancient Remington manual typewriters. Pretentious, prehistoric nonsense. Try as he might, Simon Close could not understand this. Perhaps they thought it would put them in touch with their inner Hemingway, the Charles Dickens fighting to get out. Simon was all digital, all the time.

From his Apple PowerBook, to his DSL connection, to his Nokia GSM phone, he was on top of the tech world. *Go ahead,* he thought, *write on your slate tablets with a sharpened rock for all I care. I'm going to be there first.*

Because Simon believed in the two basic tenets of tabloid journalism:

It's easier to get forgiveness than it is to get permission.

It's better to be first than it is to be accurate.

That's what corrections are for.

He flipped on the TV, cruised the channels. Soaps, game shows, shout shows, sports. Yawn. Even the esteemed BBC America had some idiot, third-generation clone of *Trading Spaces* on. Maybe there was an old movie on AMC. He looked it up in the listings. *Criss Cross* with Burt Lancaster and Yvonne De Carlo. A goodie, but he'd seen it. Besides, it was half over.

He cruised the dial one more time, and was just about to flip it off when a breaking news flash came on a local channel. Murder in Philly. What a shock.

But it wasn't another victim of the Rosary Killer.

The on-the-scene camera was showing something else altogether, something that made Simon's heart beat a little faster. Okay, a *lot* faster.

It was the alley in Gray's Ferry.

The alley out of which Kevin Byrne had stumbled the night before.

Simon hit the RECORD button on his VCR. A few minutes later, he rewound and freeze-framed a shot of the mouth of the alley, and compared it, side by side, to the photo of Byrne on his laptop.

Identical.

Kevin Byrne had been in that same alley the night before, the night that a black kid had been shot dead. So it *hadn't* been a backfire.

This was so deliriously delicious, so much better than the possibility of catching Byrne at a crack house. Simon paced back and forth across his small living room a few dozen times, trying to figure the best way to play this.

Had Byrne committed a cold-blooded execution?

Was Byrne in the throes of a cover-up?

Was this a drug deal gone wrong?

Simon opened his e-mail program, calmed himself, somewhat, organized his thoughts and began to type:

Dear Detective Byrne:

Long time no see! Well, that's not entirely true. As you can see by the attached photo, I saw you yesterday. Here's my offer. I get to ride along with you and your scrumptious partner until you catch this very bad boy who has been killing Catholic schoolgirls. Once you do catch him, I want an exclusive.

For this, I will destroy these photographs.

If not, look for the pictures (yes, I have many) on the front page of the very next issue of *The Report*.

Have a great day!

As Simon looked it over—he always cooled off a bit before sending his most inflammatory e-mails—Enid meowed and leapt onto his lap from her perch on top of the file cabinet.

"What's up, dolly-doll?"

Enid seemed to peruse the text of Simon's mail to Kevin Byrne.

"Too strident?" he asked the cat.

Enid purred a response.

"You're right, kitty-kitty. Not *possible*."

Still, Simon decided he would read it over a few more times before sending it. Maybe he'd wait a day, just to see how big the story of the dead black kid in the alley would get.

He could afford twenty-four more hours if it meant he could get a thug like Kevin Byrne under his thumb.

Or maybe he should send the e-mail to Jessica.

Brilliant, he thought.

Or maybe he should just copy the photos to a CD and head down to the paper. Just publish them and see how Byrne liked it.

Either way, he should probably make a backup copy of the photos, just to be safe.

He thought about the headline, huge type over a photo of Byrne walking out of that alley in Gray's Ferry.

Vigilante cop? would read the headline.

Detective in death alley on night of murder! would read the deck. *God,* he was good.

Simon walked over to the hall closet and fished out a clean CD-R.

When he closed the door and turned back to the room, something was different. Maybe not so much different as off-center. It was like the feeling you get when you have an inner-ear infection and your balance is just that little bit tipsy. He stood in the archway leading to his tiny living room, trying to pin down the feeling.

Everything seemed to be as he had left it. His PowerBook on the coffee table, his empty demitasse cup next to it. Enid purring on the throw rug near the heat register.

Maybe he was mistaken.

He looked at the floor.

He saw the shadow first, a shadow that mirrored his own. He knew enough about key lighting to know that you need two light sources to cast two shadows.

Behind him, there was only the small ceiling fixture.

Then he felt the hot breath on his neck, smelled the faint scent of peppermint.

He turned, his heart suddenly in his throat.

And stared straight into the eyes of the devil.

5 0

Byrne had made a few stops before returning to the Roundhouse and briefing Ike
Buchanan. He then arranged for one of his
registered confidential informants to call him
with the information about Brian Parkhurst's
whereabouts. Buchanan faxed the DA's office and arranged for a search warrant of
Parkhurst's building.

Byrne called Jessica on her cell phone and
found her at a café near her father's house in
South Philly. He swung by and picked her up.

He briefed her at the Fourth District head-quarters at Eleventh and Wharton.

The building Parkhurst owned was a former florist shop on Sixty-first Street, itself converted from a spacious brick row house built in the 1950s. The stone-front structure was a few battered doors down from the Wheels of Soul clubhouse. The Wheels of Soul was an old and venerable motorcycle club. In the 1980s, when crack cocaine had hit Philly hard, it was the Wheels of Soul MC, as much as any law enforcement agency, that had kept the city from burning to the ground.

If Parkhurst was taking these girls somewhere for short periods of time, Jessica thought as they approached the property, this place would be ideal. There was a rear entrance large enough to pull a van or mini-van partially inside.

When they arrived at the scene, they drove slowly behind the building. The rear entrance—a large, corrugated-steel door—was padlocked from the outside. They circled the block and parked on the street, under the El, about five addresses west of the location.

Two patrol cars met them. Two uniformed officers would cover the front; two, the rear.

"Ready?" Byrne asked.

Jessica felt a little shaky. She hoped it didn't show. She said: "Let's do it."

Byrne and Jessica approached the door. The front windows were whitewashed, impossible to see through. Byrne slammed a fist into the door three times.

"Police! Search warrant!"

They waited five seconds. He pounded again. No response.

Byrne turned the handle, pushed on the door. It eased open.

The two detectives made eye contact. On a count, they rolled the jamb.

The front room was a mess. Drywall, paint cans, drop cloths, scaffolding. Nothing to the left. To the right, stairs leading up.

"Police! Search warrant!" Byrne repeated.

Nothing.

Byrne pointed to the stairs. Jessica nodded. He would take the second floor. Byrne mounted the stairs.

Jessica worked her way to the rear of the building on the first floor, checking every alcove, every closet. The interior was half renovated. The hallway behind what was once a service counter was a skeleton of open studs, exposed wiring, plastic water lines, heat ducts.

Jessica stepped through a doorway, into what had once been the kitchen. The kitchen was gutted. No appliances. Recently drywalled and taped. Beneath the pasty smell of the drywall tape, there was something else. Onions. Jessica then saw a sawhorse in the corner of the room. On it sat a half-eaten take-out salad. Next to it was a full cup of coffee. She dipped a finger into the coffee. Ice cold.

She walked out of the kitchen, inched toward the room at the back of the row house. The door was only slightly ajar.

Drops of sweat rolled down her face, her neck, then laced her shoulders. The hallway was warm, stuffy, airless. The Kevlar vest felt confining and heavy. Jessica reached the door, took a deep breath. With her left foot she slowly edged the door open. She saw the right half of the room first. An old dinette chair on its side, a wooden toolbox. Smells greeted her. Stale cigarette smoke, freshly cut knotty pine. Beneath it was something ugly, something rank and feral.

She kicked the door open fully, turned into the small room, and immediately saw a figure. Instinctively she spun and pointed her weapon at the shape, silhouetted against the whitewashed windows in the rear.

But there was no threat.

Brian Parkhurst was hanging from an I-beam in the center of the room. His face was a purplish brown, swollen, his extremities distended, his black tongue lolling out of his mouth. An electrical wire was wrapped around his neck, digging deep into the flesh, then looped over a support beam overhead. Parkhurst was barefoot, shirtless. The sour smell of drying feces filled Jessica's sinuses. She dry-heaved once, twice. She held her breath, cleared the rest of the room.

"Upstairs is clear!" Byrne yelled.

Jessica nearly jumped at the sound of his voice. She heard Byrne's heavy boots on the stairs. "In here," she yelled.

In seconds, Byrne entered the room. "Ah *fuck*."

Jessica saw the look in Byrne's eyes,

read the headlines there. Another suicide. Just like the Morris Blanchard case. Another suspect hounded into taking his own life. She wanted to say something, but it was not her place, and not the time.

A diseased silence filled the room. They had been batted back to square one and both of them, in their own way, attempted to reconcile that fact with all they had contemplated on the way over.

The system would now go about its business. They would call the medical examiner's office, the Crime Scene Unit. They would cut Parkhurst down, transport him to the ME's office where they would perform an autopsy on him, pending notification of family. There would be a notice in the papers and a service at one of Philadelphia's finer funeral homes, followed closely by interment on a grassy hillside.

And exactly what Brian Parkhurst knew, and what he had done, if anything, would forever be cast in darkness.

They milled around the Homicide Unit, loose aggies in an empty cigar box. There were always mixed feelings at times like these, when a suspect cheats the system with suicide. There would be no allocution, no admission of guilt, no punctuation. Just an endless Möbius strip of suspicion.

Byrne and Jessica sat at adjoining desks.

Jessica caught Byrne's eye.

"What?" he asked.

"Say it."

"Say what?"

"You don't think it was Parkhurst, do you?"

Byrne didn't answer right away. "I think he knew a hell of a lot more than he told us," he said. "I think he was seeing Tessa Wells. I think he knew that he was going to do time for statutory rape, and that's why he went into hiding. But do I think he murdered these three girls? No. I don't."

"Why not?"

"Because there wasn't a single shred of physical evidence anywhere near him. Not one fiber, not one drop of fluid."

The Crime Scene Unit had combed every square inch of both of Brian Parkhurst's properties, yielding nothing. They had pinned a great deal of their suspicions on the possibility—actually, the certainty—that incriminating scientific evidence would be found in

Parkhurst's building. Everything they had hoped to find there simply did not exist. Detectives had interviewed everyone in the vicinity of his home and the building he was renovating, yielding nothing. They had yet to find his Ford Windstar.

"If he was bringing these girls to his house, someone would have seen something, heard something, right?" Byrne added, "If he was bringing them to the building on Sixty-first Street, we would have found *something*."

When they had searched the building, they had discovered a number of items, including a box of miscellaneous hardware that contained an assortment of screws, nuts, and bolts, none of which precisely matched the bolts used on the three victims. There was also a chalk box, the carpenter's tool used for snapping lines in the rough-framing stage of construction. The chalk inside was blue. They had sent a sample to the lab, to see if it matched the blue chalk found on the victims. Even if it did, carpenter's chalk could be found at every construction site in the city, and in half the home remodelers' toolboxes. Vincent had some in his toolbox in the garage.

"But what about his call to me?" Jessica asked. "What about telling me that there are 'things we need to know' about these girls?"

"I've been thinking about that," Byrne said. "Maybe there *is* something that they all have in common. Something that we're not seeing."

"But what happened between the time he called me and this morning?"

"I don't know."

"Suicide doesn't exactly fit the profile, does it?"

"No. It doesn't."

"Which means there's a good chance that . . ."

They both knew what it meant. They sat mute for a while, the cacophony of the busy office flowing around them. There were at least a half dozen other homicides being investigated, and those detectives inched and plowed forward. Byrne and Jessica envied them.

There are things you need to know about these girls.

If Brian Parkhurst was not their killer, then the possibility existed that the man they were looking for had murdered him. Perhaps for taking the spotlight. Perhaps for some reason that spoke to the basic pathology of his madness. Perhaps to prove to authorities that he was still out there.

Neither Jessica nor Byrne had as yet mentioned the similarity in the two "suicides," but it permeated the air in the room like a noxious cloud.

"Okay," Jessica broke the silence. "If Parkhurst was murdered by our doer, how did he know who he was?"

"Two ways," Byrne said. "Either they knew each other, or he got his name off TV when he left the Roundhouse the other day."

Score another one for the media, Jessica thought. They batted around the idea that Brian Parkhurst was another victim of the Rosary Killer for a while. But even if he was, it didn't help them figure out what was coming next.

The time line, or lack of it, made the killer's movements unpredictable.

"Our doer picks Nicole Taylor off the street on Thursday," Jessica said. "He dumps her at Bartram Gardens on Friday, right around the time he picks up Tessa

Wells, whom he holds until Monday. Why the lag time?"

"Good question," Byrne said.

"Then Bethany Price was grabbed Tuesday afternoon, and our one and only witness saw her body dumped at the museum on Tuesday evening. There's no cycle. No symmetry."

"It's almost like he doesn't want to do these things on the weekend."

"That may not be as far-fetched as you think," Byrne said.

He got up, approached the white board, which was now covered in crime scene photos and notes.

"I don't think our boy is motivated by the moon, the stars, voices, dogs named Sam, any of that shit," Byrne said. "This guy has a plan. I say we learn his plan, we find him."

Jessica glanced at her pile of library books. The answer was in there somewhere.

Eric Chavez entered the room, got Jessica's attention. "Got a minute, Jess?"

"Sure."

He held up a file folder. "There's something you should see."

"What is it?"

"We ran a background check on Bethany Price. Turns out she had a prior."

Chavez handed her an arrest report. Bethany Price had been arrested as part of a drug sting operation about a year earlier, having been found with nearly a hundred hits of Benzedrine—the illicit diet pill of choice for overweight teenagers. It certainly had been when Jessica was in high school, and it remained so now.

Bethany pled out and received two hundred hours of community service and a year's probation.

None of that was surprising. The reason Eric Chavez had brought it to Jessica's attention was the fact that the arresting officer in the case was Detective Vincent Balzano.

Jessica absorbed this, considered the coincidence.

Vincent knew Bethany Price.

According to the sentencing report, it was Vincent who recommended the community service in lieu of jail time.

"Thanks, Eric," Jessica said.

"You got it."

"Small world," Byrne said.

"I'd still hate to paint it," Jessica replied, absently, reading the report in detail.

Byrne checked his watch. "Look, I've got to pick up my daughter. We'll start fresh in the morning. Tear this all apart and start at the beginning."

"Okay," Jessica said, but she saw the look on Byrne's face, the concern that the firestorm that had erupted in his career after the Morris Blanchard suicide might be igniting all over again.

Byrne placed a hand on Jessica's shoulder, then slipped on his coat and left.

Jessica sat at the desk for a long time, looking out the window.

Although she didn't want to admit it, she agreed with Byrne. Brian Parkhurst was not the Rosary Killer.

Brian Parkhurst was a victim.

She tried Vincent on his cell phone, got his voice mail. She called Central Detectives and was told that Detective Balzano was out on the street.

She didn't leave a message.

51

When Byrne brought up the boy's name, Colleen went four shades of red.

"He is *not* my *boyfriend,*" his daughter signed.

"Uh, okay. Whatever you say," Byrne signed back.

"He's *not.*"

"Then why are you blushing?" Byrne signed, a huge smile on his face. They were on Germantown Avenue, heading to the

Easter party at the Delaware Valley School for the Deaf.

"I'm not *blushing*," Colleen signed, ever redder.

"Oh, okay," Byrne said, letting her off the hook. "Somebody must have left a stop sign in my car."

Colleen just shook her head, looked out the window. Byrne noticed that the vents on his daughter's side of the car were blowing around her silky fine blond hair. When had it gotten so long? he wondered. And were her lips always this red?

Byrne got his daughter's attention by waving his hand around, then signed: "Hey. I thought you guys went on a date. My mistake."

"It wasn't a date," Colleen signed. "I'm too young to date. Just ask Mom."

"Then what was it, if it wasn't a date?"

Big eye roll. "It was two kids going to see the fireworks with, like, a hundred million adults around."

"I'm a detective, you know."

"I know, Dad."

"I have sources and snitches all over town. Paid, confidential informants."

"I know, Dad."

"I just heard that you guys were holding hands and stuff."

Colleen replied with a sign that was not to be found in *The Handshape Dictionary* but was well known to all deaf kids. Two hands shaped like razor-sharp tiger claws. Byrne laughed. "Okay, okay," he signed. "Don't scratch."

They drove in silence for a while, enjoying each other's nearness, despite their sparring. It wasn't often that it was just the two of them. Everything was changing with his daughter, she was a teenager, and the idea scared Kevin Byrne more than any armed gangbanger in any dark alley.

Byrne's cell phone rang. He answered. "Byrne."

"Can you talk?"

It was Gauntlett Merriman.

"Yeah."

"He's at the old safe house."

Byrne took it in. The old safe house was five minutes away.

"Who's with him?" Byrne asked.

"He's alone. At least for now."

Byrne glanced at his watch, saw his daughter looking at him out of the corner of his eye. He turned his head to the window.

She could read lips better than any kid at the school, probably better than some of the deaf adults who taught there.

"You need some help?" Gauntlett asked.

"No."

"Okay, then."

"Are we good?" Byrne asked.

"All fruits ripe, my friend."

He closed the phone.

Two minutes later, he pulled to the curb in front of the Caravan Serai deli.

Although it was too early for the dinner trade, there were a few regulars scattered about the twenty or so tables at the front of the deli, sipping the thick black coffee and nibbling on Sami Hamiz's famous pistachio baklava. Sami was behind the counter, slicing lamb for what appeared to be a huge order he was preparing. When he saw Byrne he dried his hands and walked to the front of the restaurant, a grin on his face.

"*Sabah al-hayri,* Detective," Sami said. "Good to see you."

"How are you, Sami?"

"I am well." The two men shook hands

"You remember my daughter, Colleen," Byrne said.

Sami reached out, touched Colleen's cheek. "Of course." Sami then signed *good afternoon* to Colleen, who signed a dutiful *hello* back. Byrne had known Sami Hamiz since his days as a patrolman. Sami's wife Nadine was also deaf, and both were fluent in sign language.

"Do you think you can keep an eye on her for a few minutes?" Byrne asked.

"No problem," Sami said.

Colleen's face said it all. She signed: "I don't need anyone to keep an eye on me."

"I shouldn't be long," Byrne said to both of them.

"Take all the time you need," Sami said, as he and Colleen walked to the back of the restaurant. Byrne watched his daughter slip into the last booth near the kitchen. When he reached the door, he turned once again. Colleen waved a weak send-off, and Byrne's heart fluttered.

When Colleen had been a mere toddler, she would rocket out onto the porch to wave goodbye as he left for his tours in the morning. He had always offered a silent prayer that he would see that shiny, beautiful face again.

As he stepped out onto the street, he found that, in the ensuing decade, nothing had changed.

Byrne stood across the street from the old safe house, which was not a house at all, nor, he thought, particularly safe at this moment. The building was a low-rise warehouse tucked between two taller buildings on a blighted section of Erie Avenue. Byrne knew that the P-Town Posse had at one time used the third floor as a refuge.

He walked to the back of the building, down the steps to the basement door. It was open. It faced a long narrow corridor that led to what was once an employee entrance.

Byrne moved down the corridor, slowly, silently. For a big man, he had always been light on his feet. He drew his weapon, the chrome Smith & Wesson he had taken from Diablo the night they met.

He made his way down the hallway to the stairway at the end, listened.

Silence.

Within a minute, he found himself at the landing before the turn to the third floor. At the top was the door leading to the safe house. He could hear the faint sounds of a rock station. Someone was definitely up there.

But who?

And how many?

Byrne took a deep breath, and started up the stairs.

At the top, he put his hand on the door and eased it open.

Diablo stood near the window overlooking the alley between the buildings, completely oblivious. Byrne could see only half the room, but it didn't look as if anyone else was there.

What he *could* see, though, sent a quick shiver through him. On a card table, not two feet from where Diablo stood, next to Byrne's service Glock, was a full-auto mini Uzi.

Byrne felt the weight of the revolver in his hand and it suddenly felt like a cap gun. If he made his move and didn't get the drop on Diablo, he would not get out of this building alive. The Uzi fired six hundred rounds a minute, and you didn't exactly have to be a marksman to annihilate your prey.

Fuck.

After a few moments Diablo sat down at the table with his back to the door. Byrne knew he had no choice. He would get the drop on Diablo, confiscate the weapons, have a little heart-to-heart with the man, and this sad and sorry mess would be over.

Byrne made a quick sign of the cross, then stepped inside.

Kevin Byrne had taken only three strides into the room when he realized his mistake. He should have seen it. There, on the far side of the room, was an old dresser with a cracked mirror above it. In it he saw Diablo's face, which meant that Diablo could see him. Both men froze for that serendipitous second, knowing that their immediate plans—one of safety, one of surprise—had been changed. Their eyes met, as they had in that alley. This time they both knew that, one way or another, things were going to end differently.

Byrne had only meant to explain to Diablo the wisdom of leaving town. He now knew that would not happen.

Diablo sprang to his feet, Uzi in hand. Without a word, he spun and fired the weapon. The first twenty or thirty rounds tore up the old sofa that sat less than three feet from Byrne's right leg. Byrne dove to his left, mercifully landing behind an old cast-iron bathtub. Another two-second burst from the Uzi nearly cut the sofa in two.

God no, Byrne thought, his eyes shut tight, waiting for the hot metal to rip into his flesh. *Not here. Not like this.* He thought about Colleen, sitting in that booth, watching the door, waiting for him to fill it, waiting for him to return so she could continue her day, her life. Now he was pinned down in a filthy warehouse, about to die.

The last few slugs caught the cast-iron tub. The ringing hung in the air for a few moments.

Sweat stung his eyes.

Then came silence.

"Just want to fucking *talk,* man," Byrne said. "This doesn't have to happen."

Byrne estimated that Diablo was no more than twenty feet away. Dead center in the room, probably behind the huge support column.

Then, with no warning, came another burst from the Uzi. The roar was deafening. Byrne screamed, as if he'd been hit, then slammed his foot on the wood floor, as if he'd fallen. He moaned.

The room was again silent. Byrne could smell the burned ticking from the hot lead in the upholstery just a few feet away. He heard a noise on the other side of the room. Diablo was on the move. The scream had worked. Diablo was coming to finish him off. Byrne closed his eyes, remembering the layout. The only path across the room was down the middle. He would have one chance, and the time to take it was now.

Byrne counted to three, leapt to his feet, spun and fired three times, head high.

The first shot hit Diablo dead center in his forehead, slamming into his skull, rocking him back on his heels, exploding the back of his head into a crimson blast of blood and bone and brain matter that sprayed halfway across the room. The second and third bullets caught him in his lower jaw and throat. Diablo's right arm jerked upward, re-flexively firing the Uzi. The burst threw a dozen rounds into the floor, just inches to the left of Kevin Byrne. Diablo collapsed, a few more rounds smashing into the ceiling.

And in that instant it was over.

Byrne held his position for a few moments, weapon out front, seemingly frozen in time. He had just killed a man. His muscles slowly relaxed and he cocked his head to the sounds. No sirens. Yet. He reached into his back pocket, retrieved a pair of latex gloves. From his other pocket he removed a small sandwich bag with an oil rag inside. He wiped down the revolver, then placed it on the floor, just as the first siren rose in the distance.

Byrne found a can of spray paint and tagged the wall next to the window with JBM gang graffiti.

He looked back at the room. He had to *move*. Forensics? This would not be high priority for the team, but they would show. As far as he could tell, he was covered. He grabbed his Glock off the table and ran for the door, carefully skirting the blood on the floor.

He made his way down the back stairs as the sirens drew nearer. Within seconds he was in his car and heading toward the Caravan Serai.

That was the good news.

The bad news was, of course, that he had probably missed something. He had missed something important, and his life was over.

The main building of the Delaware Valley School for the Deaf was an early American design, constructed of fieldstone. The grounds were always well groomed.

As they approached the grounds, Byrne was once again struck by the silence. There were more than fifty kids between the ages of five and fifteen, all running around, expending more energy than Byrne could remember ever having at their age, and it was all completely quiet.

When he had learned to sign, Colleen had been nearly seven and already proficient in the language. Many times, at night, when he tucked her in, she had cried and decried her fate, wishing she could be normal, like the hearing kids. Byrne had just held her at those times, not knowing what to say, not being able to say it in his daughter's language even if he had. But a funny thing happened when Colleen turned eleven. She stopped wishing she could hear. Just like that. Total acceptance and, in some odd way, arrogance about her deafness, proclaiming it to be an advantage, a secret society composed of extraordinary people.

It was more of an adjustment for Byrne than it was for Colleen, but this day, when she kissed him on the cheek and ran off to play with her friends, his heart almost burst with love and pride for her.

She would be fine, he thought, even if something terrible happened to him.

She was going to grow up beautiful and polite and decent and respectable, despite the fact that one year, on Holy Wednesday, while she sat in a pungent Lebanese restaurant in North Philadelphia, her father had left her there, and gone off to commit murder.

5 2

She is summer, this one. She is water.

Her white-blond hair is long, pulled back into a ponytail, fastened with an amber cat's-eye bolo. It reaches the middle of her back in a glistening waterfall. She wears a faded denim skirt and a burgundy wool sweater. She carries a leather jacket over her arm. She has just emerged from the Barnes & Noble at Rittenhouse Square, where she works part time.

She is still quite thin, but it looks like she has put on weight since the last time I saw her.

Good for her.

The street is crowded, so I am sporting a ball cap and sunglasses. I walk right up to her.

"Remember me?" I ask, lifting the sunglasses momentarily.

At first, she is not sure. I am older, so I belong to that world of adults who could, and usually do, mean authority. As in—the end of the party. After a few seconds, recognition alights.

"Sure!" she says, her face brightening.

"Your name is Kristi, right?"

She blushes. "Yep. You have a good memory!"

"How have you been feeling?"

The blush deepens, morphing from the demure demeanor of a confident young woman to the embarrassment of a little girl, her eyes ringed with shame. "I'm, you know, a lot better now," she says. "That was—"

"Hey," I say, holding up a hand, stopping her. "There's nothing for you to be ashamed of. Not one single thing. I could tell you stories, believe me."

"Really?"

"Absolutely," I say.

We walk down Walnut Street. Her posture changes slightly. A little self-conscious now.

"So, what are you reading?" I ask, pointing to the bag she carries.

She blushes again. "I'm embarrassed."

I stop walking. She stops with me. "Now, what did I just tell you?"

Kristi laughs. At this age, it is always Christmas, always Halloween, always the Fourth. Every day is the day. "Okay, okay," she concedes. She reaches into the plastic bag, takes out a pair of Tiger Beat magazines. "I get a discount."

On the cover of one of the magazines is Justin Timberlake. I take the magazine from her, scrutinize the cover.

"I haven't liked his solo stuff as much as 'NSYNC," I say. "What about you?"

Kristi looks at me, her mouth half-open. "I can't believe you know who he is."

"Hey," I say in mock rage. "I'm not that old." I hand the magazine back, mindful of the fact that my prints are on the glossy surface. I must not forget that.

Kristi shakes her head, still smiling.

We continue up Walnut.

"All ready for Easter?" I ask, rather inelegantly changing the subject.

"Oh, yes," she says. "I love Easter."

"Me, too," I say.

"I mean, I know it's still real early in the year, but Easter always means summer is coming, to me. Some people wait till Memorial Day. Not me."

I fall behind her for a few steps, allowing people to pass. From the cover of my sunglasses, I watch her walk, as covertly as I can. In a few years, she would have been what people refer to as coltish, a long-legged beauty.

When I make my move, I am going to have to be fast. Leverage will be paramount. I have the syringe in my pocket, its rubber tip firmly secured.

I glance around. For all the people on the street, lost in their own dramas, we might as well be alone. It never fails to amaze me how, in a city like Philadelphia, one can go virtually unnoticed.

"Where are you headed?" I ask.

"Bus stop," she says. "Home."

I pretend to search my memory. "You live in Chestnut Hill, right?"

She smiles, rolls her eyes. "Close. Nice-town."

"That's what I meant."

I laugh.

She laughs.

I have her.

"Are you hungry?" I ask.

I watch her face as I ask this. Kristi had done her battles with anorexia, and I know that questions like this will always be a challenge to her in this life. A few moments pass, and I fear I have lost her.

I have not.

"I could eat," she says.

"Great," I say. "Let's get a salad or something, then I'll drive you home. It'll be fun. We can catch up."

A split second of apprehension settles, veiling her pretty face in darkness. She glances around us.

The veil lifts. She slips on her leather jacket, gives her ponytail a flip, and says: "Okay."

5 3

Eddie Kasalonis retired in 2002.

Now in his early sixties, he had been on the force nearly forty years, most of them in the zone, and had seen it all, from every vantage, in every light, having worked twenty years on the streets before moving to South detectives.

Jessica had located him through the FOP. She hadn't been able to reach Kevin, so she went to meet Eddie on her own. She found him where he was every day at this time. At a small Italian eatery on Tenth Street.

Jessica ordered a coffee; Eddie, a double espresso with a lemon peel.

"I saw a lot over the years," Eddie said, clearly as a preface to a walk down memory lane. A big man, with moist gray eyes, a navy tattoo on his right forearm, and shoulders rounded with age. Time had slowed his stories. Jessica had wanted to get right to the business about the blood on the door at St. Katherine but, out of respect, she listened. Eventually, he drained his espresso, called for another, then asked: "So. What can I do for you, Detective?"

Jessica took out her notebook. "I understand you investigated an incident at St. Katherine a few years ago."

Eddie Kasalonis nodded. "You mean the blood on the door of the church?"

"Yes."

"Don't know what I can tell you about it. Wasn't much of an investigation, really."

"Can I ask how it was that you came to be involved? I mean, it's a long way from your stomping grounds."

Jessica had asked around. Eddie Kasalonis was a South Philly boy. Third and Wharton.

"A priest from St. Casimir's had just gotten transferred up there. Nice kid. Lithuanian, like me. He called, I said I'd look into it."

"What did you find?"

"Not much, Detective. Someone painted the lintel over the main doors with blood while the congregation was celebrating midnight mass. When they came out, it dripped onto an elderly woman. She freaked, called it a miracle, called an ambulance."

"What kind of blood was it?"

"Well, it wasn't human, I can tell you that. Some kind of animal blood. That's about as far as we pushed it."

"Did it ever happen again?"

Eddie Kasalonis shook his head. "That was it, far as I know. They cleaned the door, kept an eye out for a while, then they eventually moved on. As for me, I had a lot on my plate in those days." The waiter brought Eddie's coffee, offered Jessica a refill. She declined.

"Did it happen at any other churches?" Jessica asked.

"No idea," Eddie said. "Like I said, I

looked into it as a favor. Church desecration wasn't exactly my beat."

"Any suspects?"

"Not really. That part of the Northeast ain't exactly a hotbed of gang activity. I rousted a few of the local punks, threw a little weight. No one copped to it."

Jessica put her notebook away, finished her coffee, a little disappointed that this hadn't led to anything. On the other hand, she hadn't really expected it to.

"Now it's my turn to ask," Eddie said.

"Sure," Jessica replied.

"What is your interest in a three-year-old vandalism case in Torresdale?"

Jessica told him. No reason not to. Like everyone else in Philly, Eddie Kasalonis was highly aware of the Rosary Killer case. He didn't press her on the details.

Jessica looked at her watch. "I really do appreciate your time," she said as she stood up, reached into her pocket to pay for her coffee. Eddie Kasalonis held up his hand, meaning: *Put it away.*

"Glad to help," he said. He stirred his coffee, a wistful look coming over his face. Another story. Jessica waited. "You know how, at the racetrack, you sometimes see the old jockeys hanging over the rail, watching the workouts? Or how when you go by a building site and you see the old carpenters sitting on a bench, watching the new buildings go up? You look at these guys and you *know* they're just dying to get back into the game."

Jessica knew where he was going. And she certainly knew about carpenters. Vincent's father retired a few years ago and these days he sat around, in front of the television, beer in hand, heckling the lousy remodeling jobs on HGTV.

"Yeah," Jessica said. "I know what you mean."

Eddie Kasalonis put sugar in his coffee, settled even more deeply into his chair. "Not me. I'm *glad* I don't have to do it anymore. When I first heard about this case you're working, I realized that the world had passed me by, Detective. The guy you're looking for? Hell, he comes from a place I've never been." Eddie looked up, fixing her in time with his sad, watery eyes. "And I thank God I don't have to go there."

Jessica wished she didn't have to go there, either. But it was a little late for that. She got out her keys, hesitated. "Is there anything else you can tell me about the blood on the church door?"

Eddie seemed to be deliberating over whether or not to say anything. "Well, I'll tell you. When I looked at the bloodstain, the morning after it happened, I thought I saw something. Everyone else told me I was imagining things, the way people see the face of the Virgin Mary in oil slicks on their driveways, things like that. But I was sure I saw what I thought I saw."

"What was it?"

Eddie Kasalonis hesitated again. "I thought it looked like a rose," he finally said. "An upside-down rose."

Jessica had four stops to make before going home. She had to go to the bank, stop at the dry cleaners, pick up something for dinner at a Wawa, and send a package to her Aunt Lorrie in Pompano Beach. The bank, the grocery store, and UPS were all within a few blocks of Second and South.

As she parked the Jeep, she thought about what Eddie Kasalonis had said.

I thought it looked like a rose. An upside-down rose.

From her readings, she knew that the term *rosary* itself was based on Mary and the rose garden. Thirteenth-century art depicted Mary holding a rose, not a scepter. Did any of this have anything to do with her case, or was she just being desperate?

Desperate.

Definitely.

Still, she'd mention it to Kevin and get his take on it.

She got the box she was taking to UPS out of the back of the Jeep, locked it, headed up the street. When she walked by Cosi, the salad-and-sandwich franchise at the corner of Second and Lombard, she looked in the window and saw someone she recognized, even though she really didn't want to.

Because the someone was Vincent. And he was sitting in a booth with a woman.

A *young* woman.

Actually, a *girl*.

Jessica could only see the girl from the back, but that was enough. She had long blond hair, pulled back into a ponytail. She wore a leather jacket, motorcycle style. Jessica knew that badge bunnies came in all shapes, sizes, and colors.

And, obviously, ages.

For a brief moment, Jessica experienced that strange feeling you get like when you're in another city and you see someone you think you recognize. There's that flutter of familiarity, followed by the realization that what you're seeing can't be accurate, which, in this instance, translated as:

What the hell is my husband doing in a restaurant with a girl who looks about eighteen years old?

Without having to think, the answer came roaring into her head.

You son of a bitch.

Vincent saw Jessica, and his face told the story. Guilt, topped by embarrassment, with a side order of shit-eating grin.

Jessica took a deep breath, looked at the ground, then continued up the street. She was not going to be that stupid, crazed woman who confronts her husband and his mistress in a public place. No way.

Within seconds, Vincent burst through the door.

"Jess," he said. "Wait."

Jessica stopped, trying to rein in her anger. Her anger would not hear it. It was a rabid, stampeding herd of emotion.

"Talk to me," he said.

"Fuck you."

"It's not what you think, Jess."

She put her package on a bench, spun to face him. "Gee. How did I know you were going to say that?" She looked at her husband, up and down. It always amazed her how different he could look, based on her feelings at any given moment. When they were happy, his bad-boy swagger and tough-guy posturing were so very sexy. When she was pissed, he looked like a thug, like some street-corner Goodfella wannabe she wanted to slap the cuffs on.

And, God save them both, this was about as pissed off as she'd ever been with him.

"I can explain," he added.

"Explain? Like you explained Michelle Brown? I'm sorry, what was that, again? A little amateur gynecology in my *bed*?"

"Listen to me."

Vincent grabbed Jessica by the arm and, for the first time since they had met, for the first time in their volatile, passionate love affair, it felt as if they were strangers, arguing on a street corner; the kind of couple who, when you are in love, you vow never to become.

"Don't," she warned.

Vincent held on tighter. "Jess."

"Take . . . your   fucking . . . hand . . . *off* me." Jessica was not at all surprised to find that she had formed both of her hands into fists. The notion scared her a little, but not enough to unclench them. Would she lash out at him? She honestly didn't know.

Vincent stepped back, putting up his hands in surrender. The look on his face, at that moment, told Jessica that they just crossed a threshold and entered a shadowy territory from which they might never return.

But at the moment, that didn't matter.

All Jessica could see was a blond pony-tail and the goofy smile Vincent had on his face when she caught him.

Jessica picked up her package, turned on her heels, and headed back to the Jeep. Fuck UPS, fuck the bank, fuck dinner. All she could think about was getting away from there.

She hopped in the Jeep, started it and jammed the pedal. She was almost hoping that some rookie patrolman was nearby to pull her over and try to give her some shit.

No luck. Never a cop around when you needed one.

Except the one she was married to.

Before she turned onto South Street she looked in the rearview mirror and saw Vincent still standing on the corner, hands in pockets, a receding, solitary silhouette against the red brick backdrop of Society Hill.

Receding, along with him, was her marriage.

5 4

The night behind the duct tape was a Dalí landscape, black velvet dunes rolling toward a far horizon. Occasionally, fingers of light crept through the bottom part of his visual plane, teasing him with the notion of safety.

His head ached. His limbs felt dead and useless. But that wasn't the worst of it. If the tape over his eyes was irritating, the tape over his mouth was maddening beyond discourse. For someone like Simon Close, the humiliation of being tied to a chair, bound with duct tape, and gagged with something that felt and tasted like an ancient tack rag finished a distant second to the frustration of not being able to talk. If he lost his words, he lost the battle. It had always been thus. As a small boy, in the Catholic home in Berwick, he had managed to talk his way out of nearly every scrape, every frightful jam.

Not this one.

He could barely make a sound.

The tape was wrapped tightly around his head, just above his ears, so he was able to hear.

How do I get out of this? Deep breath, Simon. Deep.

Crazily, he thought about the books and CDs he had acquired over the years, the ones dealing with meditation and yoga and the concepts of diaphragmatic breathing, the yogic techniques for fighting stress and anxiety. He had never read a single one, nor listened to more than a few minutes of the CDs. He had wanted a quick fix for his occasional panic attacks—the Xanax made him far too sluggish to think straight—but there was no quick fix to be found in yoga.

Now he wished he had stuck with it.

Save me, Deepak Chopra, he thought.

Help me, Dr. Weil.

Then he heard the door to his flat open behind him. He was back. The sound filled him with a sickening brew of hope and fear. He heard the footsteps approach from behind, felt the weight on the floorboards. He smelled something sweet, floral. Faint, but present. A young girl's perfume.

Suddenly, the tape was ripped from his eyes. The grease-fire pain made it feel as if his eyelids came off with it.

When his eyes adjusted to the light, he saw, on the coffee table in front of him, his Apple PowerBook, opened and displaying a graphic of *The Report*'s current web page.

MONSTER STALKS PHILLY GIRLS!

Sentences and phrases were highlighted in red.

. . . depraved psychopath . . .

. . . deviant butcher of innocence . . .

Behind the laptop, on a tripod, sat Simon's digital camera. The camera was on and pointed right at him.

Simon then heard a click behind him. His tormentor had the Apple mouse in his hand and was clicking through the documents.

Soon, another article appeared. The article was from three years earlier, a piece he had written about blood being splashed on the door of a church in the Northeast. Another phrase was highlighted:

. . . hark the herald assholes fling . . .

Behind him, Simon heard a satchel being unzipped. Moments later, he felt the slight pinch at the right side of his neck. A needle. Simon struggled mightily against his bindings, but it was useless. Even if he could get loose, whatever was in the needle took almost immediate effect. Warmth spread through his muscles, a pleasurable weakness that, were he not in this situation, he might have enjoyed.

His mind began to fragment, soar. He closed his eyes. His thoughts took flight over the last decade or so of his life. Time leapt, fluttered, settled.

When he opened his eyes, the cruel buffet displayed on the coffee table in front of him arrested the breath in his chest. For a moment, he tried to conjure some sort of benevolent scenario for them. There was none.

Then, as his bowels released, he recorded the final visual entry in his reporter's mind—a cordless drill, a large needle, threaded with a thick black thread.

And he knew.

Another injection took him to the edge of the abyss. This time, he willingly went along with it.

A few minutes later, when he heard the sound of the drill, Simon Close screamed, but the sound seemed to come from somewhere else, a disembodied wail that echoed off the damp stone walls of a Catholic home in the time-swept north of England, a plaintive sigh over the ancient face of the moors.

5 5

Jessica and Sophie sat at the table, pigging out on all the goodies they had brought home from her father's house—panettone, *sfogliatelle,* tiramisu. It wasn't exactly a balanced meal, but she had blown off the grocery store and there was nothing in the fridge.

Jessica knew it wasn't a good idea to let Sophie eat so much sugar at this late hour, but Sophie had a sweet tooth the size of Pittsburgh, just like her mother, and, well, it was so hard to say no. Jessica concluded long ago that she had better start saving for the dental bills.

Besides, after seeing Vincent mooning with Britney or Courtney or Ashley, or whatever the hell her name was, tiramisu was just about the right medicine. She tried to exile the image of her husband and the blond teenager from her mind.

Unfortunately, it was immediately replaced by the picture of Brian Parkhurst's body, hanging in that hot room, the rank smell of death.

The more she thought about it, the more she doubted Parkhurst's guilt. Had he been seeing Tessa Wells? Perhaps. Was he responsible for the murders of three young women? She didn't think so. It was nearly impossible to commit a single abduction and homicide without leaving behind trace evidence.

Three of them?

It just didn't seem feasible.

But what about the P A R on Nicole Taylor's hand?

For a fleeting moment, Jessica realized that she had signed on for a lot more than she felt she could handle with this job.

She cleaned the table, plopped Sophie down in front of the TV, popped in the *Finding Nemo* DVD.

She poured herself a glass of Chianti, cleared the dining room table, then spread out all her notes on the case. She walked her mind over the time line of events. There was a connection among these girls, something other than the fact that they attended Catholic schools.

Nicole Taylor, abducted off the street, dumped in a field of flowers.

Tessa Wells, abducted off the street, dumped in an abandoned row house.

Bethany Price, abducted off the street, dumped at the Rodin Museum.

The selection of dump sites seemed in turn random and precise, elaborately staged and mindlessly arbitrary.

No, Jessica thought. Dr. Summers was right. Their doer was anything but illogical. The placement of these victims was every bit as significant as the method of their murder.

She looked at the crime scene photographs of the girls and tried to imagine their final moments of freedom, tried to drag those unfolding moments from the dominion of black and white to the saturated color of nightmare.

Jessica picked up Tessa Wells's school photograph. It was Tessa Wells who troubled her most deeply; perhaps because Tessa had been the first victim she had seen. Or maybe because she knew that Tessa was the outwardly shy young girl that Jessica had once been, the chrysalis ever yearning to become the imago.

She walked into the living room, planted a kiss on Sophie's shiny, strawberry-scented hair. Sophie giggled. Jessica watched a few minutes of the movie, the colorful adventures of Dory and Marlin and Gill.

Then her eyes found the envelope on the end table. She had forgotten all about it.

The *Rosarium Virginis Mariae*.

Jessica sat down at the dining room table and skimmed the lengthy letter, which seemed to be a missive from Pope John Paul II, affirming the relevance of the holy rosary. She glossed over the headings, but her attention was drawn to one section, a segment titled "Mysteries of Christ, Mysteries of His Mother."

As she read, she felt a small flame of understanding ignite within her, the realization that she had crossed a barrier that, until this second, had been unknown to her, a barricade that could never be breached again.

She read that there are five "Sorrowful Mysteries" of the rosary. She had, of course, known this from her Catholic school upbringing, but hadn't thought of it in years.

The agony in the garden.

The scourge at the pillar.

The crown of thorns.

The carrying of the cross.

The crucifixion.

The revelation was a crystalline bullet to the center of her brain. Nicole Taylor was found in a garden. Tessa Wells was bound to a pillar. Bethany Price wore a crown of thorns.

This was the killer's master plan.

He is going to kill five girls.

For a few anxious moments she didn't seem to be able to move. She took a few deep breaths, calmed herself. She knew that, if she was right about this, the information would change the investigation completely, but she didn't want to present the theory to the task force until she was sure.

It was one thing to know the plan, but it was equally important to understand why. Understanding why would go a long way toward knowing where their doer would strike next. She took out a legal pad and made a grid.

The section of sheep bone found on Nicole Taylor was intended to lead investigators to the Tessa Wells crime scene.

But how?

She thumbed through the indices of some of the books she had taken from the Free Library. She found a section on Roman customs, and learned that scourging practices in the time of Christ included a short whip called a flagrum, to which they often attached leather thongs of variable lengths. Knots were tied in the ends of each thong, and sharp sheep bones were inserted into the knots at the ends.

The sheep bone meant there would be a scourge at the pillar.

Jessica wrote notes as fast as she could.

The reproduction of Blake's painting *Dante and Virgil at the Gates of Hell* that was found inside Tessa Wells's hands was obvious. Bethany Price was found at the gates leading into the Rodin Museum.

An examination of Bethany Price had found that she had two numbers written on the insides of her hands. On her left hand was the number 7. On her right hand, the number 16. Both numbers were written in black magic marker.

716.

Address? License plate? Partial zip code?

So far, no one on the task force had had any idea what the numbers meant. Jessica knew that, if she could divine this secret, there was a chance they could anticipate where the murderer's next victim would be placed. And they could be waiting for him.

She stared at the huge pile of books on the dining room table. She was certain the answer was somewhere in one of them.

She walked into the kitchen, dumped the glass of red wine, put on a pot of coffee.

It was going to be a long night.

5 6

The headstone is cold. The name and date are obscured by time and wind-borne debris. I clean it off. I run my index finger along the chiseled numbers. The date brings me back to a time in my life when all things were possible. A time when the future shimmered.

I think about who she would have been, what she might have done with her life, who she might have become.

Doctor? Politician? Musician? Teacher?

I watch the young women and I know the world is theirs.

I know what I have lost.

Of all the sacred days on the Catholic calendar, Good Friday is, perhaps, the most sacred. I've heard people ask: If this is the day that Christ was crucified, why is it called good? Not all cultures call it Good Friday. The Germans call it Charfreitag, *or* Sorrowful Friday. *In Latin it has been called* Parasceve, *the word meaning* preparation.

Kristi is in preparation.

Kristi is praying.

When I left her, secured and snug in the chapel, she was on her tenth rosary. She is very conscientious and, from the way she earnestly says the decades, I can tell that she wants to please not only me—after all, I can only affect her mortal life—but the Lord, as well.

The chilled rain slicks the black granite, joining my tears, flooding my heart full of storms.

I pick up the shovel, begin to dig the soft earth.

The Romans believed that there was significance to the hour that signaled the close of the business day, the ninth hour, the time when fasting began.

They called it the Hour of None.

For me, for my girls, the hour is finally near.

5 7

The parade of police cars, both marked and unmarked, that snaked their way up the rain-glassed street in West Philadelphia where Jimmy Purify's widow made her home seemed endless.

Byrne had gotten the call from Ike Buchanan at just after six.

Jimmy Purify was dead. He had coded at three that morning.

As he walked toward the house, Byrne fielded hugs from other detectives. Most people thought it was tough for cops to show emotion—some said the lack of sentiment was a prerequisite for the job—but every cop knew better. At a time like this, nothing came easier.

When Byrne entered the living room he considered the woman standing in front of him, frozen in time and space in her own house. Darlene Purify stood at the window, her thousand-yard stare reaching far beyond the gray horizon. The TV babbled in the background, a talk show. Byrne thought about turning it off, but realized that the silence would be far worse. The TV indicated that life, somewhere, went on.

"Where do you want me, Darlene? You tell me, I go there."

Darlene Purify was just over forty, a former R&B singer in the 1980s, having even cut a few records with an all-girl group called La Rouge. Now her hair was platinum, her once slight figure given to time. "I stopped loving him a long time ago, Kevin. I don't even remember when. It's just . . . the *idea* of him that's missing. Jimmy. Gone. *Shit*."

Byrne walked across the room, held her. He stroked her hair, searching for words. He found some. "He was the best cop I ever knew. The *best*."

Darlene dabbed her eyes. Grief was such a heartless sculptor, Byrne thought. At that moment, Darlene looked a dozen years older than she was. He thought about the first time they had met, in such happy times. Jimmy had brought her to a Police Athletic League dance. Byrne had watched Darlene shake it up with Jimmy, wondering how a player like him ever landed a woman like her.

"He loved it, you know," Darlene said.

"The job?"

"Yeah. The job," Darlene said. "He loved it more than he ever loved me. Or even the kids, I think."

"That's not true. It's different, you know? Loving the job is . . . well . . . *different*. I spent every day with him after the divorce. A lot of nights, too. Believe me, he missed you more than you'll ever know."

Darlene looked at him, as if this were the most incredible thing she had ever heard. "He did?"

"You kidding? You remember that mono-grammed hankie? The little one of yours with the flowers in the corner? The one you gave him on your first date?"

"What . . . what about it?"

"He never went out on a tour without it. In fact, we were halfway to Fishtown one night, heading to a stakeout, and we had to head back to the Roundhouse because he forgot it. And believe me, you didn't give him lip about it."

Darlene laughed, then covered her mouth and began to cry again. Byrne didn't know if he was making it better or worse. He put his hand on her shoulder until her sobbing began to subside. He searched his memory for a story, any story. For some reason, he wanted to keep Darlene talking. He didn't know why, but he felt that, if she was talking, she wouldn't grieve.

"Did I ever tell you about the time Jimmy went undercover as a gay prostitute?"

"Many times." Darlene smiled now, through the salt. "Tell me again, Kevin."

"Well, we were working a reverse sting, right? Middle of summer. Five detectives on the detail, and Jimmy's number was up to be the bait. We laughed about it for a week beforehand, right? Like, who the hell was ever gonna believe that big slab of pork was sellin' it? Forget sellin' it, who the hell was gonna *buy*?"

Byrne told her the rest of the story by rote. Darlene smiled at all the right places, laughed her sad laugh at the end. Then she melted into Byrne's big arms and he held her for what seemed like minutes, waving off a few cops who had shown up to pay their respects. Finally he asked: "Do the boys know?"

Darlene wiped her eyes. "Yeah. They'll be in tomorrow."

Byrne squared himself in front of her. "If you need anything, anything at all, you pick up the phone. Don't even look at the clock."

"Thanks, Kevin."

"And don't worry about the arrangements. The association's all over it. It's gonna be a procession like the pope."

Byrne looked at Darlene. The tears came again. Kevin Byrne held her close, felt her heart racing. Darlene was tough, having survived both her parents' slow deaths from lingering illness. It was the boys he worried about. None of them had their mother's backbone. They were sensitive kids, very close to each other, and Byrne knew that one of his jobs, in the next few weeks, would be shoring up the Purify family.

When Byrne walked out of Darlene's house, he had to look both ways on the street. He couldn't remember where he had parked the car. The headache was a sharp dagger between his eyes. He tapped his pocket. He still had full scrip of Vicodin.

You've got a full plate, Kevin, he thought. *Shape the hell up.*

He lit a cigarette, took a few moments, got his bearings. He looked at his pager. There were still three calls from Jimmy that he'd never returned.

There will be time.

He finally remembered that he had parked on a side street. By the time he reached the corner, the rain began again. Why not, he thought. Jimmy was gone. The sun dared not show its face. Not today.

All over the city—in diners and cabs and beauty parlors and boardrooms and church basements—people were talking about the Rosary Killer, about how a madman was feasting on the young girls of Philadelphia, and how the police couldn't stop him. For the first time in his career, Byrne felt impotent, thoroughly inadequate, an impostor, as if he couldn't look at his paycheck with any sense of pride or dignity.

He stepped into the Crystal Coffee Shop, a twenty-four-hour spoon he had frequented many mornings with Jimmy. There was a pall over the regulars. They'd heard the news. He grabbed a paper and a large coffee, wondering if he'd ever be back. When he exited, he saw that someone was leaning against his car.

It was Jessica.

The emotion almost took his legs.

This kid, he thought. *This kid is something.*

"Hey there," she said.

"Hey."

"I was sorry to hear about your partner."

"Thanks," Byrne said, trying to keep it all in check. "He was . . . he was one of a kind. You would've liked him."

"Is there anything I can do?"

She had a way about her, Byrne thought. A way that made questions like that sound sincere, not like the bullshit that people say just to go on record.

"No," Byrne said. "Everything's under control."

"If you want to take the day . . ."

Byrne shook his head. "I'm good."

"You sure?" Jessica asked.

"Hundred percent."

Jessica held up the *Rosarium* letter.

"What's that?" Byrne asked.

"I think it's the key to our guy's mind."

Jessica briefed him on what she had learned, along with details of her meeting with Eddie Kasalonis. As she talked, she saw a number of things crawl across Kevin Byrne's face. Two of them mattered most.

Respect for her as a detective.

And, more importantly, determination.

"There's somebody we should talk to before we brief the team," Jessica said. "Somebody who could put this all in perspective."

Byrne turned and looked once, briefly, toward Jimmy Purify's house. He turned back and said: "Let's rock."

They sat with Father Corrio at a small table near the front window of Anthony's, a coffeehouse on Ninth Street in South Philly.

"There are twenty mysteries of the rosary in all," Father Corrio said. "They are grouped into four groups. The Joyful, The Sorrowful, The Glorious, and the Luminous."

The notion that their doer was planning twenty murders was not lost on anyone at that table. Father Corrio didn't seem to think that was the case.

"Strictly speaking," he continued, "the mysteries are assigned days of the week. The Glorious Mysteries are observed on Sunday and Wednesday, the Joyful Mysteries on Monday and Saturday. The Luminous Mysteries, which are relatively new, are observed on Thursday."

"What about the Sorrowful?" Byrne asked.

"The Sorrowful Mysteries are observed on Tuesday and Friday. Sundays during Lent."

Jessica did the math in her head, counting back the days from the discovery of Bethany Price. It didn't fit the pattern of observance.

"The majority of the mysteries are celebratory," Father Corrio said. "They include the Annunciation, the baptism of Jesus, the Assumption, the resurrection of Christ. It is only the Sorrowful Mysteries that deal with suffering and death."

"And there are only five Sorrowful Mysteries, right?" Jessica asked.

"Yes," Father Corrio said. "But keep in mind that the rosary is not universally accepted. There are objectors."

"How so?" Jessica asked.

"Well, there are those who find the rosary unecumenical."

"Not sure what you mean," Byrne said.

"The rosary celebrates Mary," Father Corrio said. "It venerates the mother of God, and some believe that the Marian character of the prayer does not glorify Christ."

"How does that apply to what we're facing here?"

Father Corrio shrugged. "Perhaps the man you seek does not believe in the virginal state of Mary. Perhaps he is, in his own sick way, trying to return these girls to God in such a state."

The thought sent a shudder through Jessica. If that was his motive, then when, and why, would he ever stop?

Jessica reached into her folio, held up the

photographs of the insides of Bethany Price's palms, the numbers 7 and 16.

"Do these numbers mean anything to you?" Jessica asked.

Father Corrio slipped on his bifocals, looked at the photos. It was apparent that the wounds caused by the drill through the young girl's hands were disturbing to him.

"It could be many things," Father Corrio said. "Nothing comes immediately to mind."

"I checked page seven hundred sixteen in the Oxford Annotated Bible," Jessica said. "It was in the middle of the book of Psalms. I read the text, but nothing jumped out."

Father Corrio nodded, but remained silent. It was clear that the book of Psalms, in this context, didn't strike a chord within him.

"What about a year? Does the year seven sixteen have any significance in the church that you know of?" Jessica asked.

Father Corrio smiled. "I minored in English, Jessica," he said. "I'm afraid that history was not my best subject. Outside of knowing that Vatican One was convened in 1869, I'm not much good on dates."

Jessica went through the scribbled notes

she had taken the night before. She was running out of ideas.

"Did you happen to find a scapular on this girl by any chance?" Father Corrio asked.

Byrne went through his notes. A scapular was essentially two small, square pieces of woolen cloth connected to each other by two strings or bands. It was worn in such a way that, when the bands rested on the shoulders, one segment rested in the front, while the other rested in the back. Usually, scapulars were given as a gift for the first communion—a gift set that often included a rosary, a chalice-and-host pin, and a satin bag.

"Yes," Byrne said. "She had a scapular around her neck when she was found."

"Is it a brown scapular?"

Byrne scanned his notes again. "Yes."

"You might want to look closely at it," Father Corrio said.

Quite often, scapulars were encased in clear plastic to protect them, as was the one found on Bethany Price. Her scapular had already been dusted for prints. None had been found. "Why is that, Father?"

"Every year there is a feast of the Scapular, a day devoted to Our Lady of Mount Carmel. It is the anniversary of the day the Blessed Virgin appeared to Saint Simon Stock and presented him with a monk's scapular. She told him that whoever wore it would not suffer eternal fire."

"I don't understand," Byrne said. "Why is that relevant?"

Father Corrio said: "The Feast of the Scapular is celebrated on July 16th."

The scapular found on Bethany Price was indeed a brown scapular, dedicated to Our Lady of Mount Carmel. Byrne phoned the lab and asked if they had opened the clear plastic case. They had not.

Byrne and Jessica headed back to the Roundhouse.

"You know, the possibility exists that we might not catch this guy," Byrne said. "He might get to his fifth victim, then crawl back into the slime forever."

The notion had crossed Jessica's mind. She had been trying not to think about it. "You think that might happen?"

"I hope not," Byrne said. "But I've been at

this a while. I just want you to be prepared for the possibility."

The possibility did not sit well with her. If this man was not caught, she knew that, for the rest of her career in the Homicide Unit, for the rest of her time in law enforcement, she would judge every case by what she would consider a failure.

Before Jessica could respond, Byrne's cell phone rang. He answered. Within seconds, he closed the phone, reached into the backseat for the deck strobe light. He put it on the dash and lighted it.

"What's up?" Jessica asked.

"They opened the scapular and dusted the inside," he said. He slammed the gas pedal to the floor. "We've got a print."

They waited on a bench outside the print lab.

There are all kinds of waiting in police work. There's the stakeout variety, the verdict variety. There's the type of waiting when you show up in a municipal courtroom to testify in some bullshit DUI case at nine in the morning, only to get on the stand for two minutes at three in the afternoon, just in time to start your tour at four.

But waiting for a print to come up was the best and the worst waiting. You had evidence, but the longer it took, the more likely it was that you would not get a usable match.

Byrne and Jessica tried to get comfortable. There were a number of other things they could be doing in the meantime, but they were bound and determined to do none of them. Their main objective, at the moment, was to keep both blood pressure and pulse rate down.

"Can I ask you something?" Jessica asked.

"Sure."

"If you don't want to talk about it, I totally understand."

Byrne looked at her, his green eyes nearly black. She had never seen a man look quite so exhausted.

"You want to know about Luther White," he said.

"Well. Yeah," Jessica said. Was she that transparent? "Kinda."

Jessica had asked around. Detectives were protective of their own. The bits and pieces she had heard added up to a pretty crazy story. She figured she'd just ask.

"What do you want to know?" Byrne asked.

Every last detail. "Whatever you want to tell me."

Byrne slid down on the bench a little, arranged his weight. "I had been on the job about five years or so, in plain clothes for about two. There had been a series of rapes in West Philly. The doer's MO was to hang out in the parking lots of places like motels, hospitals, office buildings. He'd strike in the middle of the night, usually between three and four in the morning."

Jessica vaguely remembered. She was in ninth grade, and the story scared the hell out of her and her friends.

"The doer wore a nylon stocking over his face, rubber gloves, and he always wore a condom. Never left a hair, a fiber. Not a drop of fluid. We had nothing. Eight women over a three-month period and we had zero. The only description we had, other than the guy was white and somewhere between thirty and fifty, was that he had a tattoo on the front of his neck. An elaborate tattoo of an eagle that went all the way up to the base of his jaw. We interviewed every tat parlor between Pittsburgh and Atlantic City. Nothing.

"So one night I'm out with Jimmy. We had just taken down a suspect in Old City and were still suited up. We stopped for a quick one at this place called Deuces, out by Pier Eighty-four. We were just getting ready to leave when I see that a guy at one of the tables by the door is wearing a white turtleneck, pulled high. I don't think anything of it right away, but as I walk out the door I turn around for some reason, and I see it. The tip of a tattoo peeking out over the top of the turtleneck. An eagle's beak. Couldn't have been more than a half-inch, right? It was him."

"Did he see you?"

"*Oh* yeah," Byrne said. "So me and Jimmy just leave. We huddle outside, right by this low stone wall that's right next to the river, figuring we'd call it in, seeing as we just had a few and we didn't want anything to get in the way of us putting this fucker away. This is before cell phones, so Jimmy heads to the car to call for backup. I decide I'm going to go stand next to the door, figuring, if this guy tries to leave, I'll get the drop on him. But as soon as I turn around, there he is. And he's got this twenty-two pointed right at my heart."

"How did he make you?"

"No idea. But without a word, without hesitation, he unloads. Fired three shots, rapid succession. I took them all in the vest, but they knocked the wind out of me. His fourth shot grazed my forehead." At this, Byrne fingered the scar over his right eye. "I went back, over the wall, into the river. I couldn't breathe. The slugs had cracked two ribs, so I couldn't even *try* to swim. I just started to sink to the bottom, like I was paralyzed. The water was cold as hell."

"What happened to White?"

"Jimmy took him down. Two to the chest."

Jessica tried to wrap her mind around the images, the nightmare every cop has of facing down a two-time loser with a weapon.

"As I was sinking, I saw White hit the surface above me. I swear, before I went unconscious, we had a moment when were face-to-face under the water. Inches apart. It was dark, and it was freezing, but we locked eyes. We were both dying, and we knew it."

"What happened next?"

"They fished me out, did CPR, the whole routine."

"I heard that you . . ." For some reason Jessica found it hard to say the word.

"Drowned?"

"Well, yeah. *That*. Did you?"

"So they tell me."

"Wow. How long were you, um . . ."

Byrne laughed. "Dead?"

"Sorry," Jessica said. "I can safely say that I've never asked that question before."

"Sixty seconds," Byrne replied.

"Wow."

Byrne looked over at Jessica. Her face was a press conference of questions.

Byrne smiled, asked: "You want to know if there were bright white lights and angels and golden trumpets and Roma Downey floating overhead, right?"

Jessica laughed. "I guess I do."

"Well, there was no Roma Downey. But there was a long hallway with a door at the end. I just knew that I shouldn't open the door. If I opened the door, I was never coming back."

"You just knew?"

"I just knew. And for a long time, after I got back, whenever I got to a crime scene, especially the scene of a homicide, I got a . . . *feeling*. The day after we found Deirdre Pettigrew's body, I went back to Fairmount Park. I touched the bench in front of the bushes where she was found. I saw Pratt. I didn't know his name, I couldn't see his face clearly, but I knew it was him. I saw how *she* saw him."

"You *saw* him?"

"Not in the visual sense. I just . . . knew." It was clear that none of this was easy for him. "It happened a lot for a long time," he said. "There was no explaining it. No predicting it. In fact, I did a lot of things I shouldn't have to try and get it to stop."

"How long were you IOD?"

"I was out for almost five months. Lots of rehab. That's where I met my wife."

"She was a physical therapist?"

"No, no. She was recovering from a torn Achilles tendon. I had actually met her years earlier in the old neighborhood, but we got reacquainted in the hospital. We hobbled up and down the hallways together. I'd say it was love at first Vicodin if it wasn't such a bad joke."

Jessica laughed anyway. "Did you ever

get any kind of professional psychiatric help?"

"Oh, yeah. I did two years with the department shrink, on and off. Went through dream analysis. Even went to a few IANDS meetings."

"IANDS?"

"International Association for Near Death Studies. Wasn't for me."

Jessica tried to take all this in. It was a lot. "So what's it like now?"

"It doesn't happen all that often these days. Kind of like a faraway TV signal. Morris Blanchard is proof that I can't be sure anymore."

Jessica could see that there was more to the story, but she felt as if she had pushed him enough.

"And, to answer your next question," Byrne continued. "I can't read minds, I can't tell fortunes, I can't see the future. No *Dead Zone* here. If I could see the future, believe me, I'd be at Philadelphia Park right now."

Jessica laughed again. She was glad she had asked, but she was still a little spooked by it all. She had always been a little spooked by stories of clairvoyance and the like. When she read *The Shining* she slept with the lights on for a week.

She was just about to try one of her clumsy segues to another topic when Ike Buchanan came blasting out of the door to the print lab. His face was flushed, the veins on his neck pulsed. For the moment, his limp was gone.

"Got him," Buchanan said, waving a computer readout.

Byrne and Jessica shot to their feet, fell into step beside him.

"Who is he?" Byrne asked.

"His name is Wilhelm Kreuz," Buchanan said.

5 8

According to DMV records, Wilhelm Kreuz lived on Kensington Avenue. He worked as a parking lot attendant in North Philly. The strike force headed to the location in two vehicles. Four members of the SWAT team rode in a black van. Four of the six detectives on the task force followed in a department car: Byrne, Jessica, John Shepherd, and Eric Chavez.

A few blocks from the location, a cell phone rang in the Taurus. All four detectives

checked their mobiles. It was John Shepherd's. "Yeah . . . how long . . . okay . . .
thanks." He slid the antenna, folded the
phone. "Kreuz hasn't been in to work for the
past two days. No one at the lot has seen
him or talked to him."

The detectives assimilated this, remained
silent. There is a ritual that attends hitting
the door, any door; a private interior monologue that is different for every law enforcement officer. Some fill the time with prayer.
Some, with blank silence. All of it intended
to cool the rage, calm the nerves.

They had learned more about their subject. Wilhelm Kreuz clearly fit the profile. He
was forty-two years old, a loner, a graduate
of the University of Wisconsin.

And although he had a long sheet, there
was nothing close to the level of violence or
the depth of depravity of the Rosary Girl
murders. Still, he was far from a model citi-
zen. Kreuz was a registered Level Two sex
offender, meaning he was considered a
moderate risk to re-offend. He had done a
six-year stint in Chester, registering with authorities in Philadelphia upon his release in
September 2002. He had a history of contact with minor females between the ages of

ten and fourteen. His victims were both known and unknown to him.

The detectives agreed that, although the victims of the Rosary Killer were older than the profile of Kreuz's previous victims, there was no logical explanation as to why his fingerprint would be found on a personal item belonging to Bethany Price. They had contacted Bethany Price's mother and asked if she knew Wilhelm Kreuz.

She did not.

Kreuz lived in a second-floor, three-room apartment in a dilapidated building near Somerset. The street entrance was beside the door to a long-shuttered dry cleaner. According to building department plans, there were four apartments on the second floor. According to the housing authority, only two were occupied. Legally, that is. The back door to the building emptied into an alley that ran the length of the block.

The target apartment was in the front, its two windows overlooking Kensington Avenue. A SWAT sharpshooter took a position across the street, on the roof of a three-story building. A second SWAT officer covered the rear of the building, deployed on the ground.

The remaining two SWAT officers would take down the door with a Thunderbolt CQB battering ram, the heavy cylindrical ram they used whenever a high-risk, dynamic entry was required. Once the door was breached, Jessica and Byrne would enter, with John Shepherd covering the rear flank. Eric Chavez was deployed at the end of the hall, next to the stairs.

They drilled the lock on the street door and gained entry in short order. As they filed across the small lobby, Byrne checked the row of four mailboxes. None was apparently in use. They had long ago been pried open, and never fixed. The floor was littered with scores of handbills, menus, and catalogs.

Above the mailboxes was a moldy cork-board. A few local enterprises barked their wares in fading dot matrix print, printed on curling, hot neon stock. The specials were dated nearly a year earlier. It seemed the people who hawked flyers in this neighbor-hood had long ago given up on this place. The lobby walls were scarred with gang tags and obscenities in at least four languages.

The stairwell up to the second floor was stacked with trash bags, ripped and scattered by a menagerie of urban animals, two- and four-legged alike. The stench of rotting food and urine was pervasive.

The second floor was worse. The heavy pall of sour pot smoke lounged beneath the smell of excrement. The second-floor corridor was a long, narrow walkway of exposed metal lath and dangling electrical wire. Peeling plaster and chipped enamel paint hung from the ceiling in damp stalactites.

Byrne stepped quietly up to the target door, placed his ear against it. He listened for a few moments, then shook his head. He tried the knob. Locked. He stepped away.

One of the two SWAT officers made eye contact with the entry team. The other SWAT officer, the one with the ram, got into position. He counted them silently down.

It was on.

"Police! Search warrant!" he yelled.

He drew back the ram then smashed it into the door, just below the lock. Instantly the old door splintered away from the jamb, then tore off at its upper hinge. The officer with the ram pulled back as the other SWAT officer rolled the jamb, his .223-caliber AR-15 rifle high.

Byrne was in next.

Jessica followed, her Glock 17 pointed low, at the floor.

The small living room was directly to the right. Byrne sidled up to the wall. They were first accosted by the smells of disinfectant, cherry incense, and moldering flesh. A pair of startled rats scurried against the near wall. Jessica noted dried blood on their graying snouts. Their claws clicked on the dry wood floor.

The apartment was sinister-quiet. Somewhere in the living room a spring clock ticked. There were no voices, no breathing.

Ahead was the unkempt living area. A stained gold crushed-velvet love seat, cushions on the floor. A few Domino's boxes, picked and chewed clean. A pile of filthy clothing.

No humans.

To the left, a door to what was probably the bedroom. It was closed. As they drew closer, from inside the room, they could hear the faint sounds of a radio broadcast. A gospel channel.

The SWAT officer got into position, his rifle high.

Byrne stepped up, touched the door. It was latched. He turned the knob slowly, then quickly pushed open the bedroom door, slid back. The radio was a little louder now.

"The Bible says without question-uh that one day everyone-uh will give an account of themselves-uh to God!"

Byrne made eye contact with Jessica. With a nod of his chin, he counted down. They rolled into the room.

And saw the inside of hell itself.

"Oh, Jesus," the SWAT officer said. He made the sign of the cross. "Oh Lord Jesus."

The bedroom held neither furniture nor furnishings of any kind. The walls were covered in peeling, water-stained floral wallpaper; the floor was dotted with dead insects, small bones, more fast-food trash. Cobwebs lined the corners; years of silken gray dust covered the baseboards. The small radio sat in the corner, near the front windows, windows covered with torn and mildewed bedsheets.

Inside the room were two occupants.

Against the far wall, a man was hung upside down on a makeshift cross, a cross that appeared to be fashioned from two pieces of a metal bed frame. His wrists, feet, and neck were bound to the frame with concertina wire that carved deep into his flesh. The man was naked and had been slit down the center of his body from his groin to his throat—fat, skin, and muscle were pulled to the sides to form a deep furrow. He was also slashed laterally across his chest, forming a cruciform shape of blood and shredded tissue.

Beneath him, at the base of the cross, sat a young girl. Her hair, which may have been blond at one time, was deep sienna. She was soaked with blood, a shiny pool of which had puddled in the lap of her denim skirt. The room was filled with the metallic taste of it. The girl's hands were bolted together. She held a rosary with only one decade of beads.

Byrne recovered from the sight first. There was still danger in this place. He slid along the wall opposite the window, peered into the closet. It was empty.

"*Clear,*" Byrne finally said.

And while any immediate threat, at least

from a living human being, was over, and the detectives could have holstered their weapons, they hesitated, as if they could somehow vanquish the profane vision in front of them by deadly force.

It was not to be.

The killer had come here and left in his wake this blasphemous tableau, a picture that would certainly live in all of their minds for as long as they drew breath.

A quick search of the bedroom closet yielded little. A pair of work uniforms, a pile of soiled underwear and socks. The two uniforms were from Acme Parking. Attached to the front of one of the work shirts was a photo ID tag. The tag identified the hanging man as Wilhelm Kreuz. The ID matched his mug shot.

At long last, the detectives holstered their weapons.

John Shepherd called for the CSU team.

"It's his name," the still-shaken SWAT officer said to Byrne and Jessica. The tag on the officer's dark blue BDU jacket read D. MAURER.

"What do you mean?" Byrne asked.

"My family is German," Maurer said, trying his best to compose himself. It was a difficult task for all of them. "*Kreuz* is *cross* in German. His name is William Cross in English."

The fourth Sorrowful Mystery is the carrying of the cross.

Byrne left the scene for a moment then quickly returned. He flipped through his notebook, looking for the list of young girls for whom missing-person reports had been filed. The reports contained photos as well. It didn't take long. He crouched down next to the girl, held a photograph by her face. The victim's name was Kristi Hamilton. She was sixteen. She lived in Nicetown.

Byrne stood up. He took in the horrific scene in front of him. In his mind, deep in the catacombs of his terror, he knew he would soon face this man, and they would both walk to the edge of the void together.

Byrne wanted to say something to the team, a squad he had been selected to lead, but he felt like anything but a leader at that moment. For the first time in his career, he found that no words would suffice.

On the floor, next to Kristi Hamilton's right leg, was a Burger King cup with a lid and a straw.

There were lip prints on the straw.
The cup was half full of blood.

Byrne and Jessica walked aimlessly, a block or so down Kensington, alone with images of the shrieking insanity of the crime scene. The sun made a brief, timid appearance between a pair of thick gray clouds, casting a rainbow over the street, but not over their moods.

They both wanted to talk.

They both wanted to scream.

They remained silent for now, the storm roiling inside.

The general public operated under the illusion that police officers can look at any scene, any event, and maintain a clinical detachment from it. Granted, the image of the untouchable heart was something a lot of cops cultivated. That image was for television and movies.

"He's laughing at us," Byrne said.

Jessica nodded. There was no doubt about it. He had led them to the Kreuz apartment with the planted print. The hardest part of this job, she was learning, was to relegate the desire for personal vengeance to the back of your mind. It was getting harder and harder.

The level of violence was escalating. The sight of Wilhelm Kreuz's eviscerated corpse told them that this would not end with a peaceful arrest. The Rosary Killer's rampage was going to end in a bloody siege.

They stood in front of the apartment, leaned against the CSU van.

After a few moments, one of the uniformed officers leaned out the window in Kreuz's bedroom.

"Detectives?"

"What's up?" Jessica asked.

"You might want to get up here."

The woman appeared to be in her late eighties. Her thick glasses prismed rainbows in the spare, incandescent light thrown by the two bare bulbs in the hallway ceiling. She stood just inside her door, leaning over an aluminum walker. She lived two doors down from Wilhelm Kreuz's apartment. She smelled like cat litter, Bengay, and kosher salami.

Her name was Agnes Pinsky.

The uniform said: "Tell this gentleman what you just told me, ma'am."

"Huh?"

Agnes wore a torn, sea-foam terry house-coat, buttoned a single button off. The left side hem was higher than the right, revealing knee-high support hose and a calf-length blue wool sock.

"When was the last time you saw Mr. Kreuz?" Byrne asked.

"Willy? He's always nice to me," she said.

"That's great," Byrne said. "When did you see him last?"

Agnes Pinsky looked from Jessica to Byrne, back. It seemed she just realized she was talking to strangers. "How did you find me?"

"We just knocked on your door, Mrs. Pinsky."

"Is he sick?"

"Sick?" Byrne asked. "Why do you say that?"

"His doctor was here."

"When was his doctor here?"

"Yesterday," she said. "His doctor came to see him yesterday."

"How do you know it was a doctor?"

"How do I *know*? Hell's a matter with you? I know what doctors look like. I don't have old timer's."

"Do you know what time the doctor came?"

Agnes Pinsky stared at Byrne for an uncomfortable amount of time. Whatever she had been talking about had slid back into the murky recesses of her mind. She had the look of someone waiting impatiently for her change at the post office.

They would send up a sketch artist, but the chances of getting a workable image were slim.

Still, from what Jessica knew about Alzheimer's and dementia, certain images were quite often razor sharp.

His doctor came to see him yesterday.

There was only one Sorrowful Mystery left, Jessica thought as she descended the steps.

Where would they go next? Into which neighborhood would they come with their guns and their battering rams? Northern Liberties? Glenwood? Tioga?

Into whose face would they peer, sullen and lost for words?

If they were late again, there was no doubt in any of their minds.

The last girl would be crucified.

Five of the six detectives gathered upstairs in the Lincoln Room at Finnigan's Wake. The room was theirs, closed off for the time being from the public. Downstairs, the juke played the Corrs.

"So, what, we're dealing with a fucking vampire now?" Nick Palladino asked. He stood at the tall windows overlooking Spring Garden Street. The Ben Franklin Bridge hummed in the distance. Palladino was a man who thought best on his feet, rocking on his heels, hands in pockets, jingling change.

"I mean, gimme a gangbanger," Nick went on. "Gimme a homeboy and his Mac-Ten, lighting up some other asshole over turf, over a short bag, over honor, code, whatever. I understand that shit. This?"

Everyone knew what he meant. It was so much easier when the motives hung on the exterior of the crime like a shingle. Greed was the easiest. Follow the green footprints.

Palladino was on a roll. "Payne and

Washington got the squeal on that JBM banger in Gray's Ferry the other night, right?" he continued. "Now I hear they found the shooter dead over on Erie. That's the way I like it, nice and neat."

Byrne shut his eyes for a second, opened them to a brand-new day.

John Shepherd came up the stairs. Byrne motioned to the waitress, Margaret. She brought John a Jim Beam, neat.

"The blood was all Kreuz's," Shepherd said. "The girl died from a broken neck. Just like the others."

"And the blood in the cup?" Tony Park asked.

"That belonged to Kreuz. The ME thinks that, before he bled out, he was fed the blood through the straw."

"He was fed his own blood," Chavez said on the tail of a full body-shiver. It wasn't a question; merely the stating of something too hard to comprehend.

"Yeah," Shepherd replied.

"It's official," Chavez said. "I've seen it all."

The six detectives absorbed this. The attendant horrors of the Rosary Killer case were growing exponentially.

"Drink of it, all of you; for this is my blood of covenant, which is poured out for many for the forgiveness of sins," Jessica said.

Five sets of eyebrows raised. Everyone turned their head toward Jessica.

"I've been doing a lot of reading," she said. "Holy Thursday was known as Maundy Thursday. This is the day of the Last Supper."

"So this Kreuz was our doer's Peter?" Palladino asked.

Jessica could only shrug. She had thought about it. The rest of the night would probably be spent tearing apart Wilhelm Kreuz's life, looking for any connection that might turn into a lead.

"Did she have anything in her hands?" Byrne asked.

Shepherd nodded. He held up a photo-copy of a digital photograph. The detectives gathered around the table. They took their turns examining the photo.

"What is it, a lottery ticket?" Jessica asked.

"Yeah," Shepherd said.

"Oh, that's fucking great," Palladino said. He walked back to the window, hands in pocket.

"Prints?" Byrne asked.

Shepherd shook his head.

"Can we find out where this ticket was purchased?" Jessica asked.

"Got a call into the commission already," Shepherd said. "We should hear from them anytime now."

Jessica stared at the photo. Their killer had placed a Big 4 ticket into the hands of his most recent victim. Chances were good that it was not simply a taunt. Like the other objects, it was a clue as to where the next victim would be found.

The lottery number itself was obscured by blood.

Did this mean he was going to dump the body at a lottery agent's location? There had to be hundreds. There was no way they could stake them all out.

"This guy's luck is unbelievable," Byrne said. "Four girls off the streets and not a single eyewitness. He's smoke."

"Do you think it's luck, or that we just live in a city where no one gives a shit anymore?" Palladino asked.

"If I believed that, I'd take my twenty today and head to Miami Beach," Tony Park said.

The other five detectives nodded.

At the Roundhouse, the task force had plotted out the abductions and the dump sites on a huge map. There was no clear pattern, no way to anticipate or discern the killer's next move. They had already regressed to the basics—serial murderers start close to home. Their killer lived or worked in North Philly.

Square one.

Byrne walked Jessica to her car.

They stood around for a short while, each rummaging for words. It was at times like these that Jessica wished she smoked. Her trainer at Frazier's Gym would kill her for the very thought, but it didn't stop her envying Byrne for the comfort he seemed to find in a Marlboro Light.

A barge lazily cruised up the river. Traffic moved in fits and starts. Philly lived, despite this madness, despite the grief and horror that had befallen these families.

"You know, no matter how this ends, it's going to be ugly," Byrne said.

Jessica knew this. She also knew that, before it was over, she would probably learn a large new truth about herself. She would probably uncover a dark recess of fear and rage and anguish that she would just as soon leave undiscovered. As much as she wanted to disbelieve it, she was going to emerge from the end of this passage a different person. She hadn't planned on this when she agreed to take the job but, like a runaway train, she found herself speeding toward the chasm, and there was no way to stop.

PART FOUR

GOOD FRIDAY, 10:00 AM

The drug nearly took off the top of her head.

The rush slammed into the back of her skull, ricocheted around for a while, in time to the music, then sawed at her neck in jagged up and down triangles, the way you might cut the lid off a pumpkin at Halloween.

"Righteous," Lauren said.

Lauren Semanski was failing two of her six classes at Nazarene. If threatened with a gun, even after two years of algebra, she couldn't tell you what the quadratic equation was. She wasn't even sure the quadratic equation *was* algebra. Maybe it was geometry. And even though her family was Polish, she couldn't point to Poland on a map. She tried once, landing her glitter-polished nail somewhere south of Lebanon. She had gotten five tickets in the past three months, both the digital clock and the VCR in her bedroom had been flashing 12:00 for nearly two years, and the one time she tried to bake a birthday cake for her little sister Caitlin, she had nearly burned down the house.

At sixteen, Lauren Semanski—and she might be the first to admit this—didn't know a whole lot about a whole lot of things.

But she did know good meth.

"Krypto*nite*." She dropped the tooter on the coffee table, leaned back against the couch. She felt like howling. She glanced around the room. Wiggers everywhere. Someone cranked up the music. Sounded like Billy Corgan. Pumpkins were old-school cool. Zwan sucked.

"Low-*rent!*" Jeff yelled, barely audible above the music, using his stupid nickname for her, ignoring her wishes for the millionth time. He air-guitared a few choice licks, drooling on his Mars Volta T-shirt, grinning like a hyena.

God, what a queer, Lauren thought. *Cute, but geek-a-roni.* "Gotta jet," she yelled.

"Naw, come *on,* Lo." He held out the tooter to her, like she hadn't already snorted an entire Rite-Aid.

"I can't." She was supposed to be at the grocery store. She was supposed to be picking up a cherry glaze for the stupid Easter ham. As if she needed food. Who needed food? No one she knew. Still, she had to fly. "She'll kill me if I forget to go to the store."

Jeff made a face, then bent over the glass coffee table and ripped a line. He was gone. She was hoping for a kiss good-bye, but when he leaned back from the table, she saw his eyes.

North.

Lauren stood, gathered her purse and her umbrella. She looked around the obstacle course of bodies, reposing in various states of hyper-consciousness. The windows were blacked out with construction paper. All the lamps held red lightbulbs.

She'd be back later.

Jeff had enough for all tweak-end *long*.

She stepped into the street, her Ray-Bans firmly in place. It was still raining—would it ever stop?—but even the overcast sky was a little too bright for her. Besides, she dug the way the sunglasses made her look. Sometimes, she wore them at night. Sometimes, she wore them to bed.

She cleared her throat, swallowed. The burn of the meth at the back of her throat gave her a second charge.

She was *way* too gakked to go home. Anyway, it was Baghdad there these days. She didn't need the grief.

She pulled out her Nokia, trying to think of an excuse she could use. All she needed was an hour or so to come down. Car trouble? Seeing as the VW was in the shop, that wouldn't fly. Sick friend? Please, Lo. Grandma B would ask for notes from the doctors at this point. What hadn't she used for a while? Not much. She had been at Jeff's maybe four days a week for the past month. Late almost every day.

I know, she thought. *I've got it.*

Sorry, Grams. I can't make it home for lunch. I've been kidnapped.

Ha-ha. Like she'd give a shit.

Ever since Lauren's parents had done the real crash test dummy scene last year, she had been living with the living dead.

Fuck it. She'd go deal with it.

She window-shopped a little, lifting the sunglasses to see. The 'Bans were cool and all, but *man* were they dark.

She cut across the parking lot behind the stores at the corner of her street, steeling herself for the onslaught that was her grandmother.

"Hi, Lauren!" someone yelled.

She turned around. Who called her? She glanced around the lot. She didn't see anyone, just a handful of cars, a couple of vans. She tried to place the voice, couldn't.

"Hello?" she said.

Silence.

She backtracked between a van and a beer delivery truck. She took off her sunglasses, looked around, turning 360.

The next thing she knew, there was a hand over her mouth. At first she thought it was Jeff, but even Jeff wouldn't take a joke this far. This was *so* not funny. She struggled to get herself free, but whoever was playing this (not at all) hilarious joke on her was strong. Really strong.

She felt a needle in her left arm.

Huh? *Oh, that's it, fucker,* she thought.

She was just about to go Vin Diesel on this guy when, instead, her legs wobbled, and she fell against the van. She tried to stay alert as she slid to the ground. Something was happening to her and she wanted to catalogue everything in her mind. When the cops busted this fucker—and bust this fucker they most assuredly would—she was going to be the best witness ever. First of all, he smelled clean. A little too clean if you asked her. Plus, he had on rubber gloves.

Not a good sign, *CSI*-wise.

The weakness made its way up to her stomach, her chest, her throat.

Fight it, Lauren.

She had taken her first drink at the age of nine, when her older cousin Gretchen had slipped her a wine cooler at the Fourth of July fireworks at Boat House Row. It was love at first buzz. Since that day she had ingested every substance known to humankind and a few that may have only been known to extraterrestrials. She could handle whatever was in that needle. The world going wah-wah pedal and rubbery around the edges was old shit. She once drove home from AC while she was one-eyed drunk on Jack and nursing a three-day amp.

She blanked.

She came back.

Now she was on her back in the van. Or was it an SUV? Either way, they were moving. Fast. Her head was swimming, but it wasn't a *good* swimming. It was like that *three in the morning and I shouldn't have done the X and the Nardil* swimming.

She was cold. She pulled the sheet over her. It wasn't really a sheet. It was a shirt or a coat or something.

From the far reaches of her consciousness, she heard her cell phone ring. She heard it chime its stupid Korn ring tone and it was just in her pocket and all she had to do was answer it like she had a billion other times and tell her grandmother to call the fucking cops and this guy would be *so* busted.

But she couldn't move. Her arms felt like they weighed a ton.

The phone rang again. He reached over and began wiggling the phone from her jeans pocket. Her jeans were tight and he was having a hard time getting the phone out. *Good*. She wanted to grab his arm, to stop him, but she seemed to be moving in slow motion. He worked the Nokia out of her pocket, slowly, keeping the other hand on the wheel, every so often glancing back at the road.

From somewhere deep inside her, Lauren felt her anger and rage begin to grow, a volcanic swell of fury that told her that if she didn't do something, and soon, she wasn't going to get out of this alive. She pulled the jacket up over her chin. She was so cold, suddenly. She felt something in one of the pockets. A pen? Probably. She took it out and gripped it as tightly as she could.

Like a knife.

When he finally got the phone out of her jeans, she knew she had to make her move. As he pulled away, she swung her fist in a huge arc, the pen catching him on the back of his right hand, the tip snapping off. He shrieked as the vehicle swerved, left, then right, tossing her body against one wall, then the other. They must have gone over a curb, because she was abruptly thrown into the air, then came crashing back down. She heard a loud click, then felt a huge rush of air.

The side door was open, but they were still moving.

She felt the cool, damp air swirl around the inside of the vehicle, bringing with it the smell of exhaust fumes and just-mowed grass. The rush revived her a bit, tamed the rising nausea. Somewhat. Then Lauren felt the drug he had injected her with grab hold again. She was still flying on the meth, too. But whatever he had shot her up with made her mind swim, dulling her senses.

The wind continued to whip around. The earth screamed by, just beyond her feet. It reminded her of the twister in *The Wizard of Oz.* Or the twister in *Twister.*

They were driving even faster now. Time receded for a moment, then returned. She looked up just as the man reached for her again. He had something in his hand this time, something metallic and shiny. A gun? A knife? No. It was *so* hard to concentrate. Lauren tried to focus on the object. The wind blew dust and debris around the inside of the vehicle, clouding her vision, stinging her eyes. Then she saw the hypodermic needle coming at her. The needle looked huge and sharp and deadly. She couldn't let him stick her again.

Couldn't.

Lauren Semanski summoned the last scrap of her courage.

She sat up, felt the strength gather in her legs.

She pushed off.

And found that she could fly.

60

The Philadelphia Police department labored beneath the microscope of the national media. The three networks, as well as Fox and CNN, had camera crews set up all over town and were running updates three or four times per cycle.

The local television news ran the Rosary Killer story in heavy rotation, complete with its own logo and theme music. They also featured a listing of Catholic churches offering Good Friday masses, as well as a handful that were holding prayer vigils for the victims.

Catholic families, especially those with daughters—whether they attended parochial schools or not—were proportionately terrified. Police expected a heavy increase in stranger shootings. Mail carriers, FedEx and UPS drivers were at particular risk. As were people with whom others had a grudge.

I thought he was the Rosary Killer, Your Honor.

I had to shoot him.

I've got a daughter.

The department held the news of Brian Parkhurst's death from the media as long as they could, but it eventually leaked, like it always does. The district attorney had addressed the media gathered in front of 1421 Arch Street and, when asked if there was evidence that Brian Parkhurst was the Rosary Killer, she had to tell them no. Parkhurst had been a material witness.

And so the carousel spun.

The news of the fourth victim brought them all out of the woodwork. As Jessica approached the Roundhouse, she saw a few dozen people with cardboard signs milling around the sidewalk on Eighth Street, most of their sentiments proclaiming the end of the world. Jessica thought she saw the names JEZEBEL and MAGDALENE on a few of the signs.

Inside it was worse. As much as they all knew that no credible leads would come out of it, they had to take all their statements. B-movie Rasputins, the requisite Jasons and Freddys. Then there were the ersatz Hannibals, Gacys, Dahmers, and Bundys to deal with. In all, there had been more than one hundred confessions.

Up in the Homicide Unit, as Jessica began to gather her notes for the task force meeting, a rather shrill female laugh from across the room drew her attention.

What kind of lunatic is this? she wondered.

She looked up, and what she saw stopped her in her tracks. It was the blond girl in the ponytail and leather jacket. The girl she had seen with Vincent. Here. In the Roundhouse. Although now that Jessica got a good look at her, it was clear that she was not nearly as young as she had originally thought. Still, seeing her in this setting was completely surreal.

"What the hell is *this*?" Jessica said, loud enough for Byrne to hear. She tossed her notebooks on the assignment desk.

"What?" Byrne asked.

"You've got to be kidding me," she said. She tried, and failed, to calm herself. "This . . . *bitch* has the balls to come down here and get in my *face*?"

Jessica took a step forward, and her posture must have taken on a certain menace, because Byrne stepped between her and the woman.

"Whoa," Byrne said. "Hang on. What are you talking about?"

"Let me by, Kevin."

"Not until you tell me what's going on."

"That's the bitch I saw with Vincent the other day. I can't believe she—"

"Who, the blonde?"

"Yeah. She's the—"

"That's Nicci Malone."

"Who?"

"Nicolette Malone."

Jessica processed the name, came up with nothing. "This is supposed to mean something to me?"

"She's a narcotics detective. She works out of Central."

Something suddenly dislodged in Jessica's chest, an ice floe of shame and guilt that chilled her. Vincent had been on the job. The blond woman was someone he *worked* with.

Vincent had tried to tell her, and she wouldn't listen. Once again, she had made a Grade-A asshole out of herself.

Jealousy, thy name is Jessica.

The task force prepared to meet.

The discovery of Kristi Hamilton and Wilhelm Kreuz had brought a call to the Homicide Unit from the FBI. The task force was scheduled to convene the following day with a pair of agents from the Philadelphia field office. The jurisdictional considerations of these crimes had been in question since the discovery of Tessa Wells, given the very real possibility that all of the victims were kidnapped, which made at least part of the crimes federal. The usual territorial objections were voiced, as expected, but none too vehemently. The truth was the task force needed all the help it could get. The

Rosary Girl murders had escalated so rapidly, and now, with the murder of Wilhelm Kreuz, promised to expand into areas the PPD was simply not equipped to deal with.

The Crime Scene Unit had half a dozen technicians in Kreuz's Kensington Avenue apartment alone.

At eleven thirty Jessica retrieved her e-mail.

In her mailbox were a few pieces of spam, along with a few pieces of e-mail from GTA knuckleheads she had put away in the Auto Squad, relaying the same invectives, the same promises to see her again one day.

Amid the same-old, same-old there was one message from sclose@thereport.com.

She had to look at the sender's address twice. She was right. Simon Close at *The Report*.

Jessica shook her head at the enormity of the brass on this guy. Why on earth would this piece of shit think she wanted to hear anything he had to say?

She was just about to delete it when she saw that there was an attachment. She ran it by the virus program and it came back clean. *Probably the only clean thing about Simon Close.*

Jessica opened the attachment. It was a color photograph. At first, she had trouble recognizing the man in the photograph. She wondered why Simon Close would be sending her a picture of some guy she didn't know. Of course, if she understood the mind of a tabloid hack to begin with, she would start to worry about herself.

The man in the photograph was sitting in a chair, with duct tape wrapped around his chest. There was also duct tape around his forearms and wrists, securing him to the arms of the chair. The man had his eyes tightly closed, as if he might be anticipating a blow, or as if he were wishing very hard for something.

Jessica blew up the picture to twice its size.

And saw that the man didn't have his eyes closed at all.

"Oh, *Christ,*" she said.

"What?" Byrne asked.

Jessica turned the monitor to face him.

The man in the chair was Simon Edward Close, star reporter for Philadelphia's leading shock tabloid, *The Report*. Someone had taped him to a dining room chair and sewn both of his eyes shut.

When Byrne and Jessica approached the apartment on City Line, there was already a pair of homicide detectives on the scene. Bobby Lauria and Ted Campos.

When they entered the apartment, Simon Close was in precisely the same position he was in the photograph.

Bobby Lauria briefed Byrne and Jessica on what they knew.

"Who found him?" Byrne asked.

Lauria looked through his notes. "Friend of his. A guy named Chase. They were supposed to meet for breakfast at a Denny's on City Line. The victim didn't show. Chase called twice, then stopped over to see if something was wrong. Door was open, he called nine-one-one."

"Did you check the phone records from the pay phone at Denny's?"

"Didn't need to," Lauria said. "Both calls were on the vic's answering machine. The caller ID matched the phone at Denny's. He's legit."

"This is the POS you had the problem with last year, right?" Campos asked.

Byrne knew why he was asking, just like he knew what was coming. "Yeah."

The digital camera that took the picture was still on the tripod in front of Close. A CSU officer was dusting the camera and the tripod.

"Check this out," Campos said. He knelt next to the coffee table and, with his gloved hand, maneuvered the mouse attached to Close's laptop. He opened the iPhoto program. There were sixteen photographs, each of them titled, successively, KEVINBYRNE1.JPG, KEVINBYRNE2.JPG, and so forth. Except none of the photographs were comprehensible. It seemed as if each one had been run through a paint program and had been defaced with a drawing tool. A drawing tool colored red.

Both Campos and Lauria looked at Byrne. "Gotta ask, Kevin," Campos said.

"I know," Byrne said. They wanted his whereabouts for the past twenty-four. Neither of them suspected him of a thing, but they had to get it out of the way. Byrne, of course, knew the drill. "I'll lay it out in a statement back at the house."

"No problem," Lauria said.

"Got a cause yet?" Byrne asked, happy to change the subject.

Campos stood up, walked behind the victim. There was a small hole at the base of Simon Close's neck. It was probably caused by a drill bit.

As the CSU officers did their thing, it was clear that whoever had sewn Close's eyes shut—and there was little doubt as to who that was—had not gone for quality of workmanship. The thick black thread alternated from piercing the soft skin of the eyelid to an inch or so down the cheek. Thin rivulets of blood had trickled down the face, giving him a Christ-like visage.

Both skin and flesh were pulled tight, in an upward direction, dragging up the soft tissue around Close's mouth, exposing his incisors.

Close's upper lip was pulled up, but his teeth were together. From a few feet away, Byrne noticed that there was something black and shiny just behind the man's front teeth.

Byrne took out a pencil, gestured to Campos.

"Help yourself," Campos said.

Byrne took the pencil and gently leveraged Simon Close's teeth slightly apart. For a moment, his mouth appeared empty, as if what Byrne thought he saw was a reflection in the man's bubbled saliva.

Then a solitary item fell out, rolling down Close's chest, over his lap, and onto the floor.

The sound it made was slight, a thin plastic click on the hardwood.

Jessica and Byrne watched it roll to a stop.

They looked at each other, the significance of what they were seeing registering at the same moment. A second later, the rest of the missing rosary beads tumbled out of the dead man's mouth like a slot machine paying off.

Ten minutes later, they had counted the rosary beads, carefully avoiding contact with the surfaces, lest they disturb what might be a usable shred of forensic evidence, although the probability of the Rosary Killer tripping himself up at this point was low.

They counted twice, just to be sure. The significance of the number of beads that had been stuffed into Simon Close's mouth was not lost on anyone in the room.

There were fifty beads. All five decades.

And that meant that the rosary for the last girl in this madman's passion play had already been prepared.

FRIDAY, 1:25 PM

At noon, Brian Parkhurst's Ford Windstar was found parked at an indoor garage a few blocks from the building in which he was found hanged. The Crime Scene Unit had spent the early afternoon combing it for trace evidence. There was no blood evidence, nor any indication that any of the murder victims had been transported in the vehicle. The carpeting was a bronze in color and did not match the carpet fibers found on the first four victims.

The glove compartment held the expected—registration, owner's manual, a pair of maps.

It was the letter they found in the visor that was most interesting, a letter containing the typewritten names of ten girls. Four of the names were already familiar to police. Tessa Wells, Nicole Taylor, Bethany Price, and Kristi Hamilton.

The envelope was addressed to Detective Jessica Balzano.

There was little debate about whether the killer's next victim would come from the ranks of the remaining six names.

There was much room for debate about why these names were in the late Dr. Parkhurst's possession, and what it all meant.

FRIDAY, 2:45 PM

The white board was divided into five columns. At the top of each was a Sorrowful Mystery. AGONY, SCOURGE, CROWN, CARRY, CRUCIFIXION. Beneath each heading, except for the last, was a photograph of the respective victim.

Jessica briefed the team on what she had learned from her research, from Eddie Kasalonis as well as what Father Corrio had told her and Byrne.

"The Sorrowful Mysteries are the last

week in Christ's life," Jessica said. "And, although the victims were discovered out of order, our doer seems to be following the strict order of the mysteries.

"As I'm sure you all know, today is Good Friday, the day Christ was crucified. There is only one mystery left. The crucifixion."

A sector car had been assigned to every Catholic church in the city. By three twenty-five, incident reports had come in from all corners. The three o'clock hour—noon to three were the hours it is believed that Christ hung upon the cross—had passed at all Catholic churches without episode.

By four o'clock they had gotten in contact with all the families of the girls on the list found in Brian Parkhurst's car. All the remaining girls were accounted for and, without causing undue panic, the families were told to be on guard. A car was dispatched to each of the girls' houses for protection detail.

Why these girls were on the list, and what they had in common to get on the list was still unknown. The task force had tried to cross-reference the girls based on the clubs they belonged to, the churches they attended, eye and hair color, ethnicity; nothing leapt off the page.

Each of the six detectives on the task force would visit one of the six girls left on the list. The answer to the riddle of these horrors, they were certain, would be found with them.

6 3

The Semanski house sat between two vacant lots on a dying street in North Philly.

Jessica spoke briefly to the two officers parked out front, then walked up the sagging steps. The inside door was open, the screen door unlatched. Jessica knocked. After a few seconds, a woman approached. She was in her early sixties. She wore a pilled blue cardigan and well-worn black cotton slacks.

"Mrs. Semanski? I'm Detective Balzano. We spoke on the phone."

"Oh yes," the woman said. "I'm Bonnie. Please come in."

Bonnie Semanski opened the screen door and let her in.

The interior of the Semanski house seemed cast from another era. There were probably a few valuable antiques in here, Jessica thought, but to the Semanski family they were most likely seen as functioning articles of furniture that were still good, so why throw them away?

To the right was a small living room with a worn sisal rug in the center and a grouping of old waterfall furniture. Sitting in a recliner was a gaunt man in his sixties. On a folding metal TV tray table next to him were a variety of amber pill bottles and a pitcher of iced tea. He was watching a hockey game, but it appeared as if he was looking near the television, not at it. He glanced over at Jessica. Jessica smiled, and the man lifted a slight arm to wave.

Bonnie Semanski led Jessica to the kitchen.

"Lauren should be home any minute now. She's off school today, of course," Bonnie said. "She's visiting friends."

They were sitting at a red-and-white chrome-and-Formica dinette set. Like everything else about the row house, the kitchen seemed a 1960s vintage. The only things that brought it into the present were a small white microwave and an electric can opener. It was clear that the Semanskis were Lauren's grandparents, not her parents.

"Did Lauren call home at all today?"

"No," Bonnie said. "I called her a little while ago on her cell phone, but all I got was her voice mail. She turns it off sometimes."

"You said on the phone that she left the house around eight this morning?"

"Yes. That's about right."

"Do you know where she was headed?"

"She went to visit with some friends," Bonnie repeated, as if this were her mantra of denial.

"Do you know their names?"

Bonnie just shook her head. It was obvious that, whoever these "friends" were, Bonnie Semanski did not approve.

"Where are her mom and dad?" Jessica asked.

"They were killed in a car accident last year."

"I'm sorry," Jessica said.

"Thank you."

Bonnie Semanski looked out the window. The rain had eased to a steady drizzle. At first Jessica thought the woman might cry, but with a closer look she realized that this woman had probably shed all her tears a long time ago. The sorrow, it seemed, had settled to the bottom half of her heart, and could not be disturbed.

"Can you tell me what happened to her parents?" Jessica asked.

"A week before Christmas, last year, Nancy and Carl were coming home from Nancy's part-time job at the Home Depot. They were hiring for the holidays, you know. Not like now," she said. "It was late and really dark. Carl must have been going a little too fast around a turn and the car slid off the road and went down into a ravine. They say they didn't linger in death."

Jessica was a bit surprised that this woman didn't tear up. She imagined that Bonnie Semanski had told this story to enough people, enough times, that she had gained some distance from it.

"Did Lauren take it very hard?" Jessica asked.

"Oh yes."

Jessica scribbled a note, noting the time line.

"Does Lauren have a boyfriend?"

Bonnie gave the question a dismissive wave of her hand. "I can't keep up with them, there are so many."

"What do you mean?"

"They're always coming around. All hours. They look like homeless people."

"Do you know if anyone has threatened Lauren lately?"

"Threatened?"

"Anyone she might have had a problem with. Someone who may have been bothering her."

Bonnie thought for a moment. "No. I don't think so."

Jessica jotted a few more notes. "Would it be okay if I took a quick look at Lauren's room?"

"Sure."

Lauren Semanski's room was at the top of the stairs, at the back end of the house. On the door was a faded sticker that said BE-WARE: SPUN MONKEY ZONE. Jessica knew enough drug terms to know that Lauren Semanski was probably not out "visiting friends" in order to organize a church picnic.

Bonnie opened the door, and Jessica stepped into the room. The furniture was quality, French provincial in style, white with gold accents; a four-poster bed, matching nightstands, dresser, and desk. The room was painted a lemon yellow, long and narrow, with a sloped ceiling that met knee walls on either side, a window at the far end. On the right were built-in bookshelves, to the left, a pair of doors cut into the half wall, presumably a storage area. The walls were covered in posters for rock bands.

Mercifully, Bonnie left Jessica alone in the room. Jessica didn't really want her looking over her shoulder when she went through Lauren's belongings.

On the desk were a series of photographs in inexpensive frames. A school shot of Lauren at about nine or ten. One was of Lauren and a scruffy teenaged boy, standing in front of the art museum. One was a magazine shot of Russell Crowe.

Jessica poked through the drawers in the dresser. Sweaters, socks, jeans, shorts. Nothing significant. Her closet yielded the same. Jessica closed the closet door, leaned against it, surveyed the room. *Think.* Why was Lauren Semanski on that list? Other than the fact that she attended a Catholic school, what was in this room that would fit into the puzzle of these bizarre deaths?

Jessica sat down at Lauren's computer, checked the bookmarks on the web browser. There was one call *hardradio.com,* dedicated to heavy metal, one called *snakenet.* But the one that caught her attention was a site called *yellowribbon.org.* At first, Jessica thought it might have been dedicated to POWs and MIAs. When she connected to the net, then clicked on the site, she saw it was about teen suicide.

Was I this fascinated with death and despair when I was a teenager? Jessica thought.

She imagined she was. It probably came with the hormones.

Back in the kitchen, Jessica found that Bonnie had made a pot of coffee. She poured Jessica a cup, then sat down opposite her. There was also a plate of vanilla wafers on the table.

"I need to ask you a few more questions about the accident last year," Jessica said.

"Okay," Bonnie replied, but her down-turned mouth told Jessica it was anything but okay.

"I promise I won't keep you too long."

Bonnie nodded.

Jessica was organizing her thoughts when a look of gradually dawning horror came over Bonnie Semanski's face. It took Jessica a moment to realize that Bonnie wasn't looking directly at her. She was, in-stead, looking over her left shoulder. Jessica turned, slowly, following the woman's gaze.

Lauren Semanski was standing on the back porch. Her clothes were ripped; her knuckles were bleeding and raw. There was a long contusion on her right leg, a pair of deep lacerations on her right arm. On the left side of her head, a large patch of scalp was missing. Her left wrist appeared to be broken, the bone protruding through the flesh. The skin on her right cheek was peeled back in a bloody flap.

"Sweetheart?" Bonnie said, rising to her feet, a trembling hand to her lips. All the color had drained from her face. "My God, what . . . what *happened,* baby?"

Lauren looked at her grandmother, at Jessica. Her eyes were bloodshot and burnished. A deep defiance shone through the trauma.

"Motherfucker didn't know who he was *dealing* with," she said.

Then Lauren Semanski collapsed.

Before the ambulance arrived, Lauren Semanski slipped in and out of consciousness. Jessica did what she could to prevent her from going into shock. When she had determined that there were no spinal injuries, she wrapped her in a blanket, then slightly elevated her legs. Jessica knew that preventing shock was infinitely preferable to treating its effects.

Jessica noticed that Lauren's right hand was clenched into a tight fist. Something was in her hand—something with a sharp edge, something plastic. Jessica tried gently to open the girl's fingers. Nothing doing. Jessica didn't press the issue.

As they waited, Lauren rambled. Jessica got a sketchy tale of what had happened to her. Phrases were unconnected. Words slipped between her teeth.

Jeff's house.

Tweakers.

Fucker.

Lauren's dried lips and ravaged nostrils, along with the brittle hair and the somewhat translucent look to her skin told Jessica she was probably a meth head.

Needle.

Fucker.

Before Lauren was loaded onto the gurney, she opened her eyes for a moment, and said one word that caused the world to stop spinning for a moment.

Rosary.

The ambulance left, taking Bonnie Semanski to the hospital with her granddaughter. Jessica called the station house and told them what had happened. A pair of detectives were on their way to St. Joseph's. Jessica had given the EMS strict instructions to preserve Lauren's clothing and, to any extent possible, any fibers or fluids. Specifically, she told them to safeguard the forensic integrity of whatever Lauren had clutched in her right hand.

Jessica remained at the Semanski house. She walked into the living room and sat with George Semanski.

"Your granddaughter is going to be all right," Jessica said, hoping she sounded convincing, wanting to believe it was true.

George Semanski nodded. He continued to wring his hands. He ran through the cable channels as if it were some sort of physical therapy.

"I need to ask you one more question, sir. If that's okay."

After a few moments of silence, he nodded again. It appeared that the cornucopia of pharmaceuticals on the TV tray had him on a narcotically induced time delay.

"Your wife told me that, last year, when Lauren's mom and dad were killed, Lauren took it pretty hard," Jessica said. "Can you tell me what she meant by that?"

George Semanski reached for a bottle of pills. He took the bottle, turning it over and over in his hands, but not opening it. Jessica noted that it was clonazepam.

"Well, after the funeral and all, after the burials, about a week or so later, she almost, well, she . . ."

"She what, Mr. Semanski?"

George Semanski paused. He stopped fidgeting with the pill vial. "She tried to kill herself."

"How?"

"She, well, she went out to the car one night. She ran a hose from the exhaust into one of the windows. She tried to breathe in the carbon monoxide, I guess."

"What happened?"

"She passed out on the car horn. It woke up Bonnie and she went out there."

"Did Lauren have to go to the hospital?"

"Oh yes," George said. "She was in there for almost a week."

Jessica's pulse quickened. She felt the puzzle piece click into place.

Bethany Price had tried to slash her wrists.

Tessa Wells had a Sylvia Plath reference in her diary.

Lauren Semanski tried monoxide poisoning.

Suicide, Jessica thought.

All of these girls tried to commit suicide.

.　.　.

"Mr. Wells? This is Detective Balzano." Jessica was on her cell phone, standing on the sidewalk in front of the Semanski house. Pacing was more like it.

"Have you caught somebody?" Wells asked.

"Well, we're working on it, sir. I have a question for you about Tessa. It's about last year, around Thanksgiving."

"Last year?"

"Yes," Jessica said. "This might be a little hard to talk about but, believe me, it won't be any harder for you to answer than it will be for me to ask."

Jessica recalled the junk drawer in Tessa's room. There were hospital bracelets in there.

"What about Thanksgiving?" Wells asked.

"By any chance, was Tessa hospitalized around that time?"

Jessica listened, waited. She found that she was clenching her fist around her cell phone. It felt as if she might break it. She eased up.

"Yes," he said.

"Could you tell me why she was in the hospital?"

She closed her eyes.

Frank Wells took a rattling, painful breath.

And told her.

"Tessa Wells took a handful of pills last November. Lauren Semanski locked herself in the garage and started the car. Nicole Taylor slashed her wrists," Jessica said. "At least three of the girls on this list attempted suicide."

They were back at the Roundhouse.

Byrne smiled. Jessica felt a charge of electricity shoot through her body. Lauren Semanski was still heavily sedated. Until they were able to talk to her, they would have to fly with what they had.

There was not yet any word on what was clasped in her hand. According to the detectives at the hospital, Lauren Semanski had not yet given it up. The doctors told them they'd have to wait.

Byrne had a photocopy of Brian Parkhurst's list in his hand. He tore it in half, handed one piece to Jessica, kept the other. He pulled out his cell phone.

Soon, they had their answer. All ten girls on the list had tried to commit suicide within the past year. Jessica now believed that Brian Parkhurst, perhaps as penance, was trying to tell the police that he knew why these girls were being targeted. As part of his counseling, these girls had all confided in him that they had attempted to take their own lives.

There are things you need to know about these girls.

Perhaps, by some twisted sense of logic, their doer was trying to finish the job these girls had started. They would worry about the why of it all when they had him in irons.

What was obvious was this: Their doer had abducted Lauren Semanski and drugged her with midazolam. What he had not counted on was that she was full of methamphetamine. The speed had counteracted the midazolam. In addition, she was also full of piss and vinegar, a fighter. He definitely picked the wrong girl.

For the first time in her life, Jessica was glad that a teenager did drugs.

But if the killer's inspiration was the five Sorrowful Mysteries of the rosary, why were there *ten* girls on Parkhurst's list? Besides attempting suicide, what did five of them have in common? Was he really going to stop at five?

They compared their notes.

Four of the girls overdosed on pills. Three of them tried to cut their wrists. Two of the girls tried to commit suicide by carbon monoxide poisoning. One girl drove her car through a guardrail and over a ravine. She was saved by the airbag.

It wasn't method that tied any five together.

What about school? Four of the girls went to Regina, four went to Nazarene, one went to Marie Goretti and one to Neumann.

As to age: four were sixteen, two were seventeen, three were fifteen, one eighteen.

Was it neighborhood?

No.

Clubs or extracurricular activities?

No.

Gang affiliations?

Hardly.

What was it?

Ask and ye shall receive, Jessica thought. The answer was right in front of them.

It was the hospital.

St. Joseph's was what they had in common.

"Look at this," Jessica said.

On the day they had tried to kill themselves, the five girls treated at St. Joseph's were Nicole Taylor, Tessa Wells, Bethany Price, Kristi Hamilton, and Lauren Semanski.

The rest were treated elsewhere, at five different hospitals.

"My God," Byrne said. "That's it."

It was the break they were looking for.

But the fact that all of these girls were treated at one hospital was not what made Jessica shaky. The fact that they all tried to commit suicide wasn't it, either.

The fact that made the room lose all of its air was this:

The same doctor had treated them all: Dr. Patrick Farrell.

6 4

Patrick sat in Interview Room A. Eric Chavez and John Shepherd handled the interview while Byrne and Jessica observed. The interview was being videotaped.

As far as Patrick knew, he was merely a material witness in the case.

He had a recent scratch on his right hand.

When they could, they would scrape beneath Lauren Semanski's fingernails, looking for DNA evidence. Unfortunately, according to the CSU, it probably wouldn't yield much. Lauren was lucky to even *have* fingernails.

They had gone over Patrick's schedule for the previous week, and, to Jessica's chagrin, they had learned that there wasn't a single day that would have prevented Patrick from abducting the victims, nor dumping their bodies.

The thought made Jessica physically ill. Was she really considering the notion that Patrick had something to do with these murders? With each passing minute, the answer was getting closer to *yes*. The next minute dissuaded her. She really didn't know what to think.

Nick Palladino and Tony Park were on their way to the Wilhelm Kreuz crime scene with a photograph of Patrick. It was unlikely that old Agnes Pinsky would remember him—even if she did pick him out of a photo lineup, her credibility would be torn to shreds by even a public defender. Nick and Tony would canvass up and down the street nonetheless.

"I hadn't been keeping up with the news, I'm afraid," Patrick said.

"I can understand that," Shepherd replied. He was sitting on the edge of the battered metal table. Eric Chavez leaned against the door. "I'm sure you see enough of the ugly side of life where you work."

"We have our triumphs," Patrick said.

"So, you're saying that you were not aware that any of these girls had at one time been a patient of yours?"

"An ER physician, especially in an inner-city trauma center, works triage, Detective. The patient needing the most immediate care is treated first. After patients are patched up and sent home, or admitted, they are always referred to their primary care physician. The concept of patient doesn't really apply. People who come to an emergency room may only be a patient of any given doctor for an hour. Sometimes less. Quite often less. Thousands of people pass through St. Joseph's ER every year."

Shepherd listened, nodding at all the appropriate cues, absently straightening the already perfect creases in his pants. Explaining the concept of triage to a veteran homicide detective was wholly unnecessary. Everyone in Interview Room A knew that.

"That doesn't really answer my question, though, Dr. Farrell."

"It seemed that I knew the name Tessa Wells when I heard it on the news. I didn't, however, make any immediate connection to whether or not St. Joseph's had provided her with emergency care."

Bullshit, Jessica thought, her anger growing. They had discussed Tessa Wells the night they had a drink at Finnigan's Wake.

"You say *St. Joseph's* as if it was the institution that treated her that day," Shepherd said. "It's *your* name on the file."

Shepherd held up the file for Patrick to see.

"The record doesn't lie, Detective," Patrick said. "I must have treated her."

Shepherd held up a second file. "And you treated Nicole Taylor."

"Again, I really don't recall."

A third file. "And Bethany Price."

Patrick stared.

Two more files in his face now. "Kristi Hamilton spent four hours in your care. Lauren Semanski five."

"I defer to the record, Detective," Patrick said.

"All five of these girls were abducted and

four of them were brutally murdered this week, Doctor. This *week*. Five female, teenaged victims who just happened to pass through your office within the past ten months."

Patrick shrugged.

John Shepherd asked, "You can certainly understand our interest in you at this point, can't you?"

"Oh, absolutely," Patrick said. "As long as your interest in me is in the nature of material witness. As long as that's the case, I'll be happy to help in any way I can."

"By the way, how did you get that scratch on your hand?"

It was clear that Patrick had an answer well prepared for this. He wasn't, however, going to blurt anything out. "It's a long story."

Shepherd looked at his watch. "I've got all night." He looked at Chavez. "How about you, Detective?"

"I cleared my schedule just in case."

They both turned their attention back to Patrick.

"Let's just say that one should always beware of a wet cat," Patrick said. Jessica saw the charm shine through. Unfortunately for Patrick, these two detectives were immune. At the moment, so was Jessica.

Shepherd and Chavez exchanged a glance. "Have truer words ever been spoken?" Chavez asked.

"You're saying a cat did that?" Shepherd asked.

"Yes," Patrick replied. "She was outside all day in the rain. When I got home tonight, I saw her shivering in the bushes. I tried to pick her up. Bad idea."

"What's her name?"

It was an old interrogation trick. Someone mentions an alibi-related person, you slam them immediately with a question regarding the name. This time, it was a pet. Patrick was not prepared.

"Her name?" he asked.

It was a stall. Shepherd had him. Shepherd then got closer, looking at the scratch. "What is it, a pet bobcat?"

"Excuse me?"

Shepherd stood up, leaned against the wall. Friendly, now. "See, Dr. Farrell, I have four daughters. They absolutely *love* cats. Love 'em. In fact, we have three of them. Coltrane, Dizzy, and Snickers. That's their names. I've been scratched, oh, at least a dozen times in the last few years. None of the scratches looked anything like yours."

Patrick looked at the floor for a few moments. "She's not a bobcat, Detective. Just a big old tabby."

"Huh," Shepherd said. He rolled on. "By the way, what sort of vehicle do you drive?" John Shepherd, of course, already knew the answer to this question.

"I have a few different vehicles. I mostly drive a Lexus."

"LS? GS? ES? SportCross?" Shepherd asked.

Patrick smiled. "I see you know your luxury cars."

Shepherd returned the smile. Half of it, anyway. "I can tell a Rolex from a TAG Heuer, too," he said. "Can't afford one of them, either."

"I drive a 2004 LX."

"That's the SUV, right?"

"I guess you could call it that."

"What would you call it?"

"I would call it an LUV," Patrick said.

"As in Luxury Utility Vehicle, right?"

Patrick nodded.

"Gotcha," Shepherd said. "Where is that vehicle right now?"

Patrick hesitated. "It's in the back parking lot here. Why?"

"Just curious," Shepherd said. "It's a high-end vehicle. I just wanted to make sure it was safe."

"I appreciate it."

"And the other vehicles?"

"I have a 1969 Alfa Romeo and a Chevy Venture."

"That's a van?"

"Yes."

Shepherd wrote this down.

"Now, on Tuesday morning, according to records at St. Joseph's, you didn't go on duty until nine o'clock in the morning," Shepherd said. "Is that accurate?"

Patrick thought about it. "I believe it is."

"Yet your shift began at eight. Why were you late?"

"Actually, it was because I had to take the Lexus in for service."

"Where did you take it?"

There was a slight rap on the door, then the door swung open.

In the doorway Ike Buchanan stood next to a tall, imposing man in an elegant Brioni pin-striped suit. The man had perfectly layered silver hair, a Cancún tan. His briefcase cost more than either detective made in a month.

Abraham Gold had represented Patrick's father, Martin, in a high-profile malpractice suit in the late 1990s. Abraham Gold was as expensive as they come. And as good as they come. As far as Jessica knew, Abraham Gold had never lost a case.

"Gentlemen," he began, using his best courtroom baritone. "This conversation is over."

"What do you think?" Buchanan asked.

The entire task force looked at her. She searched her mind for not only the right thing to say, but the right words to say it. She truly was at a loss. From the moment that Patrick had walked into the Roundhouse an hour or so earlier, she knew this moment would arrive. Now that it was here, she had no idea how to deal with it. The notion that someone she knew might be responsible for such horror was bad enough. The notion that it was someone she knew *intimately*—or thought she did—seemed to immobilize her brain.

If the unthinkable was true, that Patrick

Farrell was indeed the Rosary Killer, from a purely a professional standpoint, what would it say about her as a judge of character?

"I think it's possible." There. It was said out loud.

They had, of course, run a background check on Patrick Farrell. Except for a pot misdemeanor in his sophomore year in college, and a penchant for driving well above the speed limit, his record was clean.

Now that Patrick had retained counsel, they would have to step up the investigation. Agnes Pinsky had said that he *could've* been the man she saw knocking on Wilhelm Kreuz's door. A man who worked at a shoe repair shop across from Kreuz's apartment building *thought* he recalled a cream-colored Lexus SUV parked out front two days earlier. He wasn't sure.

Regardless, there would now be a pair of detectives on Patrick Farrell 24/7.

6 5

The pain was exquisite, a slow rolling wave that inched up the back of his neck, then down. He popped a Vicodin, chased it with rancid water from the tap in the men's room of a gas station in North Philly.

It was Good Friday. The day of the crucifixion.

Byrne knew that, one way or another, this was all probably coming to an end soon, probably tonight; and with it, he knew he would face something inside himself that had been there for fifteen years, something dark and violent and troubling.

He wanted everything to be in order.

He needed symmetry.

He had one stop to make first.

The cars were parked two deep on both sides of the street. In this part of the city, if the street was blocked, you didn't call the police or knock on doors. You definitely didn't want to blow your horn. Instead, you quietly put your car in reverse, and found another way.

The storm door of the ramshackle Point Breeze row house was open, all the lights burning inside. Byrne stood across the street, sheltered from the rain beneath the tattered awning of a shuttered bakery. Through the bay window across the street he could see the three pictures that graced the wall over the strawberry velvet Spanish modern sofa. Martin Luther King, Jesus, Muhammad Ali.

Right in front of him, in the rusted Pontiac, the kid sat alone in the backseat, completely oblivious to Byrne, smoking a blunt, rocking gently to whatever was coming through his headphones. After a few minutes he butted the blunt, opened the car door, and got out.

He stretched, flipped up the hood of his sweatshirt, straightened his baggies.

"Hey," Byrne said. The pain in his head had settled into a dull metronome of agony, clicking loud and rhythmically at either temple. Still, it felt as if the mother of all migraines was just a car horn or flashbulb away.

The kid turned, surprised but not scared. He was about fifteen, tall and rangy, with the kind of body that would serve him pretty well in playground hoops, but take him no further. He wore the full Sean John uniform—full-cut jeans, quilted leather jacket, fleece hoodie.

The kid sized up Byrne, assessed the danger, the opportunity. Byrne kept his hands in plain sight.

"Yo," the kid finally offered.

"Did you know Marius?" Byrne asked.

The kid gave him the twice-over. Byrne was way too big to mess with.

"MG was my *boy*," the kid finally said. He flashed a JBM sign.

Byrne nodded. This kid could still go either way, he thought. There was a simmering intelligence behind his now bloodshot eyes. But Byrne got the feeling the kid was too busy fulfilling the world's expectations of him.

Byrne reached slowly inside his coat—slowly enough to let this kid know there was nothing coming. He removed the envelope. The envelope was of a size and shape and heft that could only be one thing.

"His mother's name is Delilah Watts?" Byrne asked. It was more like a statement of fact.

The kid glanced at the row house, at the bright bay window. A thin, dark-skinned black woman in oversized gradient sunglasses and a deep auburn wig dabbed at her eyes as she received mourners. She was no more than thirty-five.

The kid turned back to Byrne. "Yeah."

Byrne absently thumbed the rubber band around the fat envelope. He had never counted the contents. When he had taken it from Gideon Pratt that night, he had no reason to think it was a penny less than the five thousand dollars they had agreed upon. There was no reason to count it now.

"This is for Mrs. Watts," Byrne said. He

held the kid's eyes for a few, flat seconds, a look that both of them had experienced in their time, a look that needed no embellishment, no footnoting.

The kid reached out, cautiously took the envelope. "She gonna want to know who it's from," he said.

Byrne nodded. Soon the kid understood that no answer was forthcoming.

The kid stuffed the envelope into his pocket. Byrne watched as he swaggered across the street, up to the house, stepped inside, hugged a few of the young men standing sentinel at the door. Byrne looked through the window as the kid waited briefly in the short receiving line. He could hear the strains of Al Green's "You Brought the Sunshine" playing.

Byrne wondered how many times this scene would be played out across the country this night—too-young mothers sitting in too-hot parlors, presiding over the wake of a child given to the beast.

For all that Marius Green may have done wrong in his short life, for all the misery and pain he may have spread, there was only one reason he was in that alley that night, and that play had nothing to do with him.

Marius Green was dead, as was the man who killed him in cold blood. Was it justice? Perhaps not. But there was no doubt that it all began the day Deirdre Pettigrew met a terrible man in Fairmount Park, a day that had ended with another young mother with a ball of damp tissue in her hands, and a front room full of friends and family.

There is no solution, just resolution, Byrne thought. He was not a man who believed in karma. He was a man who believed in action and reaction.

Byrne watched as Delilah Watts opened the envelope. After the initial shock set in, she put her hand to her heart. She composed herself, then looked out the window, directly at him, directly into Kevin Byrne's soul. He knew that she could not see him, that all she could see was the black mirror of night, and the rain-streaked reflection of her own pain.

Kevin Byrne bowed his head, then turned up his collar and walked into the storm.

6 6

As Jessica drove home, the radio predicted a huge thunderstorm. High winds, lightning, flood warnings. Parts of Roosevelt Boulevard were already inundated.

She thought about the night she had met Patrick, so many years ago. She had watched him work in the ER that night, so impressed with his grace and confidence, his ability to comfort the people who came in those doors, looking for help.

People responded to him, believed in his

ability to relieve their pain. His looks certainly didn't hurt. She tried to think rationally about him. What did she really know? Was she able to think about him in the same terms she had thought about Brian Parkhurst?

No, she was not.

But the more she thought about it, the more it became *possible*. The fact that he was an MD, the fact that he could not account for his time at crucial intervals in the time line of the murders, the fact that he had lost his kid sister to violence, the fact that he was a Catholic, and, inescapably, the fact that he had treated all five girls. He knew their names and addresses, their medical histories.

She had looked again at the digital photographs of Nicole Taylor's hand. Could Nicole have been spelling out F A R instead of P A R?

It was possible.

Despite her instincts, Jessica finally admitted it to herself. If she didn't know Patrick, she would be leading the charge to arrest him, based on one immutable fact:

He knew all five girls.

6 7

Byrne stood in the ICU watching Lauren Semanski.

The ER team had told him that Lauren had a lot of methamphetamine in her system, that she was a chronic user, and that when her abductor had injected her with the midazolam, it did not have quite the effect it might have had if Lauren had not been full of a powerful stimulant.

Although they had not yet been able to talk to her, it was clear that Lauren Semanski's injuries were consistent with those that might have been incurred by someone leaping from a moving vehicle. Incredibly, although her injuries were numerous and serious, except for the toxicity of the drugs in her system, none was life threatening.

Byrne sat down next to her bed.

He knew that Patrick Farrell was a friend of Jessica's. He suspected that there was probably more to their relationship than mere friendship, but he would leave that for Jessica to tell him.

There had been so many false clues and blind alleys in this case so far. He was not sure that Patrick Farrell fit the mold, either. When he had met the man at the Rodin Museum crime scene, he had not gotten a feeling of any kind.

Still, that didn't seem to matter much these days. Chances were good that he could shake hands with Ted Bundy and not have a clue. Everything pointed to Patrick Farrell. He'd seen many an arrest warrant issued on much less.

He took Lauren's hand in his. He closed his eyes. The pain settled above his eyes, high and hot and murderous. Soon, the images detonated in his mind, shunting the breath in his lungs, and the door at the end of his mind swung wide . . .

68

Scholars believe that a storm rose over Calvary on the day of Christ's death, that the sky grew dark over the valley as He hung upon the cross.

Lauren Semanski had been very strong. Last year, when she tried to take her own life, I had looked at her and wondered why such a determined young woman would do such a thing. Life is a gift. Life is a blessing. Why had she tried to throw it all away?

Why had any of them tried to throw it away?

Nicole had lived with the ridicule of her classmates, an alcoholic father.

Tessa had survived her mother's lingering death, and faced her father's slow descent.

Bethany had been the object of scorn for her weight.

Kristi had problems with anorexia.

When I had treated them, I knew that I was cheating the Lord. They had set themselves on a path and I had diverted them.

Nicole and Tessa and Bethany and Kristi.

Then there was Lauren. Lauren had survived her parents' accident only to walk out to the car one night, start the engine. She had brought her stuffed Opus with her, the plush little penguin toy her mother had given her for Christmas in the fifth year of her life.

Today she had resisted the midazolam. She was probably back on the meth. When she punched open the door we were moving at approximately thirty miles an hour. She jumped out. Just like that. There was far too much traffic for me to turn around and get her. I had to just let her go.

It is too late to change plans.

It is the Hour of None.

And although Lauren was the final mystery, another girl would do, one with shiny curls and a halo of innocence around her head.

The wind picks up as I pull over, cut the engine. They predict a massive storm. There will be another storm tonight, a dark reckoning of the soul.

The light inside Jessica's house . . .

6 9

. . . is bright and warm and inviting, a solitary ember in the dying coals of dusk.

He sits outside in a vehicle, sheltered from the rain. In his hands is a rosary. He thinks about Lauren Semanski, and how she got away. She was the fifth girl, the fifth mystery, the final piece in his masterwork.

But Jessica is here. He has business with her, too.

Jessica and her little girl.

He checks the items he has prepared: the hypodermic needles, the carpenter's chalk, the sail maker's needle and thread.

He prepares to step into the wicked night . . .

The imagery came and went, teasing with clarity, like the vision of a drowning man looking up from the bottom of a chlorinated pool.

The pain in Byrne's head was fierce. He walked out of ICU and into the parking lot, got into his car. He checked his weapon. Rain pelted his windshield.

He started his car and headed to the expressway.

FRIDAY, 9:00 PM

Sophie was terrified of thunderstorms. Jessica knew where she'd gotten it, too. It was genetic. When Jessica was small, she used to hide under the steps at their house on Catharine Street whenever it thundered. If it got really bad, she used to crawl under the bed. Sometimes she would bring a candle. Until the day she set the mattress on fire.

They had eaten dinner in front of the television again. Jessica had been too tired to object. It didn't matter anyway. She had picked at her food, disinterested in such a routine event when her world was cracking at the seams. Her stomach churned with the events of the day. How could she have been so wrong about Patrick?

Was she wrong about Patrick?

The images of what had been done to these young women would not leave her alone.

She checked the answering machine. There were no messages.

Vincent was staying with his brother. She picked up the phone and dialed the number. Well, two-thirds of it. Then she put the phone down.

Shit.

She did the dishes by hand, just to give her hands something to do. She poured a glass of wine, poured it out. She made a cup of tea, let it get cold.

Somehow, she'd made it until Sophie's bedtime. Outside, thunder and lightning raged. Inside, Sophie was scared.

Jessica had tried all the usual remedies. She had offered to read her a story. No luck. She had asked Sophie if she wanted to watch *Finding Nemo* again. No luck. She didn't even want to watch *The Little Mermaid.* This was rare. Jessica had offered to color her Peter Cottontail coloring book with her (no), offered to sing *Wizard of Oz* songs (no), offered to put decals on the colored eggs in the kitchen (no).

In the end, she just tucked Sophie into bed and sat with her. Every time there was a crack of thunder, Sophie looked at her as if it were the end of the world.

Jessica tried to think of anything but Patrick. So far, she had been unsuccessful.

There was a knock at the front door. It was probably Paula.

"I'll be right back, sweetie."

"No, Mom."

"I won't be more than—"

The power flickered off, then back on.

"That's all we need." Jessica stared at the table lamp as if she could will it to stay on. She held Sophie's hand. The kid had her in a death grip. Mercifully, the lights stayed on. *Thank you, Lord.* "Mommy just has to answer the door. It's Paula. You want to see Paula, don't you?"

"I do."

"I'll be right back," she said. "Gonna be okay?"

Sophie nodded, despite the fact that her lips were trembling.

Jessica kissed Sophie on the forehead, handed her Jools, her little brown bear. Sophie shook her head. Jessica then grabbed Molly, the beige one. Nope. It was hard to keep track. Sophie had good bears and bad bears. She finally said yes to Timothy, the panda.

"Be right back."

"Okay."

She walked down the stairs as the doorbell rang once, twice, three times. It didn't sound like Paula.

"All *right* already," she said.

She tried to look through the beveled glass in the door's small window. It was pretty well fogged over. All she saw were the parking lights of the EMS van across the street. It seemed that even typhoons didn't deter Carmine Arrabiata from having his weekly heart attack.

She opened the door.

It was Patrick.

Her first instinct was to slam the door. She resisted. For the moment. She glanced out at the street, looking for the surveillance car. She didn't see it. She didn't open the storm door.

"What are you doing here, Patrick?"

"Jess," he said. "You've got to listen to me."

The anger began to rise, dueling with her fears. "See, that's the part you don't seem to understand," she said. "I really don't."

"Jess. Come on. It's *me*." He stamped from one foot to the other. He was thoroughly soaked.

"Me? Who the hell is *me*? You treated every one of these girls," she said. "It didn't occur to you to come forward with this information?"

"I see a lot of patients," Patrick said. "You can't expect me to remember them all."

The wind was loud. Howling. They were both almost yelling to be heard.

"Bullshit. These were all within the last year."

Patrick looked at the ground. "Maybe I just didn't want to . . ."

"What, get involved? Are you fucking *kidding* me?"

"Jess. If you could just—"

"You shouldn't be here, Patrick," she

said. "This puts me in a really awkward situation. Go home."

"My God, Jess. You don't really think I had anything to do with these, these . . ."

It was a good question, Jessica thought. In fact, it was *the* question.

Jessica was just about to answer when a crack of thunder boomed, and the power browned out. The lights flickered on, off, on.

"I . . . I don't know what to think, Patrick."

"Give me five minutes, Jess. Five minutes, and I'll go."

Jessica saw the world of pain in his eyes.

"Please," he said. He was soaking wet, pitiful in his pleading.

Crazily, she thought about her weapon. It was in the hall closet upstairs, top shelf, where it always was. She was actually thinking about her weapon, and whether she could get to it in time if needed.

Because of *Patrick*.

None of this seemed real.

"Can I at least come inside?" he asked.

There was no point in arguing. She cracked open the storm door as a sheer column of rain swept through. Jessica opened the door fully. She knew that there was a team on Patrick even if she didn't see the car. She was armed and she had backup.

Try as she did, she just couldn't believe Patrick was guilty. This wasn't some crime of passion they were talking about, some moment of insanity when he lost his temper and went too far. This was the systematic, cold-blooded murder of six people. Maybe more.

Give her a piece of forensic evidence, and then she'd have no choice.

Until then . . .

The power went out.

Upstairs, Sophie wailed.

"Jesus *Christ,*" Jessica said. She looked across the street. Some of the houses still seemed to have power. Or was that candlelight?

"Maybe it's the circuit breaker," Patrick said, walking inside, walking past her. "Where's the panel?"

Jessica looked at the floor, hands on hips. This was all too much.

"Bottom of the basement stairs," she said, resigned. "There's a flashlight on the dining room table. But don't think that we—"

"Mommy!" from upstairs.

Patrick took off his raincoat. "I'll check the panel, then I'm gone. I promise."

Patrick grabbed the flashlight and headed to the basement.

Jessica shuffled her way to the steps in the sudden darkness. She headed upstairs, entered Sophie's room.

"It's okay, sweetie," Jessica said, sitting on the edge of the bed. Sophie's face looked tiny and round and frightened in the gloom. "Do you want to come downstairs with Mommy?"

Sophie shook her head.

"You sure?"

Sophie nodded. "Is Daddy here?"

"No, honey," Jessica said, her heart sinking. "Mommy's . . . Mommy's going to get some candles, okay? You like candles."

Sophie nodded again.

Jessica left the bedroom. She opened the linen closet next to the bathroom, felt her way through the box that held the hotel soaps and sample shampoos and conditioners. She remembered when she used to take long, luxurious bubble baths with scented candles scattered around the bathroom, back in the stone age of her marriage. Sometimes Vincent would join her. Somehow it seemed like someone else's life at the moment. She found a pair of sandalwood candles. She took them out of the box, returned to Sophie's room.

Of course, there were no matches.

"I'll be right back."

She went downstairs to the kitchen, her eyes somewhat adjusted to the dark. She rummaged in the junk drawer for some book matches. She found a pack. Matches from her wedding. She could feel the gold embossed JESSICA AND VINCENT on the glossy cover. Just what she needed. If she believed in such things, she might imagine that there was a conspiracy afoot to drag her into some deep depression. She turned to head back upstairs when there was a slash of lightning and the sound of shattering glass.

She jumped at the impact. A branch had finally snapped off the dying maple next to the house and smashed in the window in the back door.

"Oh, this just gets better and better," Jessica said. The rain swept into the kitchen. There was broken glass everywhere. "Son of a *bitch*."

She got out a plastic trash bag from under the sink and some pushpins from the kitchen corkboard. Fighting the wind and gusting rain, she tacked the bag around the opening in the door, trying not to cut herself on the shards that remained.

What the hell was next?

She looked down the stairs into the basement, saw the Maglite beam dancing about the gloom.

She grabbed the matches and headed into the dining room. She looked through the drawers in the hutch, found a variety of candles. She lit half a dozen or so, placing them around the dining room and the living room. She headed back upstairs and lit the two candles in Sophie's room.

"Better?" she asked.

"Better," Sophie said.

Jessica reached out, dried Sophie's cheeks. "The lights will be on in a little while. Okay?"

Sophie nodded, thoroughly unconvinced.

Jessica looked around the room. The candles did a fairly good job of exorcising the shadow monsters. She tweaked Sophie's nose, got a minor giggle. She just got to the top of the stairs when the phone rang.

Jessica stepped into her bedroom, answered.

"Hello?"

She was met with an unearthly howl and hiss. Through it, barely: "It's John Shepherd."

He sounded as if he was on the moon. "I can barely hear you. What's up?"

"You there?"

"Yes."

The phone line crackled. "We just heard from the hospital," he said.

"Say again?" Jessica said. The connection was horrible.

"Want me to call on your cell?"

"Okay," Jessica said. Then she remembered. The cell was in the car. The car was in the garage. "No, that's okay. Go ahead."

"We just got a report back on what Lauren Semanski had in her hand."

Something about Lauren Semanski. *"Okay."*

"It was part of a ballpoint pen."

"A what?"

"She had a broken ballpoint pen in her hand," Shepherd shouted. "From St. Joseph's."

Jessica heard this clearly enough. She didn't want to. "What do you mean?"

"It had the St. Joseph's logo and address on it. The pen is from the hospital."

Her heart grew cold in her chest. It couldn't be true. "Are you sure?"

"No doubt about it," Shepherd said. His voice was breaking up. "Listen . . . the surveillance team lost Farrell . . . Roosevelt is flooded all the way to—"

Quiet.

"John?"

Nothing. The phone line was dead. Jessica toggled the button on the phone. "Hello?"

She was met with a thick black silence.

Jessica hung up, stepped over to the hallway closet. She glanced down the stairs. Patrick was still in the basement.

She reached inside the closet, onto the top shelf, her mind spinning.

He's been asking about you, Angela had said.

She slipped the Glock out of the holster.

I was on my way to my sister's house in Manayunk, Patrick had said, not twenty feet from Bethany Price's still-warm body.

She checked the weapon's magazine. It was full.

His doctor came to see him yesterday, Agnes Pinsky had said.

She slammed the magazine home, chambered a round. And began to descend the stairs.

The wind continued to bay outside, trembling the windowpanes in their cracked glazing.

"Patrick?"

No response.

She reached the bottom of the stairs, padded across the living room, opened the drawer in the hutch, grabbed the old flashlight. She pushed the switch. Dead. Of course. Thanks, Vincent.

She closed the drawer.

Louder: *"Patrick?"*

Silence.

This was getting out of control really fast. She wasn't going into the cellar without light. No way.

She backed her way to the stairs, then made her way up as silently as she could. She would take Sophie and some blankets, bundle her up to the attic, and lock the door. Sophie would be miserable, but she would be safe. Jessica knew she had to get control of herself, and the situation. She would lock Sophie in, get to her cell phone, and call for backup.

"It's okay, sweetie," she said. "It's okay."

She picked up Sophie, held her tight. Sophie shivered. Her teeth chattered.

In the flickering candlelight, Jessica thought she was seeing things. She *had* to be mistaken. She picked up a candle, held it close.

She wasn't mistaken. There, on Sophie's forehead, was a cross made of blue chalk.

The killer wasn't in the house.

The killer was in the *room*.

FRIDAY, 9:25 PM

Byrne pulled off Roosevelt Boulevard. The street was flooded. His head pounded, the images came roaring through, one after the other: a demented slaughterhouse of a slide show.

The killer was stalking Jessica and her daughter.

Byrne had looked at the lottery ticket the killer had put in Kristi Hamilton's hands and not seen it at first. None of them had. When the lab uncovered the number, it became clear. The clue was not the lottery agent. The clue was the number.

The lab had determined that the Big 4 number the killer had chosen was 9–7–0–0.

The address of St. Katherine Church rectory was 9700 Frankford Avenue.

Jessica had been close. The Rosary Killer had defaced the door at St. Katherine three years ago and had fully intended to end his madness there tonight. He intended to take Lauren Semanski to the church and fulfill the final of the five Sorrowful Mysteries on the altar there.

The crucifixion.

That Lauren had fought back and escaped only delayed him. When Byrne had touched the broken ballpoint pen in Lauren's hand, he knew where the killer was ultimately headed, and who would be his final victim. He had immediately called the Eighth District, which had dispatched a half a dozen officers to the church and a pair of patrol cars to Jessica's house.

Byrne's only hope was that they were not too late.

. . .

The streetlights were out, as were the traffic lights. Accordingly, as always when things like this happened, everyone in Philly forgot how to drive. Byrne took out his cell phone and called Jessica again. He got a busy signal. He tried her cell phone. It rang five times, then switched over to her voice mail.

Come on, Jess.

He pulled over to the side of the road, closed his eyes. To anyone who had never experienced the exacting pain of a rampant migraine, there could be no explanation rich enough. The lights of the oncoming cars seared his eyes. Between the flashes, he saw the bodies. Not the chalk outlines of the crime scene after the sanitization of investigation, but rather the human beings.

Tessa Wells having her arms and legs positioned around the pillar.

Nicole Taylor being laid to rest in the field of bright flowers.

Bethany Price and her crown of razors.

Kristi Hamilton soaked with blood.

Their eyes were open, questioning, pleading.

Pleading with *him*.

The fifth body was not clear to him at all, but he knew enough to shake him to the bottom of his soul.

The fifth body was just a little girl.

FRIDAY, 9:35 PM

Jessica slammed shut the bedroom door. Locked it. She had to begin with the immediate area. She searched beneath the bed, behind the curtains, in the closet, her weapon out front.

Empty.

Somehow Patrick had gotten upstairs and made the sign of the cross on Sophie's forehead. She had tried to ask Sophie a gentle question about it, but her little girl seemed traumatized.

The idea made Jessica as sick as it did enraged. But at the moment, rage was her enemy. Her life was under siege.

She sat back down on the bed.

"You have to listen to Mommy, okay?"

Sophie stared, as if she was in shock.

"Sweetie? Listen to Mommy."

Silence from her daughter.

"Mommy is going to make up a bed in the closet, okay? Like camping. Okay?"

Sophie had no reaction.

Jessica scrambled over to the closet. She pushed everything to the back, yanked the bedclothes off the bed, and created a makeshift bed. It broke her heart to have to do this, but she had no choice. She pulled everything else out of the closet and tossed it on the floor, everything that might cause Sophie harm. She lifted her daughter out of the bed, fighting her own tears of fury and terror.

She kissed Sophie, then closed the closet door. She turned the church key, pocketed it. She grabbed her weapon, and exited the room.

All the candles she had lighted in the house were blown out. The wind howled outside, but in the house it was deathly quiet. It was an intoxicating dark, a dark that seemed to consume everything it touched. Jessica saw everything she knew to be there in her mind, not with her eyes. As she moved down the stairs, she considered the layout of the living room. The table, the chairs, the hutch, the armoire that held the TV and the audio and video equipment, the love seats. It was all so familiar and all so foreign at the same moment. Each shadow held a monster; each outline, a threat.

She had qualified at the range every year she had been a cop, had taken the tactical, live-fire training course. But it was never supposed to be *her* house, *her* refuge from the insane world outside. This was the place where her little girl played. Now it had become a battleground.

When she touched the last step, she realized what she was doing. She was leaving Sophie alone upstairs. Had she really cleared the entire floor? Had she looked everywhere? Had she eliminated every possibility of threat?

"Patrick?" she said. Her voice sounded weak, plaintive.

No answer.

Cold sweat latticed her back and shoulders, trickling to her waist.

Then, loud, but not loud enough to frighten Sophie: "Listen. Patrick. I've got my weapon in my hand. I'm not fucking around. I need to see you out here right now. We go downtown, we work this out. Don't do this to me."

Cold silence.

Just the wind.

Patrick had taken her Maglite. It was the only working flashlight in the house. The wind rattled the windowpanes in their mullions, resulting in a low, keening wail that sounded like a hurt animal.

Jessica stepped into the kitchen, trying her best to focus in the gloom. She moved slowly, keeping her left shoulder to the wall, the side opposite her shooting hand. If she had to, she could put her back to the wall and swing the weapon 180, protecting her rear flank.

The kitchen was clear.

Before she rolled the jamb, into the living room, she stopped, listened, cocking her ear to the night sounds. Was someone moaning? Crying? She knew it wasn't Sophie.

She listened, searching the house for the sound. It was gone.

From the opening in the back door, Jessica smelled the scent of rain on early-spring soil, earthen and damp. She stepped forward in the darkness, her foot crunching the broken glass on the kitchen floor. The wind kicked, flapping the edges of the black plastic bag pinned over the opening.

When she edged back into the living room, she remembered that her laptop computer was on the small desk. If she wasn't mistaken, and if any luck could be found this night, the battery was fully charged. She edged over to the desk, opened the laptop. The screen kicked to life, flickered twice, then threw a milky blue light across the living room. Jessica shut her eyes tightly for a few seconds, then opened them. It was enough light to see. The room opened before her.

She checked behind the love seats, in the blind spot next to the armoire. She edged open the coat closet near the front door. All empty.

She crossed the room to the armoire that held the television. If she wasn't mistaken, Sophie had left her electronic walking puppy in one of the drawers. She eased it open. The bright plastic snout stared back.

Yes.

Jessica took the D-cell batteries out of the back, walked into the dining room. She slipped them into the flashlight. It blazed to life.

"Patrick. This is serious business. You've got to answer me."

She didn't expect a reply. She received none.

She took a deep breath, centered herself, then gradually descended the steps into the basement. The cellar was pitch black. Patrick had turned off the Maglite. Halfway down, Jessica stopped, ran the flashlight beam across the width of the room, cross-handed with her weapon. What was ordinarily so benign—the washer and dryer, the utility sink, the furnace and water softener, the golf clubs and summer furniture and all the other jumble of their lives—was now fraught with peril, etched out of long shadows.

Everything was exactly where she expected it to be.

Except Patrick.

She continued down the steps. She had

a blind alcove to her right, the recess that held the circuit breakers and electrical panel. She ran the light as far into the niche as she could, and saw something that made her breath catch in her throat.

The telephone junction box.

The telephone had not gone out due to the storm.

The wires dangling from the junction box told her that the line had been *cut*.

She eased her foot onto the concrete floor of the basement. She ran her light around the room again. She began to back up, toward the front wall, when she nearly tripped over something. Something heavy. Metallic. She spun around to see that it was one of her free weights, the ten-pound barbell.

And that's when she saw Patrick. He was lying facedown, on the concrete. Near his feet was the other ten-pound weight. It appeared that he had fallen over it as he was backing up from the telephone box.

He was not moving.

"Get up," she said. Her voice sounded raspy and weak. She pulled the hammer back on the Glock. The click echoed off the block walls. "Get . . . the fuck . . . *up*."

He didn't move.

Jessica stepped closer, nudged him with her foot. Nothing. No response at all. She eased the hammer back down, kept it pointed at Patrick. She bent down, slipped her hand around his neck. She felt for a pulse. It was there, strong.

But there was also dampness.

Her hand pulled back blood.

Jessica recoiled.

It appeared that Patrick had cut the phone line and then tripped over the barbell, knocking himself unconscious.

Jessica grabbed the Maglite on the floor next to Patrick, then ran upstairs and out the front door. She had to get to her cell phone. She stepped onto the porch. The rain continued to batter the awning overhead. She glanced up the street. The lights were out on the whole block. She could see branches lining the street like bones. The wind picked up in a fierce gust, drenching her in seconds. The street was deserted.

Except for the EMS van. The parking lights were off, but Jessica heard the engine, saw the exhaust. She holstered her weapon, ran across the street, through the torrent.

The medic was standing behind the van, just about to shut the doors. He turned to face Jessica as she approached.

"What's wrong?" he asked.

Jessica could see the ID tag on his jacket. His name was Drew.

"Drew, I want you to listen to me," Jessica said.

"Okay."

"I'm a police officer. There is a wounded man in my house."

"How bad?"

"I'm not sure, but I want you to listen to me. Don't talk."

"Okay."

"My phone is out, the power is out. I need you to call in a nine-one-one. Tell them an officer needs assistance. I need every cop and his mother out here. Call it in, then get over to my house. He's in the basement."

A huge gust of wind blew a sheet of rain across the street. Leaves and debris swirled around her feet. Jessica found that she had to yell to be heard.

"Do you understand?" Jessica shouted.

Drew grabbed his bag, shut the back doors on the EMS van, held up his handheld radio. "Let's go."

7 3

Traffic crawled up Cottman Avenue. Byrne was less than half a mile from Jessica's house. He approached a few of the side-streets, found them blocked by branches and electrical wires, or too flooded to pass.

Cars were cautiously approaching inundated sections of the road, all but idling through. As Byrne approached Jessica's street, the migraine bloomed fully. A car horn made him grip the wheel tightly, realizing he had been driving with his eyes closed.

He had to get to Jessica.

He parked the car, checked his weapon, and got out.

He was just a few blocks away.

The migraine surged as he turned his collar up against the wind. As he fought the gusts of rain, he knew that . . .

He is in the house.

Close.

He has not expected her to invite someone else inside. He wants her all to himself. He has plans for her and her daughter.

When the other man walked in the front door, his plans became . . .

7 4

. . . altered, but not changed.

Even Christ had his obstacles this week. The Pharisees tried to trap Him into uttering blasphemy. Judas had, of course, betrayed Him to the chief priests, telling them where Christ could be found.

Christ was not deterred.

I will not be deterred, either.

I will deal with the intruder, this Iscariot.

In this dark cellar I will make this intruder pay with his life.

FRIDAY, 9:55 PM

When they entered the house, Jessica pointed Drew to the basement.

"He's at the bottom of the stairs, and to the right," she said.

"Can you tell me anything about his injuries?" Drew asked.

"I don't know," Jessica said. "He's unconscious."

As the paramedic descended the stairs into the basement, Jessica heard him call in the 911 emergency.

She mounted the stairs to Sophie's room. She unlocked the closet door. Sophie was awake and sitting up, lost in a forest of coats and slacks.

"You okay, baby?" she asked.

Sophie remained unresponsive.

"Mommy's here, sweetie. Mommy's here."

She picked Sophie up. Sophie put her little arms around her neck. They were safe now. Jessica could feel Sophie's heart beating against her.

Jessica crossed the bedroom to the front windows. The street was only partially flooded. She watched for backup.

"Ma'am?"

Drew was calling her.

Jessica walked to the top of the stairs. "What's wrong?"

"Uh, well, I don't know how to tell you this."

"Tell me what?"

Drew said, "There's no one in the basement."

FRIDAY, 10:00 PM

Byrne turned the corner onto the pitch-black street. Fighting the wind, he had to walk around the huge tree limbs lying across the sidewalk and the road. He could see flickering lights in some windows, capering shadows dancing on the blinds. In the distance he saw a sparking electrical wire across a car.

There were no patrol cars from the Eighth. He tried his cell again. Nothing. No signal at all.

He had only been to Jessica's house once. He had to look closely to see if he remembered which house it was. He did not.

This was, of course, one of the worst parts of living in Philadelphia. Even Northeast Philadelphia. At times, everything looked alike.

He stood in front of a twin that looked familiar. With the streetlights out, it was difficult to tell. He closed his eyes and tried to recall. The images of the Rosary Killer obscured everything else, like the hammers falling on an old manual typewriter, soft lead on bright white paper, smeary black ink. But he was too close to see the words.

FRIDAY, 10:00 PM

Drew waited at the bottom of the basement stairs. Jessica lit the candles in the kitchen, then sat Sophie on one of the dinette chairs. She put her weapon on top of the fridge.

She descended the steps. The blood-stain on the concrete was still there. But Patrick was not.

"Dispatch said there's a pair of patrol cars on the way," he said. "But I'm afraid there's no one down here."

"Are you sure?"

Drew flashed his light around the basement. "Uh, well, unless you have a secret way out of here, he must have gone up the steps."

Drew aimed his flashlight up the stairs. There were no bloody footprints on the treads. Wearing latex gloves, he knelt down and touched the blood on the floor. He slicked two fingers together.

"You're saying he was just here?" he asked.

"Yes," Jessica said. "Two minutes ago. As soon as I saw him, I ran upstairs and down the driveway."

"How did he receive his injury?" he asked.

"I have no idea."

"Are you all right?"

"I'm fine."

"Well, the police will be here any second. They can give the place a good going over." He stood up. "Until then, we'll probably be safe down here."

What? Jessica thought.

We'll probably be safe down here?

"Is your little girl okay?" he asked.

Jessica stared at the man. A cold hand

squeezed her heart. "I never told you I had a little girl."

Drew peeled off the gloves, tossed them into his bag.

In the flashlight beam, Jessica saw the blue chalk stains on his fingers and the deep scratch on the back of his right hand, at the same moment she noticed Patrick's feet emerging from beneath the stairs.

And she knew. This man had never called in the 911. No one was coming. Jessica turned to run. To the stairs. To Sophie. To safety. But before she could move a hand shot out of the darkness.

Andrew Chase was upon her.

FRIDAY, 10:05 PM

It wasn't Patrick Farrell. When Byrne had gone through the files at the hospital, it had all fallen into place.

Besides being treated by Patrick Farrell in the St. Joseph's emergency room, the one thing that all five girls had in common was the ambulance service. They all lived in North Philly. They all used Glenwood Ambulance Group.

They were all treated first by Andrew Chase.

Chase had known Simon Close, and Simon had paid for that proximity with his life.

On the day she died, Nicole Taylor was not trying to write P-A-R-K-H-U-R-S-T on her palm. She was trying to write P-A-R-A-M-E-D-I-C.

Byrne flipped open his cell phone, tried 911 one final time. Nothing. He checked the status. No bars. He wasn't getting a signal. The patrol cars were not going to make it in time.

He'd have to go it alone.

Byrne stood in front of a twin, trying to shield his eyes from the rain.

Was this the house?

Think, Kevin. What were the landmarks he had seen the day he had picked her up? He could not remember.

He turned and looked behind him.

The van parked out front. Glenwood Ambulance Group.

This was the house.

He drew his weapon, chambered a round, and hurried up the driveway.

7 9

Jessica struggled up from the bottom of the impenetrable fog. She was sitting on the floor in her own basement. It was nearly dark. She tried to enter both of these facts into an equation, and got no acceptable results.

And then reality came roaring back.

Sophie.

She tried to get to her feet, but her legs would not respond. She was not bound in any way. Then she remembered. She had been injected with something. She touched her neck where the needle had penetrated, pulled back a dot of blood on her finger. In the faint light thrown by the flashlight behind her, the dot began to blur. She now understood the terror that the five girls had experienced.

But she was not a girl. She was a woman. A police officer.

Her hand went instinctively to her hip. Nothing there. Where was her weapon?

Upstairs. On top of the refrigerator.

Shit.

She felt nauseated for a moment, the world swimming, the floor seeming to undulate beneath her.

"It didn't have to come to this you know," he said. "But she fought it. She tried to throw it away herself once, but then she fought it. I've seen it over and over."

The voice came from behind her. The sound was low, measured, edged with the melancholy of deep personal loss. He still held the flashlight. The beam danced and played about the room.

Jessica wanted to respond, to move, to lash out. Her spirit was willing. Her flesh was unable.

She was alone with the Rosary Killer. She had thought that backup was on the way, but it wasn't. No one knew they were there together. Images of his victims flashed through her mind. Kristi Hamilton soaked in all that blood. The barbed-wire crown on Bethany Price's head.

She had to keep him talking. "What . . . what do you mean?"

"They had every opportunity in life," Andrew Chase said. "All of them. But they didn't want it, did they? They were bright, healthy, whole. It wasn't enough for them."

Jessica managed to look to the top of the stairs, praying that she would not see Sophie's little form there.

"These girls had it all, but they decided to throw it all away," Chase said. "And for what?"

The wind howled outside the basement windows. Andrew Chase began to pace, the beam of his flashlight bouncing in the blackness.

"What chance did my little girl have?" he asked.

He has a child, Jessica thought. *This is good.*

"You have a little girl?" she asked.

Her voice sounded distant, as if she were talking through a metal pipe.

"I *had* a little girl," he said. "She didn't even get out of the gate."

"What happened?" It was getting harder to form her words. Jessica didn't know if she should make this man relive some tragedy, but she didn't know what else to do.

"You were there."

I was there? Jessica thought. *What the hell is he talking about?*

"I don't know what you mean," Jessica said.

"It's okay," he said. "It wasn't your fault."

"My . . . fault?"

"But the world went mad that night, didn't it? Oh, yes. Evil was unleashed on the streets of this city and a great storm descended. My little girl was sacrificed. The righteous reaped reward." His voice was rising in pitch and cadence. "Tonight I settle all debts."

Oh my God, Jessica thought, the memory of that brutal Christmas Eve rushing back on a wave of nausea.

He was talking about Katherine Chase.

The woman who miscarried in her squad car. Andrew and Katherine Chase.

"At the hospital they said things like 'Oh don't you worry, you can always have another baby.' They don't know. It was never the same for Kitty and me. With all the so-called miracles of modern medicine, they couldn't save my little girl, and the Lord denied us another child."

"It . . . it was nobody's fault that night," Jessica said. "It was a horrible storm. You remember."

Chase nodded. "I remember all right. It took me nearly two hours to get to St. Katherine. I prayed to my wife's patron saint. I offered a sacrifice of my own. But my little girl never came back."

St. Katherine, Jessica thought. She'd been right.

Chase grabbed the nylon bag he had brought with him. He dropped it to the floor next to Jessica. "And do you really think that society is going to miss a man like Willy Kreuz? He was a pederast. A barbarian. He was the lowest form of human life."

He reached into his bag, and began to remove items. He put them on the floor next to Jessica's right leg. She slowly lowered her eyes. There was a cordless drill. There was a spool of sail maker's thread, a huge curved needle, another glass syringe.

"It's amazing what some men will tell you as if they were proud of it," Chase said. "A few pints of bourbon. A few Percocets. All their terrible secrets bubble over."

He began threading the needle. Depite the anger and rage in his voice, his hands were steady. "And the late Dr. Parkhurst?" he continued. "A man who used his position of authority to prey on young girls? Please. He was no different. The only thing that separated him from men like Mr. Kreuz was the pedigree. Tessa told me all about Dr. Parkhurst."

Jessica tried to talk, but couldn't. All her fear bottlenecked. She felt herself fade in and out of consciousness.

"Soon you will understand," Chase said. "Easter Sunday there will be a resurrection."

He placed the threaded needle on the floor, got within inches of Jessica's face. In the dim light, his eyes looked burgundy. "The Lord asked Abraham for his child. And now the Lord has asked me for yours."

Please, no, Jessica thought.

"It is time," he said.

Jessica tried to move.

She couldn't.

Andrew Chase walked up the steps.

Sophie.

Jessica opened her eyes. How long had she been out? She tried again to move. She could feel her arms, but not her legs. She tried to roll onto her side, failed. She tried to drag herself to the base of the steps, but the effort was too great.

Was she alone?

Had he left?

There was now a single candle lit. It sat on top of the dryer and threw long, shimmering shadows on the unfinished ceiling of the basement.

She strained to hear.

She nodded off again, startling herself awake seconds later.

Footfalls behind her. It was so hard to keep her eyes open. *So* hard. Her limbs felt like stone.

She turned her head as far as she could. When she saw Sophie in the arms of this monster, a freezing rain rinsed her insides.

No, she thought.

No!

Take me.

I'm right here. Take *me*!

Andrew Chase put Sophie down on the floor next to her. Sophie's eyes were closed, her body limp.

Inside Jessica's veins, the adrenaline fought the drug he had given her. If she could just get up and get one clear shot at him, she knew she could hurt him. He was heavier than her, but just about the same height. One blow. With the rage and anger roiling inside her, it was all she needed.

When he turned away from her momentarily, she saw that he had found her Glock. He now had it in the waistband of his pants.

Out of his field of vision, Jessica moved an inch closer to Sophie. The effort seemed to exhaust her completely. She had to rest.

She tried to see if Sophie was breathing. She couldn't tell.

Andrew Chase turned back to them, the drill now in his hand.

"It is time to pray," he said.

He reached into his pocket, removed a carriage bolt.

"Prepare her hands," he said to Jessica. He knelt down, put the cordless drill in Jessica's right hand. Jessica felt the bile rise in her throat. She was going to be sick.

"*What?*"

"She is only sleeping. I've given her only a small amount of midazolam. Drill her hands and I'll let her live." He took a rubber band out of his pocket and put it around Sophie's wrists. He placed a rosary between her fingers. A rosary with no decades. "If you don't do it, I will. Then I will send her to God right in front of you."

"I . . . I can't . . ."

"You have thirty seconds." He leaned forward, depressed Jessica's right forefinger on the trigger of the drill, testing it. The battery was fully charged. The sound of the steel twisting in the air was nauseating. "Do it now and she will live."

Sophie looked at Jessica.

"She's my daughter," Jessica managed.

Chase's face remained implacable, unreadable. The dancing candlelight drew long shadows over his features. He took the Glock from his waistband, drew back the hammer, and placed the gun to Sophie's head. "You have twenty seconds."

"*Wait!*"

Jessica felt her strength recede, return. Her fingers trembled.

"Think of Abraham," Chase said. "Think of the determination that compelled him to the altar. You can do it."

"I . . . I can't."

"We all must sacrifice."

Jessica had to stall.

Had to.

"Okay," she said. "Okay." She closed her hand around the grip of the drill. It felt heavy and cold. She tested the trigger a few times. The drill responded, the carbon bit whirring.

"Bring her closer," Jessica said weakly. "I can't reach her."

Chase walked over, lifted Sophie. He put her down just a few inches from Jessica. With her wrists banded together, Sophie's hands were steepled in prayer.

Jessica lifted the drill, slowly, resting it for a moment on her lap.

She recalled her first medicine-ball training session at the gym. After two or three reps, she wanted to quit. She was on her back, on a mat, the heavy ball in her hands, completely spent. She couldn't do it. Not one more rep. She would never be a boxer. But before she could give up, a wizened old heavyweight who had been sitting there, watching her—a longtime fixture in Frazier's Gym, a man who had once taken Sonny Liston the distance—told her that most people who fail don't lack strength, they lack *will*.

She had never forgotten him.

As Andrew Chase turned to step away, Jessica summoned all of her will, all of her resolve, all of her strength. She would have one chance to save her daughter, and the time to take that chance was now. She pressed the trigger, locking it in the ON position, then thrust the drill upward, hard and fast and strong. The long drill bit dug deep into the left side of Chase's groin, puncturing skin and muscle and flesh, roaring far into his body, finding and shredding his femoral artery. A warm gush of arterial blood erupted into Jessica's face, blinding her momentarily, making her gag. Chase shrieked in pain as he reeled back, spinning, his legs starting to give, his left hand jammed against the tear in his trousers, trying to stanch the flow. Blood pumped between his fingers, silken and black in the dim light. Reflexively he fired the Glock into the ceiling, the roar of the weapon huge in the confined space.

Jessica fought her way to her knees, her ears ringing, fueled now by adrenaline. She had to get in between Chase and Sophie. Had to move. Had to get to her feet somehow and plunge the drill into his heart.

Through the scarlet film of blood over her eyes, she saw Chase slam to the floor, dropping the gun. He was halfway across the basement. He screamed as he removed his belt and slipped it around the top of his left thigh, the blood now covering his legs, pooling on the floor. He tightened the tourniquet with a shrill, feral howl.

Could she drag herself to the weapon?

Jessica tried to crawl toward him, her hands slipping in the blood, fighting for each inch. But before she could close the distance, Chase picked up the blood-slicked Glock, and slowly rose to his feet. He stumbled forward, manic now, a mortally wounded animal. Just a few feet away. He waved the gun in front of him, his face a tortured death mask of agony.

Jessica tried to rise. She couldn't. She had to hope that Chase would get closer. She raised the drill with two hands.

Chase stumbled in.

Stopped.

He was not close enough.

She couldn't reach him. He would kill them both.

Chase looked heavenward in that moment and screamed, the unearthly sound filling the room, the house, the world, just as that world came back to life, a bright and raucous coil suddenly sprung.

The power had returned.

Upstairs, the television blared. Next to them, the furnace clicked on. Above them, the light fixtures blazed.

Time ceased.

Jessica wiped the blood from her eyes, found her attacker in the miasma of crimson. Crazily, the effects of the drug played havoc with her eyes, splitting Andrew Chase into two images, blurring them both.

Jessica closed her eyes, opened them, adjusting to the sudden clarity.

It wasn't two images. It was two *men*. Somehow Kevin Byrne was standing behind Chase.

Jessica had to blink twice, just to make sure she wasn't hallucinating.

She wasn't.

80

In all his years in law enforcement, Byrne was always surprised to finally see the size and shape and demeanor of the people he sought. Rarely were they as big or grotesque as their deeds. He had a theory that the volume of someone's monstrousness was often inversely proportional to his or her physical size.

Without debate, Andrew Chase was the ugliest, blackest soul he had ever encountered.

And now, as the man stood in front of him, not five feet away, he looked small, inconsequential. But Byrne would not be lulled or fooled by this. Andrew Chase was certainly not inconsequential in the lives of the families he had destroyed.

Byrne knew that, even though Chase was severely wounded, he did not have the drop on the killer. He did not have the upper hand. Byrne's vision was clouded; his mind was a mire of indecision and rage. Rage over his life. Rage over Morris Blanchard. Rage over the way the Diablo affair had played out, and how it had turned him into everything he fought against. Rage over the fact that, had he been a little better at this job, he might have saved the lives of a number of innocent girls.

Like an injured cobra, Andrew Chase sensed him.

Byrne flashed on the old Sonny Boy Williamson track "Collector Man Blues," on how it was time to open the door, because the collector man was here.

The door opened wide. Byrne fashioned his left hand into a familiar shape, the first one he learned when he began studying sign language.

I love you.

Andrew Chase spun around, red eyes ablaze, the Glock held high.

Kevin Byrne saw them all in this monster's eyes. Every innocent victim. He raised his weapon.

Both men fired.

And, as it had once before, the world fell white and silent.

For Jessica, the twin explosions were deafening, stealing the rest of her hearing. She folded to the cold basement floor. There was blood everywhere. She could not lift her head. As she fell into the clouds, she tried to find Sophie in the charnel house of torn human flesh. Her heart slowed, her eyesight failed.

Sophie, she thought, fading, fading.

My heart.

My life.

EASTER SUNDAY, 11:05 AM

Her mother sat on the swing, her favorite yellow sundress accentuating the deep violet flecks in her eyes. Her lips were claret, her hair a lush mahogany in the summer sun.

The aroma of just-lit charcoal briquettes filled the air, carrying with it the sound of a Phillies game. Beneath it all—the giggles of her cousins, the scent of Parodi cigars, the aroma of *vino di tavola.*

Softly came forth the scratchy voice of

Dean Martin crooning "Come Back to Sorrento" on vinyl. Always on vinyl. The technology of CDs had not yet moved into the mansion of her memories.

"Mom?" Jessica said.

"No, honey," Peter Giovanni said. Her father's voice was different. Older somehow.

"Dad?"

"I'm here, baby."

A wave of relief washed over her. Her father was there, and everything was going to be fine. Wasn't it? He's a police officer, you know. She opened her eyes. She felt weak, fully spent. She was in a hospital room but, as far as she could tell, she was not hooked to machines, nor an IV drip. Memory plodded back. She remembered the roar of the gunfire in the confines of her basement. It did not appear that she had been shot.

Her father stood at the foot of the bed. Behind him stood her cousin Angela. She turned her head to the right to see John Shepherd and Nick Palladino.

"Sophie," Jessica said.

The silence that followed exploded her heart into a million pieces, each one a burning comet of fear. She looked from face to face, slowly, dizzyingly. Eyes. She needed to see their *eyes*. In hospitals, people say things all the time; usually the things that people wanted to hear.

There's a good chance that . . .

With proper therapy and medication . . .

He's the best in his field . . .

If she could just see her father's eyes, she would know.

"Sophie's fine," her father said.

His eyes did not lie.

"Vincent's down in the cafeteria with her."

She closed her eyes, the tears now flowing freely. She could survive whatever news came her way. Bring it on.

Her throat was raw and dry. "Chase," she managed.

The two detectives looked at her, at each other.

"What happened . . . to Chase?" she repeated.

"He's here. In ICU. In custody," Shepherd said. "He was in surgery for four hours. The bad news is, he's going to make it. The good news is, he's going to stand trial, and we have all the evidence we need. His house was a petri dish."

Jessica closed her eyes for a moment, absorbing the news. Were Andrew Chase's eyes really burgundy? She had a feeling they would be in her nightmares.

"Your friend Patrick didn't make it, though," Shepherd said. "I'm sorry."

The insanity of that night seeped into her consciousness slowly. She had actually suspected Patrick of these crimes. Maybe, if she had believed him, he wouldn't have come to her house that night. And that meant he would still be alive.

An overwhelming sorrow ignited deep within her.

Angela picked up the plastic tumbler of ice water, brought the straw to Jessica's lips. Angie's eyes were red and puffy. She smoothed Jessica's hair, kissed her on the forehead.

"How did I get here?" Jessica asked.

"Your friend Paula," Angela said. "She came over to see if your power had come back on. The back door was wide open. She went downstairs and she . . . she saw everything." Angela teared up.

And then Jessica remembered. She almost could not bring herself to say the name. The very real possibility that he had traded his life for hers tore at her from the inside, a hungry beast fighting to get out. And, in this big, sterile building, there would be neither pill nor procedure that could ever heal that wound.

"What about Kevin?" she asked.

Shepherd looked at the floor, then at Nick Palladino.

When they looked back at Jessica, their eyes were grim.

CHASE ENTERS PLEA, RECEIVES LIFE SENTENCE

by Eleanor Marcus-DeChant,
The Report Staff Writer

Andrew Todd Chase, the so-called Rosary Killer, pleaded guilty Thursday to eight counts of first-degree murder, bringing to a close one of the bloodiest crime sprees in the history of Philadelphia. He was immediately remanded to the State Correctional Institution in Greene County, Pennsylvania.

In a plea agreement with the Philadelphia District Attorney's office, the 32-year-old Chase pleaded guilty to the murders of Nicole T. Taylor, 17; Tessa A. Wells, 17; Bethany R. Price, 15; Kristi A. Hamilton, 16; Patrick M. Farrell, 36; Brian A. Parkhurst, 35; Wilhelm Kreuz, 42; and Simon E. Close, 33, all of Philadelphia. Mr. Close was a staff reporter at this paper.

In exchange for the plea, numerous other counts, including kidnapping, aggravated assault, and attempted murder, were dropped, along with the death penalty provision. Chase was sentenced by Municipal Court Judge Liam McManus to a life sentence, without the possibility of parole.

Chase remained silent and impassive at the hearing, during which he was represented by Benjamin W. Priest, a public defender.

Priest said that, considering the horrific nature of the crimes, and the overwhelming evidence against his client, the agreement was the best thing for Chase, a paramedic with the Glenwood Ambulance Group.

"Mr. Chase will now be able to receive the treatment he so desperately needs."

Investigators revealed that Chase's wife Katherine, 30, was recently committed to the Ranch House Mental Health Facility at Norristown. They believe that this event may have triggered the spree.

Chase's so-called signature included leaving a rosary at the scene of each crime, as well as the mutilation of the female victims' hands.

8 3

There is a principle in sales, that being the Rule of 250. They say that, in one's lifetime, one becomes acquainted with around 250 people. Make one customer happy, and that just may lead to 250 sales.

The same might be said for hatred.

Make one enemy . . .

It is for this reason, and, perhaps, many others, that I am segregated from the general population here.

At just before eight I hear them coming. I

am brought to the small exercise yard for thirty minutes each day, right around this time.

The officer arrives at my cell. He reaches through the bars and shackles my hands. He is not my usual guard. I have never seen him before.

The guard is not a big man, but he looks to be in great physical shape. He is about my size, my height. I might have known he would be unremarkable in every way but his resolve. In this, we are surely kin.

He calls for an open cell. My door slides, I exit.

Hail Mary, full of grace . . .

We walk down the corridor. The sound of my chains echoes off the dead walls, steel conversing with steel.

Blessed art thou amongst women . . .

Every step resonates with a name. Nicole. Tessa. Bethany. Kristi.

And blessed is the fruit of thy womb, Jesus . . .

The pills I take for pain barely mask the agony. They bring them one at a time to my cell, three times a day. I would have taken them all today if I could have.

Holy Mary, mother of God . . .

This day trembled to life just a few hours ago, a day with which I have been on a collision course for a very long time.

Pray for us sinners . . .

I stand at the top of the steep iron stairs as Christ stood on Calvary. My cold, gray, solitary Golgotha.

Now . . .

I feel the hand at the center of my back.

And at the hour of our death . . .

I close my eyes.

I feel the push.

Amen.

8 4

Jessica rode to West Philly with John Shepherd. They had been partners for two weeks, and were en route to interview a witness to a double homicide that left the owners of a variety store in South Philly shot, execution style, and dumped in the cellar beneath their store.

The sun was warm and high. The city was finally throwing off the shackles of early spring and embracing the day—windows open, convertible tops down, fruit vendors open for business.

Dr. Summers's final report on Andrew Chase held a number of interesting findings, not the least of which was the fact that workers at the St. Dominic Cemetery reported that a grave had been dug up on the Wednesday of that week, a plot owned by Andrew Chase. Nothing was removed from the ground—the small casket remained untouched—but Dr. Summers believed that Andrew Chase truly expected the resurrection of his stillborn daughter on Easter Sunday. She theorized that the motivation behind his madness was to offer the lives of five girls as sacrifice to bring his daughter back from the dead. In his twisted reasoning, the five girls he chose had already attempted suicide, had already welcomed death into their lives.

About a year before he killed Tessa, as part of his job, Chase had transported a body from the row house right next to the Tessa Wells crime scene on North Eighth. It was then that he had most likely seen the pillar in the basement.

As Shepherd parked on Bainbridge Street, Jessica's phone rang. It was Nick Palladino.

"What's up, Nick?" she asked.

"Hear the news?"

God, she hated conversations that began with that question. She was fairly sure she hadn't heard any news that would warrant a phone call. "No," Jessica said. "But give it to me gently, Nick. I haven't had lunch yet."

"Andrew Chase is dead."

At first, the words seemed to carom around in her mind a bit, the way unexpected news, good and bad, tends to do. When Judge McManus had sentenced Chase to life, Jessica had assumed that *life* would be forty or more years, decades to reflect on the pain and suffering he had inflicted.

Not weeks.

According to Nick, details surrounding Chase's death were a little sketchy, but Nick heard that Chase had fallen down a long flight of steel steps and had broken his neck.

"A broken neck?" Jessica asked, trying to keep the irony from her voice.

Nick read it. "I know," he said. "Karma's a bitch with a bazooka, sometimes, eh?"

That she is, Jessica thought.

That she is.

.   .   .

Frank Wells stood in the doorway to his row house, waiting. He looked small and brittle and terribly pale. He wore the same clothes he'd had on the last time she'd seen him, but now he seemed even more lost in them than he had before.

Tessa's angel pendant had been found in Andrew Chase's bedroom dresser and had just cleared the miles of red tape attendant in capital cases such as this. Before she got out of the car, Jessica slipped it out of the evidence bag and into her pocket. She checked her face in the rearview, not so much to see if she looked okay, but rather to make sure she had not been crying.

She had to be strong here one final time.

"Is there anything I can do for *you*?" Wells asked.

Jessica wanted to say: *What you can do for me is get better.* But she knew it wasn't going to happen. "No, sir," she said.

He had asked her in, but she had declined. They stood on the steps. Above them, the sun warmed the corrugated-aluminum awning. Since she had been here last, she noticed Wells had put a small flower box beneath the window on the second floor. Bright yellow pansies grew toward Tessa's room.

Frank Wells had taken the news of Andrew Chase's death the way he had taken the news of Tessa's death—stoic, impenetrable. He had simply nodded.

When she had given him the angel pendant back, she thought she might have seen a brief flourish of emotion. She had turned to look up the street, as if she were waiting for a ride, giving the man his moment of privacy.

Wells looked down at his hands. He held out the angel pendant.

"I want you to have this," he said.

"I . . . I can't take it, sir. I know how much it means to you."

"Please," he said. He put the pendant in her hand, wrapped his hand around hers. His skin felt like warm tracing paper. "Tessa would want you to have it. She was like you in many ways."

Jessica opened her hand. She looked at the inscription engraved on the back.

Behold, I send an angel before you,
to guard you on the way.

Jessica leaned forward. She kissed Frank Wells on his cheek.

She tried to keep her emotions in check as she headed to her car. As she neared the curb, she saw a man exiting a black Saturn, parked a few cars behind her on Twentieth Street. He was about twenty-five, medium height, slender, but toned. He had thinning dark brown hair, along with a trimmed mustache. He wore mirrored aviators and a tan uniform. He headed towards the Wells house.

Jessica placed him. Jason Wells, Tessa's brother. She recognized him from the photo on the living room wall.

"Mr. Wells," Jessica said. "I'm Jessica Balzano."

"Yes, of course," Jason said.

They shook hands.

"I'm very sorry for your loss," Jessica said.

"Thank you," Jason said. "I miss her every day. Tessa was my light."

Jessica couldn't see his eyes, but she

didn't have to. Jason Wells was a young man in pain.

"My father has a great deal of respect for you and your partner," Jason continued. "We're both very grateful for all you've done."

Jessica nodded, not knowing what to say. "I hope you and your dad can find comfort."

"Thank you," Jason said. "How is your partner doing?"

"He's hanging in there," Jessica said, wanting to believe it.

"I'd like to stop in and see him sometime, if you think that would be okay."

"Sure," Jessica replied, although she knew that the visit would not be acknowledged in any way. She looked at her watch, hoping it didn't appear as clumsy as it felt. "Well, I've got a few errands. It was nice to meet you."

"Same here," Jason said. "Take care."

Jessica walked to her car, got in. She thought about the rebuilding process that would now begin in the life of Frank and Jason Wells, along with the families of all of Andrew Chase's victims.

As she started the car, it hit her. She remembered where she had seen the crest before, the crest she had first noticed in the photograph of Frank and Jason Wells on the living room wall, the crest on the black windbreaker the younger man wore. It was the same crest she had just seen on the patch sewn onto the sleeve of Jason Wells's uniform.

Did Tessa have any brothers or sisters?

One brother, Jason. He's much older. He lives in Waynesburg.

SCI Greene was in Waynesburg.

Jason Wells was a corrections officer at SCI Greene.

Jessica glanced at the front door to the Wells house. Jason and his father stood in the doorway. They held each other.

Jessica took out her cell phone, held it in her hand. She knew that the Greene County sheriff's office would be very interested in learning that the older brother of one of Andrew Chase's victims worked at the facility where Chase was found dead.

Very interested indeed.

She looked one last time at the Wells house, her finger poised to make the call. Frank Wells watched her with his damp, ancient eyes. He lifted a thin hand to wave. Jessica waved back.

For the first time since she had met him, the look on the older man's face was not one of grief or apprehension, or sadness. Instead, the look on his face was one of tranquility, she thought, of resolution, of an almost preternatural serenity.

Jessica understood.

As she pulled away, and dropped the cell phone back into her purse, she looked into the rearview mirror and saw Frank Wells framed in his doorway. It was how she would always remember him. For that brief moment, Jessica thought that Frank Wells was finally at peace.

And if you were someone who believed in such things, so was Tessa.

Jessica believed.

EPILOGUE

MAY 31, 11:05 AM

Memorial Day brought a punishing sun to the Delaware Valley. The sky was clear and azure blue; the cars that lined the streets around Holy Cross Cemetery were polished and tuned for summer. Hard gold sunlight glinted off the windshields.

The men were dressed in bright polo shirts and khakis; the grandfathers wore suits. The women wore spaghetti strap sundresses and JCPenney espadrilles in a rainbow of pastels.

Jessica knelt and put the flowers at her brother Michael's grave. She planted the small flag near the headstone. She looked across the expanse of the cemetery; saw other families planting their flags. Some of the older men saluted. Wheelchairs gleamed, their occupants deep in private remembrance. As always on this day, across the shimmering breadth of green, families of fallen servicemen and service-women would find each other, their eyes meeting in understanding, in shared sorrow.

In a few minutes Jessica would join her father at her mother's stone, and they would file silently back to the car. This is how they did things in her family. They grieved sepa-rately.

She turned and looked at the road.

Vincent leaned against the Cherokee. He was not good at grave sites, and that was okay. They had not worked it all out, they might never, but for the last few weeks he had seemed like a new man.

Jessica said a silent prayer and made her way through the headstones.

"How's he doing?" Vincent asked. They both glanced over at Peter, his broad shoul-ders still powerful at sixty-two.

"He's a rock," Jessica said.

Vincent reached out, took Jessica's hand softly in his. "How are *we* doing?"

Jessica looked at her husband. She saw a man in sorrow, a man laboring beneath the yoke of failure—failure to honor his marriage vows, failure to protect his wife and daughter. A crazy man had come into Vincent Balzano's house, threatened his family, and he had not been there. This was a special corner of hell for police officers.

"I don't know," she said. "I'm glad you're here, though."

Vincent smiled, held on to her hand. Jessica didn't pull away.

They had agreed to attend marriage counseling; their first session was in just a few days. Jessica wasn't ready to share her bed, or her life, with Vincent again just yet, but it was a first step. If they were meant to weather these storms, they would.

Sophie had picked some flowers at the house and was methodically distributing them on the grave sites. Because she hadn't gotten to wear the lemon-yellow Easter dress they had bought at Lord & Taylor's on the day itself, she seemed determined to wear it every Sunday and holiday until it was too small. Hopefully, that was a long way off.

As Peter began to make his way to the car, a squirrel darted out from behind a headstone. Sophie giggled and gave chase, her yellow frock and chestnut curls radiant in the springtime sun.

She seemed happy again.

Maybe that was enough.

It had been five days since Kevin Byrne had been moved from intensive care at HUP, the hospital at the University of Pennsylvania. The bullet Andrew Chase had fired that night had lodged in Byrne's occipital lobe, missing his brain stem by just over a centimeter. He had endured more than twelve hours of cranial surgery, and since that time he had been in a coma.

The doctors said his vital signs were strong, but confided that every week that went by significantly reduced the likelihood that he was going to regain consciousness.

Jessica had met Donna and Colleen Byrne a few days after the incident at her house. They were developing a relationship that Jessica was starting to feel might last a long time. Either in sorrow, or joy. It was too early to tell. She had even learned a few words in sign language.

Today, as Jessica came for her daily visit, she knew she had a lot to do. As much as it made her feel bad to leave, she knew that life would, and must, go on. She'd stay about fifteen minutes. She sat in the chair in Byrne's flower-filled room, thumbed through a magazine. For all she knew it could have been *Field & Stream* or *Cosmo*.

From time to time, she glanced up at Byrne. He was much thinner; his skin had a deep gray pallor. His hair was just starting to grow back.

Around his neck he wore the silver crucifix that Althea Pettigrew had given him. Jessica wore the angel pendant she had received from Frank Wells. It seemed that they both had their talisman against the Andrew Chases of the world.

There was so much she wanted to tell him, about how Colleen was voted valedictorian at her deaf school, about the death of Andrew Chase. She wanted to tell him that, a week earlier, the FBI had faxed the unit with the information that Miguel Duarte, the man who confessed to the murder of

Robert and Helen Blanchard, had an account at a New Jersey bank under a false name. They had traced the money back to a wire transfer received from an offshore account belonging to Morris Blanchard. Morris Blanchard had paid Duarte ten thousand dollars to kill his parents.

Kevin Byrne had been right all along.

Jessica turned back to her magazine, and an article about how and where walleyes spawn. She supposed it was *Field & Stream* after all.

"Hey," Byrne said.

Jessica nearly jumped out of her skin at the sound of his voice. It was low and raspy and terribly weak, but it was *there*.

She scrambled to her feet. She leaned over the bed. "I'm here," she said. "I'm . . . I'm *here*."

Kevin Byrne opened, then closed his eyes. For a horrifying moment, Jessica was certain he would never open them again. But after a few seconds he proved her wrong. "Got a question for you," he said.

"Okay," Jessica said, her heart racing. "Sure."

"Did I ever tell you why they call me Riff Raff?" he asked.

"No," she said, softly. She would not cry. She would *not*.

The slightest smile graced his parched lips.

"It's a good story, partner," he said.

Jessica took his hand in hers.

She squeezed gently.

Partner.

ACKNOWLEDGMENTS

Publishing a novel is truly a team effort, and no writer was ever blessed with a deeper bench.

Thanks to the Honorable Seamus McCaffery, Detective Patrick Boyle, Detective Jimmy Williams, Detective Bill Frazier, Detective Michele Kelly, Detective Eddie Rocks, Detective Bo Diaz, Sgt. Irma Labrice, Catherine McBride, Cass Johnston, and the men and women of the Philadelphia Police Department. Any mistakes in police procedure are mine and, if I ever get arrested in Philly, I hope this admission counts for something.

Thanks also to Kate Simpson, Jan Klincewicz, Mike Driscoll, Greg Pastore, JoAnn Greco, Patrick Nestor, Vita DeBellis, D. John Doyle, M.D., Vernoca Michael, John and Jessica Bruening, David Najfach, and Christopher Richards.

A huge debt of gratitude to Meg Ruley, Jane Berkey, Peggy Gordijn, Don Cleary, and everyone at The Jane Rotrosen Agency.

Special thanks to Linda Marrow, Gina Centrello, Rachel Kind, Libby McGuire, Kim Hovey, Dana Isaacson, Arielle Zibrak, and the great team at Random House/Ballantine Books.

Thanks to the city of Philadelphia for letting me create schools as well as mayhem.

As always, thanks to my family for living the writer's life with me. It may be my name on the cover, but it is their patience, support, and love on each and every page.